MURDOCH

MYSTERIES

Poor Tom is Cold

MAUREEN JENNINGS

TITAN BOOKS

Murdoch Mysteries: Poor Tom is Cold
Print edition ISBN: 9780857689894
E-book edition ISBN: 9780857689962

Published by Titan Books
A division of Titan Publishing Group Ltd
144 Southwark St, London SE1 0UP

First edition: March 2012
2 4 6 8 10 9 7 5 3 1

Names, places and incidents are either products of the author's imagination or used fictitiously. Any resemblance to actual persons, living or dead (except for satirical purposes), is entirely coincidental.

Maureen Jennings asserts the moral right to be identified as the author of this work.
© 2001, 2012 Maureen Jennings

Visit our website:
www.titanbooks.com

What did you think of this book? We love to hear from our readers. Please email us at: readerfeedback@titanemail.com, or write to us at the above address.
To receive advance information, news, competitions, and exclusive offers online, please sign up for the Titan newsletter on our website: **www.titanbooks.com**

A CIP catalogue record for this title is available from the British Library.

Printed and bound in Great Britain by CPI Group Ltd.

To Iden with love and gratitude, as always

GLOUCESTER: *Our flesh and blood, my lord,*
is grown so wild
That it doth hate what gets it.

EDGAR: [pretending to be a lunatic]
Poor Tom's a-cold

FROM *KING LEAR* (III. IV.)

PROLOGUE

SINCE THE BOY HAD DIED, SHE DIDN'T SLEEP AND MANY nights she prowled around the house, searching. She was quiet so as not to wake any of the others, but they knew and talked about it when she wasn't there. This night was particularly bad. It was long past midnight and she had heard the grandfather clock in the hall chime. She counted out the number of gongs, not wanting the sound to die away as it was comforting, like a voice. After a while the snuffles and groans of her sleeping husband were insufferable and she got out of bed. She didn't put on her dressing gown or slippers, even though the room was chill. She went out to the landing. A slit of light was showing beneath the door opposite and she knew he was not yet in bed. She walked over and went in without knocking. He was seated at his desk, writing, and turned quickly when he heard her enter. She was glad she had startled him. She smiled, a false smile, hiding her fear. He regarded her coldly. He didn't get up, didn't exclaim in concern or bewilderment; he merely sat and waited for her to say something.

She moved closer. "You are up late," she said.

"And you."

"You must be cold."

"Not at all."

He indicated the fire, which was still burning in the hearth, and the woollen shawl that was around his shoulders.

She wanted to flee, to run from that icy stare, but she knew this might be her only chance.

"I have seen the looks you give me. They burn my skin like the hot sun."

"I must disillusion you. I have no such desire."

Some of her earliest memories were of witnessing the power her mother could exercise over the many men who visited her, and Peg knew she had no other recourse. She slipped her arms out of her nightgown, letting it fall to her ankles. She tried to take a bold stance, feet apart, the way she had long ago seen her mother do. But her legs were quivering and she couldn't force herself to stand other than with her knees pressed together. Cupping her small breasts in her hands, she pushed them up.

"I ache for your suck," she said. She tried to make her voice coy and sweet, but even to her own ears, she sounded unconvincing.

He scanned her thin body, studying her dispassionately, critically, making it clear how much the choice was his. Then he took the candleholder from his desk and came over to her. She tried not to flinch but she couldn't help herself. He bent down and pulled up the nightgown.

"Allow me to take you back to your room," he said.

CHAPTER ONE

IT WAS STILL DARK OUT, NOT YET DAWN, AND THE flickering street lamps made little dint in the sodden November darkness. Acting Detective William Murdoch pulled his astrakhan hat tighter over his ears, thrust his bare hands deep into his pockets and, shoulders hunched against the cold driving rain, plodded up Ontario Street toward the police station. Pain from an infected tooth had sent him from his bed, and in an attempt to distract himself, he had dressed and set out for work well ahead of his duty time.

He turned onto Wilton just as a cab was going by and stepped back to avoid being splashed. The cabbie slowed his horse in case Murdoch was a potential fare, realised he wasn't, and tipped his whip in acknowledgment as he passed by. He was wrapped in a voluminous black oiled slicker, the high collar masking his lower face and the hood pulled down so low over his forehead that only his eyes were visible. The horse had no such protection and its coat was dark from the rain. Like a lot of cab horses, the beast looked underfed, as if it had barely a trot left in it, but the driver snapped the reins and they heaved into a faster clip. Murdoch watched the rear lamp swaying, warm and bright in the gloom, until the carriage turned south on Parliament, leaving him alone on the dark street.

What if I am the last man on the earth? he thought. *What if I'm really dead and in purgatory? Is this what it is?* Physical pain and loneliness melded together until he couldn't separate one from the other. Suddenly, somebody, probably a servant, lit a lamp in the upstairs room of one of the houses he was passing and the light winked out through a crack in the curtain. Murdoch was somewhat embarrassed at the relief he felt and he grinned at his own nonsense. He shook his head to clear out the morbid thoughts and was rewarded by a current of white-hot pain along his jaw, so severe he yelped. Trying to move cautiously to avoid aggravating matters, he continued on his way. He was heartily glad to reach the steps of the station. The outside lamp was burning and the windows were bright.

He pushed open the door, greeted by the familiar smell of woodstove, sawdust, and a lingering sourness from the old clothes and unwashed bodies of the local constituents. The fourth division served Toronto from the working-class streets of River and Sackville in the east, to the nobs who lived in grand houses on Jarvis and Church streets in the west. The east-siders were the ones whose backsides polished the wooden benches in the station hall.

The night-duty sergeant, Gardiner, was seated on a high stool behind the counter, entering his report in the register. He glanced up in surprise to see Murdoch.

"Gawdelpus, you're the early bird."

The detective grunted, not feeling up to a long-winded explanation. His tooth had started hurting about a week ago, but he'd managed to ignore it until yesterday, when the pain had worsened. His landlady, Mrs. Kitchen, sent him to bed with a brown paper and vinegar poultice to hold to his face and had padded his gum with some cotton wool soaked in carbolic. That had helped for a while, but at five o'clock he had been dragged to consciousness with the sensation that every nerve in his body had gathered at a point on his lower jaw and was pulsing there.

He took off his fur hat and shook the rain out of it.

"What's up?" asked the sergeant.

Gardiner was regarding him curiously and Murdoch knew he must look like a pauper's pal.

"Got a toothache," he mumbled. He tried to talk without moving his mouth very much.

"Awful things them toothaches. Keep you up, don't they?"

Murdoch blinked in agreement.

"Better get yourself into the dentist. There's a fellow right at the corner. You could drop in on him."

Murdoch grunted. Not if he could help it. George Crabtree had been forced to visit Dr. Brodie last year and, big and tough as a moose though he might be, the constable had almost fainted when he staggered out of the chair. His face was swollen for weeks.

"My landlady's good," said Murdoch. "Knows a lot... carbolic..."

"Wondered what it was I could smell. Helped, did it?"

"Hm."

The sergeant sniffed. "Or is it fish? Did the cat bring something in?"

Murdoch shrugged. The smell was from his sealskin coat, which developed a distinctive odour when it was wet. He'd got it from an old lag a couple of years ago, in exchange for some tobacco, and he considered it a good bargain in spite of the pong.

He started to head for the sanctuary of his office, which was a tiny cubicle across from the cells.

"While you're over there, put some more coal in, will you?" called out Gardiner.

Murdoch opened the stove door, picked up a pair of tongs, seized a large piece of coal and dropped it into the red maw. The action hurt.

There was a waft of chill air as the hall door opened and Ed Hales, the patrol sergeant, came in. He hung his dark lantern on a hook.

"Perishing cold out there."

"It's nothing to what it will be," said Gardiner. "Wait till we get winter."

"You're early this morning, Will."

"He's got toothache," Gardiner answered for him. "Kept him up. He's going to have to have it pulled."

"Hey, I don't know that yet," protested Murdoch.

The sergeant grinned at him. "That kind of pain means abscess. If you don't look after it, you could be in bad trouble. Second cousin of the wife's nearly died from an abscess. Poison got into her blood. She was bad for months after, still not right. It affected her mentally. She cries all the time."

"Glad to know that, Gardiner. Lifted my spirits no end did that little tale."

The duty sergeant shrugged, undaunted. "It's the truth, I tell you."

"How about I brew up a pot of tea, Will?" interjected Hales. "Cheer us both up. Come on."

Murdoch was about to refuse but Hales, out of sight of the duty sergeant, nodded warningly. He had something to say.

"I wouldn't mind a mug myself," Gardiner called after them. "I'm parched."

Murdoch followed Hales through to the small back room where the officers ate their meals. The morning shift hadn't arrived yet and the fire was low in the grate, the room chilly.

"Why don't I look after the pot and you see to the fire; you're better at it than me," he said.

"All right," said Hales but he didn't move. He pulled at the ends of his moustache. He was a tall man, ruddy-faced. He was invariably pleasant and even-tempered, qualities that made him popular in the station, but this morning he was visibly distressed.

"Need your ear a minute, Will…I didn't want to say anything in front of Gardiner, he's got a sniffer for trouble like a rat on offal but," he hesitated, reluctant to admit the bad news, "fact is, young Wicken seems to have gone missing."

"Missing?"

"Well, he don't seem to be on his beat." He rubbed at his moustache. "I did my first check on him at twenty-five minutes past eight. All correct. Did the second at a quarter past ten like normal. Again all correct. But when I went to check in on him at a quarter past two, he was nowhere to be seen. Supposed to be up at River and Gerrard. I thought maybe he'd stepped into a laneway to have a piss, even though he shouldn't, and I waited a bit. No sign of him. I walked back along Gerrard. Not a whisker. I put pebbles on the doorknobs. You know that little trick."

Murdoch nodded. The constable on the beat was supposed to check the doors of the vacant houses to make sure they were secure, no vagrants camping out. The patrol sergeant sometimes tested the officers with a small stone or piece of dirt. If it was still there at the next round, heaven help the constable on duty.

"When he wasn't at the four o'clock checkpoint, I walked his entire beat in reverse but he was nowhere to be seen. All of the pebbles were still there."

Murdoch frowned. "That's bloody strange. Is he playing up,

d'you think? Hiding?"

The younger constables sometimes teased the good-natured patrol sergeant by hiding out until he went by, then innocently meeting him on the return route. It was childish but it relieved the boredom. Murdoch had done it himself when he was on the beat.

Hales shook his head. "He's never done it before and it's past a joke by now. If he isn't here at changeover, he could be put on a charge."

"Ill then? Could he have been taken ill? Gone home?"

Even as he said it, Murdoch knew how unlikely that was. Wicken would have gone to the closest alarm box and telephoned in to headquarters.

"He looked healthy as a doctor when I saw him last. He wasn't drunk neither."

The two men looked at each other, mirroring each other's uneasiness.

Murdoch reached for his hat. "I'll go and have another gander. You've got your report to do."

"Thanks, Will. If he is just acting batchy, I'll overlook it as long as he's back on the beat when the next shift comes in. But if he's not there without a damn good reason, it'll be dire."

"Where should he be right now?"

"Coming down River Street from Gerrard. Maybe you could try going the reverse way."

Murdoch stood up. "Save me some tea."

"The whole pot if you find him safe," said Hales. "And you'd better take my lamp. But don't let Gardiner see you if you can help it."

Murdoch went back to the hall. He managed to whip the lantern off the hook while the duty sergeant was turned away, getting a file from the cabinet. However, Gardiner saw him at the door.

"Where's my tea? What are you doing, growing it?"

"Hales's doing it," muttered Murdoch. "Got-tuh go."

The sergeant called after him. "Have them all pulled out. You'll be better off in the long run."

Murdoch waved his hand.

Outside, dawn was coming in begrudgingly and the rain had slowed to a drizzle. He set off at as fast a pace as he could manage, heading east along Wilton to River Street. Even though moving quickly caused the pain to pulse through to his eye socket, he felt the need to hurry. He couldn't imagine why the young constable wasn't on his beat. No one with a brain in his head would take a joke this far and risk losing his job. That left the possibility that something had happened to him and that wasn't good either.

River Street wasn't as heavily populated as the other streets in the division and there were several vacant lots. They reminded him of missing teeth, a gap between molars. Quickly, he checked the doors of the houses that were boarded up. On each knob was balanced a small pebble. Wicken's beat started at the corner of Parliament Street and Gerrard and would have taken him in an easterly direction toward River Street, where he turned south to Queen, back west, then north again up Parliament. During the long night, he walked this square many times, making sure all the God-fearing were safe in their beds. If he had the bad luck to miss any criminal occurrence, such as a break-in, he was held accountable. As far as the chief constable, Lieutenant-Colonel Henry Grasett, was concerned, a crime meant the constable on the beat was remiss in his duty and he was always reprimanded.

Murdoch turned left onto Gerrard and paused, looking down the deserted street. More lamps were showing in the houses now, welcome smudges of light. If the constable had run into any kind of trouble, it had been silent. No one had raised an alarm.

He continued to Parliament Street, past Toronto General and the Burnside lying-in hospital on the north side of Gerrard. *Even as I'm going by, an infant might be squawling its first cry.* His mind skittered away from the thought because that led straight to Liza, and what they had hoped for. *Four children, Will, and then we'll see. I'm not going to be one of those women whose job in life is to be a breeding mare.* Murdoch sighed. *Fat lot of good all that nattering did us. There won't be any at all now.* The memory of her sudden death from typhoid fever, two years ago, was still a cause for anguish.

He forced himself to focus on what he was doing. Across from the hospital grounds was the medical school. Quite a lot of lights burning there. It took him about fifteen minutes to reach Parliament Street but there was absolutely no sign of

Wicken. He stopped for a moment until the throbbing in his jaw subsided. On the southeast corner there was another vacant house. It had once been quite grand, but now the windows were boarded up and the front fence was protecting only weeds, colourless and drooping. He squeezed by the stiff iron gate and walked down the path to the front door. Shrubs, heavy with raindrops, brushed against him as he went up a short flight of steps into a deeply recessed porch. Hales's pebble was where he'd put it. Murdoch knocked it off, turned the doorknob and shoved. The door had lost much of its paint but was solid wood and it didn't yield. He stepped back, fished out a box of matches from his pocket, and lit the dark lantern. The bull's-eye beam was bright and strong and he directed it at the windows. They too looked intact, no sign of breakage.

There was a flagged path that branched off to the rear of the house and, pushing his way through the long grass that had overgrown it, Murdoch tramped around to a high gate that opened into a walled garden. This was neglected and overgrown, but like the house, suggested a former grandeur. To his right was a patio with a fancy design of yellow and red brick. He walked over to the back door. Around the lintel there was a climbing rose bush, two or three frostbitten buds still on their stems. An image of the church window, Christ's blood on the thorns, jumped into his mind, taking him by surprise with its intensity.

He turned the handle and the door opened easily. He stepped inside.

The light shone on Wicken's body.

He was lying on his left side, facing the door; his head was uncovered and surrounded by a halo of blood, which had soaked much of his blond hair. His legs were crossed at the ankles and between his thighs was wedged his revolver, barrel uppermost, stiff and protruding like a grotesque symbol of manhood.

CHAPTER TWO

PEG HAD ALREADY WEDGED ONE OF THE ARMCHAIRS underneath the doorknob, but in a sudden rush of fear, thinking she heard Nathaniel's voice, she dragged over the chiffonier and pushed it so that it toppled against the chair. There were two doors she had to worry about. This one, which connected with the master bedroom, the other, which opened onto the landing. The latter had been fitted with a bolt some time ago. Nathaniel said this was so he and Harmony could have some privacy from the children. Everything he said had an implied reproach. His previous wife had liked nothing better than to spend time with him alone; she had been loving and compliant.

Not like you. Never like you.

She went back to reassure herself that the bolt was in place. They would have to break the door down to get in. She stood still as she could, listening. Whatever she'd heard had gone. The house was silent.

She shivered. There was no longer any heat in the room as she had used up the last piece of coal the night before. The tips of her fingers were cold. Suddenly she caught a glimpse of herself in the chiffonier mirror and she stared, hardly recognising herself. There was a crust of dried blood at the corner of her mouth where his ring had cut her lip. She touched it gingerly with her tongue and shuddered. The salty taste of her own blood frightened her. He was an old man but still strong and made more so by his rage.

She looked again at her reflection. Her eyelids were reddened from lack of sleep, her hair unpinned and lank. The sight repelled her – a doxy's face if ever there was one. She could have been looking at her own mother. She snatched the crocheted antimacassar from the Morris chair and draped it over the mirror.

You and the boy will be well looked after, my sweet. I promise. That's what he'd said when he first came courting, and foolishly, desperate, she had given in. She moaned. That promise would not be kept now. His feeling for her had withered away, corroded by his own humiliation.

She's a whore, Father. You've married a whore.

Jarius was calm, his voice as dispassionate as if he were

reciting the order of hymns for the day. And they had stared at her from the table, all of them there, even the child.

Did you do this? Did you go to Jarius's room and offer yourself like some Jezebel?

And all she could answer was, *He is trying to murder me. He put poison in my food. He killed Charley.*

But he repeated, *Did you go to his room?*

When she said yes, Nathaniel hit her hard across the face.

One of the candles in the wall sconces sputtered and Peg's heart thudded.

I must save them for nighttime. They're burning down too fast. She reached for the candle snuffer but stopped herself.

It's all right. He'll be back long before then…he believed you.

She returned to the couch, suddenly so tired she thought she would fall down. She would rest for a moment, just a moment, then she had to think. She had to make plans. She lay back and closed her eyes.

Off the dining room of the Village Home was a tiny pantry that the matron referred to as "the calming room". Naughty children were put in there, in the dark, until they thought better of their behaviour and were willing to act like grateful Christian children and not heathens. Not too long after she had been admitted, Peg was locked in there for using bad language and for scratching and biting another child.

She stole my cup. The bint took it. It's mine. The matron, Mrs. Southgate, was firm.

Nobody owns the furnishings here. The cups and plates, the knives and forks, belong to everybody. You have behaved most wickedly and you must pray for forgiveness.

Although Peg had kicked and fought, the matron and two of the bigger girls easily subdued her. She was closed inside the pantry to think about her wrongdoing. Perhaps Mrs. Southgate did indeed forget; she was a busy woman with many cares. Perhaps the time in the darkness was not as long as Peg experienced it. However, when she was finally let out, she had messed in her drawers and was hoarse with crying. Overnight, she became a model child and was frequently paraded before visitors as an example of the miracle of love and Christian teaching. When she was sent to Canada as one of the quotient of child emigrants, Mrs. Southgate handed her a splendid testimonial and kissed her.

Peg sat up. The memory burned like acid in her gut.

She got off the couch, went over to the window, and raised the blind. The sky was lighter and relief ran through her body. The night was over. She gave a quick, hard tug on the window sash but she knew it was futile. Frank had nailed it shut earlier in the week. She leaned forward, pressing her forehead against the glass. Even if she smashed it, there was nobody to call to, nobody who would help her. She hadn't been friendly with the neighbours, sensing their disapproval. If word of Jarius's accusation ever got out, they would turn away completely. And she knew he would make sure it did get out.

He was young, fair-haired. His eyes were kind and she could tell he was listening so she tried to speak calmly. She told him everything. About Charley, about the poison she'd tasted the two nights she'd become ill. How they all hated her. She also told him about Jarius and lastly about Frank. "Show me," he'd said to the others and they took him off. "I'll come back," he had said. And he would, she trusted he would.

She felt short of breath, as if the air was being sucked away, and she returned to the couch and lay down again. She'd brought this piece of furniture with her when she'd married Nathaniel and its familiarity was a comfort. She stroked the plush surface as if it were a creature and pulled the velour cover over her face. Under the tent of it, she could smell her own stale flesh.

All she had to do was wait.

Suddenly, there was a sharp rapping on the door and she jumped.

"Stepmother? Stepmother?" the voice outside called to her and the doorknob rattled. "Please let me in, Stepmother. I've made you some porridge for your breakfast…You must eat something."

Augusta was speaking softly, falsely, as if she were trying to trick a child to take foul medicine. But Peg knew it wasn't medicine that she wanted her to swallow.

She didn't answer and the doorknob shook again. Augusta's voice was less patient this time.

"Stepmother, open the door." Another rap.

A rush of white-hot rage surged through Peg's body and she jumped off the couch and ran over to the door.

"Sod off," she screamed. "You can all sod off. All the frigging lot of you."

She banged with her fists on the unyielding wood.

CHAPTER THREE

MURDOCH BROUGHT THE LANTERN CLOSE TO THE ravaged face. The source of the injury seemed to be a small circular wound near the right temple, and the blood which was covering the right eye was from that wound. The left eye was open.

What in God's name happened?

Slowly, he swung the beam along the length of the body. The metal of the gun barrel gleamed in the light and abruptly Murdoch tugged the gun loose from between the thighs. Placing the lantern beside him on the floor, he crouched down and snapped open the cylinder. All police pistols had six chambers but, for safety reasons, officers were allowed only five cartridges. The hammer was always to rest on the empty chamber. Wicken's gun held four undischarged cartridges; the fifth had been fired. Near his right shoulder was the empty shell case. Murdoch left it where it was. Hurriedly, he tugged off his own glove and held the back of his hand beneath Wicken's nose to check for any indication of breath, although he knew there could be none. He touched the chin; the skin was grey and cold, and when he tried to move the jaw from side to side, it was stiff. The rigor of death had already started. The constable must have died four or five hours earlier. More carefully, his hands steadying, Murdoch began to scrutinise the body.

Wicken was lying with his left arm underneath him and the right arm was flung across his chest, the gloved hand touching the floor. Just beyond the reach of his fingers was his notebook and underneath that was tucked a piece of paper.

Gingerly, Murdoch extricated it. Printed neatly in pencil were the following words:

LIFE IS UNBEARABLE WITHOUT YOUR LOVE.

FORGIVE ME.

He felt a rush of anger. *You stupid boy. May God forgive your sin. I won't.*

He stared at the note again as if there was some answer in the terse words.

LIFE IS UNBEARABLE WITHOUT YOUR LOVE.

Whose love? Why had it been withdrawn?

Murdoch didn't know much about Wicken's personal life. As an acting detective, his rank was above the constable's, and off-duty they were not expected to have much to do with each other. On the occasions when they had met, however, he'd liked the young man. And in fact, he'd talked to him only last evening when Wicken had come on duty. What was it they'd chatted about? He couldn't remember because his toothache had obliterated everything else. No, of course, that's what it was. Wicken expressed sympathy. Said he'd had a tooth pulled when he was young. Murdoch was too proud to ask if it had hurt but Wicken had told him cheerily, "Hurt like the deuce at first but the pain doesn't last that long." The constable had seemed in perfectly good spirits. Quite normal.

And now look at him.

He took out his own notebook and placed the piece of paper inside. He was tempted to inspect the body further but Wicken's rubber cape was wrapped tightly around him, which meant he'd have to be lifted. Murdoch decided to wait until the coroner arrived.

He picked up the lantern and started to walk around the kitchen. The room was totally bare of furnishings, although the original rush matting remained. He examined the door and the window next to it. Dust was thick on the sill and there was no sign of forcing around the frame. How had Wicken got into the house? And why choose this particular place to take his own life? Murdoch looked out of the window at the neglected garden, forlorn and grey in the pre-dawn light. The fence was high all around and the house abutted a laneway on the east side. Parliament Street was on the west. There was no other house overlooking this one. Wicken had made sure his sin was a private one.

He turned back to the body. *Who was the note addressed to?* It didn't sound as if the beloved person had died – more likely rejected him. *You get over it, my lad. Nothing is worth committing such a mortal sin. You might want to die to escape your pain but God says that is according to His will, not yours.* But Murdoch knew he himself had thought such things not so long ago when his fiancée had died. And he wasn't completely sure he was over it.

A few feet away was Wicken's helmet, standing upright as if he'd put it tidily on a shelf. Murdoch picked it up and held it in the light of the lantern. It seemed clean, free of blood. He replaced it in the same spot, then he paced around a second time, saw nothing more, and returned to the body.

He was about to say a brief prayer but he stopped. He could as yet find no forgiveness for Wicken. His pity was with those left behind. He'd heard that the boy's mother was a widow and that there was a younger sister. And he wondered also how the unnamed woman would feel when she learned she had precipitated this self-murder.

He left the house, closing the door tightly behind him. The sky had turned from black to dull grey but the drizzle was unalleviated. He started to jogtrot back to the front gate and along the street to the neighbouring house. There was a plaque on the wrought-iron gate proclaiming this was a livery stable and he could see into a long yard. At the far end was a low building, which he supposed housed the horses. He tried the gate but it was bolted on the inside and he shook it impatiently, prepared to knock the shicey thing off its hinges if need be. However, at that moment a man emerged from the stable, leading a saddled horse.

"Hey you, come over here," Murdoch shouted.

The man hesitated, then approached slowly, the horse swaying behind him, its hooves clacking on the cobblestones.

"Who the sod are you? What d'you want?"

He was quite young, perhaps in his mid-twenties, short and wiry, dressed in corduroy trousers and jacket. His cap was low on his forehead.

"I'm sodding William Murdoch, acting detective, that's who. Now open up."

The fellow's expression changed.

"Sorry, Officer. What's up? Here –"

He threw back the bolt on the gate and started to swing it open.

"What's your name?" Murdoch asked.

"Eakin, Frank Eakin."

"Well, Mr. Eakin, I'm commandeering you. I need somebody to run over to the police station. At once. Ask for Sergeant Hales. Got that? Hales."

"Yes, sir."

"Tell him I've found Wicken. Tell him we need the ambulance and the coroner."

"Somebody dead then?" He shifted nervously.

"That's what it usually means when you get the coroner. Now hurry." He pointed. "I'm in the empty house on the corner. Tell them to come to the back door."

Eakin indicated the horse standing listlessly behind him.

"I was just going to exercise Sailor. Shall I take him?"

"Of course take him, unless you can run faster. Get going. Scorch!"

The man swung himself into the saddle, kicked his heels hard into the horse's sides, and lunged into a gallop out of the gate.

Murdoch turned around and half-ran, half-skittered back to the scene of death.

CHAPTER FOUR

JARIUS GIBB PULLED THE CANDLESTICK CLOSER, SELECTED a fresh pen, and dipped it into the inkwell. He did these actions deliberately, watching his own hand to determine if it would betray him with a sign of human weakness. It didn't and, as he entered the date in the ledger, his writing was steady, even and precise as always.

TUESDAY, NOVEMBER 12, 1895

I write this entry in good health. My tongue is furred but my pulse is quite steady. I have pissed copiously in the chamber and my water is of good colour. I have slept for at least four hours but fitfully. I had expected to experience a natural fatigue but so far that is not the case. In fact, I would say I am quite invigorated.

He paused. Even in his own diary, he had difficulty writing down the absolute truth. He blotted what he had written so far, and continued.

I doubt Father will be with us much longer. He looks more aged every day, although, I regret to say, his temper is unabated. This failing is made worse, of course, by the present situation. I must admit, even I quailed when we spoke on Saturday night. But he has brought it all on himself so I have no pity. So utterly, utterly unsuitable.

His hand had betrayed him and the writing was suddenly untidy. She was a young woman, it was true, but plain as a mouse, skin like lard, no diddies or arse to rouse a man, no wit or liveliness to explain Nathaniel's infatuation with her.

Frank said in his delicate way that Father was "cuntstruck". To me it was less of the human. Father lusted after her like a dog after a bitch in heat. I thought he would take her on the dining room table that first night he brought her here. "This is your new mother," he said. None of us had an inkling. He was barely out of mourning. She is younger than Frank. A widow, she said, and she brought her own by-blow with her. A vile boy who immediately made it apparent he carried criminal blood.

Within a week, I was missing several coins from my trousers. Frank said he stole from him also. All this denied of course; Father was determined to side with the boy at all costs.

He had written an account of these events several times before but he found himself returning over and over again to that day and the weeks that followed.

I thought at first my "stepmother" must practice whore tricks to keep him panting the way he did but I stood shamelessly outside their bedroom and I heard her refusing him, crying "no" while he grunted and rutted like the goat he had become. I might have felt pity except I thought her coyness must be a way to keep him hot. Augusta says she has not yet conceived but I thought she would when it suited her.

The thought was still so unbearable, Jarius had to lay down his pen and stand up. He went to the table beside the bed where he'd left his pipe and, not bothering to fill it, stuck the stem in his mouth and clenched down hard. He returned to his desk.

I am glad to say the possibility is now remote. I am almost able to rest.

Once again he noticed a tremor in his hand and he forced himself into steadiness.

I cannot pretend I was sorry when the boy died but I must admit it was quite convenient. She plays so easily, I almost feel compunction for her state. Of course, nobody believes her. She has given up any pretext of affection for dear Papa and this has been bringing about a rapid cure of his obsession. I have seen his distaste, although he attempts to hide it whenever I am present, cooing and caressing with her as he did before.

The memory filled him with contempt. She was as unresponsive as stone. An unpaid whore would have more life.

Like a preening peacock he seems intent on proving his feathers are the brightest. How sweet, then, that she revealed what she really is. How beautifully she has played into my hands. I could hardly wait to tell him. I had expected he would throw her out immediately but he didn't go that far. And what a pity that has proved to be!

Another pause, another struggle to contain the surge of excitement through his body.

There was quite a scene, I must say. Worthy of the stage. She screaming that I was a liar, which ironically is true but not in this case. Poor Augusta had to hurry Lewis from the room with her hands over his ears. I was not surprised. Only a whore knows language like that and it is my conviction that is what she is.

He had checked the marriage registry and discovered she had been, in fact, legally married and her son was legitimate.

That does not eliminate the fact that she was and still is a tart.

Unfortunately, it didn't mean Nathaniel wouldn't continue even now to dip his sugar stick in her honey pot. And she could catch. She had shown she was fertile.

"Fertile – capable of producing issue."

Jarius had insisted on having connections with his wife, Caroline, almost daily, but even his most vigorous pushing and shoving could not create the heir he yearned for. Her monthly courses had arrived with the regularity of the moon. Then she became ill and there was no possibility.

I will now write down the events of last night.

He was distracted by the sound of somebody talking outside in the hall. Augusta's voice, although he couldn't quite make out what she was saying. Then there was an enraged scream that he knew came from his stepmother, followed by the sound of bangs and thumps. He closed the ledger quickly and waited, listening. Almost at once, there was a sharp rap at the door.

"Jarius! Are you awake?"

"Yes."

"Can I come in?"

"Yes."

Augusta entered, a tray in her hands. Her eyes were bright with anger.

"Did you hear her?"

"How could I not?"

"She was shouting at me in the foulest language. Listen, she's still banging on the door."

"What did you do to provoke her?"

"How can you ask that? I did nothing. I thought she might want something to eat and I brought her up some porridge. She's had nothing since Saturday night. She spewed filth at me for thanks."

"How odd. I was under the impression she liked her porridge."

"Jarius, please! I will not tolerate her behaviour any longer. We have to do something."

"What do you suggest?"

"I don't know. Perhaps you can speak to Papa. He will listen to you. He always does."

"Is he up yet?"

"Not so far."

"And the others?"

"Frank has not shown his face...nor has my husband."

He lifted his hands in a placating gesture. "I understand how difficult it is for you, my dear, I do truly understand."

In contrast to his soothing voice, his thoughts were full of irritation and contempt for his half-sister. Regrettably, Augusta did not live up to the grandeur of her name; she was short with an unprepossessing figure. Even at this hour, she was already fully dressed and her hair was pinned in a tight coil on top of her head. She insisted on remaining in mourning for her mother and was wearing a black bombazine gown – even though the woman had died more than a year ago. The dull colour didn't suit her fair complexion and she looked washed out.

Augusta gave the tray she was holding a shake, as if it were a live creature and responsible for the situation.

"I have Lewis to consider. He is being exposed to the worst kind of language and behaviour in his very own home."

"That won't do." Jarius clutched the woollen shawl tight around his neck as if he were a woman going to market. "But the poor soul needs our love and sympathy, Aggie. She needs special care. More than we can possibly provide."

She gaped at him. "What do you mean?"

"I have been thinking and praying most of the night. I think we should send for Dr. Ferrier. I fear for her mental stability."

"Oh, dear, Jarius, I don't know if we should go that far."

He came over to her, removed the tray from her hands, and drew her to his chest. "Try not to fret, little Cissie. It will be for the best. Think of your son."

She stood leaning against him. "Jarius, why did he do this to us? My mother was as good a Christian woman as you could wish for. She was devoted to him. Your mother was the same. How could he marry such a one as this?"

He stroked her cheek tenderly. "Hush, little one. He is an old man in his dotage, that's why. But I promise the situation won't continue. Now, why don't you go and stir up Cullie to make me some breakfast."

Augusta stepped back and picked up her tray.

"I had better do that. She's a clumsy girl. She'd set us all on fire if I didn't watch her."

"I'll come down shortly."

She left, closing the door softly behind her.

Jarius went back to the ledger and opened to his last entry.

So far all is proceeding beyond my greatest imaginings. I am sure we will have no difficulty in persuading Ferrier that she belongs in an asylum. In my deepest heart I know it has all been worth it.

In spite of what he wrote, for a brief moment, quickly controlled, he quailed.

The Eakins' servant girl, Janet Cullie, was grating sugar from the loaf into a bowl. Because she was near-sighted, she was bent over close to what she was doing. The low kitchen windows didn't let in much light at the best of times and this morning the rain was virtually obliterating the dull early morning light. There was one oil lamp, which hung from the ceiling, but the wick was turned low. Augusta watched every expenditure, making Janet's life miserable by her constant carping about wastage.

There was the sound of a footstep on the uncarpeted stairs

and, involuntarily, the girl flinched.

Sure enough the door was thrust open and her mistress entered. She was carrying a tray, which she put on the kitchen table.

"Clear this away, Janet."

Her voice was cool but the girl knew her well enough by now not to be fooled. Something had riled her bad. Worse even than she'd been for the last two days and Janet thought that was very bad. Very high-up riling.

"Must I finish this first, ma'am?"

"Of course, finish. You should have been done by now."

"Yes, Mrs. Curran. Sorry, ma'am."

She gave a quick curtsey as she had been taught to do in the school. Janet Cullie was only fourteen and this was her first placement. Augusta had taken her from the Industrial Refuge for Girls, a school where orphan girls who might be in danger from bad influences were set to rights by being trained in working skills, mostly domestic service. Janet knew she should be grateful to Augusta, but many nights she cried herself to sleep, her head pushed into the pillow so as not to wake anybody. The school had been strict but there were other girls to chatter with and the work was not anywhere near as hard as what she was expected to do here. Besides, no matter how much she tried not to, she seemed to irritate her mistress and Augusta's voice became sharp and impatient. This only made the girl more nervous and ingratiating.

Augusta picked up the porridge dish from the tray.

"No sense in throwing this out; it wasn't touched." She scraped the porridge back into the pot that was cooking on the stove. "You can start the bacon for Mr. Jarius."

"Shall I do up some for you, ma'am?"

"No, just toast and coffee will suffice. Why isn't the pot on?"

The girl grimaced. "We've run out of coffee, ma'am. There isn't any."

It wasn't Janet's job to order supplies but she was supposed to tell Augusta when they were getting low.

"Make me tea then."

Augusta dropped the porridge dish into the pail of water which stood beside the sink.

"I have a task for you after you have served breakfast."

Janet glanced over at her nervously. Her tone of voice suggested something disagreeable.

"Yes, ma'am."

"I want you to go for Dr. Ferrier. Mrs. Eakin has been taken poorly."

"Yes, ma'am. I'm sorry to hear that, ma'am."

She meant it. Ever since Peg had come to the house, she had felt an affinity for her. The new Mrs. Eakin was a watcher the same as Janet. She knew the poor woman had shut herself up in her sitting room for the past two days, but so far nobody had said a word about it.

"Come from losing her little one, doesn't it?" she continued.

"What?" Augusta turned to stare at her.

"Our under-matron had a little girl that died. Only two she

was. Missus never came back to work after. We heard she'd lost her mind. She had –"

She halted. Even though Augusta was standing a few feet away, Janet felt the sudden rage that came from her body.

"Whatever gave you the notion that this was any of your business?"

"I, er…I'm sorry, ma'am, I didn't mean anything –"

"Don't ever, ever, overstep your position like this again, or you will be dismissed instantly without reference. Do you understand me?"

Janet curtsied. "Yes, ma'am."

"You are a very ignorant girl. There are many women who have the misfortune to lose their children and they do not become lunatics. They continue on with their lives." There was a fleck of spittle at the corner of Augusta's mouth. "Is that clear?"

The girl ducked her head. "Yes, mistress."

Augusta looked as if she could have said much more, but with an ostentatious gesture of self-control, she turned and swept out of the kitchen. Janet sniffed hard, trying not to cry in case Augusta came back in and saw her. But she couldn't help herself and the tears welled up in her eyes. She used her sleeve to wipe away the dribble from her nose. Then she dipped her forefinger in the soft, shiny sugar and stuck it in her mouth. The sweetness on her tongue was comforting and she sucked on her lips to make it last. She wished desperately that she had somewhere else to go but she didn't.

CHAPTER FIVE

WHILE THE CORONER DID A PRELIMINARY INVESTIGATION, Murdoch went to inform Oliver Wicken's mother that her son was dead. They lived on Wilton Street, not far from the police station. He found himself inwardly rehearsing the words he would use.

The house was narrow-fronted with brown gables that even in the dulling rain looked freshly painted. The small yard behind the iron fence was neat and the shrubs trim. At the door, Murdoch took a deep breath, then knocked on the door. There was no response and he was forced to knock again, harder. This time the door opened. A tall woman of middle age stood looking at him enquiringly. The resemblance between her and the dead constable was striking and he assumed this was Mrs. Wicken. He raised his hat.

"Ma'am. My name is Murdoch. I'm a detective at number four station. I, er..."

His words stuck in his mouth. The truth was too dreadful to say while he was on the doorstep. "May I have a word with you?"

Fear flashed across her face but, perhaps with some instinct of self-preservation, she suppressed it immediately and nodded graciously. "Of course. Please come in. We're in the back."

She led the way down the narrow hall toward the rear of the house. There was an elegance to her that Murdoch hadn't anticipated. Her abundant fair hair was stylishly dressed, her silk wrapper a smart sky-blue stripe with cherry-red yoke and flounces.

"We can talk in here," she said and she drew back the portieres that covered the door to the kitchen. They were velvet and a rich garnet colour. Like the outside of the house, the interior gave the impression of care and pride. Green durrie strips had been placed on the linoleum of the hall and there were several framed paintings on the walls, mostly equestrian portraits as far as he could tell.

"You must excuse us, we were just finishing breakfast."

By the window was an invalid chair, tilted back to a reclining position. Murdoch blinked, fighting the reflexive impulse to look away. There was a child lying in the chair, although it was impossible to tell whether it was male or female. The head was enormous and virtually bald, except for a few sparse strands of white hair that straggled across the forehead. The neck seemed thin as a stalk, although it was probably normal size, and he saw that there was a leather brace under the chin to hold the weight of the head. The pale blue eyes beneath the bulging forehead were vacant.

"This is my daughter, Dora."

She bent over and held a sipping cup to the girl's mouth. Murdoch waited. The kitchen seemed to serve a double function as a sitting room; it was crammed with furniture.

Mrs. Wicken concentrated on her task, wiping away the dribbles from the child's chin. Then she turned around and regarded him.

"I beg your pardon, Mr. Murdoch, please have a seat." She indicated a comfortable armchair but he was reluctant to take it.

"Is there somewhere we could speak in private?"

She shook her head. "It makes no matter where we talk; Dora can neither hear nor see."

She met his eyes and what she saw there frightened her dreadfully.

"What is it? Is Oliver hurt?"

He plunged in and his mouth was dry. "I'm afraid I have very bad news, Mrs. Wicken. Oliver has met with" – He was going to say, "met with an accident", but that wasn't true. He tried again. "I deeply regret to tell you that your son is dead."

The words were out unsoftened and he would have given anything in the world to call them back, to make them palatable. As if that were possible.

She didn't cry out, or show any immediate sign of grief. She simply stared at him.

"I'm not sure I heard you correctly, sir. Are you referring to my son, Oliver Wicken? He is a police constable."

"Yes, ma'am, I know him well."

Her face had gone the colour of chalk. "I don't understand. What has happened?"

"I myself discovered his body in a vacant house a little while ago…he had been shot."

"Shot? By whom?"

"I, er…" Murdoch didn't want to tell her. "He was shot through the head. The bullet was from his own revolver."

He could see her absorbing the implications of what he said but she shook her head.

"I still cannot comprehend what you are saying. Was this an accident?"

"I'm afraid that doesn't seem likely."

"Then I don't understand."

"There was a note beside his body."

He removed it from his notebook and handed it to her. She took it reluctantly and read the message.

"This is preposterous. It makes no sense to me. Who is this addressed to?"

"Did he have a sweetheart?"

"He did not."

"Are you certain, ma'am? That is what the letter implies."

"Of course I am certain. Do you think I don't know my

own son? He was devoted to me and his sister. Her care was a vital part of his life." Her chin and lower lip were shaking uncontrollably and she turned abruptly to the crippled girl and began to fuss with her covers. The child gurgled some sounds of distress, sensing what she couldn't hear or see. Her mother picked up the sipping cup again but held it suspended in the air. Her hand was trembling so badly, however, she couldn't hold the cup steady and she put it down on the table. Murdoch wanted to reach out and comfort her but he couldn't. Finally, she turned back to face him.

"I know what you are implying, Mr. Murdoch. You think he took his own life."

"We won't know for certain until after the inquest but I'm afraid it does seem that way."

"That is utterly impossible. He isn't that kind of boy. My son would never commit suicide. He loved both of us too much."

Murdoch did not reply.

"Let me see that letter again." She examined it. "I am not even sure if that is his hand."

He knew printed letters were hard to distinguish but he didn't contradict her. Abruptly, she returned the letter to him.

"Where is he?"

"At the moment he is still where I found him in the empty house on Gerrard Street. After the jurors have viewed the body he will probably be taken to Humphrey's Funeral Home for the inquest."

Suddenly, she sat back in her chair. "I beg your pardon..."

She put her hand to her mouth, turned to the side, and retched violently, two or three times.

Murdoch crossed over to her and put his hand on her shoulder.

"I am so terribly sorry, Mrs. Wicken."

CHAPTER SIX

WITH A GRUNT, THE CORONER, ARTHUR JOHNSON, GOT to his feet. He was getting on in years and his knees were plaguing him. The wet weather made the ache worse and his temper fractious. He had been examining the wound in Wicken's temple. Murdoch was standing to his right and jammed around the room were the thirteen members of the jury. Constable George Crabtree was at the door. He had been appointed constable of the court and commissioned to find and swear in at least twelve men to serve as jurors. Because of the early hour, he'd managed to net thirteen, catching them before they went to work. For most of the men, this meant missing a day's wages and they had griped and complained. Only two of them were genuinely willing. Albert Chamberlin, retired and lonely, was more than happy to do his duty, and Jabez Clarke, a traveller, was eager because he knew the situation would make for a good tale to recount at a dinner party. However, the sight of the corpse had silenced all of them, even the vociferous labourer, Sam Stevenson, who would sorely miss the money he would have earned that morning.

Johnson beckoned to them irritably. "All of you men, come in closer. What you expect to see from over there is beyond me."

Reluctantly, the men shifted and shuffled forward.

"Come on, come on. Unlike the constable here I haven't got all day."

Murdoch thought for a moment Johnson was referring to Crabtree, then the flippant remark hit him. He would've loved to have made some sharp retort but he daren't show his disapproval too openly. He already had a dickey relationship with his inspector and if he antagonised Johnson, he ran the risk that the coroner would report him. The fine for insubordination was hefty.

"Have you chosen a foreman?" asked the coroner.

"Yes, sir. I am he." The speaker was a tall, lean-faced man, middle-aged, who was dressed in the sombre clothes of a clerk.

"Your name, sir?"

"Jarius Gibb."

"Mr. Gibb, are you prepared to be sworn in?"

"I am."

"Constable, please address the jury."

Crabtree clasped his official papers and in a voice that would have been easily heard in the rear seats of the new Massey Hall, he read:

"'Gentlemen, hearken to your foreman's oath; for the oath he is to take on his part is the oath you are severally to observe and keep on your part.' Mr. Gibb, take this Bible in your right hand."

Gibb did so. He had a rather prissy face with tightly pursed lips, as if he was used to disapproving of the transgressions of humanity. Murdoch wondered where he was employed. Crabtree continued:

"'You shall diligently inquire and true presentment make of all such matters and things as shall be here given you in charge, on behalf of our Sovereign Lady the Queen, touching on the death of Oliver Wicken now lying dead, of whose body you shall have the view; you shall present no man for hatred, malice, or ill will nor spare any through fear, favour, or affection; but a true verdict give according to the evidence, and the best of your skill and knowledge. So help you God.'"

"Amen."

Crabtree addressed the remaining jurors:

"'The same oath which Jarius Gibb, your foreman upon this inquest, hath now taken before you on his part, you and each of you are severally well and truly to observe and keep on your parts. So help you God.'"

There was a varied chorus of "Amens" and then the jury was sworn and ready. Johnson had been waiting impatiently for it all to be concluded.

"All right then. Pay attention all of you." He indicated the wound at the right temple. "The bullet entered here, exited here." He raised Wicken's head releasing trapped blood, which dripped onto the floor.

"Blasted butcher's shop," the labourer muttered to his neighbour.

"Watch your language, Stevenson," Crabtree warned. "This is Her Majesty's court now present."

Johnson pushed at the dead man's shoulder. "See, he's getting stiff as a statue. That's what we call 'rigor mortis'. Happens to all of us when we die – man, woman, or babe." He started to warm to his role as demonstrator. "Anybody know what we can tell from the development of rigor?"

The men avoided his eye.

Murdoch said, "When I found him, at about six o'clock this morning, rigor had started in the chin and neck. I figured he'd been dead for approximately five to six hours."

He didn't want to show off, just let Johnson know there was somebody else in the room he couldn't lord it over.

The coroner nodded. "That's right. So let's see. Rigor is now more advanced. I would agree with the detective. He probably died some time between midnight and two o'clock last night. It's quite cold in here so that slows down the stiffening. Now what else can you tell me about the body? Hm? One of you men speak up. What do you see?"

The jurors stared at him, trying to figure out what he wanted. Johnson shook his head impatiently.

"Well, it's obvious, isn't it? He's in uniform. He was on duty. Isn't that right, Murdoch?"

"Yes, sir. The patrol sergeant last spoke to him at a quarter past eleven."

Sergeant Hales had seen Wicken's body before the coroner arrived and he had been very upset. Saying he didn't want to watch them poking and prodding, he'd put himself in charge of keeping back the curious onlookers who had gathered outside.

"His helmet is about six feet away from him. You didn't move it, did you, Murdoch?"

"I did examine it, sir, but I replaced it in the same spot."

"You said the constable's pistol was wedged between his thighs. Show us exactly where it was, will you."

Murdoch had no desire to do so but he couldn't refuse. He walked over to the body, picked up the gun and, holding it by the handle, tried to push it between the rigid thighs. It was obscenely difficult.

"All right," said Johnson. He scanned the jurors, then pointed to one of them, a short, squat man who looked as if he were trying to make himself invisible. "You at the back. Yes, you. You with the scars."

The man's nose was wide and flattened across his face and the lower lid of his right eye was pulled down by the pucker of a scar, exposing the red. The pupil was dull and unseeing.

Murdoch hoped the fellow wasn't sensitive about his appearance.

"What's your name?" asked the coroner.

"Peter Curran, sir."

"Occupation?"

"I work in the livery stable next door, sir."

"What happened to you? A horse kick you?"

"It was a cow actually, sir. I was just a nipper at the time."

"Unfortunate," said the coroner, his tone brisk as if Curran might be one of those malingerers who are always pleading for sympathy. "Now, then." He held up the note that Murdoch had given him. "The detective found this close to the right hand, under the constable's notebook. What did it say again, Murdoch?"

"Life is unbearable without your love. Forgive me."

"Rather poetic, wouldn't you say? You can all have a look at it."

Murdoch handed the note to the closest juror, who took it gingerly, studied it, and then passed it on. One of the men raised his hand as if he were in the classroom. He had a chubby, weather-roughed face and bright, dark eyes.

"Excuse me, sir. But do we have the pencil that this note was wrote with?"

Johnson frowned. "Do you, Murdoch?"

"No, sir. Perhaps he returned it to his pocket."

"We'll look in a minute."

"I do have another question, sir."

"Yes? State your name so I know who I'm dealing with."

"Stevenson, labourer."

"Speak out."

"Why was the gun between Wicken's legs? It seems an odd place for it to be."

"It must have fallen there as he collapsed, then it was fixed in the grip of death. Don't you agree, Mr. Murdoch?"

"Actually, I was wondering about that myself, sir. It would seem more likely to fall beside him."

There was a palpable ripple of uneasiness among the jurors, who sensed the coroner would not take kindly to contradiction. Most of them had learned to be intimidated by authority.

Johnson shook his head. "Typically, in the case of sudden death, the body can go into seizures. The gun must have been trapped at that moment. Let's move on. The spent casing was here, as you see. What now, Stevenson?"

"Where is the bullet?"

"I don't know, still lodged in his head probably. The post mortem examination will tell us."

"Beg pardon, sir."

It was Constable Crabtree who had spoken. "There is a hole in the wall right here beside the door. Can I examine it?"

"Do, please do."

The constable felt into the small hole and, breaking off some of the plaster, he fished out a bullet and brought it over to Johnson.

"Probably the one that killed him. Take care of it, will you, Mr. Murdoch?"

Murdoch took out one of the envelopes he had at the ready in his pocket and put the bullet into it.

"The entrance of the bullet into the wall seems rather low, sir. Certainly not six feet."

Johnson stared at the spot he indicated. "What religious denomination was the young man?"

"I don't know, sir."

"Hm, an important facet of a man's life, I would say. Strange not to know. Constable?"

"He was Episcopalian, I believe, sir."

"So there. He was no doubt kneeling and saying his prayers. At least he stands a chance of divine forgiveness. Lucky for him he wasn't a Papist. He would head straight to hell for a sin like this."

Murdoch didn't think the coroner could possibly know that he was Roman Catholic but he was stung by the contempt in the man's voice.

"Excuse me, Mr. Johnson." He tried to keep his voice devoid of expression. "At this juncture, we are not absolutely sure he did shoot himself, are we? Won't that be determined at the inquest?"

As soon as the words were out of his mouth, he regretted saying them. They were more likely to close up Johnson's mind than open it.

"No, we are not *absolutely* sure but as close to as makes no difference. We have a farewell note and the position of the wound is consistent with suicide. I fail to see how we can come to any other conclusion."

The jurors were quiet, aware of the rebuke, sympathetic. Then one of them, an elderly man with an old-fashioned full beard, indicated he had a question. Johnson nodded at him.

"Chamberlin, sir. Retired. I was wondering why his helmet was beside him."

"You are most perspicacious. If he were wearing it, the strap would prevent it from being blown off. Conclusion, Wicken must have placed it where he did prior to shooting himself. As to why he did, I have no idea. Some kind of mental preparation, I suppose. People who drown themselves often take off their clothes and fold them up neatly. Like going to bed."

"Can we see his notebook, sir?" This was again from Stevenson.

"As you wish." Johnson handed him the book. A couple of the other men looked over his shoulder.

"There are two entries with yesterday's date. *Monday, November 11.9.07 Gerrard and River. All secure.* The second entry says *Monday, November 11.11.12 Queen and Parliament. All secure and accounted for.* He sounds quite normal here, sir."

"Come, man, what do you expect? He's not going to use his official notebook to write down his inner turmoil. Typically self-murderers vacillate, sometimes for days, until the actual moment."

Stevenson handed back the notebook.

"Let's move on. We'll examine his clothes, then we'll call it a morning."

Murdoch signalled to Crabtree to help him. He undid the neck button of the rubber cape and tugged it away so they could reach into Wicken's pockets. He started with the trousers and pulled out a clean handkerchief from the right-hand pocket and, from the left, a small brown paper package that contained a half slice of cheese. The pencil was here and an iron key.

"Constable, see if it fits the back door," said the coroner.

Crabtree, who seemed even bigger than usual in the cramped room, walked to the door and tried the key. It fit the lock perfectly.

Johnson glanced around at the jurors. "I don't know if there's any more to be done here. We will request a post mortem examination and you will hear that report at the inquest. Murdoch, will you take charge of the effects?"

"Yes, sir."

"Excuse me, Mr. Johnson, could I ask something?" Once again it was the labourer Stevenson who spoke.

"What now? I've got to be getting on. I don't have all day to speculate."

"I've just been thinking, you see."

Johnson made a surprised face that caused some of the other jurors to titter sycophantically.

"What I mean is, I'm wondering why Wicken didn't do himself in the first time."

"What on earth are you talking about?"

His tone was so withering, the man was abashed. Murdoch interjected.

"If I may speak for Mr. Stevenson, sir, I was about to ask the same question. If we are to assume that Wicken was so despondent, why did he wait so long to kill himself? He could have come into the house immediately."

Mr. Johnson smiled. "You weren't listening, Detective. As I said, people can shilly-shally for a long time. To me it is very clear. He is ambivalent about what he is thinking of doing. He knows it is a blasphemy against the Divine Will. He walks his beat, round and round through the empty streets, trying desperately to decide. His sweetheart has abandoned him. His heart is broken. He does not want to live. He has the means at hand to commit the act but he cannot make up his mind. Finally in the darkest hours of the night, he can bear it no longer. He enters the house and…well, you can see the rest."

"Where did he get the key?" asked Murdoch.

Johnson frowned, annoyed that Murdoch had spoiled the effect of his little speech. "I don't know. Don't the police keep the keys to vacant houses?"

"Occasionally we do, but I don't recall ever seeing this one at the station."

The coroner waved his hand dismissively. "We might not be able to tie up all the loose ends. This is something you, yourself, can investigate. Now, I'm setting the inquest for tomorrow morning at eleven o'clock, Humphrey's Funeral Home." He pulled on his fur-lined kid gloves. "Constable, please read the jurors their duties and obligations. And Mr. Murdoch, as you seem so anxious to have this case absolutely certain, you have my permission to investigate further. You can tell your inspector I have requested it."

He made his way to the door, then he paused and turned

around, a bemused look on his face.

"You're not Roman Catholic by any chance, are you, Detective?"

If Murdoch could have controlled his own flush by sheer willpower, he would have done so, but he couldn't. All the other men were gazing at him curiously. The coroner had a fine sense of an exit line.

"As a matter of fact I am, sir. But I don't understand why you ask."

"It's just that you people are so jumpy about suicide. Mortal sin or something in your religion, isn't it? Go to everlasting damnation, don't you?"

"That is the teaching, yes, sir."

"Well, don't let it blind you to the truth, that's all I ask. Remember the oath. We want a true verdict."

Johnson was busy wrapping himself in his muffler or he would have seen the expression on Murdoch's face. Crabtree saw and said loudly, "Off you go then, you men. And don't forget to report in tomorrow. No feeble excuses. You don't show up, you'll be fined."

The jurors shuffled out and Murdoch was left alone with the constable.

"Don't let him get to you, sir. He's a first-class fart if I can put it that way."

"You certainly can, George."

"Do you think it's a suicide, Mr. Murdoch?"

"Let's say I'm keeping an open mind."

"Shall I have him off to the morgue now?"

"Yes. Ask Hales to go for the ambulance. I'll wait here."

The constable left and when the door had closed behind him, Murdoch crouched down beside the dead man.

"May our Lord have mercy on your immortal soul."

He made the sign of the cross with his thumb on Wicken's cold forehead.

CHAPTER SEVEN

FRANK EAKIN SLICED A PIECE OFF THE APPLE HE WAS holding and held it underneath the mare's nose. She sniffed at the fruit and went to take a nibble but Frank stepped back quickly and put the slice between his own teeth.

"Kiss me," he said and he poked his head forward. The horse tossed her head but didn't move. Frank said again, "Come on, Duchess, kiss me."

Peter Curran was leaning against the stable partition watching. "Doesn't want to, does she? Can't say I blame her."

Suddenly, Frank kicked out and his heel caught Curran right on the shin. He yelped and grasped his leg.

"For God's sake, Frank. What are you doing?"

Eakin didn't deign to answer but he made more seductive noises at the mare and this time she stretched her neck and gently nibbled the piece of apple away from his mouth. He grinned.

"See, she's learning."

"That's wonderful," said Curran sullenly. "You can both join the frigging circus."

However, he made sure he had stepped out of reach as he spoke.

"And you could join the freak show," said Frank, "but I doubt they'd take you. Your face would scare the nippers off."

Peter Curran was used to his brother-in-law's jibes but he didn't ever like them. Only fear of the younger man's temper kept him from retaliating.

"So are we going to twitch her or not? Fellow said he'd come by tomorrow."

Frank gave Duchess the remainder of the apple and stroked the horse's soft nose.

"She's a lovely little tart, isn't she?"

Then he grasped her upper lip and twisted it, holding it tightly pinched between his fingers. Far from shying off, the mare stood motionless as if she had gone into a trance. Curran picked up an iron file from the shelf and started to rub at the exposed front teeth, which were splayed out with age.

"There you go, my pretty. You're going to look like a filly all over again," said Eakin.

"Only in the dark. They'll notice for sure."

"You're a cheerful Charley, aren't you? Is something the

matter? Is there something darkening your view of life?"

"Leave off, Frank."

He worked on in a sullen silence, while Frank spoke soothingly to the horse.

"Almost done. You just keep your mind on one of those enormous stallion dongs."

"Do you need to be so crude?"

"You only say that because you aren't stopping your beak in my sister. The mares like knee tremblers. And speaking of that, is Aggie still giving you the go-by?"

Curran shrugged but didn't respond.

"I'll give you some advice, even though she's my own flesh and blood. You've got to show her the whip. Give her a goffer about the head. She'll start talking to you."

Curran scooped out the filings from the mare's mouth. "I didn't notice I'd asked for any advice."

"Suit yourself. But she's a mule when she wants to be. Look, you did me a favour by marrying her. I've never seen a woman more anxious to snare a husband. Before you came along, she'd take things out on me. Wouldn't speak to me once for almost two months. Not that I gave a piss about her stupid conversation but it got to be aggravating that she wouldn't answer anything. One day, I just got fed up and I picked up the slop pail in the kitchen and dumped it all over her. That brought her voice back fast."

Curran rubbed away in silence, the mare still transfixed by Eakin's grip on her lip.

"I'm done," he said and Eakin let go. Duchess ducked her head a few times and snuffled. "Do you think we should puff her glims?"

Frank regarded the mare's sunken eyes. The upper skin had collapsed with age.

"No. She'll have to do. Keep the lamp down low. This fellow is nothing but a country sot. He won't notice." He stroked the horse's neck. "She'll look beautiful."

"Why'd the old gasser pick on me at the viewing?" Curran asked suddenly.

Frank shrugged. "Must have been your open and honest face."

"He made a comment about my eye. I told him the cow kicked me."

"You should have said the truth – it was some poor heifer you were trying to stick it to."

Curran scowled. "Leave off, Frank. I mean it."

"I was joking, for Jesus' sake. Just trying to lighten the mood."

"You needn't bother. You'd be low too if you'd been there when they were examining him. It'll haunt me for the rest of my days."

"Like I said, you should have made yourself scarce when the frog came around recruiting."

"You know I didn't have a chance. The fella came right into the stable and nabbed me."

"Well, put it this way, one good thing is you'll be up on all what's going on, won't you? You and Jarius both."

"He don't show much, does he? Didn't even blink an eye

when one of the fellas nominated him as foreman. 'I'll be honoured' was his very words."

"Don't surprise me. He don't have blood in his veins like normal people. I should know."

"Know what?"

Jarius had entered the stable unheard. Frank jumped as if there was a loud noise. "Nothing," he said.

"We need some help," said Jarius.

"What with?"

"Dr. Ferrier's come but she won't open the door. She's screaming like a street slut." He nodded at Frank. "Where's the axe?"

"In the back."

"Bring it."

"What does Pa say?"

"Nothing. He's leaving everything up to me. Hurry up, I don't have all day. I want to get to my office before the day's wasted completely." He was dressed in outdoor clothes – a smart plaid cape and a black crusher.

Frank tapped his forehead in a mock salute and went to do what he was told. As he went past the last stall, the big grey gelding poked his head over the gate and gave him a quick, hard bite on the shoulder. Frank yelled, spun around, and fetched the horse a savage punch on the side of the head.

CHAPTER EIGHT

AFTER THE AMBULANCE HAD TAKEN AWAY WICKEN'S body, Murdoch and Crabtree started the tedious process of knocking on doors. The constable took the west side of the street and Murdoch the east. There was a string of stores from Gerrard down to Wilton Street and he was able to speak to the shopkeepers, who for the most part were huddled by their stoves with the lamps fully burning. None of them could give him any information. Two or three were familiar with the constable and one confirmed he had seen Wicken walking the beat at ten o'clock last night and said he had seemed quite normal. They had heard nothing. Mrs. Bail, the widow lady who ran a confectionery at number 327, was particularly upset.

"Oh dear, oh my word," she kept repeating. "He came in here once a week on Friday night without fail. He'd catch me just before I closed when he was on his way to work. Very partial to my buttercups with the nut centre. Oh dear, oh my."

She had seen Wicken as usual on Friday last. "He bought a box of chocolate creams. Raspberry flavoured. For his sister, he said, but I suspect it was a sweetheart. They are my best candies."

She was so distressed, Murdoch felt sorry that he had to press her. "In your opinion, Mrs. Bail, did the constable seem in any way despondent or out of sorts?"

She eyed him, puzzled. "Not at all. He was cheery as always. 'Good evening to you, Mrs. Bail,' he'd say. 'What have you got for me to try today?' I experiment with new candies, you see, and I'd let him taste them. I'd made some maple toffee and he really liked it. Oh my, Mr. Murdoch, why are you asking such a thing?"

Murdoch had said little about the way Wicken had died but she picked up the implications of his question immediately. He hesitated.

"I'm afraid there are indications that he may have taken his own life."

"Oh, no. I cannot believe that. He was too happy. No, Mr. Murdoch, that cannot be."

"Did he ever mention to you that he had a sweetheart?"

"No, he never did. But as I said, I wondered sometimes when he would buy a special box of chocolates. I knew he lived with his mother and a sister who is poorly." She indicated one of the large jars on the shelf behind the counter that was filled with small, brightly coloured candies. "His sister was partial to the Tom Thumb mix and his mother liked the marshmallow drops."

She was close to tears and Murdoch wished he could offer her some solace but he couldn't.

"The coroner's inquest is tomorrow and we hope we'll learn what exactly happened. For now, I'm just trying to find out if anybody heard or saw anything that might have to do with him."

She shook her head. "I did not. I closed up the shop as usual at seven o'clock and retired for the night at a half past nine. Saves the lamp oil."

She gave him a wan smile that nevertheless had the ghost of the coquette in it. She was a small woman, grey-haired and neat in her green silk waist and crisp white apron. She reminded him of his landlady, Mrs. Kitchen, and he responded warmly.

"Indeed it does, ma'am."

She went on to express concern for Wicken's widowed mother. She was as adamant as Mrs. Wicken had been that Oliver was not the kind of man to take his own life.

Finally, as Murdoch was leaving, she took some barley sugar sticks from a jar, put them in a brown paper bag, and thrust it into his hand.

"Freshly made this morning."

The shop had a wonderful sweet smell of boiled candy.

Because of his painful jaw, Murdoch didn't want to risk eating anything now but he thanked her and stowed the bag in his pocket.

The next half hour was unforthcoming. From across the road, Crabtree indicated he'd had no success either. They continued making their way south and Murdoch was glad the constable had the dentist Brodie on his side of the street. He wondered if revisiting the scene of his pain would distress him but Crabtree emerged looking much the same.

About half a block below Wilton Street, there was a Chinese laundry and when Murdoch stepped through the front door he was immediately enfolded by the hot moist air. A Chinaman was working on an abacus behind the counter. He was wearing a traditional blue smock and round black hat and his hair was braided into a long queue.

"Can help you?"

Murdoch tapped his own chest. "Me police officer. Need to ask questions."

The man looked at him uncomprehendingly. Murdoch paused, trying to think how to communicate. "Me police officer," he repeated in a louder voice. "Ask questions."

"Washing very cheap. Very clean."

Behind him in the long narrow shop were two large steaming washtubs. Another man was forking out piles of boiled linen with a long stick and dumping them into a basket, ready for mangling. To his right was a large iron range where a variety of irons were heating.

Murdoch pointed. "He speak English?" He made motions at his mouth but realised he looked as if he was wanting to eat. He called out instead. "Hey, you back there. Do you speak English?"

The Chinaman stopped what he was doing and approached Murdoch. He was young and seemed as wary as a dog with a stranger.

When he was close enough, Murdoch asked, "Speak English?"

"Ay. What ken I do for ye?"

For a moment, Murdoch was confused by his accent, expecting Chinese. Then he realised the man had spoken with a strong Scottish burr.

"Early this morning, a police constable was found dead up at the corner of Gerrard Street. He was on duty last night and I was wondering if you saw him at all or had anything to do with him. He would probably have been walking past here on his beat at various times during the night. Any information you can give me would be much appreciated."

The older man apparently asked a question and there was a spirited exchange between the two of them. Murdoch couldn't tell if they were excited or if it was the rhythm of the language. The younger man turned back to Murdoch.

"I perhaps should present my father, Mr. Sam Lee. I myself am called Foon Lee."

He bowed in such a formal way that Murdoch almost reciprocated. He nodded an acknowledgement.

"I'm Acting Detective William Murdoch from number four station."

"My father would like to know a description of the officer in the case."

"He was young, about the same height as me, but he had a

blond moustache, not dark."

"And this unfortunate officer has been the victim of an accident?"

"Something to that effect."

Sam Lee spoke to his son and Murdoch wondered if he understood English better than he was letting on. Foon bowed.

"I must tell you that I myself had got myself off to my bed but my father did encounter the constable last night. The officer opened the door. Apparently it was not locked and he was concerned that all was well. When he was sure that all was as it was intended to be, he left."

He stopped and they both watched Murdoch, waiting for the next move.

"What time was that?"

Foon translated the question to his father.

"It would have been at approximately twenty minutes past eleven o'clock. Mr. Lee is quite assured of the correctness of this time." He indicated a large clock that was hung on the wall, its glass face obscured by steam.

"Will you ask him if there was anything strange about the constable. Was he calm? Distracted in any way? Do you understand what I mean?"

"Ay, I do."

Again the exchange in Chinese.

"My father says the officer has come here on two prior occasions to check on his well-being and they have had pleasant words. Last night was not an exception. The constable seemed

74

quite equal in his temper."

Mr. Lee senior interceded, saying directly to Murdoch, "Lady. Had lady."

"I don't understand."

"Lady, was a lady with him."

Exasperated, Murdoch turned to Foon. "What is he saying?"

"The officer was accompanied by a young woman. She was standing back but he saw her clearly, then they walked up the street together."

Murdoch sighed. It was strictly against regulations for anyone to accompany constables on their beat. However, in spite of what Mrs. Wicken believed, the evidence was pointing to her son having a lover. Someone he was willing to risk his job over.

"Please inform Mr. Lee that he will have to be a witness at the inquest. A constable will come back today with a subpoena."

There was a flurry of talk, both of them obviously alarmed.

"Mr. Lee wishes to ask what is the charge he is under? He has paid his licence most recently."

"No, no. He isn't being charged with anything. At an inquest anybody with information has to tell it. There will be others doing the same. Then the jury can decide what has happened."

"My father is now wondering if he was not in truth mistaken. That it was not this night that he saw the officer."

Murdoch faced the older man, gave him a little bow, and spoke slowly and distinctly.

"Mr. Lee. You need not be afraid. You are not in any trouble.

All I want you to do is to tell the coroner, the judge, what you have just said to me. That's all."

He turned his hands palms up in a universal gesture of openness. As far as he could tell, the Chinaman calmed down.

"You will have to come as his translator," Murdoch said to the son.

"Very well."

Both the Lees bowed deeply and Murdoch gave a quick bob himself. It was infectious.

He left. Outside on the grey street, the air was even more chill after the warmth of the laundry and he shivered. He wondered when the mysterious woman was going to turn up and he hoped he wouldn't be the one to give her the news.

CHAPTER NINE

BY THE TIME HE GOT TO THE END OF THE BEAT, MURDOCH was getting tired. His jaw was still pulsing and when he touched his cheek, it felt swollen. He would have to find a dentist soon and stop being such a lily liver. His moustache was dripping and his hands were freezing because he'd left his lodgings without his gloves, and to make matters worse, he was overly conscious of the fishy miasma all around him from his wet coat. He took out one of the barley sugar sticks and stuck it in his mouth. As long as he kept it away from the bad side of his jaw it seemed fine, and the sweetness filled his mouth.

He had almost reached the corner of Gerrard and Parliament streets, when two men emerged from the house that was next to the livery stable. They were carrying a chair between them on which was sitting a young woman. She was squirming and it took a moment for Murdoch to realise she was strapped to the chair. Her actions were peculiarly lethargic, as if she were a mechanical piece that was winding down. A frightened-looking girl, dressed in servant's grey, was endeavouring to hold an umbrella over all of them while an older man, a doctor by the look of him, followed behind. He was speaking in a quick, anxious voice to the woman in the chair.

"Calm yourself, madam. Please calm yourself."

One of the men carrying her was Frank Eakin, the other, the scarred juror whom Murdoch had seen earlier.

The bizarre entourage was heading for a carriage drawn up at the gate but, even as he watched, Murdoch saw the woman's struggles begin to subside completely. They came through the gate and he waited to let them pass. The woman's head was lolling back against the chair, but she turned in his direction and her eyes, wide with terror, met his.

"Help me," she whispered. "Please, mister, help me."

He had no chance to respond because the doctor stepped in front of him. The coachman opened the door of the carriage and she was lifted in, chair and all. The doctor climbed in himself, immediately pulled down the window blind, and they drove off. The two men, both of them panting from their exertion, watched.

"What's going on?" Murdoch asked.

Curran realised who Murdoch was and he gave him a quick salute.

"Morning, Officer. That's Mrs. Eakin. I'm afraid she's lost her slates. We're getting her to the loony bin."

Murdoch was about to make some polite murmur of condolence but he didn't get the chance.

Eakin snapped at the servant girl. "For God's sake, Cullie. We're getting soaked. You're as useless as a stuck pig. Bring the frigging thing over here."

She jumped to obey and Eakin took the umbrella. "Anything we can do for you, sir?"

"I was coming to speak to the members of the household concerning the death of Constable Wicken. I'm sorry if this is not an appropriate time. I can come back later."

"What is it you're after?"

"Any information. Whether anybody heard the gunshot. That sort of thing."

"Nobody's said anything about it."

"I'd still like to talk to them. We're asking questions of everybody in the vicinity."

Eakin managed to produce a friendlier expression. "Of course. Terrible tragedy, that."

He was studying Murdoch from the shelter of the umbrella and the detective began to get irritated. He was sorry for the man's circumstances but he didn't feel like spending more time in the rain than he had to.

"It shouldn't take too long," he said.

Eakin looked toward the house. The front door was open and a woman was standing on the threshold watching them.

She was dressed in mourning clothes and her hands were clasped in front of her as if in prayer. Whatever Eakin saw there made up his mind.

"You might as well come in now. Get it out of the way."

He extended the umbrella to cover Murdoch and they walked toward the door in awkward intimacy.

"Augusta, this is Detective Murdoch. He wants to ask us all some questions about the fellow they found in the empty house." He was closing up the umbrella as he spoke. "This is my sister, Mrs. Curran." He gestured with his thumb. "Hitched to him."

She stepped back so they could enter, then over his shoulder, she noticed the servant girl who was trailing behind them.

"Janet, you can get back to work. Go in the side entrance."

She bobbed. "Yes, ma'am." She scurried off.

"Come this way, Mr. Murdoch," said Mrs. Curran. "We can talk in the drawing room."

She turned and led the way down the narrow hall but not without a quick glance at Murdoch's boots to determine just how wet they were. He wiped them hurriedly on the doormat and set off after her. Peter Curran was at his heels, and at the door, he tapped Murdoch on the shoulder.

"You don't want me, do you, sir?" asked Curran. "Me being on the jury and all."

"Yes, as a matter of fact I do. It won't affect anything. It can all be repeated for the inquest."

He'd found that asking questions of an entire family at the

same time tended to yield a lot of information, if not about the case, certainly about them.

The drawing room fire was laid but unlit and the air was chill. Frank went straight to the fireplace and reached for the box of matches standing by the fender.

"That won't be necessary," said his sister. "I'm sure Mr. Murdoch won't keep us."

Eakin turned to her, glaring in a little spurt of anger.

"Aggie, it's frigging freezing in here. I'm going to light the bloody fire."

His sister didn't retaliate for his rudeness except by a visible tightening of her lips.

"Mr. Murdoch, will you take that chair?" She indicated an armchair next to the fireplace. He sat down, took off his damp hat, and placed it beside the chair. The mantel was draped with black crepe and the mirror above was covered with a grey gauze. He wondered who had died.

Eakin had got a blaze going right away and stretched out his hands to the flames. Then, predictably, he turned to warm his backside. Mrs. Curran took a seat on the Turkish couch opposite him, while her husband remained by the door.

"Shall I light the lamps, Augusta?" In the gloom, Peter Curran would have been a sinister-looking fellow except that his whole bearing was so hangdog, Murdoch felt sorry for him.

She didn't look in his direction at all but addressed the air in front of her. "I would have thought it was obvious we need some light."

Murdoch took a quick glance around the room. There were other crepe trimmings on the sideboard and around the pictures on the walls. The furniture was dark hued and, although the plush green coverings were thick and patterned with gilt flowers, the effect was gloomy. The house wasn't that grand and he had the impression the drawing room wasn't much used. Probably a family aspiring to a lifestyle beyond their class. Fine furniture but not fine manners. On the other hand, to be fair, it had been his experience that ungraciousness could be found at any level of society.

Curran lit a lamp from the sideboard and brought it closer to where they were sitting. Augusta pointed wordlessly at a small japanned table and he placed it there.

Murdoch took out his notebook to indicate he was ready to start. Frank Eakin, smelling slightly of singed corduroy, came and sat beside his sister. The family resemblance was strong. Short nose and round chin, fair complexion. Augusta had light brown hair that she wore pinned tightly in a knot on top of her head. Eakin was trying without much success to sport side whiskers and a moustache.

"Is this everybody in the house?" asked Murdoch.

"No, there's Mr. Eakin, our father, but I'm afraid he is indisposed. Besides, I'm sure he could not help you. He always takes a sedative at night. Nothing would wake him."

"Anyone else?"

"There's Mr. Jarius Gibb. You must have met him. He's the foreman of the coroner's jury. He is our older brother."

"Stepbrother," interrupted Eakin. "His mother was a widow when she married our father. Unfortunately, she did not live too much longer afterward. Father married for the second time. This Mrs. Eakin, Harmony by name and nature, was our mother."

He was offering this information in a chatty way that Murdoch found odd. As did his sister, obviously, because she frowned at him.

"Frank, really! I doubt that is relevant to the officer's enquiry."

Murdoch had a vivid image of the two of them as small children ready to squabble at any moment. But that early animosity seemed to have hardened into mutual disdain.

He addressed Eakin, trying to be as delicate as he could. "And your wife, sir? She was in the house last night, I assume."

"Who?"

"Mrs. Eakin, the lady who…" He waved vaguely in the direction of the door.

"That's not my wife. She's married to my father. As I said, Mother died last year. My father married again this April. Quick you might say. Properly speaking, the woman you saw is my stepmother, young as she is."

There was a strange sound from Curran, and Murdoch could have sworn he had guffawed and stifled it immediately. He looked over at Curran but he was sitting in the shadows behind the light and he couldn't see his expression.

"Mrs. *Nathaniel* Eakin was indeed in the house," answered Augusta. "But as you saw, she is dreadfully ill. Her doctor has been forced to commit her to the provincial lunatic asylum. I doubt she would be aware if Beelzebub himself visited us."

Her tone was sharp. *No love lost there,* Murdoch thought.

"Do you have other servants?" he asked.

"Only Janet, the girl you saw. We hire extra help as we need."

Murdoch felt a twinge of pity for the young servant. He could imagine the amount of work that was foisted on her.

"I assume your husband has spoken to you about the tragedy I am investigating, Mrs. Curran?"

"My brother told me. But I thought the coroner declared him a suicide."

"We won't know anything for certain until after the inquest. That is why I am conducting this investigation."

"'Scuse me." Frank got up and went to the fire. He grabbed the poker and gave a recalcitrant piece of coal a couple of good thwacks. Flames leaped out. He stayed where he was, watching the fire.

"I am interested in any information you can give me," said Murdoch. "We think the constable died some time between midnight and one o'clock. Did any of you hear anything?"

"I for one am a very sound sleeper," said Augusta. "I heard nothing at all."

"Where is your bedroom, ma'am?"

"On the third floor. My husband and I have a suite there."

Murdoch nodded at Curran. "What about you, sir?"

"Not a peep. I sleep like the dead."

"You were on the third floor as well?"

Augusta looked at Murdoch as if he had said something

quite rude but his guess was right.

Curran chuckled in embarrassment. "Not last night I wasn't. I snore. Keeps my wife aggravated. I was in the stable loft. Better."

"So was I," added Frank. "I have a room there so I can keep an eye on the horses. I didn't hear anything except them farting."

This remark was obviously intended to offend his sister, who took the bait.

"Frank, how many times must I ask you not to be so coarse?"

"That's not coarse, Aggie. It's a fact of nature. Horses fart all the time. Noisy buggers."

Any further argument was halted by the mantel clock which began to announce the hour in such a deep-toned gong, it was impossible to speak. Involuntarily they all looked in its direction. It was a massive bronzed piece, more than two feet high, and the clock face nestled in the middle of the bust of a smiling woman, rather Roman in appearance. Her hair and collar were lavishly hung with imitation coins and the word "Fortune" was embossed on the base. As the sound died away, Murdoch closed his notebook, picked up his hat, and stood up.

"I won't keep you any longer. What time might I catch Mr. Gibb?"

"He works at the city offices. He issues marriage licences. He is usually home by six o'clock."

"Either I or a constable will come back then. For now, I'll just have a word with your servant before I go."

Frank Eakin grinned. "Janet's a fanciful girl, Mr. Murdoch.

Don't take everything she says as gospel. She believes in ghosts. She's always going on about hearing them wandering round the house."

"I'll take that under advisement. Where would I find her, ma'am?"

Augusta stood up. "I'll take you. She should be in the kitchen."

"We'll get back to the stable," said Eakin. "You won't want us any more, will you, Officer?"

"Not for now."

At the door, Mrs. Curran paused and apparently speaking to nobody in particular, she said, "It won't be necessary to leave the lamp lit."

Her husband hurried to obey and blew out the light. The sour, smoky smell of the extinguished wick wafted on the air.

Murdoch left with a feeling of relief. Being with this family was like sticking your hand in a wasp's nest.

CHAPTER TEN

PEG THOUGHT SHE MUST HAVE BEEN IN THE BATHTUB for a very long time but it was hard to be sure. There was no clock in the room and her memory of coming here, of being put into the tub, was not quite real, as if she had been dreaming violent, vivid dreams. However, her eyes were focusing properly now and even though her head felt as if she were inside a blanket, she was no longer under the influence of the sedative. She knew she was in an institution.

She shivered. The water had cooled to the point of discomfort. She turned her head. There were three large bathtubs in the room and she was in the middle one. On her left was a woman whose face, with its well-defined nose and chin and good wide brow, showed some refinement of features. She wasn't young but her hair was still brown and abundant, braided and pinned into a crown on top of her head.

"Hello," said Peg softly.

The woman's eyes were closed and she didn't respond. "Good girl." The woman in the other tub had spoken loudly. "You'll go to heaven, my dear." Her hair was white and stringy and Peg could see there were large bare patches on her scalp, the skin showing pink.

"Hello," she said.

The woman looked over at her but her eyes were blank and unseeing. Suddenly she burst into harsh crying. Peg could offer no comfort but the tears stopped as abruptly as they'd begun and the woman started to sing a cheerful hymn.

All three women were in the same position. A canvas cover was stretched across the iron tub. There was a hole for the patient's head; the rest of the body was completely immersed. There was a canvas harness which sloped backward and Peg was fastened to it by a strap at the waist. Her arms were tied at the wrists and her legs were similarly restrained at the ankles. The bonds weren't tight but she couldn't slip out of them. Even if she had been able to get loose, she knew she wouldn't be able to lift the canvas cover because it was tied to rings at the side of the tub.

Somebody will come soon. Keep calm, keep calm.

But the panic swept over her and she couldn't stop it bursting out of her mouth.

A woman in attendant's uniform came hurrying in. She was large and her features were strong to the point of being masculine but her expression was kind. She clucked sympathetically.

"What's this now?"

"Let me out, please let me out."

"Are you cold?" the attendant asked.

"Yes, yes, I am. Can I get out?"

"I'll just warm up the water a bit and that'll feel better. All our ladies show great improvement after a time in the tub. Wish I could do it myself; my beaters get real sore at the end of the day."

"I don't care a frigging toss about your feet. I want to get out of this goddam tub."

The woman wagged her forefinger. "Nasty words like that won't get you anywhere except into trouble."

Peg felt a wave of terror pinch her stomach. This attendant seemed quite kind really but she was like all of them. If you offended, retribution was inevitable. Sometimes it was angry and overt, more often subtle. Small withholdings. Leave her there longer, just fifteen minutes longer in the solitary room. Fifteen minutes that would make the difference between sanity and madness.

She tried to gain back some control. "I'm sorry, truly I am. Please forgive me. I didn't mean it. I was..."

She was interrupted by her neighbour bursting into sobs again. The attendant nodded over at her.

"Don't worry about Miss Anderson. She's quite harmless."

"Why is she crying like that?"

"She is afraid she won't go to heaven. She was a missionary most of her life."

She went over to the white-haired woman and leaned over close to her face.

"Why don't you sing us another hymn now, Miss Anderson? I do dearly love to hear 'Waiting by the River.'"

Almost without pause, the woman changed from crying to singing. Her voice was hoarse but the rendition was tuneful, years of habit still strong. The attendant came back to Peg and turned on the taps at the end of the tub.

"Is that better? Do you want it hotter?"

"No, thank you. I'm sorry I was so rude. What is your name please?"

"Trayling."

"How long have I been in here?"

"In the bath or in the asylum?"

"The bath."

Trayling consulted the steel watch pinned to her grey apron. Peg noticed the swell of her large breasts which seemed soft even beneath the starched bib. Her sleeve was rolled up past the plump forearm and her skin was freckled and reddened from the water. Peg had to fight hard to keep back a rush of tears. The attendant reminded her of somebody but she couldn't quite recover the memory. It was somebody who had appeared in her dreams many times. Familiar yet unidentifiable, like a place you know you must have visited some time in the past, but cannot name. She'd been told a neighbour had delivered her to Dr. Barnardo's orphanage when her mother disappeared and she thought it might be her she dreamed of.

"You were admitted this afternoon. Dr. Clark thought a bath would calm you and you've been in here for two hours. He wants you to stay for at least three."

She must have seen the fear because she picked up a sponge from a basket beside the tub, and dipping it in a bowl of cool water, she wiped Peg's brow.

"Best thing is not to fight so. You'll feel better before you know it."

"What is going to happen to me?"

"That's for the doctors to decide. If you act like a good Christian woman, no cussing like you did just now, do what you're told, and you'll soon be allowed to go home."

"And if I'm not good?"

"Then you'll have to stay in here with all the other lunatics."

As if in answer, the woman who hadn't said a word up to now burst into loud laughter. They could hear her splashing her feet in the water. Trayling clucked her tongue disapprovingly.

"Mrs. Stratton, stop that noise. You sound like a heathen if ever I heard one."

She got up stiffly from her stool, rolled down her sleeve, and started to dry her hands on the piece of holland towelling on the chair. She smiled down at Peg. "I'll leave you for now. See if you can get some rest."

She left, her clogs splashing against the water-splattered brick floor.

Peg was so afraid again, she felt nauseated. Her mouth was dry and she wished she had asked for a drink of water. She didn't want to call again, though. She couldn't risk using up the goodwill that the attendant was showing toward her. She lay back, her eyes open wide, looking at the ceiling, which was stained with watermarks from the steam. She forced herself to be calm, to think.

Her memories were returning and at first she wanted to shy away from them, to get lost in the fog of the drug.

No! Think. Get it back.

They'd broken down the door. It had splintered when somebody, Frank probably, wielded an axe. They had all come in, Dr. Ferrier behind them with his black bag. He had talked to her, she remembered that, but she didn't know how long that had taken. He had turned away to his bag, and when he faced her again, he was holding a syringe. She had screamed and kicked it out of his hand. Then Frank and Peter had held her in the chair and Dr. Ferrier got another syringe.

At that moment, she had stepped out of her body and stood to one side, watching. The two men holding her were exerting painful pressure and Frank was cursing because she was fighting so. "I must ask you to temper your language," said the doctor, and she thought what an old-fashioned expression that was. The woman who was struggling to get free was very strong and could easily throw them off if she wanted to but somehow she was being slowed down. She was falling asleep; she was so tired she couldn't help herself.

If you go to sleep now you will die, said the separate self. She moved further away from her body as if she were actually floating near the ceiling. She saw the other Peg tied to the chair with some binding the doctor had brought with him. Then they were carrying her downstairs.

Don't give in. Stay awake.

But sleep was inviting – safe and irresistible. They were outside. She saw Cullie and was sorry the young servant was afraid. Then she was looking at a tall man in a fur hat and a long coat. He had a dark moustache and his eyes were noticing. The Peg in the chair spoke to him.

Help me. Please help me.

He was worried. "I'll help you," he said, although his lips didn't move.

"Psst, you, new woman."

She turned her head to the left. Mrs. Stratton was watching her.

"Yes?" She tried to make her voice friendly.

"Allow me to introduce myself. I'm Mrs. Harold Stratton of Chatham, Ontario. What is your name?"

"Margaret Eakin."

"Are you married?"

"Yes."

"Children?"

"Ye-no. That is, I did have a son but he died."

Mrs. Stratton gazed over at her; her eyes were fierce. "Murdered, was he?"

Peg turned her head away as abruptly as if she had been struck.

"Yes," she said. "Yes, he was."

CHAPTER ELEVEN

WEARILY, MURDOCH HEADED FOR ONTARIO STREET AND the comfort of Mrs. Kitchen's parlour. He was cold and hungry, his back ached from walking so long, and the pain in his jaw was all-consuming. Between them, he and Crabtree had questioned virtually every household member on Wicken's beat, but nothing significant had come of it. Many of the people were familiar with the young constable; some of them were sincerely distressed. One or two of the women wept openly. "Such a nice, polite young man," cried Mrs. Jackson, who was the cook at a grand house on Gerrard Street. But she hadn't seen him since the end of the summer when she'd been sitting on the front veranda, it was so scorching that day. "Madam allowed all us servants, even young Eddie, to come outside after evening chores. Very kind it was. The constable went by and we joked at him. He looked so hot, he did, in his uniform."

Most people tried to be helpful, would have manufactured information if they could, but essentially nobody told him anything new. Nobody other than Mr. Lee had actually seen Wicken or his companion. It was a night when everybody was as snug as they could be in their own houses.

Lamps were lit along the street, the macadam black and slick in the rain. Not for the first time Murdoch wished he were coming home to Liza. Closely following on that thought, however, like a herding dog on the heels of a sheep, was an image of Enid Jones, the young widow who was also a boarder at the Kitchens'. Under different circumstances, Murdoch had to admit he would have been paying court to her but she was a devout Baptist, he, a Roman Catholic, although not so devout. Those differences of faith seemed irreconcilable.

He was passing one of the big houses on Wilton Street. The curtains were not drawn and he could see into the front sitting room. Two men, one about his own age, were lounging in their armchairs in front of the fire. They were wearing claret-coloured smoking jackets and he saw them both, in unconscious unison, take a protracted luxurious pull on their respective cigars. The furnishings were opulent and the room was golden from the bright firelight. Murdoch knew the two men slightly, knew they were both lawyers and that the son had joined his father's firm. He felt a sharp stab of envy. He walked on by, realising it wasn't the affluence of the men that he was jealous of, so much as the feeling of security surrounding them and how comfortable they seemed to be in each other's company. He hadn't thought about his own father in a while, deliberately keeping his memories as buried as possible, but he wondered if he was even still alive. The life of a fisherman was a dangerous one, after all. However, he assumed somebody would have informed him of any catastrophe.

Murdoch didn't particularly like his own envy. He'd seen too much of it in his father and had experienced over and over again the man's rancour, his unrelenting jealousy of his own son. Once again his thoughts flew to Liza. If she had lived they would be married by now, probably with a babe, and he himself would have been struggling with the complexity of fatherhood.

Oh, but I would have wanted it. The words were so strong in his mind, he thought for a moment he'd said them out loud. At times, his grief at her death seemed as fresh as ever. He looked for her in the women he passed on the street, dreamed of holding her in his arms, dreamed that she wasn't dead but merely gone away. After those dreams he awoke angry; after the loving dreams he awoke aching.

However, over the past few months he had found himself actively seeking for a sweetheart. He had started dancing lessons, taken to it quite well really, even though his only dancing partner at first was the instructor himself, Professor Otranto, who took the lady's part. Then in the summer he'd attended his first mixed class and met a young woman who worked at the music store on King Street. She had seemed most receptive toward him until she discovered he was Roman Catholic. She was Methodist. "My father would disown me. And I'm all he's got now," she had said sadly. As a result, Murdoch had given up his dancing classes, reluctant to see her there and be tantalised by what he couldn't have.

And now, stronger all the time, were his feelings for Enid. Would he change his faith in order to fit with a woman's? He tried to be honest with himself, sighed, and had to admit, fair or not, he couldn't see himself doing that. He'd never even set foot in a church other than a Catholic one. In that respect he'd been thoroughly indoctrinated by the priests of his childhood. *About time I gave this some thought,* he said to himself, again not for the first time. But later, not when his head was pounding, not when the rain had washed all colour from the world, and certainly not on the same day a fine young man had been ripped from life before he'd even lived much of it.

As he approached the house, he experienced a rush of pleasure. The lamps were lit in the front parlour and he knew Mrs. Kitchen would have his supper waiting for him. She prided herself on being a "plain cook", which meant that the meat was often overdone and the potatoes boiled into tastelessness, but he didn't mind. Since he had moved in with the Kitchens three years ago, they had become dear friends. The closest thing to a family he had ever known. He opened the door and entered the narrow hall, also well-lit tonight. He had hardly taken off his hat and coat when his landlady came hurrying out of the kitchen.

"Oh my, what dreadful weather. Come and get yourself

warm this minute. The fire's going in the parlour and your tea is all ready. I'll bring it right in."

Murdoch blew on his cold hands.

"I forgot my gloves this morning."

Then he noticed that the chenille curtains across the rear door were lowered.

He nodded in that direction. "How's Arthur?"

"A bit poorly. This damp weather is hard for him."

She took his astrakhan hat from the coat tree where he'd hung it and shook off the raindrops. "I've minced up some lamb for you and mashed potatoes. And I've boiled up the rutabaga. I thought you'd be glad of soft food. I'm sure that tooth is bothersome. I don't suppose you've had it tended to, have you?"

"I confess I have not. Cowardice won out."

"I'll bring you some more clove oil."

"Thank you, Mrs. K. Can I go and see him?"

"Of course. He's been brooding too much. See if you can take his mind off things."

As he lifted the curtain aside, Mrs. Kitchen said, "He asked me to close them, said the draft was bothering him. Fact is he's wrapped up tight so I don't know what it could be."

The ever-present worry about her husband was close to the surface tonight. Usually, she acted as if he were suffering from a bad head cold that would clear up before long.

She returned to the kitchen and Murdoch went into the room. Arthur Kitchen was wrapped in a tartan blanket, sitting in his wicker Bath chair. He seemed to be asleep, but at Murdoch's entrance, he opened his eyes and grinned with pleasure.

"Hello, Will. You're late tonight. Something happen?"

"I'm afraid so. I'll tell you about it after my tea."

They both knew Mrs. Kitchen wouldn't let them talk until Murdoch had been properly fed. But he valued their chats and both the Kitchens loved to hear about his experiences with what Arthur termed "the fascinating diversity of the criminal strand in the fabric of society". Arthur almost never went out and certainly hadn't stirred from home during the entire last six weeks of wet, chilly weather.

"How's your tooth?"

"Making itself known. You've been a bit poorly today, Mrs. K. said."

Arthur nodded and suddenly coughed. He had a cloth which he held close to his mouth, but Murdoch could see how much blood he expectorated. There was a fetid odour in the room that not even the bucket of carbolic Mrs. Kitchen had placed in the corner of the room could disguise. The window was closed tonight. Another deviation from the usual routine. Even in the bitterly cold winter months, Mrs. Kitchen had kept the window open in the hope that fresh air would arrest the progress of the disease. She tried out every treatment she heard of and Murdoch couldn't tell whether it was, in fact, the efficacy of these cures or her desire that had kept Arthur alive this long.

A fire was burning in the hearth but there was only one lamp lit on the mantelpiece and the room was gloomy. He was about to offer to light a lamp when Mrs. Kitchen came in. She was carrying a jug and a glass.

"Good heavens, what are you doing sitting in the dark like this?"

Arthur shrugged listlessly.

"I'll light the sconces, shall I?" asked Murdoch.

"Yes, please, and those two lamps on the sideboard. Poor light is unhealthy."

Murdoch set to and Beatrice poured water from the jug into the glass.

"Here you are, Arthur. Drink it right down." She saw the bloodied rag and whisked it away into the bucket that stood beside the chair. She handed her husband a fresh piece of cloth.

"Mrs. O'Brien's niece has a friend who was completely cured of the consumption by drinking several glasses of hot water every day. We're going to try it," she said to Murdoch.

"Mother, it's a good thing my kidneys aren't in the same condition as my lungs. I have to make water on the hour every hour."

"Arthur! Mind what you're saying."

Mrs. K. treated Murdoch the same way she treated the priest – as if their ears must be kept pure from any reference to body parts or functions and, God forbid, any obscenity.

Arthur sipped the hot water, then immediately went into a fit of coughing. This time the fresh cloth was filled. The water had spilled all over him and Mrs. Kitchen wiped at the blanket. There was blood there too.

"I'll get another glass. Won't be a minute."

Arthur shook his head. "No, Mother, please. I can't."

"Of course you can. It was too hot was the problem."

"I thought it was supposed to be hot," he whispered.

She ignored his remark, shaking her head in disapproval as if he were being a finicky child.

"Mr. Murdoch, your tea will be ready in just a minute."

"Has Mrs. Jones eaten yet?" Murdoch kept his voice as casual as he could, knowing his landlady's avid interest.

"Yes, she was down at six. She has a big piece of work to do."

"Another legal brief?"

"I believe so. Such a hard-working young woman. She hasn't stopped all day."

She held out her hand for the empty glass. "I'm going to bring you some of Arthur's medicine. It'll help you sleep until you get that tooth looked after. If I may say so, you look quite exhausted."

She left for the kitchen. As soon as the door closed, Arthur turned to Murdoch and gave him a wry grin.

"There's something makes you sleep better than any laudanum and it's natural."

"What is this, a riddle?" asked Murdoch, pleased by the revival in his landlord's spirits.

"No riddle. I'm referring to conjugal relations. The best cure for insomnia is to have connections with the woman you love."

Murdoch could feel himself blushing like a green youth. Arthur had never spoken so personally to him before.

"I am assuming from your expression this is not a joy you have yet experienced, Will?"

"Well...I..."

Murdoch thought his passionate but unconsummated caresses with Liza didn't count, and before her there had only been awkward fumblings with a neighbour's daughter when he was seventeen.

"I must say I don't have the interest right now," continued Arthur. "But I miss it. So I am being so bold as to give you some advice, Will. Don't let the differences get in the way."

Murdoch was confused as to what he meant by that.

"She's a good woman, no matter that she's Baptist. Still young. Her face lights up whenever she sees you."

"You're referring to Mrs. Jones?"

"Who else? I saw the way she was at the police games when we were all watching the tug-of-war." He spoke in a good imitation of Enid's lilting Welsh accent. "What does the blue marker indicate, Mr. Murdoch?" Ha. She didn't care a jot. She just didn't want you paying attention to that other young woman."

Mrs. Kitchen came in and overheard these last words. "He's better off without that one. Flighty, I thought. Here you go, Arthur."

While she stood over him, Arthur drank all the hot water. This time he didn't cough it back. "There, you see!" said his wife.

"I'll go and change into my slippers," said Murdoch, glad to escape any further talk about his love life.

Mrs. Jones's room was at the top of the stairs, across the

landing from his. Her door was closed but he could hear the rapid clack of the typewriting machine. Her face lit up, did it? His too probably. But what on earth was he going to do about it?

The clove oil and the vinegar compress had relieved the toothache somewhat, and although he could hardly stop himself from yawning, Murdoch felt better. He and the Kitchens were in their sitting room. All three of them were tucked under covers, as Mrs. K. had opened the window. Arthur's mood had swung in the opposite direction, typical of a consumptive. Murdoch had just finished telling them about Wicken's death and the subsequent round of questioning he and Crabtree had gone through.

"How's the latest arrival?" asked Mrs. Kitchen, referring to the constable's newborn son.

"Healthy as a horse and growing like a weed according to George."

"That's good."

Her husband glanced over at her and Murdoch knew they were both thinking about the son they had lost so many years ago. He had lived for only three weeks.

"When's the inquest going to happen?" asked Arthur.

"Tomorrow."

"Your Inspector Brackenreid isn't going to be too happy if the inquest comes in with a suicide verdict. Not on his force."

Arthur carefully removed a dried pansy from the waxed paper where it had been pressed and started to glue it onto a strip of stiff cardboard. He was helping his wife make bookmarks. She earned a little money by selling handmade articles to the fancy-goods shop on Queen Street.

"I feel sorry for his sweetheart. Poor thing, having that on her conscience. Suicides are always hardest for the survivors," said Mrs. Kitchen.

"Not as far as the Lord is concerned," said Arthur.

Beatrice selected an ivy leaf for the bottom of the bookmark. "Of course. But I do wonder why she would reject such a nice young man."

Mrs. Kitchen had never met Wicken but it was enough for her that Murdoch had liked him and that he had had a widowed mother.

"I'll light a candle tomorrow for the sake of his mother. How ever she will cope I don't know. She won't get any insurance compensation, will she?"

"Not if the verdict is suicide."

Murdoch yawned again.

"Off to bed with you, this instant," said Mrs. Kitchen.

"Yes, ma'am." He pushed away his blanket.

"I put the portable oil heater at the end of the landing. Why don't you leave your door open and you'll be warmer. And don't forget to take two spoonfuls of the syrup. It'll make you sleep like a baby," said Beatrice.

"That or the other thing I mentioned," added Arthur.

Mrs. Kitchen looked at him with curiosity. "What other thing?"

"Nothing," said Murdoch. "He means counting the rosary beads."

"Really? That shouldn't be so boring as to put us to sleep though, should it?"

Mrs. Kitchen was very devout, especially when it suited her.

"You're quite right, Mrs. K. But toothache or not, I think I'll be out the minute I put my head on the pillow."

He shook hands good night. Arthur's skin was hot with the fever but at least he wasn't moping.

Murdoch left them and went to his room. Enid's door was slightly ajar and he could hear the sounds of sleep from her and the boy. He undressed quickly and got into bed but he closed his door. He thought that even drugged with laudanum he might be kept awake with what the priest would call impure thoughts.

CHAPTER TWELVE

CULLIE KNOCKED ON THE DOOR SOFTLY. ON DAMP DAYS such as this one, Jarius liked to take a foot-bath before bed in the conviction that it kept away colds and influenza. She had brought up the pitcher of water.

"Come in."

She could hear the impatience in his voice and she shrank. Jarius never shouted at her or slapped her the way Frank did, but she was more afraid of him than anybody else in the household. Whenever she had a task to do, like build up the fire or, as now, bring him hot water, he never allowed her to get on with it but sat watching. She sensed something in that scrutiny not exactly malevolent, but not kind either, and her nervousness always made her clumsy.

She entered the room. He was sitting by the fire, wrapped in his shawl, already undressed for bed. His nightshirt was pulled up to his knees, exposing his spindly calves.

"Ah Janet, good. I've been waiting."

"Sorry, Mr. Gibb, I had the water bottles to fill for Missus."

He waved his hand, indicating she should pour the water into the enamel bowl that he'd placed by his feet. She came closer but, as she poured the water, it splashed over his legs.

He yelped. "Damn it, girl, what are you doing?"

"Oh I'm sorry, sir, I..."

"Get a cloth."

She put the pitcher on the floor and scurried to the washstand by the bed to fetch a towel. He didn't take it from her but pointed at his legs.

"Wipe them off."

"Yes, sir."

She dabbed at the pale, hairy shanks, all too aware of the parted knees protruding from the flannel nightshirt. Jarius made no attempt to assist her or to do it himself.

"That's enough. Finish pouring the water and be more careful."

She tried again but he didn't move back, which forced her to bend closer to the bowl on the floor. This time she managed not to splash. He eased his feet into the water. Gibb was of middle age but his feet were old man's feet, his toes bent, reddish corns on the joints.

Janet hovered beside him waiting for her release.

"Where's the mustard?"

She gasped. "I, er, I-I'm sorry, Mr. Jarius, I'll go get it."

"No! It's too late now. Remember next time."

"Yes, sir."

The girl squirmed in her misery.

Jarius hitched his nightshirt up his thighs. He was looking into the fire, not at her, and when he spoke his voice was quite gentle.

"I hope you weren't too frightened by the police officer today."

"No, sir. He was very kind. Not frightening at all."

"I see. That explains it."

She waited but he didn't seem as if he were going to continue. The silence was unbearable. Like a fly caught in a web, Janet could only hold out for so long.

"Beg pardon, sir. What does it explain?"

Now he looked up at her. "My sister tells me you had a lot to say to the kind detective. You seem to have told him all sorts of things about the family. Unnecessary things."

"I'm sorry, Mr. Jarius. It sort of burst out. He asked me to tell him anything I could."

Gibb reached over and caught her hand. He started to stroke it with his thumb.

"Janet, you are a silly girl to imagine gossip is of any importance to the police. But tell me truthfully, what exactly did you say?"

"Nothing really, sir. Just that there'd been a big row on Saturday night and that Mrs. Eakin had shut herself up in her room. Wouldn't eat nor drink."

He continued to stroke the back of her hand and his touch burned.

"Did you by any chance also load the poor man's ear with why there was a quarrel?"

"No, I didn't. If you remember, Missus sent me out of the room when it all started."

"Quite so. Was the detective at all curious?"

"I can't say especially. He listened to everything and wrote down things in his book."

Jarius released her hand.

"I'm sure that is the last we will see of him, but if by chance he does come back, you will be more discreet, won't you, my dear? You will keep family matters to yourself from now on."

"Yes, sir. I'm sorry, sir. I didn't mean no harm."

"Of course you didn't. Now get off to bed with you. It's eleven o'clock."

Janet curtsied and headed gratefully for the door. Her legs were trembling. In fact, she did know what the quarrel was about because she had listened at the dining room door. But she hadn't told Murdoch that. Her mistress had insisted on being present during the interview and she knew, if she had told everything, she would have been dismissed sure as houses.

She was just about to close the door behind her when Jarius called out.

"Janet, you forgot to bring me my writing box."

He indicated the scribe's desk that was on the dresser. She

hurried back and he waited for her to place it in his lap.

"Thank you, my dear. Good night."

"Good night, sir."

She hurried off.

Jarius waited a moment, then fished under the chair cushion and pulled out a flat leather pouch. He untied the thongs, removed a key, and unlocked the lid of the desk. He took out his ledger and the fountain pen. Then, momentarily distracted, he watched the fire. As a child he'd sat like this many an evening, making up stories about the castles and cliffs he saw in the glowing coals. He had created that imaginary world to escape from the misery of his life. A mother who was never well, hardly ever laughed that he could recall, and who demanded from her young son an emotional sustenance he could not provide. His eyes were starting to itch and he looked away. Then, taking up his pen, he began.

So draws to a close this most difficult of days. I had little patience with any of my customers today, which I suppose is not surprising. There were five all together wanting to marry before the year is out. One of the women showed clearly that she was already with child, but she and the prospective groom dabbled in each other's palms as if the prize was still to be had. The men smack their lips when they name the wedding date. You can practically see their members quivering in their breeches. Most of the girls, for that is what they are, act coy, but I can always tell the ones that are pretending. Who are as eager for a screw as their men. There are more of that kind than we think.

Jarius paused. He'd understood at once when Peg came into his room that it was not from desire for him. He hated her even more that she thought he would be brought down by such a pitiful display. He was not the least like the eager men he saw in his office every day.

They said she fought like a trapped vixen when Ferrier came. She had to be sedated. "A needle right into her arse" was how Frank put it, in his usual delicate way. They intend to keep her in the asylum for several days to assess her state.

He stopped writing and wiped his pen with a piece of felt. The clock on his dressing table chimed the hour. He heard the sound of footsteps coming up the stairs. Augusta was going to bed. She paused and he knew she was considering coming in to talk to him, but she thought better of it.

Father has stayed in his room all day. I went to see him before supper but he had little to say. "A peck of trouble," was all he would offer. I am sure he is sick of her but who knows if that will stop him rutting. It is strange to write this but I am quite exhilarated. Tired yes, but excited. It seems as if I am able to resolve these same troubles.

He had been out of mourning for one month for my

wretched stepmother when he claims to have met up with the tart. However, I strongly suspect he was dallying with her long before. And she of course would have no respect for his state. The sooner married, the better for her. A chance for his money.

The memory of that first meeting was bitter to him. Peg, small and plain, but dressed in a cream silk and lace gown for her wedding day. His father doting over her, kissing her on the mouth without heed to anyone else. Her child, silent and watchful, ugly.

He blotted his page and closed the ledger. There was a carafe of water and a glass on his desk and he poured out some water, swilled it around in his mouth, and spat into his handkerchief as if he had a foul taste in his mouth.

For a moment he wavered, wanting to go to bed but his need was too great, overriding the desire for sleep. He took up his lamp and left his room quietly, hurrying down the backstairs as if he were a harried servant.

CHAPTER THIRTEEN

SHE WAS TRYING TO WAKE UP BUT HER EYELIDS WERE stuck together and she couldn't open them. She'd been crying, she knew that; the salty taste of tears was caught in her nostrils. She could hear her mother talking to somebody, a man. "Shut her up," he said. "Give her something to shut her up else she'll get what for." Her mother was clad only in her drawers, her breasts swinging as she bent over the bed. The man was naked. "I did. She'll be out in a minute," said her mother. But Peg fought against the weight of sleep until she could do so no longer.

She opened her eyes and lay still, listening. Where was she? She could hear the sounds of other people, a soft snore, a bed creaking as somebody turned over. She was in a narrow bed that felt hard, the sheets rough. She wasn't at Dr. Barnardo's – she was too old – nor at home with Harry. The bed wasn't the soft luxuriant feather mattress that he loved.

Think. What has happened?

Then, as suddenly as if the stereoscope had come into focus, she found the details.

I'm not married to Harry any more. He died. I married Mr. Nathaniel Eakin.

As fast as she registered that knowledge, she felt everything she was trying to keep at bay rush toward her, bringing such desolation the pain was almost physical.

I have been committed to the lunatic asylum. I have been here since yesterday.

The occupant in the adjoining bed, Mrs. Mallory, turned, muttering some unintelligible words. Peg waited to see if she had woken up, but she hadn't. She was a farmer's wife who had been in the asylum for several months suffering from mental anxiety. She wouldn't talk above a whisper and sat in a chair, rocking ceaselessly.

Over by the window were Miss Anderson, whom she'd met last night in the baths, and Mrs. Foster, an elderly woman who confessed she'd been in the asylum for six years. She knew everyone's history and was curious to know about Peg. She had insisted on taking her by the arm and leading her down the corridor where the patients were taking a walk before lights out.

"It's the change of life that's affected her," she said, referring to the farmer's wife. "You've got that to look forward to, dear. It comes to us early in here."

Peg knew from her experience in the orphanage that there was always somebody who wanted to befriend the newcomer, somebody who knew the ropes. So she'd been glad to stroll along the corridor with Mrs. Foster, listening to her talk about the other inmates and the attendants.

"Reid is a good sort but she's strict. Furness is cold as a frozen cod. Try not to cross her. Oh, there's poor Miss Green. She thinks she's related to Her Majesty, a distant cousin or some such. Do give her a nod; she gets very upset if you snub her."

Peg wanted to ask Mrs. Foster why she herself was in the asylum but she knew it was best to wait. She'd find out sooner or later.

She put her hands between her knees to warm them. There was a steam radiator in the room, but there was a strong draft blowing from the window and the cotton quilt on the bed was thin. What time was it? The blinds were lowered, shutting out all light, but she sensed that it was close to morning. There was a night candle on the windowsill and it had burned low.

She felt wide awake now. Ever since she could remember, at times of great distress, she couldn't sleep. Paradoxically, she felt worse if she was sharing the room or bed with somebody else. The sound of the regular breathing of the sleeper created more and more anxiety. She was awake in a world that slept; she was abnormal in a normal world. When she was in the cottage home, she never dared to wake one of the other girls, afraid of possible anger, and she had slept so badly for weeks that finally the matron had prescribed a daily tonic, convinced that the dark circles underneath Peg's eyes were from anaemia. Later, when she was married to Harry, desperate, ready to risk wrath if it meant somebody would talk to her, she had awakened him. He was always impatient, didn't understand, and soon turned away, putting his pillow over his head to shut her out.

There was a sound from the other bed. She raised her head. Mrs. Foster had gotten out of bed. She trotted over to Mrs. Mallory and opened the door of her bedside cupboard. Then she realised Peg was watching her and she stopped, glancing over her shoulder with a mischievous grin.

"She had some bonbons," she whispered. "She won't eat them and she's always offering them to me. I was feeling a bit peckish." She reached in and helped herself to one of the candies, popped it into her mouth, and took another handful.

"Do you want one?"

"No, thank you," said Peg.

Mrs. Foster scampered back to her own bed and stashed the stolen candy in her own cupboard.

"Good night, dear."

She was so childlike in her pleasure and lack of guilt that Peg smiled. She wanted to go on talking, to engage her, but the older woman immediately pulled up her quilt and turned over.

Peg curled up tighter, trying to will herself into sleep. She must have been lying like that for a while when she heard the soft creaking of footsteps outside the door. There was a gleam of light through the small window and she heard the key turn in the lock. Somebody came into the room with a lamp, sweeping it back and forth over the beds. The person came nearer to her and she could hear wheezing in the chest. It was the night attendant, Reid. Her skirt rustled as the hem dragged on the rush matting. The light became brighter and Peg knew she was standing next to her bed, watching. She rolled over onto her back.

"Oh dear, Mrs. Eakin, not asleep?"

"I was, the light woke me."

"Try to go back to sleep. It's not time to get up yet."

"Yes, Mrs. Reid." She closed her eyes obediently, listening as the other woman checked on the remaining occupants. She heard her blow out the night candle, then she left, locking the door behind her.

Peg sat up and waited until her eyes grew accustomed to the darkness, then she swung her legs over the side of the bed. She hitched up her nightgown. When she arrived she had been issued a flannel gown and a grey dressing robe, both too large for her.

"When you're feeling better, you can wear your own clothes," said the matron. "Your gown did need to be laundered," she added, and Peg knew that she must have been filthy when she'd been admitted.

Keeping her in nightclothes ensured she was conspicuous and vulnerable. The better you behaved, the better you were treated and the more privileges you got. Peg had soon realised the asylum was run on very similar principles to the orphanage where she'd grown up.

She went quietly over to the window. The sash was stiff but she managed to push it open. There were bars that smelled metallic and they were cold and wet with rain. She knew she was on the third floor and, as she sniffed the damp night air, she caught the smell of livestock. She must be facing the south side of the building, which overlooked the vegetable gardens and stables. Mrs. Foster had told her proudly that the asylum tried to be as self-sufficient as possible and that they raised pigs and a few milch cows.

"The bacon's really quite excellent," said the old lady with glee.

Suddenly, Miss Anderson sat bolt upright.

"Good morning," she said to Peg in a loud voice. "How are you, Annabel?"

Miss Anderson called everybody Annabel, which was apparently the name of the family household maid, long since dead.

"I'm very well, thank you."

Miss Anderson burst into song.

"Onward Christian soldiers, marching as to war…"

She was well launched into the first verse when the two other women in the room both woke up. Mrs. Foster called out, "Please be quiet over there. I'm trying to sleep."

Miss Anderson was oblivious and began to sing louder. "With the cross of Jesus going on before."

Mrs. Foster glared, then flung back her covers and jumped

out of bed. Before Peg realised what she intended, she ran over to Miss Anderson and attempted to put a hand over her mouth.

"I'll make you be quiet, then, you silly canary."

The older woman grabbed at the hand across her mouth, trying to pry the fingers loose. Mrs. Foster wasn't big but she was much more vigorous than her victim. She started to push her back into the pillows.

"I'll shut you up once and for all."

Her ferocity was so alarming, Peg had to do something. She rushed over and tried to pull her away.

"Stop it! Come on now, stop it."

The woman let go and turned her fury on Peg. Her fingernails hadn't been cut for some time and the claws aimed straight for Peg's cheeks. She would have inflicted a serious injury, but Peg managed to grab her by the wrists and keep her at bay.

Next to them, Miss Anderson was trilling at full voice. "Forward into battle, see His banners go."

Mrs. Foster was trying to get at Peg's face, spitting at her and kicking. Her toenails were likewise untrimmed and she scratched Peg's shins badly. Suddenly, the door opened and Reid swept in.

"What's going on in here? Stop that at once. Mrs. Foster! Let go of her, Mrs. Eakin."

Peg grunted, too intent on protecting herself to answer. The attendant caught hold of Mrs. Foster's arms from behind and, quickly and expertly, spun her around and two paces back.

"Mrs. Eakin, please get into bed," she managed to call over

her shoulder. Panting, Peg retreated and at that moment another attendant who had heard the noise came hurrying into the room. Reid was holding Mrs. Foster tightly but she was bucking and struggling like a wild creature. Miss Anderson sang on. The second attendant went straight over to her, took out a strip of linen from her pocket and in one swift movement, bound it around Miss Anderson's mouth. She made no attempt to remove the gag, but continued to sing in a much muffled way, staring at the ongoing struggle between Reid and Mrs. Foster. Abruptly, the fight stopped; Mrs. Foster went limp and sagged in the attendant's arms. Reid spoke to her soothingly.

"That's my good girl. Shush now."

The fourth occupant of the room, Mrs. Mallory, had covered her head with her quilt but she was moaning to herself. Reid led Mrs. Foster back to her bed.

"Are you going to be good, now? I don't have to tie you down, do I?"

"No, dear, not me." She pointed at Peg. "It's her who's the troublemaker. Tie her down."

Peg shrank back, shaking her head. "Please, I was just trying to help Miss Anderson. Mrs. Foster was hurting her." She spoke in her best English manner. "She began to sing and Mrs. Foster got angry."

"And why shouldn't I?" interjected the other woman. "That's the third time this week she's started bellowing and woken us all up. Listen to poor Mrs. Mallory over there."

The two attendants exchanged glances and Mrs. Reid went

over to Miss Anderson, who immediately became silent.

"It's too early to be singing. You're just being naughty. You can sing after dinner. Now do you promise to be a good girl and go back to sleep?"

Miss Anderson nodded, her blue eyes wide and bright above the gag. The attendant removed the linen strip from her mouth. She waited until the elderly woman lay down, patted her lightly on the head, and went back to Mrs. Foster's bed. She brought her face so close their noses were almost touching.

"You will not move a muscle until morning bell or you will have only bread for breakfast. And tomorrow is Wednesday and it's ham. You know how much you like ham, don't you?"

Mrs. Foster nodded. "I have to use the commode."

"Are you sure?"

"Yes, it's coming fast."

Reid sighed. "Very well." She turned to the other attendant. "Thank you, Mrs. Furness, I think we'll be all right. I'll keep her with me until morning."

"What about that one?" Furness indicated Peg, talking as if she were invisible.

"I just want to get back to sleep, if you don't mind." She suited her actions to her words and quickly got into bed and under the covers. Her legs were stinging from the scratches but she wasn't about to add to the trouble by mentioning it.

Reid, who was the senior of the two, was satisfied, and holding Mrs. Foster by the arm, she led her away to the water closet. Furness wagged her finger in a warning at Peg and followed.

The room seemed to rock as unsteadily as a dinghy in the wake of a steamer. Peg lay staring at the ceiling.

Be calm. Think! You've got to think!

CHAPTER FOURTEEN

THE CHAPEL AT HUMPHREY'S FUNERAL HOME WAS USED regularly for coroner's inquests because the post mortem examination could be easily conducted on the premises. The room was panelled in dark oak with a sober brown carpet and pews. A large portrait of Her Majesty and the prince consort, surrounded by their young children, was hung at the front of the room. Murdoch assumed Mr. Humphrey had chosen this particular reproduction because of the family aspect. Queen Victoria and Prince Albert as a source of parental comfort to the bereaved.

The chapel could comfortably hold about forty people but there were at least sixty jammed into the room, extra benches having been provided. Word had spread about Wicken's death and Murdoch also recognised many of the people he had been questioning the previous day. There were four or five constables from the station and Inspector Brackenreid himself was present. He was looking quite disgruntled and Murdoch knew he considered Wicken to have brought disgrace to the force and particularly his station. He gave a curt nod as the detective went to take his seat near the front with the other witnesses.

In the first pew were the thirteen jurors. Murdoch slipped into the aisle seat in the second row and was almost knocked over by the various odours of camphor, violet pomade, and shaving soap. Several of the men had cleaned themselves up and taken out their Sunday-best suits, as befitted their important role in the proceedings.

Across from him was Oliver's mother. She was in deep mourning and a heavy crepe veil fell to her shoulders. Her head was bowed and she was very still. She didn't acknowledge anyone and she seemed alone and friendless, even though there was a woman next to her who Murdoch assumed was a neighbour. She too was in black and he saw her wiping her eyes with a black-edged handkerchief. Mrs. Wicken was not weeping.

Beside the neighbour was the patrol sergeant Hales, who had to testify, and next to him was a young woman who Murdoch didn't recognise. She was soberly dressed in a dark grey walking suit and plain black felt hat with a short veil to the chin. He wondered if this was the woman that Wicken had apparently died for. She seemed to be alone and her head was bowed in prayer. He could imagine what an ordeal the inquest was going to be for her.

The spectators were behaving with respect and there was only a subdued murmur as they waited for the proceedings to start. A table had been placed at the front of the chapel for the coroner and the constable of the court. The side door opened and Crabtree strode in, followed by Mr. Johnson.

"Oyez! Oyez! Everybody please rise."

There was a rustling of garments and creaking of seats as the spectators obeyed.

"An inquisition is now in session, taken for Our Sovereign Lady, the Queen, at the house of Benjamin Humphrey, situated in the city of Toronto in the county of York on the thirteenth day of November in the fifty-eighth year of the reign of Our Sovereign Lady, Victoria, before Arthur Edward Johnson, Esquire, one of the coroners of our said Lady to inquire when, how, and by what means Oliver Wicken came to his death. All of the jurors here present being duly sworn and having viewed the body."

Johnson took his seat behind the table.

"Everyone may now sit."

Crabtree's booming voice filled the chapel. There was an expectant silence; nevertheless, the constable picked up the rubber mallet on the desk and banged it. He addressed the jurors.

"Oyez! Oyez! Oyez! You good men of this county, answer to your names as you shall be called, every man at the first call, upon pain and peril that shall fall thereon."

He checked off their names as they answered.

Johnson waited impassively for Crabtree to finish, staring at a spot three feet in front of him. The roll call finished, he blinked and spoke out in his raspy nasal voice.

"I shall proceed to hear and take down the evidence respecting the fact, to which I crave your particular attention."

He nodded at Crabtree, who turned slightly to face the row where the witnesses sat. Murdoch felt a slight quiver of stage fright in his stomach. Crabtree declaimed, "If anyone can give evidence on behalf of our Sovereign Lady the Queen, when, how, and by what means Oliver Wicken came to his death, let him come forth and he shall be heard."

He beckoned to Patrol Sergeant Hales, who stood up and approached the table.

"State your name, place of abode, and occupation."

"Edward Hales, number fifty, Sydenham Street. I am night patrol sergeant at number four police station, which is located on Wilton Street."

"That your full name?"

"No, sir. My full name is Edward George Wilbur Hales."

"Say so then. This is her Majesty's court now convened."

Johnson frowned at the rest of the witnesses as if they too had transgressed. Crabtree waited until the coroner had finished entering the information in his ledger, then picked up the Bible that was on the desk and held it out. Hales took it in his right hand.

"The evidence which you shall give to this inquest on behalf of our Sovereign Lady the Queen touching the death of Oliver Wicken shall be the truth, the whole truth, and nothing but the truth. So help you God. Do you so swear?"

"I do."

"Stand over there and address the coroner and make sure the jurors can hear you."

Hales moved so that he was at an angle to the court.

"Constable, second class, Oliver Wicken went on duty at a quarter to seven on the night of Monday last, the eleventh of November..."

"Don't gabble," interrupted Johnson. "I have to write this down, you know."

Hales continued, trying to speak more slowly. "I did my first check at twenty-five minutes past eight at the corner of Queen and River streets. The second was at twenty past ten when I met up with him at Parliament Street. Constable Wicken was present and correct. He was not under the influence of liquor. He showed me his report book and to that point his beat had been without incident."

"Did he seem in any way morose or dispirited?"

"No, sir, he did not."

"Other than giving his report, did he say anything to you?"

"Just about the weather."

"His exact words, if you please, Sergeant."

"I can't say as I remember them exactly, sir. Something like, 'Good weather if you're a duck. I'll be glad to be done.'"

"In your opinion was there anything at all in Mr. Wicken,

either that night or on any other previous occasion, that would have indicated a man with suicidal tendencies?"

"Absolutely not. He was always a good-natured fellow, never whinged like some of them do. I would say he was of a cheerful disposition. And if I might add, Mr. Johnson, in all my experience as a police officer, I have never known a pistol to end up stuck between a man's legs in the way it was found…"

Johnson stopped him. "Members of the jury, I should remind you that we demonstrated this point to our mutual satisfaction. The gun could in fact fall into that position. I am not suggesting this would happen every time. Of course not. We are not talking about an arcade. But there is quite sufficient probability. However, Patrol Sergeant Hales is entitled to his opinion. Nobody wants to accept the fact that a fellow officer was a weakling."

Murdoch could see Mrs. Wicken had bent her head and he cursed Johnson for his lack of tact.

The sergeant had turned even redder than usual. "I returned to the station to make my report and went out again at about two o'clock. At this time I did not encounter the constable, who should have been in the vicinity of Gerrard Street east between Parliament and River streets. I went around his beat the reverse way expecting to meet him but he was nowhere visible. I returned to the station."

"Hold on," said Johnson. "Why didn't you sound the alarm?"

Hales hesitated. "Sometimes the younger constables liven up the dullness of the watch by playing tricks – harmless, sir, quite harmless and don't affect their duty at all. Monday was a drear, wet night."

"What sort of harmless little tricks, pray tell?"

The sergeant shifted uncomfortably. "Sort of hide-and-seek. They might duck into the laneway when they hear me coming, then jump out as I go past."

"I see. So you thought Constable Wicken was simply playing games with you?"

"Yes, sir."

"Had he done that on other occasions?"

"No, sir. No, he hadn't."

"But this night, as it was, as you say, so drear, you thought he had got it into his head to act like some child with his tutor?"

Hales was stung by Johnson's tone.

"It crossed my mind as an explanation. Wicken was a responsible young fellow. I didn't think there was any harm if he did want a bit of a laugh. I did the rest of my rounds, made my report, and then I went out again at four o'clock. There was no sign of him. At this point I was getting worried. I started a bit of a search, thought he might have been taken ill and be in one of the laneways. I didn't find him."

"Didn't you think to inspect the empty house?"

"No, sir. For one, there were several vacant properties along the beat, and second, my pebble was still on the doorknob..."

"Explain if you please, Sergeant."

"Sometimes just to test that the constables are doing what they're supposed to do, I place a pebble on the doorknob of the vacant houses on the beat. It's small so as they can't really see it in the dark but, if it's still there when I come round next, I know they haven't bothered to check."

"And you put a pebble on the doorknob of the Gerrard Street house?"

"Yes, sir. When I went by at two o'clock."

"Did you do the same to the back door?"

"No, sir."

"So when did you finally decide something might be seriously the matter?"

"When Wicken hadn't shown up at the end of his shift or called in. That's when Detective Murdoch offered to go in search of him."

Johnson frowned. "Long after the horse had left the barn, wouldn't you say?"

Murdoch felt like throttling the coroner. He knew that the patrol sergeant had been chastising himself severely. All the "if onlys" tearing at him. Not that it would have made any difference if he had raised the alarm, unless he'd happened on Wicken in the act of aiming his revolver at his own head.

"You can step down, Sergeant. Constable of the court, call the next witness."

"Acting Detective William Murdoch, please come forward to be sworn."

Hales went back to his seat and Murdoch stood up and went to the table. He tried to give Hales a sympathetic glance as they passed but the sergeant averted his eyes.

He made sure to give his full name of William Henry Murdoch, then Crabtree handed him the Bible and swore him in.

Johnson laced his fingers together and cracked his knuckles.

"Address the jury and give your statement. Please be clear and precise."

Murdoch faced the jurors, who were still highly attentive, and related his discovery of Wicken's body. Most of this ground had already been covered at the viewing, so there were no questions. He assumed he had been clear enough.

"Do you yourself have an opinion as to the manner of death?"

"I do not, sir. I have known Constable Wicken for some time and, like Sergeant Hales, I have always found him to be uncommonly even-tempered. It is hard to conceive of him committing such a violent act as self-murder. However, the situation in which I found him does seem to indicate that is the case. I am frankly puzzled by it."

"Are you indeed? Well, as I remarked to the sergeant, we are not visiting an arcade. Men do not function like mechanical pieces. Perhaps any one of us is capable of irrational acts at times in our lives when we are unbalanced by our passions."

There was no answer to that.

"You can step down, Mr. Murdoch."

Johnson addressed the jurors. "There was a post mortem examination of the body conducted by Dr. Grieg, a licenced physician. Unfortunately, he is not able to be here in person today but I do have his written report. Members of the jury, you will be able to study this said report when you are deciding on your verdict, but I will ask the constable of the court to read it out for the benefit of the rest of the people here present."

Crabtree did so, handling the medical terminology remarkably well. "...The anterior fossa of the base of the skull was much shredded. The base of the brain was torn and lacerated almost to a pulp...in the interior of the brain was a pepiculer of bone about the size of three quarters of an inch long and one half an inch broad..." Again, Murdoch felt bad for Oliver's mother. No matter how Latinate the language, what she was listening to was a description of her son's head being shattered.

Crabtree concluded with "...abdominal organs healthy. Heart healthy."

The only new piece of information for Murdoch was that Wicken had eaten shortly before he died. There was partially digested meat and bread in his stomach.

"Thank you, Constable. Mr. Samuel Lee is our next witness, I believe. Please swear him. His son will act as interpreter."

Crabtree called out their names and the two Chinamen approached the desk. There was a murmur from the spectators, many of whom had probably never seen such a sight.

Both of the men were wearing padded silk jackets of red silk embroidered with green and gold thread. On their heads were black tri-cornered hats. They were like exotic birds among the sparrows and crows. And the rustle of whispers expressed a rather hostile curiosity.

Johnson said to the young man, "State your name and address first, then his, and the constable will swear him in."

The son's name was Foon. "This is my father, Samuel Lee. We live at number two hundred plus twenty-four on Parliament Street. We run the laundry."

There was a giggle from somebody in the crowd and Murdoch guessed it was because of Foon's accent.

Crabtree took a flat box from the desk and lifted out a china saucer.

"Tell Mr. Lee he must kneel down."

Foon translated and rather stiffly his father obeyed. Crabtree handed him the saucer. Bewildered, the Chinaman took it in his hand.

"Instruct him he must break the saucer in two," said Crabtree. "He can smash it on the floor if he likes."

A short, fast exchange took place between Foon and his father, and with a slight shrug, Mr. Lee slammed the saucer hard, breaking it in two.

"Now repeat to him the following," said the constable. "You shall tell the truth and the whole truth. The saucer is cracked and, if you do not tell the truth, your soul will be cracked like the saucer."

Foon translated.

"Does he understand?"

Lee nodded.

"You can stand up now," said Johnson.

Crabtree picked up the broken pieces and returned them to

the box.

The audience had watched this ritual as avidly as if they were at a magic show. The coroner looked at Lee. "As a witness in this investigation you are required to tell the jury exactly what you told the detective when he came to question you yesterday."

Foon repeated what he'd said and his father answered animatedly. Foon translated it all back into English. When he mentioned seeing a young woman with Wicken, a ripple of excitement ran through the crowd. When he had finished, Stevenson put up his hand.

"What now?" asked the coroner in exasperation.

"Just want to make sure the gentleman knows what he is saying. That there's no mistake. How did he know for certain it was twenty minutes past eleven o'clock when Constable Wicken came to the door?"

Lee spoke at once to his son.

"My father says he looked at the clock, wondering who was coming so late."

"He tells the time, then, does he?"

Johnson saved Foon the embarrassment of a reply.

"Mr. Stevenson, you are revealing an appalling ignorance. The Chinese invented clocks, isn't that so, Mr. Foon?"

"Ay, sir."

There was a titter at Stevenson's expense but Murdoch had the impression most of the listeners were surprised to hear this.

"Any other questions for the witness?"

Jarius Gibb, the foreman, indicated he had one.

"In the opinion of the Chinaman, was the constable in low spirits or good spirits?"

Foon translated and his father paused for a moment before he answered.

"My father regrets to say he could not distinguish what sort of demeanour the constable was in. Nor the lady. But he must emphasize, he only glimpsed them as they walked up the street together."

"Talking or not talking?"

"He believes talking."

The coroner consulted a sheet of paper in front of him. "He can step down but he is still sworn. Remind him, Mr. Foon. Call the next witness."

"Miss Mary Ann Trowbridge, please come forward."

The young woman edged her way along the row. As she crossed in front of Mrs. Wicken, she hesitated, made as if to reach out her hand, thought better of it, and went on.

Crabtree swore her in and she answered in a soft, light voice.

"Give your statement, Miss Trowbridge," said Johnson. "And please speak up; I won't bite."

She nodded but more volume seemed beyond her and Murdoch had to strain to hear.

"I am, that is to say, I was betrothed to Oliver Wicken." She glanced over at Mrs. Wicken. "It was a secret betrothal. Nobody knew, not even his mother. We became engaged two months ago but…" She stopped, swallowing back tears. "On Monday evening I broke off our engagement. Oh, if only I hadn't." Her voice trailed off.

"You really must speak louder, my dear young lady. The jurors need to hear you." Johnson was being most solicitous.

Miss Trowbridge lifted her veil to wipe her eyes and Murdoch had a good view of her face. She was a pretty girl with fair skin and light-coloured brows. Her eyes were well shaped, blue or grey, and her chin was rounded. He judged her to be less than twenty.

"Oliver was most upset. He begged me not to abandon him...He said his life was nothing without me. I was dreadfully worried but I could not go back on my decision. I felt we were not suited to each other and that eventually he would be happier with another. He did not think so...We quarrelled dreadfully."

"Did he make threats at that time to take his own life?" Johnson asked.

Mary Ann nodded. She reached into her reticule and took out a folded piece of paper.

"I live with my aunt, Mrs. Avison. She would have come here today but she is in poor health. However, she wrote out a letter to you, Your Honour. I spoke to her the moment I returned home, so she can vouch for what I said."

Johnson took the missive, scanned it quickly, and put it into the folder that was on his desk.

"So, the last time you saw Oliver Wicken was this Monday past?"

"Yes, that is correct."

"And where did you see him?"

"I must confess, Your Honour, I met him on his beat. I know I should not have done this as he was on duty but...I felt safer. I did not think he would dare to pursue me. So I arranged to meet him in the empty house. I knew he had the key because he'd begged me to meet him there before, which I had not done...When we were inside, in the former kitchen, I told him my intention...He became very angry. He began to shout at me, dreadful cruel things...I was afraid he would actually strike me. I ran off..." She was having a hard time speaking. "I wish now I had stayed, tried to talk to him until he was in a more reasonable frame of mind, but I was afraid..."

Suddenly, Mrs. Wicken burst out, "That girl is not telling the truth. Oliver was not like that. He would never have become engaged without informing me."

Her voice was harsh and she was panting as if she had been running. Unnecessarily, Johnson thumped the table with the mallet.

"Order please. Mrs. Wicken, I do appreciate your distress but you cannot call out like that. This is a law court. If you wish to make a statement, you have to be properly sworn. Is that what you want?"

Her neighbour touched her arm and whispered at her but Mrs. Wicken shrugged her off.

"Yes. I would like to testify."

"Very well. When Miss Trowbridge has finished you can come up. But I must ask you to control yourself. I will not allow any hysterics."

He turned back to the young woman. "Do continue."

She wiped at her eyes again. "I'm sorry, sir. I cannot bear to upset Oliver's mother in this way but I can't lie because of that, can I?"

"Absolutely not. Is there anything else you want to add?"

"No, sir. That's all that happened. He must have remained in the house until…until he…"

"That's all right, Miss Trowbridge. We understand. Now, does any member of the jury have a question? Oh no, Mr. Stevenson, not again?"

"Yes, sir. I just wanted to know how long this encounter lasted."

The girl answered. "Not long. Ten or twelve minutes at the most. As I said, I was afraid and I left as soon as I could."

"And what time of night was this?"

"I'm afraid I can't say exactly. I don't carry a watch. It was after midnight, I believe."

"One more question, Miss. Isn't that very late for a young woman to be out unescorted?"

She turned to Johnson. "Would it be too much to ask for a glass of water?"

"Of course not." There was a glass and a carafe of water on the table, and Johnson poured some out and handed the glass to the young woman. She sipped some of the water.

"I'm sorry, sir, what was your question?"

Stevenson repeated it.

"You are quite right, sir, and believe me I would not have

done such a thing if I were not desperate. As I mentioned, my aunt is in ill-health and I am the sole watcher. I could not leave her any earlier. But where I live isn't too far away and I hurried as fast as I could."

Miss Trowbridge was looking more and more frightened. Murdoch wished for her sake that the ordeal was over.

Chamberlin waved his hand. "One question, sir…Ma'am, how did you find out what had happened to the constable?"

"I read about it in the newspaper this morning. I came directly to the coroner, as I thought it was my duty to say what had occurred, even though there were those who might blame me."

"Nobody of a reasonable mind would blame you, Miss Trowbridge," said Johnson.

Murdoch thought he was acting like a besotted old fool and it added to the list of grievances he held against the man.

Gibb indicated he had a question. "Miss Trowbridge, had Wicken shown any previous signs of mental instability?"

"I regret to say that he did. If I even had a cross word for him, which was not often, he would become distraught. He said he could not rest until I had forgiven him. He was horribly jealous and made mountains out of molehills over everything…That is why I broke off our engagement. I know he didn't show that part of his nature to the world, but please believe me, I saw it all too often."

"I think we've heard what we need," said Johnson. "You may return to your seat, Miss Trowbridge."

She did so, this time ignoring Oliver's mother.

Johnson pulled out a large gold watch from his waistcoat pocket and consulted it.

"We will hear from Mrs. Wicken."

She stood up, swayed for a moment on her feet. Murdoch was afraid she was going to fall. But she held tightly onto the back of the pew in front of her until she was composed and then she approached the table. When Crabtree swore her in her voice was audible, in spite of the encumbering veil.

Johnson nodded at her and ostentatiously dipped his pen at the ready for her statement.

"I know of no such engagement entered into by my son and I am entirely unacquainted with Miss Trowbridge. However, even if Oliver were betrothed to her, I cannot believe for a moment he would kill himself because she rejected him. From an early age, Oliver was a sensible boy."

In spite of the sympathy that was her due as bereaved mother, Mrs. Wicken was not endearing herself to the spectators. Her composure, which had momentarily deserted her, was now firmly in place and Murdoch knew that most of those listening would see her as unnatural and unfeeling. They far preferred a story of love and passion and the evidence of heartbreak that Miss Trowbridge had given them. However, he knew how Mrs. Wicken had reacted when she'd heard of her son's death and his heart went out to her.

The indomitable Stevenson raised his hand again and Johnson nodded permission for him to speak. "Excuse me, ma'am, for asking, but was your son's life insured?"

"Yes, it was. After my husband died, Oliver became the sole support of me and his sister. We took out modest policies for both of us."

"Thank you, that is all."

He didn't have to press the point. Everybody knew that, if it was determined that Wicken had killed himself, there would be no payout from the insurance company.

"I myself wish to ask one thing, Mrs. Wicken," said Johnson. "I commiserate with you most sincerely but this is a court of law and you are sworn under oath to tell the truth…you do understand that, don't you?"

"Of course."

"Did your son show any signs of a melancholy disposition at any time prior to his death?"

"No, he did not. Never."

"Thank you, madam. That is all."

Tall and erect she returned to her seat.

Stevenson's hand was in the air immediately.

"I'd like to ask the previous witness, Mr. Lee, a question, Your Honour."

Johnson sighed. "Is this the last?"

"Yes, sir."

"Very well. Mr. Foon, please tell your father to stand up. Remind him he is under oath."

Foon spoke to his father and he obeyed the instruction.

"I do want to make it clear, Your Honour, that I mean no

disrespect to Miss Trowbridge in any way at all," said Stevenson. "This is strictly for confirmation, you understand…"

"Spit it out, man. We don't have all day."

"Mr. Lee, is the young woman who has here testified the same person that you saw when Oliver Wicken came to your laundry? Miss, would you be so good as to stand and raise your veil again. Thank you."

Mr. Lee regarded her for a few moments, then spoke quickly to his son. Foon nodded.

"My father says that is of certainty the young woman he saw on the street with the constable."

A sigh of gratification went through the room. Mrs. Wicken only sat straighter.

Johnson banged the mallet on the table. "We will adjourn for fifteen minutes."

Crabtree stepped forward. "Court, please rise."

With much shuffling and scuffling of boots, the spectators stood up while Johnson left.

CHAPTER FIFTEEN

THE JURORS WERE SEATED AROUND A TABLE IN THE viewing room of the funeral parlour. On two shelves at the back were displayed empty coffins, the quality ranging from expensive polished oak lined with white satin to plain pine with no brass and thin cotton lining. At first these eternity boxes had served as silent memento mori, but now they had assumed the same invisibility as a sideboard.

The men had taken out their pipes and the air was thick.

"Has everybody now read over the witness statements?" asked Gibb. There were murmurs of agreement.

Gain, a porter, called out, "Wonder if they could bring us a bite, Mr. Gibb? It's past my dinner time and my belly is starting to eat itself." There were some grins at this. Thomas Gain was a stout man with heavy jowls and an abundant stomach. "And as for Peter Curran here," he continued, "his is growling so loud I can't hear the half of what's being said."

The man beside him answered before Gibb could respond.

"If you want to eat, you'd better hurry up and settle the verdict. They're not going to give us anything until you come to a decision. It's the rule." His name was James Slade and he owned a grocery store on Jarvis Street. He wasn't at all happy at being subpoenaed to serve on the jury, but at the least he thought he should have been foreman, given the social standing of his clientele. He spoke in a condescending tone that had already set the rest of them on edge.

"That used to be the practice, Mr. Slade," said Gibb, "but I don't believe it's the case nowadays. If you men want some refreshment, I'll order it right away."

"They won't, you'll see."

Stevenson, who was next to him, groaned, glanced around for somewhere to spit, caught Gibb's eye, and refrained.

"Can we at least have a jug or two of Dominion?" asked John Shaw, who was a coal merchant. His jacket and flannel shirt were clean enough, but around his neck and wrists the skin was dark with coal dust. He considered it weakened you to bathe more than once a month. A tarry odour of coal emanated from him but it wasn't totally unpleasant. Better than the smell of hides coming from Emery Nixon, the tanner.

"Why don't we just get on with it? Cast our vote now," said

Chamberlin, who was an avid temperance man.

"You're the one who's been insisting on going over everything like you're combing your head for lice," interjected Jabez Clarke. "In my view the constable was a silly arse lad who thought it mattered what woman you get a bit of dock with. As for me, I'm as confused as a priest in a brothel. In other words, gentlemen, soon as the lassie with the lovely tiddies stood up, I knew at once where to put my vote – and my member." Clarke was a corset salesman for Mr. Simpson's store. Perhaps in reaction to the need to be constantly deferential and discreet, when in male company he was unremittingly vulgar. Some of the men considered him a wag, some did not.

"Show some respect, Mr. Clarke," said Gibb.

"No offence meant." He flicked his heavy moustache, which was an unnaturally black tint, as was his thick, glossy hair.

Gibb laid down his pipe and picked up the ledger where he'd been taking notes.

"Is everybody ready then?"

A chorus of "ays" but one man shook his head.

"I hate to see the lad's mother destitute. And she will be if she don't get that insurance money," said Mr. Bright, an elflike man with large ears. He was a druggist who had his shop on Parliament Street.

"I feel the same way," said Gibb, "but our job is to find the truth and we must present that unflinchingly. I'm afraid we cannot worry about the consequences."

"Why not?" interjected James Slade. "We are decent Christian men after all."

Gibb took a long pull on his pipe but, before he could answer, Chamberlin spoke up.

"Jarius is right. Unpleasant as that may prove to be, our duty is to present the truth as we see it. What happens after that is out of our hands. I say we should vote."

"Hear, hear," agreed Stevenson. "I might even be able to get to work and not be totally out of pocket."

Gain, who was at the far end of the table, waved his pipe to get Gibb's attention.

"There's something niggling at me, Mr. Foreman. It's about the food."

"I promise I'll send for dinner as soon as we're done…"

"No, I don't mean that. I mean the food the doctor said was in Mr. Wicken's stomach. When did he eat it?"

"I don't quite follow…"

"According to what I'm looking at here, the constable ate his meat and cheese shortly before he died. If he shot himself at one o'clock, after his sweetheart had given him the push, when did he eat?"

The rest of the jurors were regarding him with some exasperation.

"You would be the one to focus on that," said Slade.

"I'm quite serious. Think about it for a minute. Here's your lady-love breaking it off; you're not going to be munching on your sandwich while she's telling you that. So she leaves; would you eat then? Doesn't seem likely to me. You'd be more likely to go off your feed than not."

"Well, it's obvious you've never been lovelorn, Mr. Gain," said Stevenson, and the others chuckled.

"Thomas has got a point," said Chamberlin. "People have been known to fade away to nothing when they're pining. But usually they're women."

"I've known the exact opposite," said Slade. "One of my customers had a cousin who lost his fiancée in a boating accident. He couldn't stop eating. Built up over fifty pounds in less than a month. It can go either way."

The jurors looked as if they were about to plunge into a lively argument, but Gibb called them to order.

"I thank Mr. Gain for bringing up this matter but we're missing the point. The time of death is approximate. It's impossible to pinpoint exactly. It could be earlier. And Miss Trowbridge was not clear as to when she left Wicken. He probably had plenty of time to polish off his sandwich before he met her." He smiled at them. "And speaking of polishing off, let's do it."

"One thing I can't get off my mind is his mother saying she wasn't aware of a fiancée," said Bright.

"Of course she's going to say that," said Slade. "She don't want a suicide verdict. She needs the money bad." He fished in his waistcoat pocket, pulled out an enamel snuffbox, took a pinch of snuff, and sneezed satisfactorily. "Don't forget, there's an invalid sister to take care of."

"Are you for a verdict of death by his own hand then?" asked Gibb.

"Absolutely. It's crystal clear that's what the fool did."

"The patrol sergeant and the detective seemed to think differently," said Bright.

"They're going to stick with their own, aren't they? Nobody wants to admit a police officer shot himself." Slade shook out another pinch of snuff onto the back of his hand and inhaled it. He didn't offer any around.

"Gentlemen? Other comments?" Gibb asked.

"You haven't said much yourself, Jarius," said Curran. "We'd like to know your views."

Gibb leaned back in his chair, tapping the stem of his pipe on the table. "If it wasn't by his own hand, whose was it by? There's no sign of a fight, or a disturbance. He didn't seem to have any more enemies than normally go to a police officer. He's in that vacant house for no other reason. Think of it, if you were going to do yourself in, where would you go? Not home where your mother is going to find you. You'd want to spare her that. Not at the station where there's people about all the time. You'd want a bit of privacy. Time to compose yourself to meet your Maker. I have to say that it all adds up the same way, no matter what direction I put the sums. He was plunged into a state of extreme melancholy by the rejection of his fiancée. She told us he was of a jealous and highly strung disposition. When she left, he must have stood there mulling things over, getting more and more het up. His mind goes completely, he takes out his revolver and shoots himself. My verdict is for suicide. I'm truly sorry for his mother and wish I could say otherwise but I can't. None of us here present is so old we don't know what it feels like to have a woman turn you down. Am I right in this?"

"Right," said George Griffin, the butcher. He spoke with such vigour, the others stared at him and he squirmed. "I had more backbone than that constable but love sure does put you in a miserable state."

"Shall we take the vote then so Mr. Shaw can have his beer before he faints away? Here's some paper; pens are in that box. Write down 'ay' and the word 'suicide', or 'nay' and 'cause of death unknown'. Add your name."

He handed around the slips of paper. Inkwells had been placed in front of each place and for a few moments there was only the sound of pens scratching.

Jarius wrote down his own vote and began to collect the slips as the men finished. All were done but one.

"Mr. Griffin, your paper, if you please."

"Coming."

The butcher was not much used to writing and he formed his letters as slowly and carefully as if he were in the classroom. Finally he passed the folded paper to Gibb, who looked at it.

"That's it then." Gibb recorded the votes on his sheet and placed them all in an envelope. He got to his feet and addressed the men in front of him, reading from a card. "By a unanimous vote, we the jury here present do upon our oath all say that at the city of Toronto on the eleventh day of November, 1895, from injuries received by a pistol fired by his own hand, the deceased, Oliver Wicken, came to his death."

"So be it," added Chamberlin and there was a corresponding murmur of "amens" from the remaining jurors.

CHAPTER SIXTEEN

MISS ANDERSON WAS AT THE PIANO, SINGING AND accompanying herself to 'Onward Christian Soldiers'. She seemed to have a small repertoire, three hymns at the most, which she had been rotating for the last hour. Immediately after luncheon, all the inmates of the ward had been shepherded into the sitting room. Peg hated it at once. It smelled like an institution – carbolic cleaner and not enough fresh air. The chairs and couches were old and shabby, the plush worn threadbare at the arms. The lamps were lit but to her it seemed as if the entire place, including the inhabitants, existed in a grey wash that leached out colours from clothes and faces.

"…with the cross of Jesus going on before." Miss Anderson's

voice was cracked but still strong enough to reach the unconverted.

If she plays that tune once more I will surely go stark staring mad.

Realising what she'd just said to herself, Peg had to smile. She got up and walked over to the fireplace where she stood and gazed at the bright, dancing flames, hoping they would burn away the grey film from her eyes. Suddenly she was aware that Shelby, one of the attendants, was watching her. There was something implacable in her attention that made Peg uneasy. So far the attendants had been quite kind but she had the feeling that in this woman's eyes, once committed as a lunatic, always a lunatic. She was alert for any evidence of what she would see as madness. In spite of the fire, Peg shivered. The knowledge of her own helplessness was cold in her stomach.

There was a tap on her shoulder and she turned around. Mrs. Foster was smiling at her.

"Would you like to take a walk around the room, Mrs. Eakin?"

The older woman seemed to have forgotten totally about their altercation of the previous night and was beaming at her happily. Glad to escape her thoughts, Peg nodded and Mrs. Foster linked arms. They strolled over to the window for all the world as if they were two well-to-do ladies promenading along King Street.

"I'm so glad I have you for a friend," said Mrs. Foster, giving Peg's arm a hard squeeze.

In spite of herself, Peg felt a thrill of pleasure. She had always had trouble making friends. She was too stiff and awkward and gave the impression of being standoffish. For as long as she could remember, she had been trying to understand the subtle signals that seemed to go back and forth between people, making some acceptable and others not.

Miss Green was sitting on the couch next to another attendant, and as they went past she called out in an affronted tone.

"I beg your pardon, I do beg your pardon."

Peg hesitated, not sure what transgression had occurred.

"Bow to her," said Mrs. Foster and bobbed in the other woman's direction.

Peg had already curtsied to Miss Green twice as they passed her in the corridor but she did so again. However, the other woman was not satisfied.

"I beg your pardon," she said in an even more indignant voice. The attendant stood up quickly and interposed herself between them.

"I think it's time for you to write your letters, madam. Her Majesty relies on you."

She led her away to a desk at the far side of the room. Miss Green was well into middle age but she had styled her hair into side ringlets more suitable for a young woman. She was wearing an out-of-fashion dress of green and blue check taffeta. The bodice was tight and the full skirt was pulled back into a bustle with a drape of blue ruffles that cascaded into a long train.

"Poor woman," said Mrs. Foster. "She gets most upset if she thinks she's been slighted."

"What did I do wrong?"

"I don't know, dear. She's quite changeable on the matter."

Mrs. Stratton, the woman Peg had talked to in the bath, was sitting alone on the window bench. She was oddly dressed in a one-piece loose garment of brown holland. It had legs like a man's trousers and was fastened at the ankles and wrists.

"Good afternoon," said Mrs. Foster. "May I introduce Mrs. Eakin?"

The woman turned her head but gave no sign of recognition.

"I believe we've met," said Peg.

Mrs. Stratton nodded. "Yes, of course. Do you have children?"

Peg recoiled. "I told you yesterday that I did."

"They're all dead, I assume. Murdered no doubt."

She was saved from answering by Mrs. Foster, who pulled at her arm.

"Come on, my dear. Good afternoon to you, Mrs. Stratton." She patted Peg's hand. "Don't mind her. She has ten fine healthy children, seven of them boys, but she fancies they're all dead and that her husband murdered them." She lowered her voice. "It's been brought on by the change. Poor thing, her flushings are very bad."

"Why is she wearing that peculiar outfit?"

"That's what they call an untidy suit. She must be in one of her bad spells. She's worse than any baby during those times. Wipes her food all over herself. Not to mention her you-know-what."

"How long has she been in the – in here?" Peg couldn't bring herself to say the word "asylum".

"Not that long. She came in last March." Mrs. Foster continued, "She probably should be on the second floor with the really bad patients. It's not nearly as nice as our floor. They don't have any singing or dancing and nobody is allowed sweets." Suddenly, she stroked Peg's cheek. "You don't want to go down there, my dear."

Peg involuntarily moved away from her touch. "I have no intention of doing so."

As they turned back toward the fireplace, the door opened and Miss Bastedo, the matron, and two nurses came in. All the attendants stood up in deference and one or two of the patients followed suit. Miss Bastedo was a tall woman, mature and strong featured. Like the rest of the staff, she wore a plain dress of blue wool but she omitted the apron and the cap. Her dark hair was pulled into a tight knot at the nape of her neck. She began her tour of the room, chatting to the patients as she went. Her assistants walked quietly behind her.

Peg could feel her heart beating faster as she approached. She felt as if she had gone backward to her own girlhood and this was one of the mistresses of the orphanage. Unexpectedly, Mrs. Foster dropped her arm and wandered off in the direction of the hearth, leaving her stranded.

Miss Bastedo halted in front of Peg. "How are you feeling today, Mrs. Eakin? The nurse tells me you are settling down quite nicely."

"Indeed I am, thank you."

"I heard you ate a hearty breakfast this morning."

"Yes, ma'am, I did."

Peg had been ravenous and she'd devoured two servings of ham and toast.

"You wouldn't take your tonic though."

"No, ma'am. I did not feel the need."

"You really must take it. You will feel so much better. All of the other ladies do."

"Yes, ma'am."

The matron's expression was kind. "I understand how new everything must seem. I know you have been very frightened. Tonight, I will come by myself and give you the tonic. And just so you will know it is perfectly safe, I will even have some myself. I could do with it these days. Will that be more acceptable to you?"

"Thank you, ma'am."

Peg had been afraid the tonic contained sedatives and she couldn't bear the drowsy, helpless state they induced.

One of the assistants came forward and said something to the matron.

"Ah, yes. Before your marriage you had the occupation of dressmaker, I understand?"

"Yes, ma'am."

"We encourage our ladies to do some simple occupation while they're with us. It calms the nerves. We have a wonderful sewing room here. Would you like to do something? Embroidery, if you wish. Or we are always in need of garments."

"I would like that, ma'am."

"Excellent. Perhaps on Friday, then, you can go to the sewing room."

"Yes, ma'am."

"And I think you can have day clothes tomorrow. You will have to make do with what the asylum provides for now, but I will send a message to your family to bring in your own clothes."

She was about to move on but Peg reached out and caught her sleeve. Both assistants tensed but Miss Bastedo stayed, looking at her calmly. Peg let her go.

"I was wondering if anybody has been to see me."

"Not yet. On the whole we prefer to see our patients settled in before they have visitors. Are you anxious to see your husband?"

Peg was quite aware that, in spite of the pleasantness of Miss Bastedo's manner, like Shelby, she was watching for any signs of delusions or unnatural behaviour. But she wanted to scream out, *No! Don't let him near me. Don't let any of them near me.* Instead, she bowed her head.

"Yes, ma'am."

Mrs. Foster had wandered back and the matron greeted her warmly.

"I see you've been taking good care of our new arrival."

The old lady beamed. "I most certainly have. She's my dear friend. We were just about to go for a walk down the corridor."

"Very good. And I must continue with my rounds. Good afternoon to you both."

She moved away and Mrs. Foster took Peg's arm.

"My dear, you are trembling. Are you cold?"

"Yes. Yes, I am rather."

There was another attendant sitting by the door. She was round-featured and rather jolly looking.

"Good afternoon, Mrs. Foster, Mrs. Eakin. Where are you going?"

"Just for a turn down the corridor and back," answered Mrs. Foster. "Matron approves."

"Very well. But don't be gone too long, will you?"

"That's Wylie," said Mrs. Foster as they went outside. "She's a good lassie; never has a cross word for anyone."

They began to walk down the corridor. There were no other patients out there except for one of the charity inmates who was sweeping the floor. She was quite elderly and bent and, as they passed, Peg heard her cough so hard, she had to stop what she was doing and lean on her broom.

"She sounds consumptive," she whispered to Mrs. Foster.

"Oh, she is, my dear. That's Effie Callahan. She was quite all right when she came in here but she caught the consumption last year from another patient. She'll probably be gone by spring, you mark my words."

They walked by her but she didn't look up.

"Who was it you wanted to see, my dear? Oh, don't be surprised. Nothing escapes me, especially where my friends are concerned. I myself only want my daughter. She is such a love. She is married now with her own family and she cannot visit as often as she would like. My husband, Mr. Foster, doesn't approve and hardly ever comes."

She reached up and pinched Peg's cheek. "You can tell me."

But she couldn't. Her protestations only got her into trouble. A dog that barked and bit was tied up and rendered helpless. It was the silent cat who moved in the darkness that remained free.

"How many grandchildren do you have?" she asked, and Mrs. Foster was diverted and chatted to her merrily until they reached the end of the corridor. Here, there was a pair of double doors. Mrs. Foster made to turn back.

"We can't go through there."

"Why not?"

"It leads onto the verandah and we're only supposed to be there in warm weather."

Peg tried the door and it wasn't locked. Mrs. Foster dithered. "We'll get into trouble."

"Don't worry. If anybody scolds, I'll tell them it was entirely my idea."

"I'll wait here then. I'm not allowed."

Peg pushed open the door and stepped through. The semicircular verandah was quite large and roofed but otherwise open. She drew in her breath sharply. Her flannel wrapper and nightgown were little protection against the chill air. She walked over to the far side and peered through the bars. In the distance, the pewter-coloured lake was hardly distinguishable from the sky. Below her stretched the sodden garden, denuded now of all vegetables. There was a thin plume of smoke coming from the chimney of the gardener's house and the hominess of it made her want to weep. She pushed up her sleeve and thrust her bare arm through the bars and held it there while the rain wet her skin.

"I don't know what will happen to me if you don't come. Please don't leave me here," she whispered.

"Mrs. Eakin? We should be getting back."

Mrs. Foster had the door partly open and was peering in anxiously. Peg turned.

"I'm coming." She returned to her companion. "There, you see, a little air has done me wonders."

In fact, she was shaking uncontrollably. Mrs. Foster took one of her hands in hers and chafed it briskly.

"My dear, you're so cold. And look at your slippers. They're quite wet. Let's go back to the fire."

She looked into Peg's face, her eyes knowing.

"I heard you say something. Were you praying?"

Peg gave a wry smile. "Yes, I suppose I was."

"That's good, dear. I myself pray all the time."

CHAPTER SEVENTEEN

THE MOOD AT THE STATION WAS SUBDUED. EVERYBODY felt bad about Wicken, who had been well liked. The discussions were ongoing, but most of the constables were resigned to the verdict and the inexplicable nature of the human mind. Murdoch retired to the cubicle behind the tea room that served as his office. He wasn't in the mood for talking. Mrs. Wicken's devastation haunted him. She had left immediately after the verdict had been delivered and he hadn't had a chance to speak to her again. Mary Ann Trowbridge had departed quickly as well and he hoped she had somebody to comfort her.

With a sigh, he turned to his battered metal filing cabinet.

He should look over his old reports at least, see if he could follow up on anything. He took out the folder labelled Piersol, which was a charge of embezzlement against a young clerk who worked for an insurance company. It was a complicated case and Murdoch had to admit he didn't much care about it. Piersol was underpaid and overworked and if he syphoned off some of the considerable profits of the company, good for him. Before Murdoch could go any further with these thoughts, there was a tap outside. His cubicle was too small for a proper door, so visitors had to signal their presence by knocking on the wall. Through the reed curtain, he could see the outline of Sergeant Seymour.

"Come in."

Seymour pushed through into the tiny space.

"Thought you could use a spot of tea." He was carrying a mug, which he held out to Murdoch.

"Thank you, Sergeant."

Murdoch took the mug and sipped at the hot brew.

"Ow."

"Will, you'd better get that tooth looked at. Your jaw is all swollen."

"Yrr, tea'sot."

The sergeant smiled at him. "Listen, it's quiet here this afternoon. I'll book you out early. Go over and see Brodie."

"He's a butcher."

"Maybe, but he does his job."

The hot drink had set up such a clamour in Murdoch's

mouth that he could hardly sit still.

"Come on, Will. You can't keep putting it off."

"Yes, I can," said Murdoch, trying to grin.

But the sergeant prevailed and he soon found himself setting off along Wilton Street in search of a dentist, any dentist other than Brodie.

A chill wind was blowing in from the lake and the sky was grey, sunless, threatening more rain to come. He wrapped his scarf around his face. *Are you a miserable coward or not?* he said to himself, and the answer was a loud *Yes.*

He remembered passing a dentist's office not too far from the station on Wilton Street and he decided to try there first. His feet had kept moving and he was now standing in front of a dry-goods shop. Just to the right of the window was a green door that looked newly painted. A shiny brass plaque announced DR. F. STEVENS, DENTIST. 2ND FLOOR. He hesitated. Well, at the least he could look at the place, determine if it looked decent. No blood and discarded teeth on the floor. He opened the door and stepped into a narrow hall which led to a steep flight of stairs. The walls were a cheery yellow tint and the oilcloth floor covering was a flowered pattern. Everything appeared to be well swept and clean. So far so good. Slowly, he mounted the stairs. At the top was a small landing with another green door and another plaque that said PLEASE ENTER. Murdoch paused and touched his sore tooth with the tip of his tongue. The resulting jolt moved him to open the door. He poked his head around. In front of him was a tiny room with just enough space for a desk and three straight-backed chairs lined up against the wall. A pretty young woman was seated at the desk and at his entrance she rewarded his courage with a welcoming smile.

"Good afternoon, do come in."

She was wearing a sober blue dress with a starched white apron over it and her auburn hair was pinned up beneath a stiff white cap.

"You're here to see the doctor, I presume?"

Murdoch mumbled. "Yes, bad toothache."

She looked at him sympathetically. "I can see your jaw is swollen. But never mind, Dr. Stevens will have you right as rain before you know it."

She stood up and came over to him. "Let me take your things. It's another nasty day, isn't it?"

She hung his hat and his coat on a brass coat stand. Murdoch added the muffler and stood awkwardly waiting. There was some kind of telephone board on the desk and she sat down, plugged in a wire, and leaned closer to the mouthpiece.

"A patient here to see you, Doctor. A Mr...?" She looked up.

"Murdoch, William Murdoch."

She repeated that into the telephone, then held the receiver to her ear. Murdoch heard crackling as the invisible doctor replied. She gave a smile, so quickly suppressed, he wondered what the man had said. He perched on one of the chairs while she took out a large ledger.

"I just need your name, address, and occupation."

He gave her the information.

"Oh, my, a detective. We haven't had one in here before. It must be exciting work."

"Sometimes." He wasn't up to explaining all the different shades of liveliness that his job entailed.

Suddenly, he noticed a shelf behind the desk. Sitting on it was a glass box, inside of which was what looked like a set of teeth. He got up and went closer to investigate. The young woman smiled.

"Those are an old set of dentures. Dr. Stevens collects them. They are what we call 'Waterloo' teeth. The back molars are made from ivory but the front teeth were taken from the corpses at the Battle of Waterloo. They were very popular as they are so natural looking. They're glued to a copper plate."

"Must have been hard to eat with those things. How did they stay in?"

"There is a little spring at the back. But you're right, they would be quite uncomfortable and we believe they were only worn for show. Special occasions. I suppose you had to eat as best you could with your gums. Nowadays we have vulcanised rubber that we use for the plate. Much better. People can have all those troublesome teeth removed and hardly know the difference."

Murdoch thought her glance fell to his lips as if sizing him up as a prospect but just then the door opposite opened and Dr. Stevens came into the waiting room. He too seemed very young and Murdoch's stomach quailed. He had hoped for an elderly man with much experience who knew what to do, who wouldn't hurt any more than necessary. Stevens looked to be barely into his mid-twenties. He was tall, clean shaven, with dark-brown hair trimmed close to his head. Seeing Murdoch he stretched out his hand and smiled, revealing perfectly white and even teeth. Murdoch supposed that was a good advertisement and he wondered if they were real. Weakly, he shook hands.

"What can I do for you, sir?"

"I've got a bad toothache." He jabbed his finger in the air, indicating the side of his jaw.

"Ah. Come this way, we'll have a look."

The nurse gave a reassuring nod and Murdoch followed the dentist through to the adjoining room. This was larger, with deep windows on two sides. Even with this much light, the afternoon was so gloomy that all the wall sconces had to be lit. In the far corner was a Chinese screen of black lacquer, hiding who knows what instruments of torture. There were two tall oaken cabinets flanking the door. However, what dominated the room was The Chair. It was on a pedestal and stood dead centre.

Stevens walked over to it and patted the backrest invitingly. "Sit here, if you please," as if Murdoch were going to get a haircut.

The chair was covered with plush, burgundy in colour. The better to hide blood stains, he thought. There was a wooden footrest with a Grecian scene painted on it. Probably nymphs chasing Zeus. He climbed in. There was a metal spittoon attached to the arm of the chair. For blood, he assumed.

"Open your mouth wide."

He did and Stevens peered into it. He'd picked up some sharp instrument from another tray without Murdoch noticing and he tapped the gum where all the pain was emanating.

"Ow." Murdoch tried not to make that a bellow.

"Hm. Did that hurt?"

His face was very close to Murdoch's, and at this intimate distance, he saw that the dentist had a small cut on his chin where he'd nicked himself shaving.

"Um," he replied.

"How long have you had the ache?"

"'Bout two weeks."

"Oh, dear, that is a long time. You really should have come in sooner. I'm afraid it looks infected. It will have to come out."

Murdoch's thoughts must have been obvious, because the dentist patted his arm.

"Don't worry. I have all the latest equipment. The extraction will be quite painless."

"How long have you been practising?" Murdoch asked.

Stevens looked disconcerted. "To tell the truth, I graduated from dental college this spring. But I was in the top five of the class."

"How many altogether, six?"

Stevens smiled uneasily and Murdoch himself grinned. "Just a joke, sir. My apologies."

He was afraid to ask him how many patients he'd had. His tooth was throbbing again. Besides, there was something jolly about the man and sympathetic. That must count for a lot surely.

"If that's the only thing to be done, then we'd better do it."

"You'll be glad. Better this than weeks of pain. And an abscess can cause the devil of a lot of problems. Look."

He pointed at his neck just below the jaw and Murdoch saw a rather deep, round scar.

"The result of an abscessed tooth. The infection went right through to the cheek. We didn't have very good dentistry the way we do now. So you see, I know what it's like." Then he shouted, "Inge!"

Almost at once, the door opened and the young woman appeared. So much for fancy telephones.

"This is Mrs., er, Mrs. Stevens. I am proud to say my wife and also my assistant."

She smiled at Murdoch shyly. "Don't worry, it will be over before you know it."

She went behind the Chinese screen and came back with a linen towel that she placed over his chest, tying the ends behind his neck. She had a nice flowery smell about her that he liked. Carnations perhaps. He could hear the dentist rooting around behind him, but he resisted the impulse to turn and investigate. Then Stevens appeared on his left-hand side. He was wheeling a small cart in which sat a long metal cylinder. There was a rubber tube looped around the top. At the end of the tube was a cone-shaped piece. He manoeuvred the cylinder closer to the chair.

"This is nitrous oxide. You've probably heard it called 'laughing gas'. It's a wonderful discovery, I must say. Most people feel completely euphoric and it utterly takes away pain. Two ticks of the clock and it will be over."

"I saw that stuff used at a music hall show a few years ago," said Murdoch. "It made people do really silly things. Is that going to happen to me?"

Stevens shook his head. "This gas is for medicinal purposes, not entertainment. All that will happen is that you'll go into a pleasant dreamlike state."

"And the alternative?"

"We could administer laudanum or chloral hydrate but those will need an hour or so to take effect."

Murdoch looked at Inge Stevens. Even in her severe cap and uniform there was a soft prettiness to her.

"I'll do the gas," he said.

The dentist nodded at his wife and she went over to the sink in the corner of the room, returning with what looked like a glass of water.

"Swill out your mouth with this and spit it out."

Murdoch did so. The liquid had a strong, tarry kind of taste.

Mrs. Stevens dabbed at his mouth as he sat back in the chair and he was reminded of Mrs. Kitchen wiping away the blood from Arthur's chin. The memory grabbed him and he sighed. Misunderstanding him, the young woman said softly, "You'll probably think I'm prejudiced but Dr. Stevens is really very good. I even let him pull one of my teeth and I didn't feel a thing."

Murdoch hoped this hadn't happened while they were on their wedding trip but he didn't comment, allowing himself to surrender to their administrations. The dentist placed the rubber cone over his nose and mouth.

"Just breathe normally."

He fiddled with a dial on the cylinder and Murdoch heard the soft hiss of the gas.

"I'm going to count backward from ten. Nice easy breaths now. Don't gasp. All right, here we go…Ten…nine…eight…"

Murdoch's head was beginning to spin as if the top part were rotating like a top. For a moment he wanted to fight it off, get back his control, but Inge touched his forehead and he relaxed. The spinning sensation stopped and he felt as if he were floating up, way up in the sky.

"Three…two…one."

He started to have a lovely dream about dancing with Liza, a waltz that he was executing effortlessly. He tried to tell her how beautiful she looked in her new white silk gown, but he had a big piece of apple in his mouth and it got in the way. He tried to roll it off his tongue but a pip stabbed him sharply. He struggled again to get rid of the fruit and suddenly it was gone. Liza was speaking to him, "Mr. Murdoch, Mr. Murdoch," and he wondered why she was being so formal.

"Wake up, Mr. Murdoch. Wake up. We're all done."

He opened his eyes. Two rather anxious-looking faces were hovering above him. Dr. Stevens had nice brown eyes, he noticed, with girlishly long eyelashes. Inge's eyes were an unusual hazel colour. Both of them beamed. *They should kiss each other,* he thought. He felt so happy that they were happy.

Perhaps they should kiss him too. He smiled and felt something wet run down his chin.

"Oops," said Mrs. Stevens, and she quickly wiped away whatever it was.

"Tooth's out," said Stevens. "Do you want to see it?"

"Why not."

The dentist had been holding the tooth behind his back and he whipped it forward and held it under Murdoch's nose. He'd used some kind of device that close up resembled a medieval thumbscrew. The ring at the end had been slipped over the tooth and then twisted. The bloody prize was firmly in its grasp.

"The infection had made the gum spongy so it lifted out like a carrot," he said. "Now you can sit there for a while longer until the gas has worn off. Told you, didn't hurt a bit, did it?"

"I didn't feel a thing," said Murdoch. He grinned broadly. What wonderful parents they will make. He wanted to put his head on the dentist's shoulder and have it stroked. Either that or curl up in Inge's lap and be rocked.

"Your gum will be sore for a few days. I've packed the hole with some absorbent cotton and you can take it out in a couple of days when the bleeding has stopped. But if it's still bad by tomorrow, come by and I'll fix it."

"Like Medusa, you mean?"

Stevens looked puzzled, but he smiled politely and waited for Murdoch to stop laughing at his own joke.

"We'll give you some laudanum and some antiseptic to rub on it. Now I should tell you that while you were under I had a check on your other teeth and you've got some bad cavities developing. When this has healed, you should come back and I'll fill them."

"Fill them?"

"Well, I can extract them if you prefer but these days we are recommending filling. Gold is good. It'll last you a lifetime."

"Can you sit up now, Mr. Murdoch?" Inge asked. He sat forward in the chair and then got to his feet rather shakily, enjoying the feeling of her cool hand in his.

"Do you want to keep the tooth?" Stevens asked.

"No, no thanks. It's never been one of my favourites."

They all chuckled, especially Murdoch, who considered he was being quite a wag today. Inge started to escort him back to the other room. At the door was a glass-fronted cabinet and he saw it was filled with shelf after shelf of denture sets. They were all grinning at him, which made him respond in kind. Outside, in the little anteroom, not even the bill dampened his good humour. He paid up, made an appointment to come in next week, and went down the stairs, armed with his bottles of medicine.

As he headed for home, he had to admit he felt happy. The experience hadn't been nearly as bad as he'd expected. Amazing what developments had happened in the last few years. He splashed vigorously through a puddle. Yes, indeed, he would recommend young Forbes to anyone that asked. No, that wasn't right. His name was Stevens. And his lovely wife was Inge. Such an adorable smile she had, such gentle hands.

A wife to be proud of. Suddenly he thought of Enid. He'd have to tell her the story of the denture sets. That would make her laugh. She had good teeth, just slightly crooked on the lowers. Perhaps she would go to Stevens as well. He chuckled at such a good idea and a passerby, bent under his black umbrella, glanced over at him with some alarm. Murdoch touched the brim of his hat.

"Good afternoon, lovely weather, isn't it?"

The man didn't respond and Murdoch continued on his way. Ahead of him was a particularly large puddle. He aimed for it and stamped through with great satisfaction. His gum was sore but the horrible white pain had gone. Hurrah for modern science.

CHAPTER EIGHTEEN

THE SILENCE THROUGHOUT DINNER WAS SO HEAVY, Lewis felt as if it had landed on the back of his own neck and was bowing his head. He had spent most of the time watching the lamp in the middle of the table. Janet hadn't cleaned it properly and it was smoking badly. A boy at his school had told him that one of their lamps had exploded, and hot oil and bits of glass flew straight into the face of their maid. "She was blinded from then on," said the boy. Lewis had been so frightened by this story that he sat as far away as possible from the lamps at home, irritating his mother, who could not reassure him. There was a second larger lamp on the sideboard behind him, but he thought he was far enough away to be safe.

As it was a Thursday, they had had a boiled leg of pork, carrots, and parsnips, also boiled, and a pease pudding which always accompanied the pork. His mother made up the menus and they were exactly the same from week to week, unless they had company, which happened rarely. Lewis loathed pease pudding but had forced himself to eat it, knowing he would draw his grandfather's wrath if he didn't clear his plate. Nathaniel was in a bad skin, worse than usual, and he had not spoken to anybody the entire meal. Mamma and Papa still weren't on speaking terms. Augusta sent all necessary requests or instructions by way of Lewis:

"Ask your father to pass the parsnips," or "Tell your father there is no more meat."

Even Uncle Jarius, who was usually talkative, had been quiet, and Uncle Frank might have been struck dumb for all he said.

Suddenly Lewis quailed, feeling his grandfather turn toward him.

"Stop fidgeting, boy. You'd think you had worms the way you've been wriggling."

Nathaniel had a long wiry grey beard that thrust out from the sides of his chin and virtually obscured his mouth. This meant that, when he spoke, the hair below his lips moved up and down in a way that made Lewis want to giggle.

Augusta intervened quickly.

"It's his new suit, Father. The wool is scratchy."

She reached over and tugged the jacket collar away from Lewis's neck.

His grandfather looked as if he were about to continue with his complaint, but Janet came into the room with her tray. She put it down on the sideboard, aware that everyone was watching her.

"What's the sweet?" asked Nathaniel.

"Baroness pudding, sir."

"I hope it tastes better than it did last week. It was a soggy mess as I recall."

Janet bobbed. "I'm sorry, Mr. Eakin. I boiled it much longer this time."

The sweet was a suet and raisin pudding that had to cook for at least four hours.

Clumsy because of the criticism, Janet clinked the dishes noisily as she cleared the table. Nobody spoke and Jarius was the only one who assisted her by handing over his plate.

"I'll serve, Janet. You can bring it to me," said Augusta.

She did so and Lewis tried to catch her eye to give her a quick grin of sympathy, but she was too intent on placing the pudding dish as delicately as she could in front of his mother.

"Shall I pour the tea, ma'am?"

"No, I'll see to it."

Janet curtsied again and returned to the sideboard, where she piled the used china on the tray. She left as fast as she could, but she had barely closed the door when Nathaniel spoke.

"That girl is not improving, Augusta. Can you talk to her?"

"I do all the time, Father. I cannot make silk out of a cow's ear…I mean, out of a sow's ear."

"Fool," muttered Nathaniel.

Hearing him, Augusta flushed as red as her own maid had. Lewis tried to pretend he'd gone deaf and stared at the pale roll of pudding that his mother was handing him. His father had managed to withdraw his presence so completely from the table, he might as well have not been there.

Nathaniel sprinkled two large spoonfuls of sugar over his own portion and began to eat, smacking his lips. In front of him was a jug of beer that was almost empty. It was the second one he'd consumed tonight. Lewis knew that his grandfather's mood was greatly affected by the number of jugs of beer that got emptied. Usually, it was only one, but two downed, and downed quickly, spelled trouble. He looked over at his Uncle Frank. He wasn't drinking anything at all, although he usually shared a carafe of wine with Jarius. Augusta only drank liquor at special occasions or if she was ill, and her husband did likewise. Lewis wished she would pour the tea. He was allowed a cup now as long as it was heavily supplemented with milk, and he enjoyed the feeling of being grown-up that it gave him. However, Augusta didn't move; instead she nibbled at her pudding. Lewis had only recently been accorded the privilege of eating with the grown-ups at the evening meal. So far he heartily wished he was in the kitchen with Cullie, even though that afternoon she had frightened him by recounting the tale of the policeman who had died. She'd heard all this from the baker's boy.

"For love. Imagine that. Shot his brains out with his very

own gun. They were all over the place. That and the blood. It was so thick you'd think the room had been painted red."

This account had disturbed Lewis almost as much as the story of the exploding lamp. He wondered if the mood in the house had anything to do with it. His father and uncle had to go and see the body. They hadn't said anything about all the blood but they must have been horrified.

He cut into the pudding. In spite of what Janet had said, it was undercooked in the centre and the suet was unpleasantly sticky. He picked out a raisin and chewed that.

Nathaniel finished eating and immediately Augusta put down her spoon. Lewis saw her exchange a glance with his Uncle Jarius, who nodded and wiped his mouth with his napkin in his fastidious way.

"Stepfather, perhaps while everyone is present we could continue our earlier discussion," Jarius said. "We do owe Dr. Ferrier an answer by tomorrow. As I understand it, delay will only make matters worse."

Nathaniel shook his head. "This is not a suitable subject at the dinner table. Especially not with the boy present." He took another helping of the pudding.

"I am confident that Lewis is old enough to hear," said Augusta. "If we don't broach it now, when will we? It is a matter that concerns all of us."

"You're wrong," said Nathaniel, his open mouth revealing partly masticated suet and raisins. "She is my wife and the decision is mine to make."

Jarius answered; his voice was calm, reasonable.

"No one would disagree but it is such an important matter, Sister and I thought it might be helpful to you if we discussed it more thoroughly. As a family. Isn't that so, Frank?"

"Yes," said Frank.

"And you agree too, don't you, Peter?"

"Yes, begging your pardon, Father."

"We all love and honour you, sir," continued Jarius. "However, we cannot pretend this new marriage has been easy on our household. To speak honestly, both her presence and her illness have been a dreadful disruption and created havoc for all of us." He paused. "Surely it is obvious that we cannot return to the situation as it has been. I'm sorry, I realise these are most unpleasant things to hear, as they are for me to say, but we must not put our heads in the sand like so many ostriches."

The image struck Lewis as funny and he could feel another giggle threatening to break free. He concentrated on the pattern of green squares on the tablecloth, jumping across them like stepping-stones.

Nathaniel pushed aside his dish. "You're a good talker, Jarius, and you always have been. But if you want to speak honestly as you say, let's go the whole hog. The truth is that under all this mealy-mouthed gabbing what my children are really concerned about is their inheritance. They're all shitting in their britches in case I get more tads." His eyes were dark under the bushy eyebrows. "And why not? She's going to be all right. It was her boy dying that unhinged her."

Lewis shrank down into his chair, trying to make himself as small as possible. He couldn't bear any mention of Charley, whom he'd loathed from the moment he'd arrived. Whenever they were left alone, he tormented the younger boy until he sobbed. When he had died so suddenly and painfully, Lewis thought it must be because of him. He'd finally confided in his mother, who had been unexpectedly gentle with him. "Bad feelings don't kill us, my chuck. If they did, nobody in this household would be alive today."

"I'm still a vigorous man," continued Nathaniel, "and she'll be fertile for a long time to come yet. I could spawn five sons before I die."

"Father, please," said Augusta, indicating her son.

"You're the one who said he was old enough. So let him hear."

Peter Curran stopped eating and sat staring at his plate as if he were a rabbit and the fox's snout was coming through the table.

"And any son she might drop would be a whole lot better than the one I have." Nathaniel addressed this remark to Jarius, ignoring Frank, who was leaning on his elbows on the table, toying with his fork.

"We all know my stepbrother has sowed a lot of wild oats," said Jarius. "I'm not condoning that, but he has settled down now. Isn't that so, Frank?"

Nathaniel didn't wait to hear a reply.

"Bollocks. He's still up to his tricks and you know it. He's hell-bent on destroying everything I've built up."

Frank didn't look up, but began tapping the fork on the side of the dish as if he were about to crack an egg. Nathaniel wouldn't stop now.

"This woman can get me children who will have respect. I'll see to that. They won't end up scragged like he's going to. Jarius, I don't count you in this. You're not my own flesh and blood, more's the pity, but you will get a nice bequest, don't worry about that. And I know you love me like you should."

"What about Lewis?" Augusta burst out. "What about your first grandson? He deserves consideration."

"Does he? I say let him earn it. Let him earn it the way I had to."

Lewis had heard his grandfather's story many times. How, at the age of fifteen, he'd fled from a poor farm in the north of England, stowed away on a steamer to Canada, and by dint of hard work and a good mind, had established himself in a livery stable, now considered one of the best in Toronto. This history usually took a long time to relate, especially after two jugs of beer, and Lewis hoped Nathaniel wasn't going to launch into it tonight.

However, he could see his mother wasn't going to tolerate storytelling. Her mouth had gone very tight and she spoke as if her jaw were stiff.

"And what about me? I am your only daughter. Surely I matter?"

Nathaniel flapped his hand as if she were an irritating fly. "I've no time for a woman who's put a twitch on her husband's tool the way you have."

Curran didn't respond, except to stuff his hands underneath his thighs out of harm's way. Nathaniel jabbed his finger in the air.

"And I've told you time and again that you're turning your lad into a prize Miss Molly. But you, you won't listen. He's getting to be more and more soft as he grows."

This wasn't the first time his grandfather had used that term, but when Lewis asked his mother what it meant, she wouldn't tell him. Uncle Frank said it meant he would turn out like the fat gelding in the stable and Lewis added that to his other pile of worries.

Suddenly, Frank sat up straight. "Young Nephew, you probably don't know what the hell we're all talking about, do you? Concerning your new grandmother, I mean."

"No, Uncle," whispered Lewis.

"Do you remember how we had to drown Fluffy because she kept getting out and having kittens? She just wouldn't stop? Always caterwauling and carrying on."

"Frank!"

"Don't worry, Aggie. I'm only trying to educate the boy. You see, Lew, your Uncle Jarius thinks Grandmother Peg should have this special operation. It's performed on women who've lost their slates. They take out their innards, their sex parts. They can't have children after that but it's said to work wonders. Dampens them right down."

"Frank, stop it. You can't talk to the boy like that."

"Why not? His future is at stake. You see, Lewis, the problem is we're not just talking about a poor woman who's gone barmy. It's worse than that. Your grandfather is in fact married to a whore who is ready to stand for any man that comes knocking."

Nathaniel cuffed his son across the side of his mouth. His knuckle caught the top of Frank's lip, cracking it.

"You piece of filth. Your mother is crying in heaven over you."

Frank touched his finger to his mouth and examined the daub of blood. "She has a lot more to cry over than just me swearing."

Nathaniel hit out again but this time Frank was ready and he caught him by the wrist. He pushed back and they locked as if they were in a wrestling contest.

"Jarius, stop them," Augusta cried.

Gibb jumped up and came around the table. He gripped Frank's shoulder.

"Let him go."

Eakin did, at the same time pushing back from his chair so he was out of harm's way.

"I believe your father is owed an apology."

"Is he? All I'm doing is telling the truth…You say you'd like more sons but how could you ever be certain of her offspring?"

"Hold your tongue."

"Look at me, Father! I'm flesh of your flesh. You look into a mirror when you see me. There is no doubt who fathered me."

Nathaniel stared at him, then he said, "Don't you think I regret that every day? What I see when I look at you disgusts me."

Frank flinched and Lewis could see the movement of his

Adam's apple in his throat. Jarius was still standing close to him and he stepped forward.

"Stepfather, I am afraid in the interest of truth I must take Frank's side in this matter. He did not want to tell you but she went to him as well as myself. On Friday." He looked over at Curran. "I regret to say she approached both of them."

"You're lying."

Jarius frowned. "How can you say that to me? We were trying to spare you."

"Is it true?" Nathaniel asked his son. His voice was quieter but to Lewis he sounded even more terrifying.

Frank reverted to studying his plate. "Yes, Father."

"Like she did with Jarius?"

"Yes, the same."

"And you, Peter?"

"Er, yes, sir." He glanced quickly at his wife.

"Why didn't you tell me?" asked Augusta.

Curran stared at a point over her right shoulder. "No point really."

"I don't believe you!" Nathaniel roared and slammed his fist on the table. Lewis was afraid he would hit Frank again. Jarius bent over him.

"It is true, Stepfather. I saw them bringing her back. I did not want to tell you. You had enough to contend with. And you can see how upset you are."

All eyes were on Nathaniel. Finally he spoke.

"The woman is a whore, that is clear. I must apologise to

you, Frank." He held out his hand, palm down, to his son.

Frank took it in his and kissed the fingers.

Lewis saw that he left behind a smudge of blood.

CHAPTER NINETEEN

SAM LEE AND HIS SON LIVED IN A ROOM TO THE REAR OF the laundry. No Westerner had ever entered this place, and, if they had, it would have fulfilled all their most riotous fantasies about Chinamen. Earlier the two had lit incense sticks and the smell was dense and pungent in the air. The light was a soft bluish red. Lee had draped scarves of violet-coloured silk over the two lamps, which were turned down low. There was little furniture and all of it Lee had made himself. He was a talented wood-carver, but it would have been impossible for him to find work other than in the expected laundry. However, he had built a massive hinged panel that covered one side of the room, and slowly, over the lonely years, he'd covered it with carvings of flowers, birds, and bats. The entire work was painted with gilt. In front of this panel was a red lacquered table on which stood the kitchen altar, three porcelain cups, and rice-filled bowls with their chopsticks. A brightly coloured picture of Choi Sun, the god of wealth, was propped beside these items, and tucked slightly to the back was a more subdued painting of Jesus ascending to heaven.

Against the opposite wall was a single wooden couch covered with a thin, padded mattress and a blue quilt. The evidence of Western life was an ugly iron range that served as cooker and heater. Foon had prepared boiled rice and greens for their dinner and they were having it, seated cross-legged on the floor. He finished eating, served his father the remaining rice, and sat quietly, waiting.

Sam gave a soft belch in a sign of appreciation of the meal his son had prepared.

"Shall I get your pipe, *baba*?"

The older man nodded and Foon got up, crossed to a cupboard beside the range, and took out a brown leather sack. He returned to his father, who had stretched out on the wooden couch.

"*Baba*, with your permission, I have a question I would like to present to you."

Lee was lying with his head on the pillow roll and his eyes were closed. "What is your question, *laoerh*?" He addressed his son in the traditional Chinese manner, according to his birth order, number-two son. Sam's oldest child had remained in Hong Kong to help support his mother and sister. Sam intended to send for them when the law changed, or smuggle them in if it didn't.

Foon opened the sack and removed the *yangqiang*, the opium pipe. It was made of bamboo with a tortoiseshell overlay. The tips were ivory and the saddle, where the bowl sat, was pewter and copper latticework studded with semi-precious stones of red and green. It was the most expensive object they owned, passed down to Lee from his uncle on his mother's side and already promised to the eldest son. Foon placed it carefully beside him and lifted the cloth that covered their eating table. Tucked underneath was a low stand of black lacquer inlaid with mother-of-pearl, which he pulled out. Resting in shallow holes were four small bowls, each a different shape and material. He slid open the drawer and took out a long steel bodkin and a tiny polished wooden box. He placed them beside the pipe.

"Do you have a preference tonight, *baba*?"

Sam studied the dampers for a moment, then lazily indicated an onion-shaped one made of jade with a carved dragon design around the edge.

Foon picked it up and snapped the stem securely onto the pipe. Next he unscrewed the top of the little box and dipped the end of the bodkin into the opium paste it contained. He had turned up the wick of the lamp and he held the blob of dark, treacly paste in the flame. As soon as it caught fire, he blew it out and rolled it in the pipe bowl, twirling the bodkin between his fingers and thumb. He repeated this procedure twice more, then handed the pipe to his father. Sam took in a deep breath, exhaled completely, then drew in the aromatic opium smoke, holding it in his lungs as long as possible. He let go of the smoke through his nostrils. Foon watched him for a moment, until he could see the pipe was to his satisfaction.

"At the inquest this morning, you instructed me to tell them that the young woman who claimed to be Mr. Wicken's fiancée was the same one that you had seen with the constable."

Sam was holding the bowl of the pipe over the lamp to heat it. He nodded an acknowledgment.

"Forgive me, *baba*, but obviously this was not the case. I too saw the woman who was walking with the constable and they were not at all alike. This first one was tall as any man. Would it not have been better to tell the truth?"

His father repeated his ritual of drawing in the smoke, then he said, "Why should I give them something they do not want? If I had said no, it is not she, that is not the one I saw, they would have continued to question me, implying I am a stupid foreigner who does not know what he is talking about. It was much simpler to agree."

"Do you think then that the young constable had two concubines?"

Sam smiled slyly. "No, I do not think so. This one we saw today is a liar."

"How do you know that, with respect, my father?"

"Chinese intuition."

Foon smiled also. "Of course. But why do you think she

was prepared to risk damnation by lying with God's book in her hand?"

"I do not have an answer. Frankly, I do not wish to know. It is no concern of ours. Let them kill each other for all I care. As far as they are concerned, we are ignorant savages with squirrel brains. Let them continue to believe so."

He passed over the pipe to Foon. "Here, my son, there is one draw left at least."

Foon hesitated. His missionary upbringing was at odds with his culture. His father was being generous and it was disrespectful to refuse, but he knew how the pastor had disapproved of opium smoking. He took the pipe while Sam watched him.

"All that nonsense about breaking a saucer. *My soul will be cracked like this vessel if I lie.* They treat us like foolish children."

Foon drew in a small amount of the smoke, retained it briefly, and returned the pipe to his father. Lee smoked in silence for about twenty minutes more, then he turned onto his side and stretched out his legs. Foon picked up the pipe, scraped out the bowl, and returned it to the stand. The *yangqiang* he placed back in the leather sack. Sam seemed to have drifted off into sleep and he looked peaceful. Sometimes the opium brought with it fearful visions that caused him to cry out in fear, but tonight the sensations were obviously pleasurable. Foon bent over him and gently lifted up the thick queue, untied the black silk cord that was braided into it, and loosened the hair completely. He drew his fingers like a comb from the base of

Sam's skull, up to the crown, and out to the ends of the hair. His father sighed with sleepy pleasure.

"With respect to Chinese intuition, *baba*, would there be another reason you are so certain the young woman was lying?"

Sam grunted; his words were almost unintelligible with sleep. "I have seen her before. At her place of employment, a brothel on King Street."

Foon's soothing actions stopped.

Sam rolled onto his back and looked at his son. "Every man has needs of the flesh, *laoerh*. Except you, who have the mind and will of a monk. I have discovered a place where a man can find comfort. They accept a Chinaman's money with quite a good grace." He chuckled. "The whores were intrigued by me. They said they had never seen a Chinese before and they insisted I display my member to the entire band of them. I think they were a little disappointed it was not so very different from the *fangui*. The girl, Mary Ann, was one of the whores. Today I gave her thanks."

He rolled back to his side and waved at Foon to continue his stroking. "Your mother would understand. I am a man." Within a few minutes he had fallen asleep. Foon rebraided his hair and tied the ribbon.

He covered Sam with another padded quilt and went to extinguish the lamps. Then, quietly, he slipped in beside him. The opium had made him sleepy too, but he did not fall into dreams immediately. His thoughts were agitating to him. Lee was wrong about his son. Foon dreamed constantly of mating with a young woman and despaired of the possibility. The missionary teaching had gone deep into his soul and he was determined to remain chaste until he could find a wife and marry in the eyes of God. As this meant returning to China, he knew it would be a long time before they had enough money. He could feel a little bubble of resentment floating to the surface of his mind. His father had committed adultery and dishonoured his mother. That was sinful.

CHAPTER TWENTY

AFTER NATHANIEL HAD GONE TO BED, FRANK HAD COME over to the stable, taken out a bottle of gin that he kept hidden in a box under his bed, and slowly and steadily drunk himself into unconsciousness. He had paid the price today.

"What time's the green arse coming?" he called over to his brother-in-law, who was in the adjoining stall working on the mare they intended to sell.

"I told you, he said he'd be here by four."

Frank took the jar of ginger, a tin of aniseed, and a bottle of turpentine from the shelf in the tack room. He carried them over to the bench where he'd already placed the measuring cup and an enamel bowl. Without thinking, he brushed his hand across his mouth and winced as he touched his lip. But he shrugged it off. He'd had worse.

He could remember the first whipping but not the reason for it and not the actual pain, although it had hurt him so badly he lost his breath. He must have been four years old, although that was hazy too. He may have been younger.

Jarius had brought him into the stable. It was winter time, he knew, because he had been outside in the yard making snowballs with Augusta. Had he thrown one at Jarius? Was that his misdemeanour? He still puzzled over it, as if knowing the transgression would make sense of the punishment. There had been many more after that, many of them severe, but it was the first one that had left the deepest scars, both physical and emotional. He had two long white marks on his right buttock where the skin had broken down.

Jarius, his stepbrother, was nineteen years his elder and Frank had always been afraid of him – his seriousness, his dark hair and skin, unlike his fairness and Augusta's, who followed after their father in looks. He didn't understand why Jarius was so different but his mother finally answered his questions.

"Your father was married before to a widow lady. She already had a son of her own – Jarius. Not too long after the marriage, the poor woman died, but Jarius was raised like his own by your father. He was thirteen years of age when I married Mr. Eakin. A sombre boy even then."

Frank remembered she had sighed when she said that.

The second Mrs. Eakin always spoke in a soft, anxious voice, as if she were perpetually afraid of being overheard. Her name was Harmony and she said many times how she loved to think that she lived up to her name. Much later, with some bitterness, Frank realised what this really meant: she strove to say nothing that would offend and avoided conflict at all costs. She never interceded when Jarius took him over to the stable and even when she was forced to put ointment on his bleeding buttocks, she only whispered to him to try to be a good boy in future and not cause trouble.

Nathaniel also beat him, but not as frequently and never in such a sustained way. He said Jarius was his lieutenant and ignored any protests. Not that Frank tried for very long. He soon learned that to cry to his father was to make matters worse with Jarius when they were alone. He also learned to read his stepbrother's mood the way a dog will immediately assess a potential threat. Woe betide Frank if Jarius was in a temper about something else. He would always find some excuse to vent that anger on the boy. The hardest thing was that Frank never knew how to react. Sometimes if he screamed, Jarius would stop sooner. At other times, the crying only seemed to incense him more. Similarly, if Frank bit his lip and choked back his pain, Jarius sometimes gave up in disgust; at other times, he went on until Frank begged for mercy.

He measured out a dram of ginger and sifted out two drams of the aniseed into the bowl. He added the turpentine to the mixture and stirred it with his fingers until it formed a ball.

When he was twelve years of age, the punishments stopped.

One afternoon, Jarius came home earlier than usual. It was a stiflingly hot summer day and Frank was in the stable. He was so uncomfortable with the heat he had stripped off his clothes and was standing naked, pouring a bucket of water over himself. He suddenly became aware that Jarius had come in and was watching him.

"My little brother is growing up, I see," he said, but his voice was so full of repulsion that Frank there and then began to think of himself as ugly; he knew it had to do with the hair that had grown in his crotch and the changes in his private parts.

Frank hadn't been paying much attention to what he was doing but suddenly the odour of the turpentine made him retch; his stomach was already so queasy from last night's binge. Then he realised he'd forgotten the other part of the recipe. Irritated, he went back to the shelf.

"Where is the frigging stuff?" he said out loud.

"What frigging stuff?" Peter Curran was in one of the stalls, working on the horse.

"The antimony. It's supposed to be here on the shelf."

"Don't blame me, I wouldn't touch it."

"Damnation."

They were interrupted by his nephew's voice.

"Uncle Frank? Shall I feed Brownie?"

Lewis was standing in the doorway. He could have been Frank's own child in appearance, with the same light brown hair and round face, but this similarity didn't endear him to his uncle. He was too quiet, inclined to be sly, and although he would never have admitted it, Frank saw himself mirrored in that cautious, wary expression with which Lewis regarded the world.

"Of course feed him. He was purged this morning. Have you been messing with the medicines?"

"No, Uncle Frank."

"This will have to do then. Put it in the mash." He held out the ball of aniseed, dropping the sticky mass into the boy's palm. "Stir it in well."

He followed the youngster to the stall and watched while he ladled mash from a pail into the horse's pan. Brownie stepped forward and Lewis leaped away, almost knocking over the pail.

Frank yelled at him and gave him a sharp rap on the side of the head.

"What's the matter with you?"

"I'm sorry, Uncle. I thought he was going to bite me."

"What a yellow-bellied little runt you are. He wanted his mash, not you. Get out of here. Go see if your father's finished."

Lewis scuttled away. Frank waited until he was sure the roan had swallowed the medicine, then followed him. Curran was in the process of blacking the mare's hooves. Earlier he had filed away the ridges in her front hooves to hide the fact she had foundered, and the blacking was to cover the signs.

"Done? Let's bring her out then. Our friend should be here soon."

Curran took the mare's halter and led her out of the stall.

Frank beckoned to Lewis. "Now, Mister Titty Suck, I want you to show the horse when the customer comes. Do you think you can do that without a big cock-up?"

"Yes, Uncle."

"This man is a stupid sod, fancies himself a bit of a buck but he's a green arse. Just the kind we like. He says he wants a lively carriage horse for his new bride. 'Course he doesn't want to pay a top price but never mind. We have the perfect mare for him. Good thing it's raining, you'll have to walk her in here. Doesn't matter if you're nervous, that'll look good, like she's spirited."

"Oh, I'm not scared of Duchess. She's quiet."

"Any more quiet and she'd be dead," put in Curran. "I'm surprised you haven't sent her to Lamb's factory. She'll make better glue than she will a 'lively carriage horse.'"

Frank laughed. "Well, we have the remedy for that, don't we? Hold on to her, Lewis, don't let her run off."

The boy stood holding the lead rein. The mare showed signs of a hard life and was slightly swaybacked. Her head drooped almost to the ground.

Frank came back with a piece of clean linen and the tin of powdered ginger. He took off the lid, twisted the cloth into a tight spindle, and dipped it into the ginger. Then, clicking his tongue softly, he approached the mare, lifted her tail, and quickly pushed the twist of cloth into her anus. She jumped, but almost immediately the ginger began to sting. She pawed at the ground.

"Walk her, Lew."

The boy tugged on the halter and she needed no urging, stepping forward in a prance, her tail held high as she tried to get away from the irritation in her backside.

Frank whistled in delight. "She's moving like a filly. We'll give her another little boost just before he gets here. He'll be totally satisfied. And he'll think he's bilking me into the bargain. 'Course in two days she'll be near death again but that won't be my fault, will it?"

"What if he brings her back, Uncle?"

"He won't. Our agreement will be final sale. Besides, he's going away on his wedding trip. When he gets back, he can blame his own groom for overriding the horse. He's not going to admit I duped him. All right, let her walk it off a bit, then put her back in the stall."

He went over to the lantern that was hanging on a hook by the door and turned down the wick. "We can see quite well enough, thank you."

Curran waited until Lewis had stabled the mare again, then he turned to Frank.

"By the way, Jarius said that Pa has made up his mind."

Eakin stared at him. "Why didn't you say so?"

"You was busy."

"Well, what's he going to do?"

Curran grinned. "I guess you persuaded him. She'll get the operation."

CHAPTER TWENTY-ONE

AS SOON AS HE OPENED THE FRONT DOOR, MURDOCH could hear Arthur coughing and immediately, almost subconsciously, he assessed the sound. No worse, maybe slightly better than usual. He was hanging up his coat and hat when the kitchen door opened and Enid Jones came out.

"Mr. Murdoch, I was hoping you wouldn't be too late. Your supper is almost ready."

He couldn't resist imitating her lilt.

"Is it now?"

She smiled. "Is it mocking me you are?"

"Not at all. I could listen to you all day long."

"I'd say that was a dreadful waste of time then." But her tone belied the words.

However, they were both suddenly awkward, standing close in the narrow hall.

"Mrs. Kitchen has gone to a prayer vigil at the church," Enid said. "I promised I would look after you in her place."

"That's kind of you, Mrs. Jones, but really I am quite capable of taking a plate out of the oven. I have done it many times before."

"Whether you are capable or not isn't the point, is it now? We both thought you could do with some tending to on a raw night like this. Especially with you having had your tooth pulled."

She scrutinised him. "Your face is still swollen. Is it hurting?"

"Very much," he said solemnly.

She stepped back. "Go get you a warm by the fire, then. I will bring in your tea."

He went into the little front parlour. The fire was crackling and there was an extra lamp on the table. The heat and light seemed dazzling after the dismal weather outside.

"Hello, Alwyn."

Enid's son was sitting at the table with some sort of games board in front of him. As Murdoch entered, the boy glanced up but he didn't look too pleased to see him.

"Good evening to you, sir."

Murdoch looked over his shoulder. "What's that you've got?"

"It's a game my mamma gave me."

"Looks interesting. *The Prince's Quest*. What do you have to do?"

Alwyn became a little more animated. "The princess is

202

asleep and she's in danger. There are four princes who want to save her. The first one to get to the bower wins her." His face was earnest. "The path is full of dangers."

"Ah, yes, I've known it to be."

There was a silence while the boy considered his options. Finally, he said, "Will you play then?"

"I would like to." He pulled out the chair next to the boy.

"We must first choose our pieces," said Alwyn.

He showed him cutout shapes of princes on little wooden stands. They wore flat hats, short embroidered jerkins, and dark stockings. Each had a sleeveless cloak, also short, which were of different colours.

"I'll take the purple one."

Alwyn looked disappointed. "That was the one I wanted."

Murdoch hesitated, trying to decide whether it would be better for character development for the boy to take his lumps or whether he could curry a bit of favour. He elected to placate.

"Green for me then. He's a handsome fellow."

"No, it's all right. My da said it wasn't manly to complain if things didn't go your way."

"Did he now? He was right, I'd say. Purple it is."

Alwyn studied the princes. "I'll take blue, no – this one, the red." He set the two chosen figures on the board, each one facing a different path. "Throw the die and move according to the number."

"Where's the princess?"

The boy pointed to a woman with extraordinarily long

hair who was reclining languidly on a couch. Her eyes were closed so he assumed she was sleeping. Or waiting and full of anticipation.

Vigorously, he shook the die in his cupped hands and tossed it down with a flourish. One.

"Hm, the story of my life."

Alwyn threw a five and gleefully counted off the spaces along the path toward the prize.

"I'm beating you already."

Murdoch's next throw landed him on a square marked Shoes of Swiftness, and he was able to shoot ahead, thereby avoiding a stint of work in the dwarf's cave. Alwyn threw a four and landed in the *Garden of Sleep*.

"Oh, dear, miss three turns," said Murdoch.

"No, that's not fair," the boy wailed.

"It's the luck of the game, titch. Remember what your father said."

He was about to throw again when Enid entered. She was carrying a big tray.

He got up quickly to help her. Alwyn said something to her in Welsh, gesturing angrily at Murdoch. She answered in a soothing voice, shaking her head.

"I didn't," said Murdoch.

"Didn't what?" she said, startled.

"Cheat."

"You know Welsh?"

"No, but I know small boys. He landed fair and square in the

Garden of Sleep. He has to miss three throws."

"Good gracious, that is hard."

"Rules are rules."

He wanted to add, *That is what your husband taught him*, but was reluctant to introduce any memory of her former love.

She turned to her son.

"Mr. Murdoch is going to have his supper. You can finish your game afterwards."

Alwyn answered in Welsh and, picking up the die, he went back to the board. He was going to play both princes. Then he was sure to win the princess. Murdoch thought it was churlish to protest. He moved over to the place set for him.

Enid lifted the lid off the tureen.

"I made a rabbit soup," she said. "It's a popular dish at home."

The food smelled so fragrant, Murdoch's mouth watered and he was afraid he'd actually be drooling if he didn't eat soon. She ladled some soup into a bowl, handed it to him, and waited for him to take his first taste. He did so, nearly scalding himself.

"Utterly delicious," he managed to mutter.

"It's hot, be careful now."

He tore off a piece of bread from the hunk on his plate and stuffed that into his mouth to ease the pain. She watched him with gratification as he made more appreciative noises.

"I thought you'd need something soft."

Alwyn looked up. "I've got a loose tooth." He opened his mouth and waggled one of his front teeth.

"Good for you," murmured Murdoch, trying to make sure

the soup wasn't getting into the gaping crater he could feel in his gum.

"I'll bring in the potatoes. I mashed them up with the rest of the rabbit," said Enid.

She went back to the kitchen, leaving Murdoch to blow air into his burning mouth.

Alwyn returned to his game, talking quietly to himself as he moved his pieces. Murdoch saw him land in the Haunted Glen. He was supposed to throw a three to get out but he ignored that and moved on. Murdoch was about to call out, "Hey, you're cheating," but thought better of it. The lad needed a firm hand, he decided. He studied him for a moment. He had his mother's dark eyes but he was sharper of feature and his hair had a curl to it. *I wonder what it's like to see your own reflection in a child's face*, thought Murdoch. *Or the face of the woman you have loved?* He stopped eating.

Enid came back into the room and he hastily dipped his spoon back into the soup.

"Is it all right then?"

"Wonderful."

She put the platter on the table.

"Thank you, Mrs. Jones. This is very kind of you."

"Not at all. I wanted to help Mrs. Kitchen."

On impulse, he caught hold of her hand, grasping it awkwardly in a semi-handshake. Then, as if his body were acting entirely on its own accord, he brought her fingers to his lips, kissing them lightly. Her skin smelled faintly of onions.

She didn't pull away but he didn't know what to do next. He wanted desperately to be eloquent but found himself tongue-tied. He looked up at her. This time she did move.

"I must go fetch the potatoes."

"You brought them in already."

"So I did." She became even more flustered and reached for the soup tureen. "I'll take this out of your way and let you finish your meal in peace."

"This is peace. I'd be honoured if you would keep me company."

She hesitated briefly, then sat down at the opposite end of the table.

"Very well."

He bought some time by spooning up more soup, which had cooled somewhat.

"Utterly delicious."

She nodded. Alwyn gave him a reprieve by getting up and going over to his mother.

"I won, Mama. I rescued the princess."

Fondly, she put her arms around him and kissed his forehead. "Well done, little one."

Murdoch was about to say that it was easy to win if you were moving both pieces but he bit his tongue. Feeling rivalrous, was he?

"If you go into the kitchen you will find a tray of lemon dumplings," she said to the boy. "You can have one for yourself. But eat it there, look you."

Alwyn took off.

"Lemon dumplings? This is a meal fit for a king."

There was another uncomfortable silence while he tackled the platter of rabbit meat and potatoes.

"Mr. Murdoch, there is something I have been wanting to ask you."

"Yes?" He was hopeful.

"In church last week, the minister was preaching about the afterlife. He pointed out that if my son were to die, God defend us, the Roman Catholic Church teaches that he would not go to heaven as he is not of the Catholic faith. He would be deprived of the sight of God for all eternity through no fault of his own. Can you explain to me how a person who believes in the Divine love can accept such a cruel doctrine?"

Murdoch almost groaned out loud. A theological discussion was not his notion of love talk. But she was regarding him earnestly, wanting an answer.

"As far as I am concerned, doctrine is man-made. We hope that it reflects God's will on earth but we can never know that for sure."

She seemed dissatisfied with his answer. "Yes, but…"

Fortunately, he was rescued by Mrs. Kitchen coming into the parlour. Her nose and cheeks were reddened from the chill air outside.

"Mr. Murdoch, I am so glad Mrs. Jones has been taking good care of you. I won't even apologise for my absence, since I can see what a splendid meal she has prepared."

Murdoch stood up to greet her. "Splendid and plentiful."

"Are you ready for your tea?"

"I am indeed."

"The kettle is at the boil," said Enid.

"Good, let me just see how Arthur is doing and I'll make us all a pot. You will join us, won't you, Mrs. Jones?"

"Thank you, but perhaps another night. I have to start getting Alwyn ready for bed."

She headed for the door.

"Perhaps I can answer your question at a later time," said Murdoch.

She nodded. "It is a discussion I am looking forward to."

Mrs. Kitchen waited until she left. "She worked all day on that soup, Mr. Murdoch. I would be careful if I were you."

"What do you mean, Mrs. K.? It tasted quite all right to me."

She tapped his hand. "Don't pretend. You know perfectly well what I am talking about. She fancies you."

Murdoch clasped both her hands in his. "Oh, dear Mrs. K., is that so terribly bad?"

"It's not so much it's bad, as that it's out of the question. Or have you forgotten she's a Baptist?"

He sighed and let her go. "No. You both seem intent on reminding me. She wanted to know how I explained limbo."

"Did she indeed? That means she's serious. She's trying to see how big the chasm is. But never you mind, some people have made successful mixed marriages. She would have to convert, of course."

He grinned. "Mrs. K., here we are talking about the lady as if she and I were courting. I'm not even at the starting line."

She smiled, knowingly. "I would say you're approaching it fast."

CHAPTER TWENTY-TWO

MURDOCH PUT HIS REPORT BACK IN THE FILE FOLDER and returned it to the cabinet. Two local ministers from Jarvis Street Baptist Church had issued a complaint. An English travelling troupe of dancers had distributed bills on the street. The photographs of the young women in the troupe were completely indecent, according to the ministers. They requested the police charge them. Murdoch thought the women, although showing a length of lower leg, were suitably clothed for dancers, assuming they had to pirouette and leap about. The ministers were indignant at his defence, and it became apparent that their complaint was not only concerning the clothing, but the very existence of the troupe. He had taken their deputation, accepted the petition with a long list of signatures, and promised to investigate further.

He found it hard to muster much enthusiasm for the case. He'd been sitting for at least a half an hour with Elizabeth's photograph in front of him. He knew it was irrational of him but he was feeling guilty at the intensity of his feelings for Mrs. Jones. It was all very well for Father Fair to say she was dead and in God's love and that she would be happy for him. In life, Liza had been prone to possessiveness, something he'd rather liked. It had made him feel wanted. He picked up the framed picture. *Liza, my dearest, you know that you had my heart and, if you had lived, no one else would ever have warranted a glance from me. But you left me and I cannot help myself. This is a woman you would have liked, perhaps befriended. I know she is not of our faith but oh, Liza, I do have to admit, I would dearly like to have her.* The blurry image of his dead fiancée showed no expression except, he was sure, some reproach.

He and Liza were of the same faith, of course, but he couldn't remember that they had discussed it much. Religion was part of the fabric of their lives, unquestioned for the most part, the rituals so familiar. They went to mass regularly and therefore to confession. They'd laughed about that together, well aware that they were committing venial sins all the time with their mutual impure thoughts. Liza insisted her penances were more severe than his but he didn't know if that was because she owned up to worse things or because she was a woman.

He touched the photograph. It was not a very good picture.

Her large-brimmed hat was shading her face too much and she'd moved just as he clicked the shutter. He returned the photograph to the drawer, feeling even more guilty that he was putting her away in that fashion.

Impatiently, he brushed off a couple of lethargic flies that were crawling over the surface of his blotter. Because of the adjoining stables, the fly population never completely disappeared. The flies just got slower, storing up energy for the spring onslaught.

He leaned back in his chair. Usually he took his surroundings for granted but today he scrutinised them with critical eyes, and his spirits sank even lower as he took in the pervading shabbiness. His desk was old, wobbly, and in need of revarnishing. He hadn't added to its appearance by constantly scratching the surface with his pen-nib when he was trying to get his thoughts straightened out. There was room for only one other chair, a decidedly shabby armchair from heaven-knows-what previous life. Part of the seat was torn and some of the horse hair was coming out. He had requested a replacement, but so far nothing had happened. According to Inspector Brackenreid, there was no money to spend, although Murdoch noticed his office was well furnished. Only last month, a splendid crimson velvet rug had arrived from the T. Eaton Company. So what if the roof still leaked over the stables and the sashes on the windows were so shrunken the snow drifted through in the winter? If Brackenreid met with members of the public they served, which was rare, he did so in impressive surroundings. The sweet fruits of power.

That taste was forever out of his reach, thought Murdoch, a little dismayed at his own bitterness. As a Roman Catholic, his chances of promotion were virtually nonexistent. He was considered lucky to have even been admitted into the recently formed detective department. The men who ran the police force were Protestant. Less acknowledged, but a significant factor, was that they were also Free Masons and belonged to one of the numerous orders that dominated the commercial and social life of the city.

He swivelled around to face the wall behind him where there were two framed portraits hanging. One was of the chief constable, Lieutenant-Colonel Henry Grasett, the other of Her Majesty, Queen Victoria. When Murdoch had first heard a rumour that the queen insisted her dead husband's clothes, shaving water, and razor be put out every morning, he'd thought such a show of grief excessive. Since Liza had died, however, he understood completely the need to cling to any vestige of that previous life, to hold on to the illusion that death was not final.

He picked up his pen and started to run the nib along a groove in the top of the desk. Some previous owner had carved the initials I.F. and, with Murdoch's help, the letters were now dark blue scars.

There was a tap outside his cubicle. Through the reed curtain he could see the large frame of Constable Crabtree.

"The inspector would like to see you at once, Mr. Murdoch. In his office."

"What for now?"

Crabtree poked his head through the reed strips. "A young lady came in a short while back asking for Wicken. Said she was his friend and she hadn't seen him lately. Wondered if he was ill."

Murdoch stared at Crabtree in dismay. "That's not good, is it!"

"Sergeant Seymour directed her right upstairs to see Inspector Brackenreid, but he's sent for you."

Murdoch stood up, followed the constable out to the front hall, and hurried up the stairs to the second floor where the inspector had his office. He was admitted at once.

A young woman was standing by the window, looking down to the street below. She was tall, her height accentuated by the long navy-blue waterproof she was wearing. Her red felt hat with its big satin bow and curled white quill was jaunty and fashionable.

Brackenreid was behind his desk. With his heavy moustache and smart uniform with the velvet frogs down the front, he was a distinguished-looking man, as long as you didn't come close enough to see the red veins in his cheeks or the stains down his jacket. Brackenreid was a toper, something, he deluded himself, nobody knew. He gave Murdoch an unusually warm greeting as he entered.

"Ah, Murdoch, glad you were available. This is Miss Isobel Brewster. She is enquiring about Constable Wicken. Miss Brewster, I'd like to present Detective Murdoch. He has, er, been, um, been involved in the case from the beginning."

The woman didn't stir; it was not clear if she had even heard what he'd said.

"I had to tell Miss Brewster what has happened," he continued. "That Constable Wicken had, er, passed away. She didn't know, so she is understandably distressed at the moment. She and Wicken were friends. She was wondering why she hadn't seen him recently and came here to find out."

"I see," said Murdoch.

The woman swung around and glared at him. "What does that mean, *I see*?"

Her fierceness was startling.

"I beg your pardon, ma'am, I meant nothing by it."

He stopped, not sure how much Brackenreid had told her. The inspector gave a slight shake of his head. He pulled a watch out of his pocket. "I do apologise, Miss Brewster, but I have an appointment I must keep. Can't be put off. Why don't you just stay here a little while and talk to Detective Murdoch. I'll have some tea sent up, and when you're ready, we'll have somebody accompany you home. Will that be all right?"

She nodded and the inspector left, fast as all cowards are to leave the place of pain.

"Won't you please come and sit down," said Murdoch.

"I prefer to stand." She turned from the window but didn't come closer. She looked to be no more than twenty or so, not a beauty by any means. Her features were sharp, the nose too long, the mouth thin. She was regarding him with frightened eyes.

"He says that Oliver Wicken has died. But how? What happened? He was quite well when I saw him last."

"When was that, ma'am?"

"Monday evening."

"His body was discovered early on Tuesday morning. I'm afraid he had been shot."

She gave a quick intake of breath. "What are you saying? Shot how?"

"It appears it was by his own hand. There was an inquest and the jury returned a verdict of suicide."

She stared at him in disbelief for a moment, then laughed derisively, as if he had said something incredibly stupid. "That is out of the question. When I saw him he was in perfectly good spirits. You are mistaken." With perceptible agitation now, she stepped closer. "Perhaps you are speaking of someone else. I am enquiring about Constable Oliver Wicken. He is blond-haired. He has a moustache and side-whiskers." She gestured at her own cheek.

"I'm sorry, Miss Brewster, but there is no mistake. I myself found his body. There is no doubt it was Oliver Wicken. I knew him."

She sat down abruptly on the edge of the chair, as if she could no longer trust herself to remain standing. Her manner became belligerent as shock hid itself in anger. "On what did the jury base their verdict of suicide?"

"Partly on the evidence of the post mortem examination. He had been shot in the right temple and the coroner felt this was consistent with a self-inflicted wound." He almost demonstrated but stopped just in time.

"And that is all the so-called evidence?"

"No. There was a note found on his person that seemed to indicate he was in an extremely despondent frame of mind."

"What did it say?"

"The exact words were, 'Life is unbearable without your love. Forgive me.'"

He paused while she absorbed this.

"Can I see the letter?"

"It is considered part of his effects and they have been returned to his mother."

"There was nothing else? No person addressed? No signature?"

"No, that was all."

She jumped to her feet again and strode back to the window. She was virtually shouting. "I don't believe it, do you hear? Ollie had no reason to feel that way."

Sobs were threatening to break through but they were suppressed almost immediately. She came back to the chair and sat down, her back as stiff as if she were in a deportment class.

"I should tell you, Mr. Murdoch, that Oliver was my…that is, what I mean to say is, we were betrothed. We have been for almost a year."

She caught the surprise in his face and misinterpreted it. "It was a secret engagement. Ollie was concerned about his mother. He supports her solely and he was afraid she would not approve, that she would worry about him marrying." Suddenly, she leaned over and caught Murdoch by the sleeve. "About the letter you found…Are you certain it was written by Oliver?"

"It was not handwritten; it was printed. He had used a piece of paper from his notebook."

Her voice dropped. "I was always on at him about how bad his hand was. He did print sometimes."

Murdoch's heart went out to her. She had come dressed in her best, worried but never suspecting the dreadful news she would receive. And that was not all of it. Suddenly, her eyes met his and he was taken off guard by the shrewdness of her next question.

"I have the feeling you are not telling me everything. Please believe me, it would help me to know all that happened. I am not going to have hysterics, I assure you. Was there something else that was said at the inquest?"

Murdoch wished he could soften the blow but he knew he couldn't. "Yes, there was. A young woman came forward who said she was Wicken's fiancée. She broke off the engagement that night, Monday, which seemed the likely cause for him to have become so despondent."

Isobel Brewster turned putty white. She could hardly form her words.

"That is impossible."

"The woman swore under oath. She said they had been engaged for the past two months."

"What was this woman's name?"

"Miss Mary Ann Trowbridge."

"I've never heard of her. I…"

She groaned and her lips and chin began to shake. She held

her fingers to her mouth as if she could barely risk hearing her own voice out loud. Whatever she was about to say, he didn't hear because, at that moment, her eyelids started to flutter and she leaned back abruptly, her eyes rolling back in her head. He jumped up and caught her just as she was about to slide off the chair.

"Put your head down on your knees."

She did as she was told and remained like that for a few moments longer, then slowly sat up. Murdoch took her right hand in his, pushed down the cuff of her glove, and rubbed the back of her wrist vigorously. The same with the left. She hardly allowed him to minister to her before she pulled away her hands.

"I'm quite all right now."

"I thought you were going to faint."

"I despise women who faint." She licked her lips. "Can I have a glass of water, please?"

"Just a minute."

He went back around to the other side of the desk. Just as he'd hoped, there was a flask in the top drawer. He shook it to make sure it wasn't yet empty and brought it over to her.

"Sip some of this."

He unscrewed the top and handed her the flask. She took a big sip of the brandy, coughing as it burned her throat.

"Good thing I'm not temperance," she said with a small smile. Her colour was better now, and satisfied she wasn't going to faint completely, he returned to his own chair. She took another drink.

"I do apologise."

"There is no need."

"What you have said is a great shock to me. It is quite unbelievable."

"The young woman has a letter from her aunt testifying to the truth of her statement and we have a witness who swore under oath that he saw the constable with Miss Trowbridge the night he died."

"What witness?"

"His name is Samuel Lee. He runs a laundry on Parliament Street. He says that Constable Wicken checked his establishment that night and he saw this young woman with him."

"When?"

"About a quarter past eleven."

"Impossible. I tell you that is utterly impossible. Oh, Mr. Murdoch, please believe me. It was me he saw. I was with Oliver then. I would often meet him on his beat. We needed to catch any time together that we could. I know it was against the rules but he didn't neglect his duty in any way; he was very responsible. On Monday night, I met him on the corner as he was coming up Parliament Street and I walked with him as far as Gerrard."

"And this was at that time?"

"Yes. It was always the same time."

"Were you with him when he went into the Chinese laundry?"

"Yes. He went inside for a few minutes while I waited on the sidewalk."

"The proprietor did identify Miss Trowbridge as the woman accompanying Wicken."

"He was mistaken."

She read Murdoch's doubt. "Please believe me. I swear I am telling the truth. I went as far as the empty house on the corner. We often met there. It gave us some privacy."

"Did you go inside?"

"No. Frankly, we would have but the doors were locked. We stood in the front doorway."

"For how long?"

"About a half an hour..." She moaned. "We had an argument."

"What was it about?"

"I assure you, Mr. Murdoch, it was not so serious. Just a tiff, a lovers' tiff, the way any couple will argue."

He waited while she sorted out in her mind the implications of what she was saying. That this was the last exchange she had had with her sweetheart.

"We have been engaged for almost a year now," she continued. "I was eager to announce it and have the bans read but we could not agree. Oliver was still procrastinating. He was always afraid to upset his mother. She depends upon him entirely."

"Did you resolve the matter?"

"No. I...er, I have a hot temper. I told him he must make up his mind or I would break off the engagement. I walked away."

She frowned. "Wait. That is not the truth, Mr. Murdoch, and

it is the pure truth that we are after, is it not? I did not *walk* away, I ran. I was furious with him."

"Where was he when you left?"

"Still in the doorway."

"Miss Brewster, sometimes in a moment of imbalance we do foolish things. In your mind is it possible that Oliver was so distressed by your quarrel he took his own life?"

"He was not that kind of weakling, Mr. Murdoch." She almost spat out the words. "You see, I know what I'm talking about...My own father hanged himself when I was a child. As a matter of fact, I was the one who found him. He was in the living room when I came home from school. He had lost his job and he never stopped moaning about it. He would sit and brood all day long, talking endlessly about how terribly he'd been treated. Suicides make sure they give you plenty of notice so you can feel sorry for them. Ollie might have been distressed when I left but he was no coward. He would never desert me or his mother and sister; he cared for us too much. I can only think there must have been a dreadful accident."

Murdoch spoke to her gently. "Miss Brewster, Wicken was inside that house when I found him."

"Where?"

"In the rear kitchen."

"But the house was locked. He tried the door."

"He had a key in his pocket."

Again he waited while she absorbed this information.

"Mr. Murdoch, I know what you're thinking; I can read

it in your face. But Oliver was not deceiving me. We shared everything. He talked a lot about the station, the inspector, you – he liked you. Besides, he had no time to be with somebody else. He has a crippled sister who requires a lot of care, and when he wasn't on duty, he was at home helping his mother. That's why I would meet him on his beat. I'd take him some supper." She plucked at the cuff on her glove. "I am certain this other woman is lying."

"Why would she do so, Miss Brewster? She came forward voluntarily."

"I don't know."

Her voice tailed off and he could see her trying desperately to sort through her memories. Was there any evidence of him being unfaithful? Small signs she might have ignored?

Isobel Brewster did not have the delicate prettiness of Mary Ann Trowbridge but there was a forthrightness to her, a promise of a passionate nature, that was attractive. He believed her when she said she was engaged to Oliver Wicken. However, that didn't mean the constable hadn't been playing fast and loose.

He realised she was regarding him anxiously.

"I'm sorry, Miss Brewster. It is possible that Mr. Lee was mistaken in his identification, but you can see that Wicken could have met with this other young lady after you left…"

"No!"

There was no point in continuing.

"What are you going to do now?" she asked. "You can't leave

it like this surely."

"The case is officially closed."

"But you didn't like the verdict, did you? I can see it. I can see it in your eyes."

She was almost sobbing again. "Please, Mr. Murdoch. Please don't leave it like this."

He hesitated, not wanting to make a promise he wouldn't be able to keep. "I must admit what you have told me changes the picture. There are some discrepancies that should be clarified. I'll see what I can do to clear them up."

Suddenly, she reached over, grasped his hand, and pressed it against her cold cheek.

"Thank you! I am quite aware that what is revealed may not be to my liking, but I would rather know the truth than not."

He hoped she wasn't deluding herself. He'd seen the truth burn like ice.

CHAPTER TWENTY-THREE

MURDOCH WALKED ISOBEL BREWSTER TO HER HOME, which was on Parliament Street, just below Queen Street. They did not speak at all and when they arrived, she dismissed him at the door. She said her mother and stepfather did not know of the engagement either, so there was nothing to be gained by telling them now. Murdoch could only guess at the anguish the young woman was going to go through alone. He promised to come back as soon as he had anything new to report and he left her.

Brackenreid had returned from his urgent appointment and Murdoch went to tell him what had happened. The inspector was surprisingly sympathetic to Isobel's plight, muttering several "poor lassies", but he was in no doubt that Wicken had deceived her.

"If you can get a bite on two ripe apples, why just have one?"

Murdoch murmured something noncommittal.

Brackenreid leaned back in his chair. "Do you think it's possible that one of the lassies found out what Wicken was up to and put the gun to his head? It wouldn't be too hard to write a note making it seem like a suicide. Miss Brewster could have returned, all weepy and wanting to make up for her harsh words. And lo, not only is he in the house he said they couldn't get into, he is the one weeping. It all tumbles out; you know how men like to confess these things. She's enraged, snatches his gun from his holster, and bang! She waits a few days, comes in with a good cover story."

"I suppose it's not out of the question, sir. Although it doesn't make a lot of sense that she would implicate herself unnecessarily. The case was closed. Besides, I would find that hard to believe about Miss Brewster." He remembered Isobel Brewster's grief-ravaged face and he felt bad they were even talking like this. Brackenreid hardly seemed to have heard him.

"On the other hand, Miss Trowbridge's story could have been all smoke and gammon. Maybe she saw them together. Brewster leaves, she confronts Wicken. He says yes, I do have another tickler. She is enraged, seizes his gun, and so on."

Unexpectedly, Brackenreid stopped being a fool. "What you said applies just the same though, doesn't it? Why be implicated if you don't have to?"

"Yes, sir."

"However, women do the strangest things when they have their cap set on a fellow."

"Is that right, sir?"

The inspector looked at him sharply but Murdoch had kept his voice neutral.

"Regardless, there are inconsistencies. Go talk to people again. See Mrs. Wicken, the Chinaman. I did wonder about his reliability, by the way. The Chinese always lie. Don't understand why, but they do."

He stroked at his moustache. "I hate to put it this way, but murder would be preferable, wouldn't it?"

"You mean rather than suicide, sir?"

"Quite. I don't like to think of one of my constables being so unmanly. Anyway, see what you can do."

Murdoch decided to visit Mrs. Wicken first. Painful as it might be to probe this question, she had a right to know this new information about her son.

The rain had stopped and a weak sun was struggling through the cloud covering, making a patch of silver in the pervading grey sky. He was warm enough today and his abscessed tooth was now only a sore gum, but he couldn't shake the feeling of heaviness in his body. Everywhere he turned, no matter what he found, somebody was going to suffer.

When he got to the Wicken house, he paused for a moment at the gate, rehearsing in his mind what he was going to say. The place looked almost abandoned. All the curtains were drawn and no crack of lamplight showed. The branches of the tree in the front were wrapped with black ribbon, and a wreath of crepe and intertwined willow branches was hung on the door. Murdoch pushed open the gate and walked up to the door. Before he had a chance to knock, it was opened by a woman he recognised as the solicitous neighbour who was with Mrs. Wicken at the inquest. She greeted him in a hushed, reverential voice.

"Good morning, sir. I'm Mrs. Morrow, one of Mrs. Wicken's neighbours. If you've come to call on her, you'll have to come later. She's not receiving until this afternoon. But I'll take your card if you wish."

Murdoch fished in his coat pocket and took out his card case. He handed her one of his cards.

"Please tell her I need to have a word."

Mrs. Morrow frowned. "She's had a dreadful shock. I don't know if she is up to talking about anything."

"I appreciate that, Mrs. Morrow, and I wouldn't trouble her if it wasn't important."

The woman shifted slightly so that she was more solidly in the doorway.

"We could all say that if we wanted to. Why, Mrs. Lynch's eldest was here just yesterday and…"

Whatever Mrs. Lynch's eldest had done, Murdoch was never to know, because at that moment Mrs. Wicken herself appeared in the hall. When she saw Murdoch, she actually smiled.

"It's all right, Mrs. Morrow, I would be happy to see Mr. Murdoch."

The guardian stood back, allowing Murdoch barely enough room to squeeze by her into the hall.

"Mrs. Morrow, will you take Mr. Murdoch's hat and coat?" There was something autocratic in her manner that he thought was not conscious to her. She had been accustomed to having servants. The other woman didn't seem to mind, however, and she did as asked, then went back to her post at the door, peering through the glass sidebars.

"We've moved in here," said Mrs. Wicken, and she ushered him through the velvet portieres into the front room. Murdoch felt a twinge of uneasiness quickly followed by guilt at his own cowardice. He didn't want to see poor Dora. However, she was in her Bath chair close to the fire. There were two lamps lit, the wicks low so that the room was full of shadows.

"Please sit down, Mr. Murdoch. It is kind of you to call."

He didn't know where to start and he procrastinated by making polite conversation. She was as well as could be expected, said Mrs. Wicken, but Dora had been poorly.

"She misses her brother dreadfully. You might not think it to look at her but she is quite aware of who is here. She began to be restless last evening when Oliver would usually have come in to play with her, before he went on his shift. I cannot, of course, explain why he is not here."

The girl made a moaning sound and turned as much as she could in Murdoch's direction; the massive head rolled too far and her neck could not control it. Mrs. Wicken reached over quickly and righted her.

Murdoch could understand why young Oliver might be reluctant to tell his mother about a forthcoming marriage. It would be difficult indeed to extricate himself from the dependency of his mother and sister. He could see how distressed the child was. A man's voice, barely heard, had stirred her.

Mrs. Wicken sat back in her chair and picked up the frame on which she was making lace.

"After the inquest I was hoping that the young woman who purported to be Oliver's fiancée would have spoken to me. I would have found some comfort in our mutual grief. However, she left at once without a backward glance."

She had given Murdoch his lead. "Mrs. Wicken, the reason I came to talk to you today has to do with that. You said you were not aware that Oliver was betrothed."

"It was, I have to admit, a great shock to me. He was such an honest boy and he gave me no indication. I suppose he was afraid to upset me. There are very few new wives who would take on such a burden as Dora. She would have insisted they live elsewhere, I am sure."

Again he hesitated, but there was no way around it if he was going to get any information at all.

"Mrs. Wicken, I was visited this morning by a young woman named Isobel Brewster. She is also claiming to be Oliver's fiancée. She says they were secretly betrothed almost a year."

"Good Lord. Am I to hear of a whole choir of fiancées?"

"I must say, she is quite credible. She says she saw him last on Monday night about eleven o'clock. They had a quarrel that she describes as trifling, and she is convinced he was not the kind of man to take his own life."

Mrs. Wicken was staring at him in utter disbelief. She put down the lace. At that moment the invalid child moaned and she was distracted for the moment as she tended to her.

"I need to move her to the couch. Will you be so good as to help me, Mr. Murdoch?"

"Of course."

"If you will take her by the legs, I will hold her head and we can swing her over."

She wheeled the chair in closer and Murdoch followed. There was a wool rug tucked around the child's legs.

"Ready?"

He nodded and with a slight heave they moved her onto the couch. Her mother turned the large head sidewards. The girl had pale blue eyes that in a normal child would have been pretty, but the pressure of the fluid made them protrude horribly. She seemed to be watching Murdoch, although he could not be sure how much she saw. She made some more guttural sounds and her lips moved.

"She probably thinks you are her brother. She wants you to touch her," said Mrs. Wicken.

"Of course, what…er…how…?"

"She likes to have her hair stroked."

There was no way Murdoch could, or would have, refused. He reached out to the sparse hair, white and downy as milkweed. Gently he stroked the enormous head. The girl smiled and quite quickly her eyes closed.

"Thank you, Mr. Murdoch. That was kind. She will sleep for a while now."

Mrs. Wicken stood up and went back to her chair by the fire. He too resumed his seat. For a few moments, he wondered if she had actually heard what he'd said or if she was going to respond at all. She picked up her lace making and without looking at him, she said:

"It is beginning to seem as if I did not know my son at all. Not one but two fiancées. It is quite extraordinary."

"Mrs. Wicken, we cannot rule out the possibility that one or even both of these young women are not telling the truth."

She frowned. "Why would they lie? They have nothing to gain. Even if he did go without my knowledge and bequeath everything to…another person, with the verdict of suicide, there will be no redemption. The hope of money cannot be a motivation."

"I have spoken to Inspector Brackenreid about the whole matter and he has asked me to investigate further. To put it bluntly, to find proof."

"What can I do to help any further?"

"Isobel Brewster is the only one of the two women that I have spoken to as yet. She says that she would meet Oliver on his day off in the afternoon. Otherwise she met him on his beat. His last day off was a week ago. Did he leave the house that day?"

He could see how much she still wanted to deny it but she

nodded. "Yes, he told me he was going to the lending library. He was an ambitious boy, Mr. Murdoch. He thought that if he was well read, it would improve his chances for advancement in the police force."

Murdoch didn't tell her that possibilities for promotion were limited these days and depended almost entirely on attrition in the ranks above.

"I'll check if anybody saw him there. And I am going to talk to the other woman, Miss Trowbridge. Also, I was wondering if I might look in Oliver's room."

"Yes, of course, if you think it will help."

"I believe his effects were returned to you. May I see them? I particularly would like to borrow the letter."

"I burned it. His uniform belongs to the station. It was stained, so I doubt it would be reused. There was nothing else of a personal kind."

She indicated a second door. "His room adjoined this one. It is not locked. When you've done, would you mind leaving by way of the hall? I don't want Dora to wake just yet; she hasn't been sleeping well. As you see, she needs care at all hours. I don't know if I will be able to manage without Oliver's support. It is quite likely that I will have to place her in the home for incurables...I cannot think how appalling that would be for her. You perhaps think she is hardly human but it is not the case. She is very attached to her family."

Murdoch could think of nothing to say. Mrs. Wicken turned back to her task.

He stood in the middle of the room, pivoting slowly, trying to get some sense of the young man who had so recently left it. Presumably for reasons of economy, the Wickens lived on the first floor of the house and rented out the second floor. This meant that Oliver occupied what would normally have been the dining room. There were connecting doors to the front room and the kitchen at the rear, both screened with tasselled chenille portieres of a rich floral pattern. The wallpaper was embossed gilt in crimson and green designs and the ceiling paper was a buff and blue glimmer. The room wasn't large and so much decoration made it seem suffocatingly small. The furnishings also would have done better in a more grand space. There was a massive wardrobe and matching bureau, both of dark mahogany. A lace-covered dining table was shoved tight against the far wall. The single concession to the actual use of the room was a mantel bed, which was alongside the window. It was neatly closed up. Wicken was tidy or had been kept so by his mother, for there was little of the debris of daily living scattered about.

What am I looking for? A diary? Love letters? Any indication into what was truly happening in the constable's life. There was no desk, but between the wardrobe and the door to the hall was a glass-fronted bookcase. Murdoch walked over to it and opened it up. On the top shelf was a small army of lead cavalry soldiers, well seasoned, and a small cast-iron bank, brightly painted. A little brown dog was sitting in front of a slotted box while a harlequin clown held a hoop in front of it. Unable to resist, Murdoch fished out a penny coin from his pocket and placed it in the dog's mouth. Then he pushed down the lever and the terrier jumped through the hoop, dropped the penny into the slot, and sat down again.

The other shelves all held books, most of them seemingly left over from Wicken's boyhood. Several novels, a mix of Sir Walter Scott, Jules Verne, and Ralph Connor; the complete works of William Shakespeare in thirty-nine volumes, rather pristine. *Little Men*, a book Murdoch always intended to read and never had. A stained and obviously well-studied edition of *Clater's Farrier*. At random, Murdoch picked out a book entitled *For Boys*. There was an inscription inside: *To my dearest Oliver on the occasion of his fifteenth birthday. With fondest regards, Mother.*

Murdoch leafed through the book, which was written by a Mrs. Shepherd. The tone was evangelical, exhorting the boy reader to have only pure thoughts in order to have a healthy body. Murdoch turned to the chapter entitled What is Sex? A doctor was quoted concerning one of his patients, a young man who complained of strange nervous symptoms. He suspected that the man's difficulties were due to some sort of sexual exhaustion. The patient replied, "Never, I never practised masturbation and never had a nocturnal emission." However, he did admit to caressing his fiancée when he visited her, and afterwards his mind became occupied with sexual fantasies. "That is the source of your problem," said the doctor. Irritated, Murdoch closed the book and returned it to the shelf. As far as he was concerned, these sorts of teachings were worth piss, the nattering of priests and women with no experience.

What else was here? Nothing remarkable. Ah, a book on etiquette that he himself had pored over years ago. He took it out with a little grin at the memory. Shy and awkward in social settings, Murdoch had tried to teach himself the rules, which unfortunately tended to make him even more self-conscious. It wasn't until he met Liza that he'd relaxed. She'd showed him what to do and laughed him out of his stiffness.

He was about to abandon the bookcase altogether when he saw that there was one book tucked away at the back of the shelf. He took it out, wondering if it had been hidden or had just fallen back there. *The Heart of Midlothian* by Sir Walter Scott. The cover matched the others in the set and this too was inscribed lovingly by Mrs. Wicken. A twelfth birthday this time. He was about to replace it when he saw that there was a thin piece of muslin pressed among the pages. He took it out. Inside the cloth was a lock of dark brown hair. Murdoch stowed the find between the covers of his own notebook. There was nothing else he could see that might be relevant, and the overfurnished room was beginning to close in on him. He went back to the hall.

Mrs. Morrow showed him out and, as soon as he was on the street, he took a long, deep breath. He had quickly developed respect for Mrs. Wicken and he could only feel compassion for her loss. However, he sensed that beneath the gracious manners there was a will of iron. He could understand why her son might have chosen to keep certain matters from her.

CHAPTER TWENTY-FOUR

HE DECIDED TO GO STRAIGHT OVER TO THE LENDING library, which was situated on Toronto Street, to the rear of St James' Cathedral. He wanted to see if he could find at least one definite confirmation of Isobel's story. Needing exercise, he walked briskly down Sackville to King Street where he could catch a streetcar. This far east, the stores were smaller, not as classy. There wasn't a line of carriages waiting outside any of them the way there always was nearer to the fancy stores on Church and Jarvis streets.

A streetcar was clanking toward him and he signalled to the driver to stop. He stepped on board into an almost empty car. The oil heater at the rear had been lit and inside was warm, smelling of the straw that was scattered on the floorboards to soak up the mud. In the middle of winter, the snow made everything a brown stew, but today the straw was still relatively fresh. Murdoch took a seat near the front and the ticket collector was on him at once, rattling his box.

"Fare please, sir."

He dropped in his ticket and the collector moved on. For a moment Murdoch almost envied him. His job seemed so clear-cut and defined. His only challenge was to keep a sharp lookout for cheaters, men who only went a couple of blocks, then, when he was busy, got off without paying. He was a young fellow, good-looking in a bold way. Destined to go far up the ranks of the Toronto Street Railway Corporation. He looked like the kind of man who would push for Sunday service. Murdoch thought the fuss about this issue was an utter waste of time. Some councillors were adamant that to have the streetcar running on the Sabbath was to propagate the work of the devil himself. Logically, this applied only to the streetcar workers, as all taverns and hotels and places of entertainment were closed on Sunday. Murdoch himself would like to have seen the cars running, taking people out to Sunnyside on hot summer days, for instance, or church even, if that's what they wanted. He sighed at the thought. He had long hated the dead space of Sunday when the entire city went into a kind of slumber.

"Church street. Who wants Church Street?" the conductor bellowed out. Murdoch got to his feet, the conductor pulled on the bell rope to alert the driver, and the streetcar halted at the corner.

On the northeast side of King and Church was St James' Cathedral. Murdoch had passed by many times without paying much attention, but now he actually looked at it. The slender copper spire, gleaming from the recent rain, soared into the pewter sky. The buff-coloured brick was warm and inviting even on this dull day. From the outside, it looked like a Roman Catholic church. The same cruciform design, the same dignity. If he had more time, he could go in and see what the inside was like. For one reason or another, not the least being a primitive superstition, he had never disobeyed the Catholic Church's teaching about the dangers inherent in the abodes of the nonbelievers. As he walked up to the library, he chided himself. It wouldn't hurt if he started exploring.

It was so quiet in the library that entering it was not unlike stepping into a place of worship. He almost looked for the holy water font.

The newspaper reading room was to the right and he decided to start there. At the far end was a high counter, and behind it, a young woman waited patiently for requests. She was wearing a white waist with a stiff high collar and a rather masculine tie. Her fair hair was pulled up into a severe knot and she was wearing gold pince-nez. She looked highly efficient. Nonetheless, her smile was friendly as she acknowledged him.

"Today's *Globe* is the only one available at the moment, sir. Would you like that?"

Murdoch assumed the rush on the daily papers was because of the shipping disaster everybody was caught up in.

"I'm not a customer, I'm afraid. I'm a detective with the police force, number four station." He handed her his card and she took it gingerly. "I'm trying to trace the movements of one of our constables. I have reason to believe he was here on Saturday last, in the afternoon. Were you on duty at that time, Miss, er…" He checked the brass nameplate that was on the counter. "…Miss Morse?"

"Yes, I was."

"Perhaps you remember him? A tall fellow, about twenty-four years of age, with a blond moustache, fresh complexion."

"Does he have a name?" she asked, reaching for a small file box in front of her.

"Oliver Wicken."

Surprisingly, she looked a little flustered. "Yes, I do remember the name. He was here about three o'clock. He took the *Huntsville Forester*. It isn't often I get a request for that newspaper, so we had a little chat about it…that's why I remember him so particularly."

Murdoch felt bad. Wicken was an attractive young man and probably not above a little harmless flirting. At least Murdoch hoped it was harmless and he wasn't going to unearth yet another fiancée.

The librarian looked at him with curiosity. "May I ask why you wish to know? He isn't in any trouble surely?"

They had both been speaking in hushed tones, but even so,

an elderly gentleman wearing check knickerbockers, who was at one of the nearby stands, hissed at them.

Murdoch sidestepped her question. "Was Mr. Wicken alone?"

"Yes, he was."

Murdoch sighed. Did this mean Isobel Brewster had lied? A man came up to the counter. His clothes were shabby and he smelled stale. Murdoch knew he had come in because the library was warm and dry.

"The *Globe*, if you please," he said to Miss Morse.

She took the rolled-up newspaper from one of the cubbyholes behind her, where they were stashed, and handed it to him.

"There's a free space in the far aisle at the back," she said.

Murdoch liked her for not discriminating against the man, who more than likely couldn't read a word.

From where she was sitting, the librarian had a good view of the entire room and who came and went. Murdoch turned back to her.

"Did you notice if Mr. Wicken spoke to anybody while he was here?"

She frowned. "I believe he did. He must have met an acquaintance. They did talk briefly, as I recall."

"Could you describe the gentleman?"

"As a matter of fact it was a lady."

Several men were standing in front of the long easels where the newspapers were hung, but as far as he could see there were no women. He didn't expect anything else. Most women were still doubtful about the propriety of being in a man's domain.

He leaned forward. "Miss Morse, you have been very helpful and I'm sorry that at the moment I am not at liberty to tell you why I am making these enquiries. However, it is very important. Can you describe this woman?"

"I barely paid her any attention."

"Anything at all that you remember would be helpful. Her age, her colouring, her costume."

"Very well." She wrinkled her forehead in concentration but he knew she was pretending. She had paid a lot of attention to Wicken's acquaintance but didn't want to admit to it.

"I believe she was quite dark, with an olive complexion, and tall. Almost as tall as Mr. Wicken himself. Perhaps a few years older than myself...I am twenty-two. She was wearing a long waterproof, a rather smart scarlet hat with a white feather and navy ribbons."

Murdoch dragged at his moustache, relieved. *Sorry, Miss Brewster, for doubting you.*

"Did they leave together?"

"Yes, now that you mention it, I believe they did."

"Did Mr. Wicken seem distressed in any way?"

"I don't understand what you mean."

"Was their exchange amicable, would you say?"

"It appeared to be." Unconsciously the young woman sighed. "He looked quite happy to see her."

Murdoch could almost read her thoughts, the doubts that his questions were raising, but he still couldn't stomach telling her what had happened. Perhaps he could come back at a later time near the end of the day. He suspected Miss Morse might be harbouring more passion in her breast than her white starched shirtwaist might indicate. Fortunately, the knickerbockered man intervened as he returned his newspaper. Murdoch whispered a quick goodbye and left. It was time to get back to Isobel Brewster. At least one part of her testimony seemed to be true.

Isobel herself answered the door and he knew she had been waiting, jumping at every knock. He asked her to get the exact clothes she was wearing on Monday night, which she did at once. He could hear a fretful child in the background and the rather sharp hushing of a woman's voice. Isobel joined him quickly. She had put on her long waterproof and a sensible black felt hat, which had only a single piece of blue ribbon for trimming. They set off up Parliament Street and he told her that the librarian had confirmed that she was with Wicken last Saturday. She made no comment but he could see how relieved she was.

At the corner of Queen Street, he stopped and took the piece of muslin from his notebook.

"Is this your hair, Miss Brewster?"

She hardly looked at it, but he could see she was affected. "Yes. I gave it to Ollie at Christmastime as a memento. At his request. He snipped off a piece himself when we were walking in the park."

Unasked, she took the curl and placed it close to her own

hair. It was an exact match. Another point on her side.

They soon reached Sam Lee's laundry and Murdoch asked her to stand where she had been on Monday night. She did, taking up a spot close to the curb.

Murdoch pushed open the door and entered. Almost at the same time, the door at the rear opened and Foon Lee emerged.

"Can I be of assistance, sir?"

"Detective Murdoch, again, Mr. Lee. I wonder if I might speak to your father for a moment?"

The young man stared at him, not recognising him at first. Then he gave a slight bow of recognition.

"Certainly. I will fetch him simultaneously."

Murdoch was about to correct his English usage, but thought it might seem rude and he let it go. Foon went back through the rear door.

He heard a murmured conversation and Mr. Lee came out, his son close at his heels.

He put his hands together and bowed in the Chinese greeting.

"Mr. Murdoch?" He pronounced it "Mulldot".

Murdoch addressed Foon. "Will you tell your father that I am still concerned about the death of the constable. Some new evidence has come to light that I am investigating. I have a witness outside and I would like to see if he can identify her."

Foon translated. Lee nodded.

Murdoch went to the door. "I am going to stand here, the way the constable did that night. Will your father come close to me? If he looks out over my shoulder he will see a young woman. I would like to know if he has ever seen her before."

Lee moved forward before his son was in mid-translation. They stood in the threshold of the laundry, the door partially open behind them. Lee was considerably shorter than Murdoch but he peered around the detective's arm and looked at Isobel.

The Chinaman shook his head and spoke to his son. Murdoch thought he was agitated.

"My father says not. He has never clapped his eyes to this woman before in her life."

"Is he positive she was not the one walking with Wicken on Monday night?"

"He is certain of that. He has made a positive identification of that woman during the inquest…He wonder why you are asking him to retract his statement. A statement he made under oath."

Murdoch sighed. "Please tell him that's not it at all. I just wanted to make absolutely sure."

"I do not know this person," interjected Lee. "I have never seen her before."

Murdoch could not tell if he was speaking the truth or not. Both of them were watching him. He was disappointed. He had put a lot of stock in this meeting.

He thanked them and went outside.

Isobel stared at him anxiously as he approached her.

"Well?"

"I'm afraid he denied it. Says you are not the woman he saw."

"Damnation. How is that possible? Of course I was. He saw

me, I know he did. I'll talk to him…"

Murdoch caught her by the arm. "No, Miss Brewster. It won't do any good. He's adamant."

She looked as if she were about to burst into tears.

"Then you don't believe me?"

"Of course I do. I think he was too afraid to change his sworn testimony." He let her go and she stood in front of him, her shoulders slumped.

"What are you going to do now?" she asked.

"I am going to talk to Miss Mary Ann Trowbridge."

He thought she was going to grasp his hand again, but she didn't, and they headed back to her house.

CHAPTER TWENTY-FIVE

JARIUS GIBB WAS NOT AT WORK. HE HAD SENT JANET with a message to say he was ill and would not be in for a few days. In a way, it was true. He felt as hot and restless as if he had a fever. He had been this way since dinner on Wednesday and nothing calmed him. Finally, he forced himself to sit at his desk, his ledger open in front of him. Janet had brought him a mug of strong coffee, milky and sweet, which he laced with a good dose of brandy. He made himself drink it slowly and deliberately before he took up his pen.

I want to fill up this page with obscenities and blasphemy, to pour out the vilest and crudest words I have ever heard, but it will not help me. He says, "You are not my own flesh and blood but you will get a bequest." As if I should be grateful, should rejoice in the pew over his generosity. He has betrayed his promise to my mother which he made in my presence. "I will treat him as my own son, my own flesh and blood. I will give him my name." And he has never. Not when he first married her, swelling with lust, he said it then. "The boy will be like my own." LIAR. And he said it at her most solemn deathbed. "He shall have my name." LIAR AGAIN. He could never love a son who did not reflect his own face back to him. He will bypass me because of the accident of blood. No son of his flesh would have behaved better than I. How many hours did I listen to him weep and complain at the loss of his wife, as if she had died on purpose to thwart him. He cared nothing that she was also my mother. And then to marry again without any consultation! It serves him right. He married weak blood and he threw weak blood. And now he would set up for more spawn. And with such a woman.

He stopped writing. He was pressing so hard he was in danger of bending his nib. He got up, went over to the fireplace, and picked up the poker. He prodded one of the lumps of coal that wasn't burning.

Fortunately, Nathaniel had agreed to have the woman spayed. Presumably that would occur soon. He hit a piece of coal hard, splitting it in two. Flames jumped up to lick at the new fuel. He pounded another piece and another until the coal was completely fractured.

Miss Trowbridge had given her address as 106 Jarvis Street. Murdoch took his second streetcar of the day and set out to talk to her. He was certain now that Mr. Lee was mistaken in his identification but afraid to admit it. However, he thought it was odd Miss Trowbridge had made no attempt to negate Lee's statement. On the other hand, witnesses often had blinkers on about matters other than their own. She must have met up with Wicken after Isobel had left.

As he headed back down Parliament toward Queen Street, he probed the hole in his gum with his tongue. His jaw was practically back to normal, as long he didn't let in too much cold air and chewed on the other side. Mrs. Kitchen had resumed her duties and sent him off with a couple of hard-boiled eggs and a jar of milk sops for his luncheon. It didn't come close to the rabbit stew that Enid had made for him, the memory of which made his mouth water. He hadn't seen her this morning but he could hear her at the typewriter quite early. Perhaps tonight they could continue the interrupted talk she so obviously wanted. Not that he was any closer to coming up with an answer, but he didn't just want to spout the church's doctrine without thinking about it.

There was a woman walking ahead of him. She halted at the corner and he saw her lift her skirt decorously to avoid a puddle as she stepped off the curb. Nevertheless, her hem dragged through the water and he suddenly had a vivid memory of himself and Liza, sitting one evening in her kitchen. She took care of her widowed father, and when he went off to bed, they had some rare and precious privacy. On this particular occasion, she was trying to clean the skirt of her best walking suit. The hem was covered with mud. "Wretched thing. It is always dirty." If she had lived, he knew she would have become an agitator for many reforms for women, including the adoption of what was currently called Rational Dress. "Why shouldn't I be able to wear a sensible shorter skirt without being leered at, or insulted?" she'd demanded. He'd stupidly tried to make light of the issue with a lewd joke and she was angry with him. "How can you be so clever about some things and so nocky about others? I wish you'd open up your mind."

They'd eventually worked their way to a reasonable talk about her point of view, but her words had stung and he still thought about them.

He was checking the house numbers now. One hundred and six was a big house of yellow brick, gables painted in the popular hunter green. Shrubs filled the large front yard, held in by a very fancy wrought-iron fence. The gate squeaked when he opened it and, on closer inspection, he could see the shrubs were shapeless and too bushy. There were weeds in the cracks of the flagstone path. The house might be grand but it looked neglected. He tugged at the bell-pull, hearing it clang inside the house. The bay windows to his right showed more care than the grounds. They were curtained with white lace, hung halfway up the window in the fashionable style. So far, nobody had answered, and he was about to ring again when the door creaked open. An elderly woman stood at the threshold, scrutinising him with a distinctly unfriendly expression. She wore a black silk dress and a white mob cap. There was a chatelaine at her waist which jingled slightly. He was somewhat surprised that the housekeeper had answered the door, but he gave her a polite smile and tipped his hat.

She frowned. "What do you want?"

"I'd like to speak to Miss Trowbridge."

"Who?"

"Miss Mary Ann Trowbridge. I understand she lives here."

"Who are you?"

Murdoch handed her his calling card. "Acting Detective Murdoch."

The housekeeper, if that was who she was, studied his card, even reversing it as if there were more information on the back.

"She isn't here."

She handed it back to him.

"When will she return? It is important I speak to her."

"She won't."

"Won't what?"

"Return."

"Do you mean she's left the city?"

"No, I mean she won't return, seeing as how she's never lived here."

Murdoch bit back a retort. If the woman needed to play games with him, he wasn't going to give her the satisfaction of getting riled up.

"Ma'am, this is an important police matter and I would appreciate your cooperation. Does a Mrs. Avison live here?"

"She does, but you can't talk to her because she hasn't finished her breakfast yet."

Murdoch reached inside his coat and fished out his watch, looking at it ostentatiously.

"My, it's half past two in the afternoon. Is your mistress an invalid then?"

She scowled at him and was about to close the door but he got his foot in just in time. He summoned as stern an expression as he could, although he had no desire to act the bully with such a tiny shrivelled old woman.

"I repeat, this is a police matter. If you don't go this minute and tell your mistress I would like to talk to her, I will be forced to come in and find her myself."

The servant stared back at him and he thought there was a glint of amusement in her eyes. *The old crow. She actually enjoyed that little contest.* He stepped into the hall.

"I'll wait here."

With a loud sniff of disapproval, she shuffled away down the hall. He watched her draw back the portieres in front of a door to the right, tap, and enter. He looked around. The hall was unusually spacious, large enough to accommodate several chairs, an imposing coat tree, and a fine marble fireplace, which was still protected by a brass screen as if it were summer. The place felt cold and gloomy. The only natural light came through the door windows, and although there was a splendid chandelier of crystal glass, none of the candles were lit. There were so many paintings on the wall, the crimson flock covering was almost obscured. As far as he could tell, they were all portraits. In spite of the grandeur of the house, there wasn't a sign of any other servants. No butler came hurrying out to take charge, no maids en route to some task. The silence, the cold musty air, made him feel as if he were in a mausoleum. It seemed an old-fashioned, gloomy house for a young, pretty girl like Mary Ann to live in.

The rear door opened and the housekeeper emerged. She beckoned to him and he approached her.

"Mrs. Avison will see you. She doesn't hear so good so make sure you speak up and don't mumble."

"I make a point of never mumbling," said Murdoch, but any irony was lost and he felt petty for even attempting it.

"Good," she said and moved a few inches out of the way so he could enter.

Like the hall, the room was dark, but at least there was a cheerful fire going in the fireplace. A woman was seated close to it in a large armchair. She was wearing a man's maroon silk dressing gown and her white hair was in a loose braid down her back. As he came in, she reached for a hearing trumpet and held it to her ear.

"What is it you want, sir? I couldn't make head nor tail of what Beulah was saying." She waved her hand at the chair opposite her. "Sit down, for goodness' sake. Beulah, go and fetch another cup. I'm sure he'd be glad of some coffee; it's perishing out there." Her voice was strident.

Murdoch did as he was told, putting his damp hat beside him on the floor. In spite of her white hair, Mrs. Avison was by no means an invalid, nor elderly; more likely she was in her late middle age. He decided her unorthodox dress and willingness to receive him the way she was must be cultivated eccentricity. She didn't wait for the housekeeper to leave before she said, "Beulah's been with me since we were both children. She started out as the nursery maid. She fusses over me in exactly the same way she did then." She aimed the trumpet in his direction. "Go on then, explain yourself."

He leaned forward. It was rather like playing a trombone in reverse.

"I want to speak to your niece, Miss Mary Ann Trowbridge. I apologise for intruding at such an unhappy time but I would like to ask her a few more questions concerning Oliver Wicken."

Mrs. Avison heard perfectly and she looked at him, puzzled.

"I don't know what in Hades you are talking about. There's no such person here. I'm a widow and I live alone except for Beulah. You've made a mistake."

It was Murdoch's turn to be taken aback. "You don't have a niece named Mary Ann who testified at the coroner's inquest on Tuesday?"

"I certainly don't. Neither niece nor nephew. Thank goodness for that, I might add."

"The young woman gave this address and produced a letter purporting to be from her aunt, Mrs. Avison."

"What sort of letter?"

"Corroborating her statement that she was engaged to a young man named Oliver Wicken."

"It certainly was not I who wrote the letter."

The housekeeper came back in carrying a china cup and saucer that could have belonged to a child's tea set.

"Beulah, listen to this story."

"Just a minute." She went to the sideboard, poured out some coffee from a silver pot, and brought the cup to Murdoch. He had only drunk coffee on three occasions in his life and then it came liquid from a bottle and was loaded with milk and sugar. Cautiously, he sipped at the dark fragrant brew.

"We always serve it black," said Mrs. Avison. "It's an abomination to do otherwise. You like coffee, don't you?"

"I do now," he said.

"So, tell Beulah what you just told me."

The housekeeper, who might also have been hard of hearing, didn't wait for him.

"I remembered while I was getting the cup. We used to have a servant here named Mary Ann. She was the upstairs maid. About ten or eleven years ago it was. But her last name wasn't Trowbridge, it was Trotter. What's this woman look like that you're after?"

"She has light brown hair, fair skin, rather dainty features, grey eyes. Probably about twenty or so."

Beulah nodded with satisfaction. "Same one. She always looked young for her age. I'm not surprised as a policeman is after her. She only lasted a couple of months with us. Got the shoot on account of immorality."

Mrs. Avison had been trying to follow the conversation but she couldn't and said in exasperation, "What are you blathering about, Beulah?"

The housekeeper shouted everything into the trumpet. Murdoch drank more of the delicious coffee.

Mrs. Avison nodded vigorously. "I recollect the girl now. Why in Hades is she pretending I'm her aunt? She was the maid here."

"I don't know the answer to that, Mrs. Avison. I wish I did."

"Looked like butter wouldn't melt in her mouth but she was as sly a minx as ever I did see."

"What exactly did she do to be dismissed?"

"Got herself in the family way, that's what," Beulah answered. "She was barely sixteen. Wicked."

"So, she married then?"

Mrs. Avison heard that one. "She did not. One of our gardeners was quite willing to take her but she refused."

"Was he the father?"

She clucked her tongue in disapproval. "He said he wasn't but she wouldn't tell us who it was. She probably didn't know."

"Did she marry anybody? I might need to seek under her married name."

Mrs. Avison waved her trumpet at Beulah, who answered for her. "As far as we know she did not. She left. The gardener's name was Crenshawe but he married somebody else soon after anyway, so there's no sense talking to him."

"Is the name Oliver Wicken familiar to you?"

She shook her head. "No. Never heard of him."

"You said they were engaged," interrupted Mrs. Avison. "Why is that of concern to the police? Has he abandoned her?"

Murdoch explained as succinctly as he could what had transpired. They listened attentively.

"Did Mary Ann stay in touch with any of the other servants? Is there anybody here that I could talk to?"

"No. I told you I live by myself with Beulah. I let them all go. Servants are an expense and a bother as far as I'm concerned. Any extra help we get in from time to time. We manage quite well, don't we, Beulah?"

The housekeeper ignored the question, intent on pursuing the more lascivious topic of Mary Ann Trotter.

"One of the maids did run into the girl the year after she'd left us. She told her the child had been stillborn. Whether that was true or not it was certainly convenient. But Agnes said she didn't look respectable at all."

"What did she mean by that?"

"She'd become a fallen woman," Beulah said in the tone of one who takes pride in calling a spade a spade.

CHAPTER TWENTY-SIX

MURDOCH WAS BEHIND HIS DESK, CONSTABLE CRABTREE seated in front of him.

"George, what's your opinion? Why'd she give us the runaround?"

"My guess is she's still in the game and doesn't want anybody to know."

"Do you think she really was engaged to Wicken?"

"Hard to tell. She might have said that to pretty it up. She wasn't about to come right out and say he was having some dock on the side and paying for it."

"Would a man kill himself over a prostitute giving him the shove?"

"Some men are stupid enough for anything. The doxy hands him a line about how he's the only one she's ever loved, all other men are as eunuchs compared to him. He makes her happy. What man wouldn't like to hear that? He believes her, gets besotted, starts to make a nuisance of himself. She's bored, says that's it, no more, and he thinks life is over. Bang."

Murdoch stared at the constable. Crabtree was a happily married man with five small children, one a newborn. He spoke with such authority, it made him wonder.

"What is puzzling me, George, is why she came forward at all. Wouldn't it have been better for her to keep quiet? She could assume nobody knew about her." He drummed his fingers on the desk. "On the other hand, we could be maligning her. We don't know for certain that she's a doxy or ever was."

"She just happened to lie under oath for no reason."

Murdoch grinned. "A point, George."

"She said she read about his death in the newspaper. Maybe she's one of those women who just want to make mischief, or get in on the limelight. She could adapt her story to whatever circumstances revealed themselves. If he'd been married she could have said the same thing. 'Oh, he loved me but I sent him back to his lawful wife.' Cow leavings like that."

"You're saying maybe Trowbridge didn't know Wicken at all."

"Yes, sir. Made it up."

"What about the letter from her aunt?"

"We haven't seen the woman in person and she certainly isn't Mrs. Avison of Jarvis Street."

"Hm. I'm wondering if Wicken was the father of the child she conceived when she was fifteen."

"That'd make him fourteen at the time."

"It happens, George. Let's say she revealed this to him. He is overcome by remorse and, after she leaves, he mulls it over to the point of despondency and takes his own life."

"That wasn't the wording of the note."

"You're right. Cancel the fathering theory. Having been in Wicken's home, I can't imagine he'd have been allowed within ten feet of a girl when he was fourteen."

"Maybe we dismissed the inspector's speculations too soon, sir."

"You mean that one of the women shot him?"

"Yes, sir."

"I have to eliminate Isobel Brewster. If she's lying to us, I'm going to throw in the towel on policing, because she's convinced me."

"Be careful what you say, sir. You always were a softie for a girl in a faint."

"Do you think so?" Murdoch asked in surprise. He rubbed his hands hard over his scalp.

"Let's go over this again." He took a piece of paper from his drawer and drew a square.

"Here's the house at the corner where we found him. Isobel Brewster has walked up Parliament with him. The timing as she told it to me fits. They stay on the porch because, for some reason, Wicken hasn't let on he has a key."

"Perhaps he didn't want her to linger. He's got an assignation with Miss Trowbridge."

"True. Anyway, they stand here for at least a half an hour, maybe longer. She is threatening to break off their relationship unless he sets a date for the wedding. A half an hour is plausible, isn't it, George? Especially if they've talked about it before."

"You can have a barney in less time than that, sir. Take it from me."

"All right, Miss Brewster leaves. Wicken now encounters Miss Trowbridge. They go inside the empty house. She is still in the game but wants to go respectable. They quarrel. She wants to marry, he spurns her, says he already has a respectable sweetheart. She grabs his revolver and shoots him. Then she prints a note that suggests suicide and cool as a cucumber comes to the inquest to reinforce her story that he was the rejected one. What about that?"

Crabtree grinned. "I'd say that's a good one, sir. 'Course, it does depend on a slip of a girl being able to get the better of a healthy six-foot-tall man."

"She took him by surprise. This would also be some explanation for the position of the gun. She was in a rage with him and stuffed the revolver in between his legs in some sort of symbol."

"You've got a good imagination, sir."

"And it's getting us nowhere. We've got to find the mysterious Miss Trowbridge. First off, I want you to go round to all the newspapers. Put an advertisement in the personal columns.

Give them her description, say we'd like to get in touch with her further to the death of Oliver Wicken. Anybody knowing her whereabouts should contact us at once."

"Are we offering a reward?"

"Probably not. There's no money. I'm going to go back to his beat; do all that again. You can join me after."

At that moment, they heard somebody coming down the hall to the cubicle.

"Murdoch?"

The reed strips were shoved aside and Inspector Brackenreid came in. He couldn't go too far with Crabtree sitting where he was and they sashayed for a moment as the constable tried to stand and get out of the way. Murdoch groaned to himself. If Brackenreid came looking for him instead of having him brought up to his office, it usually meant trouble. He, too, stood respectfully. Crabtree managed to squeeze against the wall and it was too awkward for the three of them to all be standing. The inspector took the chair. Murdoch sat down again.

"Yes, sir?"

"I was wondering how you're getting on with the Wicken case?"

"I was just going over the possibilities with Constable Crabtree."

"Go over them with me."

Murdoch related his visit to Mrs. Avison. Brackenreid looked gloomy.

"I see. That's all we need, a Jezebel mixed up with one of our officers."

"None of this is proven, sir. The housekeeper was relating another servant's judgement on the young woman. However, this has cast doubt on her testimony."

"It's beginning to look like it was a pack of lies. Our young buck must have got himself mired in some tail. I've seen it before. Men who get wet-eyed over a fen, promising to give them a better life. As if they ever want it!"

Murdoch tried not to look at Crabtree. The inspector was notorious for his cynical statements about human nature. "*I've seen it before*" was a covert catch-all phrase among the officers.

Brackenreid tapped the piece of paper in front of Murdoch.

"You fancy drawings, don't you? You should have been a general. But you can sit here and draw pictures until the cows come home and it won't get us any closer to knowing what the hell happened. You need to find that Trowbridge girl."

"That's a good idea, sir."

Crabtree winced. Will was at it again.

Brackenreid glanced up sharply at the detective, but Murdoch was a master at the blank look when he needed to be.

"I think you're on to something. It's not unlikely we are, in fact, looking at a murder."

It was a tidy proposition, but even though he was the one who'd presented it, Murdoch knew the danger of prejudice. Mary Ann Trotter may have been a prostitute at one time in her life. It didn't mean she still was or that immorality and murder were always bedfellows.

"I want a report on my desk by tomorrow afternoon."

"Yes, sir."

The inspector got up. He obviously wanted to leave in a commanding way, but it was impossible as he had to press himself past Crabtree with uncomfortable intimacy.

As soon as he was out of earshot, both men grinned at each other.

"You'll go too far one of these days, Mr. Murdoch. He's not as thick as he likes to pretend."

"I know. It's the only thing that keeps me from asking for a transfer. He hasn't completely lost his wits."

He reached for his sealskin coat. "You get off to the papers. I'm going to see if Miss Trowbridge-Trotter was noticed by anybody, anywhere, anytime."

CHAPTER TWENTY-SEVEN

FRANZ LIEPMAN WAS EATING HIS BREAKFAST. HE'D toasted two slices of bread in front of the fire and made a pot of strong tea with lacings of sugar and a tot of rum against the damp. He yawned. For more than ten years he had not had a complete night's sleep. Four hours in the evening before he went to the Foresters building where he was the night watchman, sometimes a nap there in the back room, but he had to be careful. Occasionally an hour or two before he went to his second job, sweeping floors at the general hospital. He was used to it, probably couldn't have slept an entire night through if it was offered. He did this all week long and never took time off unless he was sick.

Once at the hall, he'd overheard two of the men talking about him. "He's a bit simple is what it is," said one of them. Franz had been hurt by this remark, but his mother was alive then and she had scoffed. "Let them think it. Clever people are noticed and you don't want that. Not as you're German." And she made him a nice apple cake to make up for the hurt. "I've told you, family is the only thing you can rely on. Blood is what counts."

For as long as he could remember, there had only been the two of them and now she was gone there was no family, no blood ties to turn to. However, the necessity of having two jobs when she became ill had turned into a habit. He continued to live frugally and the extra money that accumulated he kept in a strongbox under his bed. There was a lot of it by now and sometimes he wondered if he should do anything and he'd take out a few dollars. But then he'd sit and think about it, and realise he could make do. His trousers got a good brush and his boots another blacking. So, most of the time, he put the money back. His mother taught him that. "Don't let any women know how much you have or they'll try to seduce you and take it all." He never quite knew what it was to seduce but he could tell it was bad. His mother had been born in Germany and had come to Canada just after he was born. She wouldn't talk about his father no matter how much he begged, and although she had received occasional letters for a while, they hadn't come for years now.

Even though force of habit had kept him up, he'd not gone to work at all since Monday night. He sent the neighbour's boy with a note to Mr. Tweedie saying as how he regretted but he was incapacitated for work. It took him almost an hour to write those two lines, but in the end he was proud of his big word. He didn't go the next day either.

"You'd better go tell the police," the secretary had said when Franz spilled out his story. But he wouldn't consider it. The police were always on the lookout for culprits, and they didn't care who they got, especially if they were foreigners. He could end up in jail for the rest of his life and nobody would be the wiser. No, he was very sorry he'd spoken up at all.

It was only because the cries he'd heard were so disturbing that he'd told Mr. Tweedie about them.

Darkness was well settled in and the street lamps were struggling without much success to throw out some light in the gloom. A few passersby, bent under their black umbrellas, hurried to get out of the drizzle that had started up again. Murdoch had started at Queen Street, knocking on every single door, and it had taken him almost two hours. He was tired and disheartened and his mouth felt dry from too much talking. Almost all of the people he spoke to had heard about Wicken's death, and they were eager to discuss it with him. Much as he would have expected, there was not much sympathy for the dead man, who was considered to be a disgrace and a coward to boot. Opinion ran cool toward Mrs. Wicken and the word "unfeeling" was said many times, even though for most of them this opinion on her conduct was based on hearsay. Enthusiasm was high for Mary Ann, and his questions concerning her engendered a great deal of curiosity, which he tried to diffuse. The Lees were mostly referred to as "the heathens" and he knew that, if he had introduced them into the investigation at all, speculation would have run riot. He was, in turn, asked questions, most of them prurient. He had no answer to "Was it true there was blood and brains splattered all over the walls?" Sometimes the question was asked as bluntly as that, sometimes with more subtlety, but the reason was the same – they wanted to feast on the morbid details. However, so far, he had no more information than when he had started out. If Mary Ann Trowbridge had met up with Wicken anywhere along this section of his beat, nobody had seen her. He gave out Isobel's description as well but with the same result. At least he didn't have to worry about the nocturnal habits of Toronto citizenry. They all seemed to enjoy the untroubled sleep of the righteous. And Mr. Lee was unusual in that he worked late into the night. No other business owner had. Murdoch groaned to himself. At this rate, he wouldn't get home until ten o'clock, certainly too late to visit with Mrs. Jones.

On the southwest corner of Parliament Street and Gerrard, directly across from the vacant house where Wicken had died, was the imposing Foresters Hall. Lights were burning in the downstairs windows and, hoping to find a caretaker who might have been awake on the night in question, he went in. The double front doors were unlocked and he entered a large foyer. There was a fine brass and crystal chandelier suspended from the ceiling, all the globes extravagantly lit. A splendid staircase curved in front of him and there was an imposing line of portraits ascending to the second floor. He assumed these were depictions of officers of the order.

There was nobody in sight, but to his right was a half-open door and he could hear the now familiar tapping of a typewriter. A plaque on the door said H. TWEEDIE, SECRETARY. He knocked and a strong male voice called, "Enter." Murdoch complied. A young man, presumably Mr. Tweedie, was seated behind a long desk. Several bound ledgers were piled around him like a barricade, and he seemed to be copying something from one of them. There was an electric light suspended above his head and he wore a green eyeshade to protect himself from its brilliance.

"Yes?"

"My name is Murdoch. I'm an acting detective at number four station and I'm pursuing some inquiries concerning the death of one of our constables. No doubt you've heard about it?"

The secretary pushed back his visor. "I'll say. Did himself in, didn't he? Don't understand that, I must say. I mean we all have our trials and tribulations, don't we? But we've got to keep going. As far as I'm concerned, suicide is a coward's way out. However, I digress. How can I be of assistance?"

"The investigation isn't completely closed and I was wondering if you employ a night watchman at all. If so, I'd like to talk to him."

"Yes, we do. Fellow by the name of Franz Liepman. Didn't he get in touch with you?"

"No. Should he have?"

"I told him to. But then again, I'm not surprised he didn't. He's a strange bird, bit slow on the uptake, German. He came in here on Tuesday with quite a story. I'd heard about the constable from one of our members so I thought it might be relevant. Told him to get to the station right away."

Murdoch stared at him. The green eyeshade made his face look sickly but his brown eyes were keen enough.

"Well, he didn't. What was his story?"

"He claims he heard somebody crying. Pitiful was the way he described it. Like this, he said." Tweedie put his head back and cried in a falsetto voice, "Don't leave me, please don't leave me."

"A woman?"

"Oh, no, it must have been the constable. He was beseeching his lady-love." Tweedie looked as if he were about to howl again. Murdoch cut him off.

"Did he say where the cries were coming from?"

"The vacant house."

"What time was this?"

"Franz was on his way here and he usually arrives about half past midnight, so it was shortly before that."

"Do you have this man's address?"

"Matter of fact, it's right here." The secretary propelled his chair toward the end of his table and rotated a card file that was sitting beside the telephone box. He rolled back and handed a card to Murdoch. "He hasn't been in since Tuesday. Sent a message to say he's ill. Too much of a coincidence, if you ask me. He looked like he'd shit his britches, begging your pardon, when I said he should speak to the police. Like I said, he's a strange sort of fellow. But he's been with us for years, no complaints. First time he's been off sick for six years. Hasn't missed a day."

Murdoch checked the address. "I'll go and have a word with him. Thank you, Mr. Tweedie."

"You're welcome I'm sure." He regarded Murdoch with keen curiosity. "Do you mind if I ask why the investigation isn't closed? I popped down to the inquest myself, my own backyard as it were. The verdict was unequivocal, wasn't it?"

"It was but there are a few discrepancies in some of the testimony that we need to clarify."

"The Chinamen's? What a pair they were."

"I'm not at liberty to go into it at the moment."

"Well, any time I can help, just drop in. Oh, by the way, I recommend you take a deep breath and hold it when you go into the fellow's place." He made a gesture of pinching his nostrils. "He doesn't believe in soap and water."

"Thanks for the warning."

Murdoch took his leave and left. The typewriter soon resumed its rapid clacking.

Mr. Liepman lived at 375 Gerrard Street, just east of Sackville. The house was a tall semi-detached with a narrow strip of paved front yard and a brown painted door that needed freshening up. The front window was dark, but slits of light came through the blinds at the second- and third-floor windows. There was an outside bell and the clapper was fastened to a frayed rope. He rang it as loudly as he could, given that the casing was cracked. He expected he'd have to repeat this several times before somebody heard him but, surprisingly, there was a response almost immediately. Through the glass, he saw light from a candle drawing closer. The door opened and an elderly man stood there, his candlestick held aloft.

"The room's taken," he said before Murdoch could speak.

"I'm not here for the room, I'm looking for Mr. Liepman."

"He's on the third floor."

The old man didn't wait for Murdoch to introduce himself or express any curiosity; he turned around and began to shuffle back to his lair. He took his candle with him.

"Wait a minute," Murdoch called but the man ignored him and entered a door on the left. Murdoch heard a bolt shoot closed. The hall was completely unlit and there was a strong smell of raw onions hanging in the air. On the other hand it could have been skunk. Cussing at the old man for his rudeness, Murdoch stood for a moment to get accustomed to the darkness. There was a staircase to his left and the room at the landing was occupied. Enough light came from beneath the door for him to make his way up. The stairs were uncarpeted and creaked loudly but nobody came out to see who he was or what he was doing. He didn't hear anything – no voices, no sounds of life behind the closed doors.

The stairs to the third floor became narrow and steep and

again the only light came from beneath a door at the top of the landing. He slid his hand along the railing and more or less felt his way to the top. Here there was some sign of life, a man's voice speaking rather softly in a language he didn't understand but assumed was German. It sounded as if he were reading aloud. Murdoch rapped hard on the door. The voice stopped abruptly but there was no movement. He knocked again.

"Mr. Liepman, I'm a police officer and I would like to talk to you."

No response. Murdoch was getting thoroughly annoyed. He thumped hard with his fist on the door. "Mr. Liepman, please open up."

A squeak and scrape of a chair, the door opened a crack, and a frightened face peered out at him. Murdoch had expected an older man but Liepman was of middle age. His hair was long about his shoulders and he had a full, untrimmed dark beard. He was wearing a red flannel combination suit under a pair of loose trousers.

"Mr. Liepman, I'm Acting Detective Murdoch from number four station. I have just come from the Foresters Hall. The secretary told me you had some information concerning the death of one of our constables."

Liepman stared at him for so long, Murdoch wondered if he had understood anything. He was about to repeat himself when the man said, "I have been ill. I couldn't have come." He had a pronounced German accent, turning his *v*'s into *f*'s.

"I'm not here to reproach you or charge you with anything,

Mr. Liepman. I'm pursuing an inquiry into the death of this officer."

"I thought the verdict was for self-murder."

The man wasn't as ignorant as he first appeared. "Yes, but there are a few matters I'd like to clear up. Can I come in?"

Reluctantly, Liepman stepped aside and Murdoch went into the tiny attic room. Tweedie was right about the smell. It was far worse than the odour downstairs. He tried to breathe lightly.

"I was just having my tea," said Liepman and he indicated a pine table tucked underneath the window. There was a cup and the remnants of a meat pie on a plate. A black book was turned face down beside it. Could have been a Bible.

"I won't keep you."

Murdoch had been annoyed with the old man who let him in, but this one's lack of manners was more forgivable. It seemed less deliberate and more as if he simply wasn't used to company. Unexpectedly, there was the sound of birdsong, a cascade of trills and chirps. At first, Murdoch couldn't see where it was coming from, then he noticed a small cage in the corner of the room, next to the hearth. Inside was a dainty yellow and black finch. It shook out its feathers, raised its beak, and let out another series of whistles. Liepman grinned. "She likes to show off. "

"That's a beautiful song."

"Yes, we've won competitions. Her name's Jenny Lind. She's named after the singer. My mother heard her when she did the only show she ever performed in Toronto. Fifty-three it was. I was only five years old but she took me too. It cost Mutter a week's wages but she didn't care. It was worth it. I name all my birds the same now. This is Miss Jenny Lind the eighth, or is it ninth?"

The little bird preened herself, then took a sip of water from the dish inside her cage, for all the world like a diva warming up for her performance.

Murdoch glanced around the tiny room. The furnishings were spare but whether that was from penury or from choice, he didn't know. The walls sloped and there was only one small window. It must be hot as Hades in summer. At the moment, however, it was comfortably warm and, in contrast to the rest of the house, well-lit and cheery. There was a fire going in the fireplace and a kettle was steaming on the hob. This was obviously where Mr. Liepman cooked his meals. He hadn't invited him to sit, but Murdoch pulled out a chair and sat down at the table.

"Mr. Tweedie said that you heard the sound of somebody crying on Monday night. Can you tell me more about it?"

"What would you like to know?" Liepman had plumped himself down in the single armchair by the fire but he jumped up again, went over to the cage, and shook out some seed for the bird.

"Could you describe this sound?"

"Oh, yes. Piteous, it was. Made my blood run cold."

"Were they words or just cries?"

"Words."

"What were they?"

"'Help me, help me.'"

That wasn't what Mr. Tweedie had said.

"Mr. Liepman, could you swear an oath that those words were exactly what you heard?"

The other man looked frightened.

"What I mean is that we often recall things differently from the way they actually happened. I may for instance insist that a friend said to me, 'We must have a chat,' when in fact what they said was 'I'd like to get together for a talk.'"

Liepman was staring at Murdoch. He tried again. "All I am asking, sir, is if, to your recollection, these were the precise words. Mr. Tweedie has reported it rather differently."

"Has he?" He scowled. "Well, he can go stuff himself in his filing cabinet for all I care. I heard plain as you're talking to me, 'Help me. Help me.' And that's the gospel truth, may I be put on the rack and not change my mind."

"Were the words repeated several times or twice like that?"

"Only twice."

"What made you think it was the constable?"

"Eh?"

"Mr. Tweedie said you thought it was the officer who died."

"I didn't say that. It was him who said it must have been."

"He imitated the sounds for me and they could have come more from a woman."

"I did think that at first. That it was a woman, but according to Mr. Clever, it couldn't have been."

"Did the cries come from the empty house?"

"Thereabouts." Liepman clicked his tongue at Jenny Lind but she didn't respond, just continued to dig into her flight feathers.

Murdoch sighed. "I must repeat what I said earlier, Mr. Liepman, you are not in any kind of trouble. But it would be more than helpful if you could be exact. You were walking by on your way to the hall; at what point did you hear the noises?"

"Just as I was going past the livery." He turned around and faced Murdoch. His face was tight with anxiety. "Mr. Tweedie said sound at night is difficult to pinpoint, travels around. He's the one convinced it was coming from the house. I'd have said it was behind me rather than in front. But he knows best."

"Did you hear a gunshot?"

Liepman was emphatic. "No. Not so much as a pop. Just the cries."

"And what time was this?"

"About twenty minutes past twelve. I get to the hall at half past."

"That is your regular route to work, I presume? Have you ever seen the constable on his beat? Tall fellow, blond whiskers and moustache."

"I see him most every night. He's regular and so am I."

"Did you see him on Monday?"

"No. I did wonder at it."

"Have you ever seen him accompanied by anybody else?"

"Once or twice he was with the sergeant."

"On Monday night, did you notice a young woman on the street?"

"No, it was too late for women to be out."

"You're certain?"

"Absolutely. Everybody is in bed by the time I go to work. I'd notice if it was different."

"When you heard these cries, did you see anything? Did you look up at the windows, for instance?"

Liepman shook his head emphatically. "Mutter said never to look at devils. If you did, you would go up in a puff of smoke."

"You thought these cries, piteous as you describe them, might have not been human?"

"Devils can take all kinds of shapes."

"Indeed they can."

He focused on the little finch again. "I don't want to get anybody in trouble. I won't, will I?"

"I don't think so, Mr. Liepman. You have been very helpful."

Murdoch looked at the book that was on the table. It was a Bible. There didn't seem to be any other books in the room, as far as he could see. He stood up. That was probably all he was going to get out of the man. Realising they were done, Liepman cheered up. He took the lamp from the mantelpiece.

"I'll see you down. Mr. Henry won't leave any candles out. He's afraid of fire."

As they left, the finch let loose with a glorious torrent of song.

An image had leaped into Murdoch's mind. A young woman tied to a chair, trying to reach out to him, whispering, "Help me, please help me."

CHAPTER TWENTY-EIGHT

SHE FELT AS IF SHE WERE RECOVERING FROM AN ILLNESS, a fever that had distorted her view of the world. The strict routine of the asylum, the orderliness, was actually helping to bring about clarity. However, this served to intensify her fear and her isolation. She could see only too well what she faced and she was threading her way like a cat on a mantel.

During the day, there was little to distract her from her thoughts. Mrs. Foster was coherent but childlike, and she soon gave up on any attempt to communicate with the other women. Trying to hold on to their sanity was like catching a bird in cupped hands. The attendants had a lot to do and were still wary of her. Fortunately, Miss Bastedo had made sure she was given some tray covers to embroider and it helped to while away the time. When she was in the orphanage, she had been taught fine sewing and she had become adept at it, enjoying the praise she garnered for her neat stitching. After Harry died she tried to support herself and Charley by doing dressmaking. Unfortunately, there was a plethora of skilled dressmakers in the city and she never had enough work. It was at this point Nathaniel Eakin had entered her life, by chance, looking for someone to sew for his ailing wife. Peg couldn't really understand why he had been so smitten with her but it was clear he was. After his wife's death and when he was scarcely out of mourning, he had proposed marriage. Seeing no alternative, she accepted.

On Friday Miss Bastedo announced that the Lippincott choir was coming to sing for them that evening. Peg felt a surge of excitement at the prospect of contact with the outside world. Then the reality of her situation rushed in on her. Nobody had visited her yet and she was still wearing the institutional clothes, cotton drawers and chemise, a petticoat, grey woollen dress and a stiff white pinafore. They were the regulation apparel worn by all the charity patients and she felt ashamed to be seen by normal people. Briefly, she considered begging off as being unwell, but after the plates were taken away, the attendants ushered all the women into the sitting room and she filed in with Mrs. Foster on her arm.

The Lippincott church choir was already there. Seven of them, five women and two men. They were used to the asylum and didn't gawk or pay any attention, instead sorting through their music sheets or chatting to each other quietly. There were four rows of chairs for the patients set up in a semicircle in front of the piano, but the rear seats were already occupied. Peg's hope of sitting inconspicuously at the back was dashed.

"Who are those women?" she whispered to Mrs. Foster. They were all in the asylum clothes, many of them with white mob caps. There was an air of restless energy surrounding them, as they fidgeted and looked around them. Various looks – bewilderment, fear, suspicion.

"They're from second floor," replied Emma. "It's not fair of Miss Bastedo to bring them in but she always does. Says it calms them down. Which it doesn't, in my opinion. They don't pay attention and shout out at the most inappropriate moments."

Peg felt afraid of the strangeness of these women and made sure that she was one row removed as she sat down. That put her in direct line of vision with the women of the choir, but it was the lesser of two evils. She scanned them quickly, relieved that there was nobody she knew in the group.

Mrs. Foster leaned up closer and spoke into her ear. "Whatever you do, don't get too close to the woman who's sitting at the end of the row at the back. The one in the bonnet."

Peg glanced quickly behind her. The woman in question was small and thin with haggard features. She was sitting quietly but her lips were moving in a conversation only she could hear.

"She's had ringworm. It's very contagious. She shouldn't be here but matron is always letting the old-timers get away with things. She's been in this place for twenty-two years."

"My Lord. She doesn't look much into middle age."

"She was twenty-six years old when she was admitted."

"The same age as me."

"There you go then," said Emma ambiguously. "I've been here seven years, three months, and fourteen days tomorrow."

That wasn't what she'd said before but Peg didn't challenge her. "Wouldn't you like to leave?"

Mrs. Foster shrugged. "I have left more than once, but I've had to come back."

"Why?"

"I didn't get along with my daughter-in-law." She hesitated and began to pleat her skirt, nervously.

"Why didn't you?" Peg asked.

"She said I stole things."

"Oh, I see."

The other woman looked up at Peg in confusion. "Sometimes I take things that I know people would give me anyway. That's not so wicked, is it?"

"I don't think so but perhaps it would be better to ask them first."

"Oh, no. They wouldn't give them to me then." Mrs. Foster's eyes filled with sudden tears. "She's a good girl, is Letty. I miss her so much. She's been like a daughter to me."

She began to weep with increasing fervour. Mrs. Reid, who was talking to the choir leader, came over.

"What is it, Mrs. Foster?"

"Hurt," said the old woman in a child's voice and touched her chest.

"Did you say something to her?" the attendant asked Peg.

She shook her head. "No, I did not. She mentioned her daughter-in-law and that seemed to upset her."

Reid took a handkerchief out of her pocket and wiped at Mrs. Foster's face. "Come on, where's my sunshine smile? We want to set a good example, don't we?"

Emma sniffed away the tears and gave her a wan little smile.

"Lovely. That's what I like to see. Now I need to have one more word with Mrs. Greenwood. Shall I ask them to sing 'Annie Laurie' for you?"

"Yes, please."

Reid straightened up, gave Peg a warning don't-do-anything-else glance, and returned to the choir mistress.

Emma examined the handkerchief, which was of good linen with a deep black border.

"Poor Reid's brother died this year. She was very fond of him." She put it in her pocket.

One of the choir members was at the piano. She struck a note; the others hummed to get the right pitch. Then Mrs. Greenwood faced them, lifted her arms, and they all rose, music held straight out in front of them. A patient from the rear seats shouted out, "Hurray."

"And..."

They burst into a boisterous rendition of 'Bringing in the Sheaves'.

Peg felt a surge of grief that tightened in her throat. If only she could get up and walk across that small patch of floor and be with them, the normal ones, the ones who could leave when they wanted to; the ones who could go to a home where they were safe.

CHAPTER TWENTY-NINE

IT WAS REMARKABLE THAT THE REAL BUSINESS THAT occurred at the house on Sydenham Street was undetected. Clara Doherty told her neighbours that she was a music teacher who lived with her four orphaned nieces and her housekeeper. She was strict about secrecy. Customers entered the house by way of a lane at the rear and were accepted by referral only. The whores were available at certain times and no other. Most of the men came directly after working hours, some few before work, although only Rose was willing to do that, the other girls preferring to sleep in.

The setup of the house was simple and practical. The four bawds shared the top two rooms, something they unfailingly grumbled about, as the attic was unbearably hot in summer and cold in winter. Clara allowed them only a small coal allowance. On the second floor were three well-furnished bedrooms which were used only for business. Clara had a private suite on the first floor that she shared with Emily Dawson, the housekeeper, who was also her long-time lover. Across the hall was the parlour, a good-sized room where the men could wait and have a drink of spirits and smoke a pipe if they wanted. However, they were rarely permitted to linger through the entire evening, and Clara was always there to ensure they obeyed. Sophie, the oldest whore, referred to this policy as, "Get up, get in, get on, and get out." The premises were closed at midnight and woe betide any man who presumed otherwise. Drunkenness was frowned upon and those leaving late were expected to be quiet. The Sabbath was always a day of rest.

On the whole, Clara treated the girls well. She let them have short holidays every so often, food was plentiful, and she performed abortions herself when necessary. She would have been comfortably off by now, except that, with dismaying regularity, she lost her heart to some young doxy and lavished such gifts on her that her savings were seriously jeopardised. This blatant favouritism created havoc in the house, but fortunately the infatuations never lasted long, and the girl disappeared to Montreal or America, where Clara had friends who also ran ill-reputes. Later, the others would hear her sobbing in Emily's arms, begging for forgiveness, promising it would never happen again, and then the house would settle down for a little while.

Every afternoon the girls were invited into Clara's sitting room and Emily served them lemon junkets and cakes as a treat. Here they would sort out petty quarrels, receive their allowances, and discuss their customers. Clara encouraged them to unburden themselves. The information gave her ammunition if she needed it at a later time.

She yawned. The others had been having a lively discussion of their toms, ever a popular topic.

"Personally, I like the fast-trigger ones the best; the grunters, no words, next; and the shouters the least. You could go deaf with some of them yelling in your ear," said Nellie, licking the last of the junket off her spoon. "You had one of them Friday, didn't you, Rose? The greenhead. I heard you."

"Ha! That humper wasn't a greenhead. He said he was sixteen, a virgin and the son of a bishop. The closest he's ever been to a bishop is his own cock."

"It's wicked to say things like that," said Sophie. She had been brought up in an orphanage run by the Sisters of St Joseph. Although she had become a prostitute at an early age, she suffered from regular attacks of guilt that sent her scuttling off to confession at St Michael's Cathedral. She was so oblique about her sins, however, that the priest never understood what she was referring to, and she always got off with a light penance. She compensated by wearing a piece of sacking next to her skin for the next week and refusing her favourite delicacies. Behind her back, the others referred to her variously as Mother-of-

God, Saint Sophie, or Jesus-Wept, which she said often.

"He was wild for it," continued Rose. "'Oh, another one, my dear, that was so bad, oh, say that again, I'm coming, I'm coming.' You'd think he was a delivery boy. I was running out of words by the end."

"That's not what it sounded like to me," said Nellie. "I thought you could have gone on for another half hour and not repeated yourself."

Rose scowled. She was notorious for her vulgarity, but she hated the scorn of the other women.

Clara intervened before a squabble could develop. "Now, dears, let's get on. They'll be arriving soon." She picked up a small wooden pail of candies and offered it around. "Everybody take one for now and one for later. They're lovely and fresh; Emily just bought them."

The women started to help themselves.

"I just wanted to reply to Rose," said Mary Ann, her mouth full of the candy. "The one I had, friend of your gull, he was the opposite. He whispered lovely things in my ear the whole time, 'You're so lovely, your eyes are extraordinary.' Never repeated himself and he was spent twice."

"How many times were you?" asked Nellie. The other two snickered. Nobody liked Mary Ann, whose childlike body appealed to a lot of customers. She milked the attraction for all it was worth – wore her hair down, kept her skirts short and flounced, and pouted like a spoiled child.

Mary Ann wasn't offended. She enjoyed stirring up the other

whores. "All men are the same. They need to think you are really enjoying yourself, that they are therefore great lovers."

"I think about the taste of the dollars they're going to leave," said Nellie. "I must look happy."

Emily came in. "Hurry up, girls. Time to get dressed. Nellie, don't you have anything cleaner to wear?"

"My other dress isn't dry."

"Well, you've got a stain all over your bodice; it's disgusting. Wear a shawl."

She clapped her hands as if she were shooing away geese. "Come on. We're late tonight."

One by one the girls started to leave. Emily went over to the dresser, pulled open a drawer, and took out a corset.

"You'd better get ready," she said to Clara. "There's a man here. Wants to talk to you."

"Who?"

"Mr. Smith."

"Which Mr. Smith?"

"One of the older ones."

"Damn. Did he say anything else?"

"No. Come on, stand up."

Clara got to her feet and Emily helped her off with her dressing robe. She held the corset so that Clara could step into it and started to tighten the laces.

"Not so tight, Emmie, I can't breathe."

"It's no tighter than usual; you've been eating too many candies."

"You're the one who bought them."

Emily planted a kiss on Clara's shoulder and grinned. "True, I like to see you enjoy them so much. It's like watching my little piggy at her trough."

"Emmie!"

"Don't get frosty. You know how much I love that pig."

She gave Clara's plump buttock an affectionate squeeze. "There you go. All done. What dress do you want to wear?"

"The pearl grey."

Emily came around and looked Clara in the face. "Be careful what you say, dearest. This man smells like trouble to me."

"I know. But we've managed this long, I'm not going to let any gull sink me."

The man calling himself Henry Smith was sitting in the front room. Clara had furnished it according to her idea of a well-to-do family parlour, and it was so crammed with furniture there was barely room to enter. There were two Turkish couches upholstered in purple velour with gold fringes, four Morris chairs, and taking pride of place a so-called courting couch. It was S-shaped and a man sat on one side and a woman the other. The notion was they could converse quite intimately without physical contact. Rose particularly liked this couch as she could whisper lewd things in her customer's ear and have him squirming in no time. There was a piano in one corner on which Emily stoically played popular songs like 'A Beautiful Dreamer' and 'Home Sweet Home', which were always in demand. The piano invariably needed tuning and she added fancy chords that changed the melody, but nobody would dare voice an objection. There were two sideboards on either side of the door, heavy and ornate with burled walnut mouldings. This was where Clara kept the more lascivious tools of her trade. Plush vellum albums of special photographs, books to make a man as randy as a goat. A stereoscope sat on one of the side tables. Just in the unlikely event that a neighbour came to call, the photos on display were innocent: a view of the Nile, a girl on a giant lily pad, children sitting on a wall. In the sideboard were the other pictures. The three-dimensional nature of the stereoscope made these pictures particularly startling. They were twenty-five cents a viewing.

Smith had been a customer of Mrs. Doherty's for seven years, following her whenever she moved to a new location for safety. Sometimes he visited once or twice a week, sometimes he would stay away for a month or more. There was something in his disdain that made the women uncomfortable. He wouldn't take liquor, ignored the books and photographs, and was never tempted by the latest special novel. They were glad when Mary Ann took him over.

Nellie was sitting on one of the Morris chairs. She had a bad cold and was hawking copiously into her handkerchief. Clara came out of her room. The man immediately took a gold watch from his waistcoat pocket and consulted it.

"Good evening, Mr. Smith. Sorry to keep you waiting. Nasty weather, isn't it? Can I get you a hot gin in the meantime, warm you up?"

"No, thank you. I'd like to speak to you in private."

"Of course. We can talk in my sitting room."

He followed her to the door, where she paused and looked over her shoulder. "Nellie! If you have to blow out that much snot, can you do it more quietly? The customers are going to vomit."

The girl coughed. "I can't help it. I've got a bad cold."

"Go back to bed then or you'll give it to everybody. It looks like it's going to be quiet tonight anyway."

Gratefully, Nellie got up, pulling down her skirt, which had been hitched to her scrawny thighs. She wasn't wearing any drawers.

The man's face contorted with contempt. "I must admit, the mere sight of female private parts has never aroused me."

"Each to his own," said Clara with a shrug.

She showed him into her sitting room. It, too, was crammed with furniture, and every surface was covered with crotchet work, each piece lovingly made by Emily. She'd left the lamps lit and the fire was cheery.

Clara took one of the armchairs close to the hearth and indicated he should take the other.

"Were things satisfactory with Mary Ann?" she asked.

"They were indeed. She was most credible. And adroit. There was a witness we didn't expect. A Chinaman. He'd seen the constable with a young woman. Fortunately, he couldn't tell the difference between one devil woman and another and swore it was Mary Ann. It made our case even more convincing."

"So I understand. The joke is that Mary Ann knew him. He has been one of our customers."

"Is that so?"

"She is sure he recognised her and decided to help her out."

"I doubt it. He was probably just confused. Nevertheless, this leads precisely to what I wanted to talk about. Mary Ann must go somewhere else. I would like you to send her away. You have places she can go, I know you do. Wait…"

He held up his hand to stem the protest Clara was about to make.

"I will pay for any inconvenience to you and her."

"She is one of my most popular wenches."

"I realise that, Mrs. Doherty, and in a way I am asking this as a favour. It would be better if she were not available should anyone come looking."

He had not told Clara the reason he'd wanted Mary Ann to appear at the inquest and perjure herself, and she had not asked. She'd long operated on the premise that what a person didn't know couldn't hurt them. Any suspicions she pushed far away from her consciousness. Life was easier that way.

"Well…" She pretended to think about his offer but she'd already accepted. It was true Mary Ann was popular but she created trouble with the other girls. She'd also had the temerity to laugh when Clara had approached her full of tenderness when she'd first arrived. It was time she visited Montreal.

"As I say, this is going to cost me a lot of money."

"Name a figure."

"I won't be able to get another girl for at least a week, that's thirty dollars lost income right there. Then there's the train fare to Montreal…"

"I said name a figure. I have no interest in the particulars."

Clara had been about to inflate the expenses but she thought better of it. This man was too fly.

"Forty dollars."

He took out a wallet and counted out the money. "I'd like to see her gone tonight."

"Tonight!"

He added another five-dollar bill. "This will cover your losses. I'll wait and accompany her to the train station myself."

"I don't even know if there is a train tonight."

"There is. She can stay in a hotel until you have a chance to notify her new…employer."

He stood up. "Thank you for your cooperation, Mrs. Doherty. I'll wait in here while she gets ready."

Clara took up the bills and put them in a porcelain box on the mantel. "It will take at least an hour for her to pack her belongings and to say goodbye."

"Make it half an hour and she and you get another two dollars."

"Very well."

Clara left. She closed the door behind her and rested against it for a moment. Then she spat into the cuspidor that was provided in the hall. Sometimes not even money could sweeten the shit she had to eat.

CHAPTER THIRTY

THE YOUNG MAID ANSWERED MURDOCH'S SECOND knock. She was wiping her hands on her apron and gaped at him in a flustered way. Her eyes and nose were reddened. He wondered if she had been crying and if this was what happened to her every day. He smiled and touched his hat politely.

"Hello, Janet. I'd like to speak to Mrs. Curran."

"She said she's not at home, sir."

"Did she? I'm afraid I have to insist. It's police business. Would you mind telling her that I'm here? I'll make it right for you."

"Yes, sir."

She scuttled away, leaving him on the threshold, afraid

to be so definite as to invite him in. He gave his feet a good wipe on the mat for her sake and stepped into the hall. The far door opened and Augusta emerged, Janet hovering anxiously behind her.

"Mr. Murdoch, we were about to go in to dinner."

Murdoch tried to appear suitably apologetic. The house was quiet, but the way she spoke, you'd think the mayor and council were lined up two by two.

"I insisted on seeing you, Mrs. Curran. Your maid did her job very well." Janet looked so alarmed at his words that he was afraid he'd made things worse for her.

"I'll get back, ma'am," she said.

Augusta fanned her hand dismissively and the girl hurried off.

"What is it you wish, Mr. Murdoch?"

Tonight, she was wearing a black silk dress with grey satin trimming down the bodice and skirt. From what they'd told him before, he assumed this mourning attire was for her mother. Devotion or defiance?

"There have been further developments in the Wicken case. I wondered if I could talk to Mrs. Nathaniel Eakin?"

"Oh no. She is still…she is no better."

"Is she able to receive visitors?"

"I believe not. We haven't seen her ourselves yet."

At that moment, a man came into the hall. He was of medium height, stocky, with a thick grey beard that jutted from either side of his chin. He was wearing a burgundy velvet smoking jacket that even from a distance appeared spotted and stained along the lapels. Although there was no physical resemblance whatsoever to Murdoch's own father, he was immediately reminded of him. It was the air that some men acquire when they have undisputed command over their domain.

"Augusta, bring the detective into my study. What are you thinking of?"

He held out his hand to Murdoch. "I'm Nathaniel Eakin. We haven't met before."

"No, you were indisposed when I came last."

"That's what they told you, was it?"

"Father, you were…"

He interrupted her. "I think you keep me from too many things that go on in this house. I'm as well as the next man."

He didn't seem that way to Murdoch. His face had an unhealthy, shiny flush to it, and his eyes were carrying enough baggage underneath to fit a traveller.

"Come this way, Mr. Murdoch."

The study wasn't large but the walls were panelled in the English style from floor to ceiling. There were glass-fronted bookcases on two sides and in one corner was a closed rolltop desk. All the wood was a dark hue; the chairs were brown leather. However, instead of conveying the snug respectability of a gentleman's library, the room was gloomy and oppressive. It reeked of cigar smoke.

Eakin followed him in with Augusta close behind.

"Have a seat, Mr. Murdoch," she said.

Murdoch took one of the big armchairs, Eakin the other.

Augusta came behind her father and stood with her hand on the back of his chair. Murdoch couldn't quite tell if she was using that as a shield or if she wanted to ensure her father was within reach. Eakin picked up a cigar that was on the table next to him. The ash was long on the end and he scraped it off against the dish. He obviously wasn't concerned about tobacco smoke damaging his books, but Murdoch had the impression they were for show anyway. He waited until the cigar was relit and drawn, the end disappearing into the thicket of Eakin's beard. Murdoch almost coughed. He liked a pipe himself on occasion, but this smoke was vile.

"You were asking after my wife?"

"Yes, I was wondering if I'd be able to talk to her."

"She's in the loony bin."

"I know. Does she have any rationality at all?"

Eakin studied the tip of his cigar. "Depends what you mean. She can form sentences, say words in English. But she's gone mad. Why the hell would you want to talk to her?"

"There are one or two things we want to clear up. We have a new witness who says that on Monday night he heard the sound of a woman crying. He thought it was coming from your house and it was roughly in the same time frame that Constable Wicken died. At the very least, it indicates somebody was awake at that hour and may have seen or heard something."

Nathaniel frowned. "You think it was my wife?"

"Possibly. The witness described the sound as cries for help. When I was here on Tuesday, I saw Mrs. Eakin. She cried out to me for help."

"She did not!" burst out Mrs. Curran.

"She didn't shout out loud, ma'am, but she did speak and what she said was, 'Help me.'"

Nathaniel put down his cigar, took out a large red handkerchief, trumpeted into it, then stuffed it back into his trouser pocket.

"Well, it's true, she moaned often enough."

"You can understand why I'd like to pursue this matter," said Murdoch.

"No, frankly I don't."

"Two reasons. Perhaps Mrs. Eakin saw the constable going by. She could corroborate whether or not he was alone. Secondly, if he did hear these cries, he may have come to investigate…"

He left the rest of the sentence, not wanting to fill in too much, waiting to see what would be their reaction.

Eakin looked up at his daughter. "Well?"

"Nobody came here."

"Is it possible you wouldn't have heard, ma'am? Your chambers are on the third floor. You didn't hear your stepmother calling out and it does seem that she was."

She thought for a moment and he had the feeling she was searching for the safest answer.

"It is possible but not likely."

Nathaniel poured himself a generous amount of wine from a decanter on the side table and took a good swallow. "I don't see the point of this, sir. Even if the officer did come to this house, which he didn't, what does it matter? It don't overturn the coroner's verdict. The man took his own life and that's all there is to it."

Murdoch decided to change tack. "As I said, there are one or two loose ends to the case. The more I know about Wicken's last movements, the better."

Eakin took another drink of wine as if it were water. "You're wasting your time here."

There was the merest slur to his words. Murdoch knew the signs, and in spite of himself, his body, which had its own wisdom, grew tense.

"I'll be able to determine that myself after I've spoken to Mrs. Eakin personally. And may I ask, what is wrong with her?"

Augusta shifted uncomfortably and involuntarily smoothed the antimacassar that was on the back of the chair. Her father made a show of staring at Murdoch as if he were a likely candidate for a freak show.

"She's been taken up the loop, that's what's wrong. She's gone batchy, barmy."

"Insanity has many faces, doesn't it? My question has more to do with the form that your wife's lunacy has taken."

"I thought you were a police officer, not a physician."

"Father..." Augusta tried to place a placating hand on Nathaniel's shoulder. He immediately shrugged it off.

"I would imagine Mr. Murdoch wants to know if Stepmother is a danger to herself or anybody else. Isn't that right, sir?"

Murdoch hadn't actually been that clear in his mind as to what he wanted, but he nodded.

"Is she?"

Nathaniel drew deeply on the cigar; the end glowed red through the ash. He didn't reply, his thoughts suddenly pulled away. His daughter answered.

"Unfortunately, Mrs. Eakin suffered a tragic loss not too long ago. Her son by her previous marriage died suddenly of peritonitis. The doctor feels that the grief has caused a temporary derailment of her faculties."

"Derangement. You mean derangement, fool."

Nathaniel had come out of his daydream as vicious as a ferret from its hole. Murdoch smiled falsely. "I can see you've been a schoolteacher, Mr. Eakin."

"No, I have not. But any fool can use words properly if they want to. She's had more education than I ever did. I never had the opportunity to continue past standard two even if I wanted to. I had to work. The family needed my wages."

Mrs. Curran attempted a feeble retaliation. "I hardly think he needs to know our personal history, Father." Her fair skin flushed with humiliation but she continued to address Murdoch.

"She began to suffer from delusions of persecution. She became convinced the child was poisoned and that she herself was in danger."

"Speak to the physician if you don't believe us," said Nathaniel. "He wrote the death certificate. Boy died from a burst appendix. Nothing could be done." He gulped down the last of the wine. Then he leaned forward toward Murdoch, fixing him with eyes that were fast becoming bloodshot. "The thing is, Margaret knows this lot is against her and she mulled that over in her mind until she went batchy."

His daughter fluttered nervously. "Nobody is 'against her', as you put it, Father. I, in particular, have tried to be welcoming. She would have none of it. She was so hostile from the very beginning."

"She was afraid. Stands to reason she would be. Here I was, a widower. Children grown. My daughter here is used to running the house. You know what women are like when another hen comes into the barnyard." He made pecking motions with his fingers. "*Cluck, cluck, cluck.* Fact is, they're all afraid she's going to get one under her apron and claim their inheritance."

Murdoch was beginning to feel sorry for Mrs. Curran. She turned her face away and moved over to the hearth. There were neither mourning crepe nor festoons of black ribbon in this room, Murdoch noticed.

"What was the name of the doctor who attended your wife?"

In spite of what he'd said, he wasn't at all sure this inquiry was going to yield anything, but Eakin was such a vile-tempered old sod, he didn't want to let him off too easily. Nathaniel didn't reply but began to puff on his cigar again. Murdoch knew the procrastination was a further attempt to intimidate him, to put him in his place, and he could feel his own temper rising. This man might have money and fancy himself a gentleman, but he had the temperament of a pugilist, and if he wasn't careful, he, Murdoch, would take up the challenge, old man or not.

Augusta answered for him. "Dr. Ferrier. He lives just across the road. Number three hundred and twelve."

Murdoch took out his notebook and wrote down the name and number.

A gong started to mark out the hour and he saw that there was another clock on one of the shelves that was identical to the one in the parlour. The coins around her bosom gleamed in the firelight.

He folded up his notebook, returned it to his pocket, and stood up.

"Are you going out to the loony bin?" asked Eakin.

"Yes, I'll go tomorrow."

Nathaniel got to his feet and came over to him. He was a good head shorter than Murdoch, which meant he had to look up and Murdoch could smell the cigar and the wine on his breath.

"What they should tell you is that my wife suffers from erotomania. Do you know what that means?"

"No, I don't."

"Well, you should write it down in your little notebook. It means as soon as she sees a pair of trousers, she's going to lift her tail for you. She went for Jarius in the same way. And my son-in-law, her husband…" He jerked his thumb in Augusta's direction. "I wouldn't recommend you take her up on the offer. She'd do it for the butcher's boy if he came by."

"I'll take that under advisement," said Murdoch.

"Yes, I would if I were you."

Sullenly, he backed off. With a nod to Mrs. Curran, Murdoch left.

CHAPTER THIRTY-ONE

MURDOCH JOGTROTTED ALL THE WAY TO ONTARIO Street in an attempt to dispel his anger. His head was filled with fantasies, all of them violent, of what he would do to Nathaniel Eakin. When he'd finished smashing the man's head against the floor for the second time, he slowed himself down. Yes, the old geezer was a horse's arse but Murdoch knew the rage he'd stirred up didn't totally belong with him. His memory of his father shouting about his mother was a tight pain in his chest and he felt short of breath. "She's a whore, a tart, cheap as a dish clout." And more, words that he didn't want to recall. She, silent as always, going about her task, head bowed in a way that made him, the boy, want to scream out, "Look up! Don't lower

306

your head like that." But when he spoke to her afterwards, she wept, and his feelings of fear and pity became overlaid with contempt for her and a burning rage toward his father that even now made him hot. According to the local magistrate, his mother had died accidentally, while she was gathering shellfish on the beach. A slip, a hard knock on the head that rendered her unconscious, and she drowned. Murdoch had gone to the shore afterwards, trying to find the pool where she'd died. He couldn't place it exactly but it didn't matter, they were all shallow, no more than splashing deep. That made her death even more meaningless.

"Evening, Mr. Murdoch." His next-door neighbour, O'Brien, was going by. He had a sailor's duffel bag slung over his shoulder and Murdoch assumed he was off once again to some exotic place. He turned and waved in the direction of his house and Murdoch could see his wife and children were crowded into the window. They all waved back with varying degrees of enthusiasm. Murdoch thought O'Brien had probably once again impregnated Mrs. O'Brien and they could expect to see child number nine.

All the little faces were watching Murdoch now and he tried to give them a cheery smile. He resolved to pick up some more barley sugar sticks from Mrs. Bail's confectionery as soon as he could.

He let himself into the house and was greeted by the sight of his landlady and landlord.

Arthur was walking slowly down the hall, Beatrice close

behind as if ready to catch him. They both turned around to welcome him.

"Evening, Will," said Arthur.

"What are you doing out here?"

"Taking in the sights. I'm getting corns on my rear end from sitting so much. I thought I'd take a stroll. I'm pretending this is King Street. Any minute now I'm going to go in one of the fancy shops and spend a lot of money."

"Good thing you've come, Mr. Murdoch," said Beatrice. "He always overdoes it and he won't listen to me. We've done quite enough for one night."

Arthur had dressed himself in trousers and a flannel shirt for the occasion. In the candlelight, with a brighter energy in his face, he looked almost healthy. Murdoch felt a rush of affection for him and would have embraced him if he hadn't known it would embarrass everybody. He tapped his foot on the floor. They had rolled up the hall rug to make walking a bit easier.

"This is perfect for doing a schottische. Mrs. K., we can practise whenever you're ready."

"I've forgotten how. Here, let me take your things," said Mrs. Kitchen, abandoning her husband. "It's been so miserable all day. I've got your dinner warming."

"Thank you. As usual, I'm famished. Will you join me, Arthur?"

"Why don't you eat first. I'll have a rest to satisfy my wife and then we can have tea."

"You can go right into the parlour," said Beatrice. "I'll just see to Father."

"No, you won't," said Arthur and he flexed his arm to make a muscle. "I am strong as the Borneo Wild Man. I will go myself and sit in my chair until called."

He was speaking jokingly but his frustration was evident. Before he became ill, Arthur Kitchen had been highly active, a keen bicyclist and walker. According to his wife, he was an excellent dancer, specialty the polka, something Murdoch was still aspiring to.

Beatrice went on down to the kitchen and Arthur into the middle room. Murdoch stood for a moment, blowing on his cold hands, but really trying to listen for sounds from upstairs – the typewriting machine, or Enid talking to her son. He was just about to go into the parlour when he heard the stairs creak. Mrs. Jones herself came down the stairs. She was holding her son's hand and they were both dressed for the outdoors in long rubber waterproof coats. There was something in her expression that he couldn't quite read. Guarded, not altogether happy to see him. He felt a rush of disappointment. Back to that again, were they?

"Mrs. Jones, Alwyn. Where are you off to on such a dreary night?"

"There is a special meeting at the church. A speaker has come up from Wisconsin. He is just returned from our mission in Nigeria. Apparently, he is most inspirational." Her voice was full of enthusiasm and Murdoch felt jealous. It made him sharp.

"I sincerely hope he is worth braving the rain."

She was aware of his tone and her face clouded. "He will be, I am sure. He has worked for Our Lord for many years."

Murdoch stepped back so she could pass him. He tapped the boy playfully on his cap but the child shrank away as if he had dealt him a blow. That irritated Murdoch as well. The boy was a mardy tit most of the time. At the door, Enid hesitated and turned back to him.

"I really don't expect us to be late, Mr. Murdoch. Perhaps you and I could have a word together if you're still up?"

"For that I'll wait till midnight."

He'd meant to be gallant but the words came out angry.

"Good evening, then."

She opened the door, letting in a surge of cold, wet air. Murdoch went into the front room, chastising himself for being such a boor. Mrs. Jones seemed highly devout to him. Not likely to change her religion. He caught himself. If it came to that, what about him? Could he denounce his faith, which is what he supposed he would have to do if…Again he stopped. Look at him, racing ahead of himself like a fanciful girl. Marriage on his mind and they didn't even use each other's first names! He went over to the table and sat down at the place set for him. Does any of it really matter? Our Lord didn't declare himself a Baptist, or a Catholic for that matter. He'd started out his life as a Jew. Who was he anyway? Murdoch had asked that question once when he was being taught his catechism. The priest had slapped him with the holy book on the side of the head. "Those sorts of heathen questions sound too close to blasphemy, young man. Go kneel down in that corner and say your Paternosters until I tell you to move."

Murdoch had stayed there until his knees screamed with pain but he had not begged for release.

He rubbed at his face hard. This seemed to be his day for chewing over old grudges. Father O'Malley was one. A big, tough priest, he had both a brogue and brain as thick as an Irish bog.

Murdoch knew his mother would have liked to have seen him enter the priesthood, but he couldn't imagine it. However, his sister Susanna had gone into a convent school and took her final vows at the age of eighteen. She lived as a cloistered nun in a convent in Montreal and he hadn't seen her for a long time. He was allowed to write and received one letter a year. Hers was impersonal, full of devout phrases. The playmate he had loved, argued with, and ultimately protected had vanished behind a veil of platitudes.

"My, you are looking very fierce, Mr. Murdoch."

Mrs. Kitchen came in carrying a tray.

He grinned at her, glad to be brought out of his thoughts. "You're right. I was thinking about the Church."

She gave him a shrewd glance. "The Church or people in the Church?"

He helped unload the dinner plate. Tonight she had cooked his favourite dish, sausages and mashed potato and baked rutabaga.

"Your sweet is an egg custard. Mrs. Jones made it. She insisted. She said your gum was probably still sore. Arthur even tried some. Very tasty too."

"Can I start with that?"

"Don't you dare." She smiled at him. "I find Mrs. Jones is a woman who grows on me. Quiet. I thought she was standoffish at first but she's just reserved. Wouldn't you agree, Mr. Murdoch?"

"I do indeed."

"I particularly like the fact that she teaches her boy proper manners. She won't take any nonsense."

Murdoch nodded noncommittally.

"She's a good mother, I'd say. Not one of these flighty women who'd stuff their children into whatever purse suits them."

He looked at her but she wasn't giving anything away.

She removed the tray to the sideboard. "I'll leave you in peace then. Ring when you're done."

When she'd closed the door, Murdoch slowed down on the gusto with which he'd approached his meal. The potatoes were cold and lumpy, the rutabaga bitter, and the sausage had turned hard as a rock. But he didn't live here on account of the food and he would never want Mrs. Kitchen to know what a dreadful cook she was.

He must have been asleep for more than an hour. The last he remembered was sitting in the armchair by the fire and putting his head back. He had the hazy impression of Beatrice covering him with a quilt, but he couldn't let go of the sleep that was pulling him down. What finally woke him was the sound of the front door opening. He sat up, groggy, trying to grab awareness. The candle had burned low in the holder and the fire was down to embers. The clock showed eleven.

He heard footsteps on the stairs and, yawning, he got up and went into the hall. Enid Jones was struggling to negotiate the hall furniture. She was carrying Alwyn, who was fast asleep.

"Here, let me." He held out his arms for the boy. At first he thought she was going to refuse but her only other choice was to put Alwyn down.

"Thank you."

Awkwardly, she passed him over, heavy with the relaxation of sleep. His head dropped against Murdoch's shoulder and he tucked him in under his chin.

"I'll hold the door," said Enid, and she whisked up the stairs ahead of him.

At the entrance to her room, he paused for her to light a lamp and pull back the coverlet from the bed. How warm and solid the boy felt in his arms, his breathing deep and regular. Murdoch gently kissed his cheek, still cool from the outdoors.

"Let me take off his waterproof." She manoeuvred the boy's arms out of the sleeves while Murdoch held him up. She was so close, he could see the shape of her mouth, a faint down on her upper lip.

"Lay him here, if you please."

He did so and Alwyn immediately rolled onto his stomach,

knee bent.

"I'll have to take off his boots, but I don't have the heart to disturb him now. I'll wait."

"Surely you didn't carry him all the way from Jarvis Street?" asked Murdoch in a whisper.

"No, just from the top of the street, but by the time we got here, he felt heavier than a sack of potatoes. I would never have managed the stairs. Thank you so much, Mr. Murdoch."

"Not at all. It was my pleasure." And he meant it.

She hesitated. "I was hoping we could talk for a few moments. If you're not too tired, that is."

"I'm wide awake. We can go down to the parlour if you like. I don't hear anything from the Kitchens so I'm assuming they are asleep."

"I am much later than I expected."

"The speaker had a lot to say then?"

"Yes. He was quite wonderful and people had many questions for him."

She took off her waterproof, unpinned her hat, put it on the dresser, and quickly smoothed back her hair.

"Shall we go downstairs?"

Nathaniel could not understand why Jarius was not answering him. He had told him twice that he wanted to get up. He had vomited on his bed, on the pillow, and the sour smell was in his nostrils. He wanted to move his face away but he couldn't. He tried to talk again but the words he heard coming out were garbled, not what he wanted to say. He could see Jarius frown uncomprehendingly. *My arm has gone to sleep, help me roll over on my back.* Somebody must have put the rug over him because he could feel the weight. It was far too heavy. He was cold though, the fire must have gone out. Had he tripped when he was going to put on another piece of coal? He wanted to turn his head to see but no matter how hard he tried, he couldn't. He could hear somebody talking gibberish. *What idiot is that?* he wondered.

"Father? Father?" Jarius was kneeling beside him, and he slipped an arm under Nathaniel's shoulders to hoist him into a sitting position. Nathaniel made an anguished effort to tell him what was happening but all that came out were grunts.

"Augusta!" yelled Jarius. "Augusta, come here quick!"

CHAPTER THIRTY-TWO

MURDOCH HEARD FOOTSTEPS COMING DOWN THE corridor toward the cell. The heavy tread could belong only to Constable Crabtree. The tiny panel in the cell door was pushed aside and he could see the constable's eyes peering in. They looked amused.

"You can come in, George, I'm awake."

Crabtree entered. He was carrying a mug of something, presumably tea.

"Thought you'd like this, sir."

Murdoch scratched his leg under his trouser leg. "Who was in here last?"

"Old Joe Baxter, I think."

"He left a lot behind."

He took the mug and drank some of the tea. It was strong and tasted as if a cup of sugar had been dumped into it. It was also scalding hot and he winced.

"Did you get any sleep at all, sir?"

"No. But at least it made me more sympathetic toward our guests. I'm going to requisition a new pallet. Some rocks have wandered into this one."

He yawned and looked around the small cell. There was a narrow bed, which had a straw mattress and an iron-hard blanket, a stool, and a bucket. "What do you say to a couple of pictures on the walls, George? Tasteful. I'll donate my portrait of Colonel Grasett. Cheer the place up a bit."

"The prisoners might want to stay on if we do that."

Murdoch scratched again. "Highly unlikely, even with decorations."

He twisted his head, trying to get the kink out of his neck. "I'd better get out of here before the others start wondering what the hell I'm doing."

"You're not the first officer to doss down in one of the cells and you probably won't be the last."

"I should have gone to the Avonmore but this was the first place I thought of."

Crabtree nodded. Ever tactful, he hadn't yet inquired why Murdoch had come to the station in the middle of the night looking for a bed to sleep in.

"George, how did you and Ellen meet each other?"

If the constable was surprised by the question, he didn't show it. "We've known each other since we were kids. Our parents were good friends. We played in each other's back yards."

"So, when did you know you were in love with each other?"

"In love? I can't say exactly. We just sort of took it for granted that we would get married."

"And you're both Methodists, aren't you?"

"Yes, sir."

"Do you believe in mixed marriages, George?"

"You mean if the parties are of different religions?"

"Yes. What if one was, say, Roman Catholic, and the other was, say, Baptist? Do you think such a marriage would work?"

"That would depend, wouldn't it?"

"On what?" Murdoch almost shouted out the question.

"I suppose on how important religion was to each person and how much they were prepared to compromise."

Murdoch groaned. He felt as if he'd been drinking for two days, with his thick tongue and head. Enid and he had gone downstairs to the parlour but he knew, he could tell, he was not going to like what she had to say. And he hadn't.

"I've been thinking and thinking, and difficult as it is for me to come to my conclusion, I have done so."

"Yes?" His heart sinking.

"You would want me to convert to Catholicism and I could not do that. I would be disloyal to my husband's memory and the solemn promise I made to him to rear Alwyn with Jesus as his Saviour. Therefore, I'm leaving. I've found another boarding house closer to the church."

"And further away from St Paul's, I suppose?"

He had to admire her – she'd shown more honesty than he had. Then, for the first time, she called him by his Christian name and the sweetness of it was almost obliterated by the hurt of what she was saying.

"Will, I must admit, I am growing very fond of you, but for both our sakes, it is better that these feelings do not continue."

Murdoch fingered his bristly jaw. He needed a shave.

"I have been turned down, George."

"By Mrs. Jones, sir? The Welsh lady?"

"That's the one. She doesn't think she can overcome the obstacle of our different religions. She also said, and I quote, 'We have both suffered loss of a loved one. It is lonely we are. We must not mistake these feelings for real love. They may have been created by mere proximity.' As if it would have happened with any man."

Crabtree cleared his throat. "Forgive me, Mr. Murdoch, but she does have a point. Perhaps when she is living somewhere else, you can determine if you have found true love or not."

Murdoch had to laugh at the solemnity with which his constable delivered this speech. "You're in the wrong line of work, George. You should have been a minister."

"I did consider that at one time, sir. But Ellen didn't fancy being a minister's wife. Too much scrutiny on you. I am assuming, by the way, sir, that you do intend to see Mrs. Jones when she is not under the same roof?"

"I don't know. I hadn't got that far."

They heard steps outside and one of the young constables came to the door.

"There's somebody here to see you, Mr. Murdoch. A Scotch lassie."

"Who?"

"The boy with the braid down his back."

"The Chinaman's son?"

"That's the one."

"Did he say what he wanted?"

"Och, no." He gave a dreadful imitation of Foon Lee's accent.

"Give me a few minutes, then bring him down to my office."

"Yes, sir." He looked around the cell curiously. "Are you doing an inspection, Mr. Murdoch?"

"Something like that."

He stood up and felt a sharp twinge in his lower back. "George, remind me from time to time, will you, that I am a grown man and I do not have to behave like a child in a temper."

He'd yelled out at her, "If you consider I am too proximate, as you put it, I will go somewhere else."

Crabtree grinned. "Why don't I see if I can dig out a razor for you? Nothing like scraping at your face to make you realise you've grown up."

Lifting the strands of reeds, Crabtree ushered Foon Lee into the cubicle. The young man bowed. Murdoch didn't quite know how to respond but he sort of bobbed his head.

"Have a seat, Mr. Lee."

Foon took the chair in front of the desk and immediately put his hands in the wide sleeves of his tunic. He was in his working clothes today, blue linen tunic and black wide trousers. Murdoch thought he seemed ill at ease, and was trying hard not to show it. Probably it was the first time he had ever been inside a police station. Murdoch suddenly had the sense of how it might look to the young Chinaman. Strange people, strange ways. He smiled, trying to put him at ease, then got self-conscious. Perhaps in China it wasn't considered good manners to smile.

"You wanted to talk to me, Mr. Lee?"

The young man nodded or bowed, Murdoch couldn't tell which it was. Maybe both.

There was an uncomfortable silence while they both looked at each other; Murdoch tried to appear encouraging.

"I have come concerning the matter of the constable who recently met with his death. On later reflection, my father has decided he is not utterly positive in his identification of the young woman accompanying the constable on that fateful night. In fact, on later reflection he has determined that the woman you, yourself, presented was more likely to be the one he had first seen standing behind the officer." He paused to await Murdoch's response, who, sensing there was more to come, didn't say anything. Foon looked away and addressed the rest of his remarks to the wall behind Murdoch's shoulder. "In the interests of helping the police officers in their quest, my father is, however, able to offer some information concerning the other woman. The ladyship who appeared at the inquest and said she was betrothed to Mr. Wicken."

"Is he now? And what might that information consist of?"

"Her name is Mary Ann Trowbridge as she stated but her address is a deceit. She does in fact live on Sydenham Street. Her profession is of ill-repute."

"I see. How does your father come to have that information?"

Foon coughed politely but still spoke to Her Majesty's portrait. "This ladyship and my father had acquaintance at a previous time. Of an entirely chaste nature, of course."

It wasn't easy to read him through the thick dialect and the apparent lack of expression on his face, but there was a hint of resentment in his tone, a tightening of his lips.

"When was this chaste encounter?"

"A few months ago, I believe."

"Did he mention at what number on Sydenham Miss Trowbridge lives?"

"Yes. She resides at number three hundred and thirty-four. The house with a blue door."

Murdoch fiddled with his moustache. Foon was corroborating what Beulah had said. Apparently Miss Mary Ann was still active. It might make matters even harder for Mrs. Wicken and Isobel if this came out.

The Chinaman finally met his eyes. "Mr. Murdoch, would it be correct for my part to assume you will not need to mention my father? We are at the mercy..." His voice trailed off and

Murdoch realised what a serious thing it was for him to come to the station.

"Does he know you have brought this information to me?"

Foon looked at him and his expression this time was revealing. "Can I say that my father would no doubt have approved, but I have not yet had the occasion to inform him. I chose to encumber myself with this errand."

Murdoch held out his hand. "Thank you, Mr. Lee. You have performed your civic duty. I will follow up on this."

Foon shook hands somewhat hesitantly. His fingers were cool, slightly damp.

CHAPTER THIRTY-THREE

ALL THE CURTAINS WERE DRAWN AT THE HOUSE WITH the blue door. A cast-iron lantern was fastened on a bracket to the side of the porch. It was placed so that no direct light fell on the person who might be standing there. Cunning. Murdoch opened the gate, which screeched a warning, and walked up to the door. There was a heavy brass knocker he thought at first was carved in the shape of a lion's head. As he lifted the ring, however, he saw that the design was that of a woman's face with snakes writhing from her brow. He thumped hard.

Almost at once, the curtain across the windows to his right lifted slightly. He couldn't see who was looking out but he smiled pleasantly so as not to frighten them. After what seemed a long wait, the door opened, barely a crack, only sufficient for him to glimpse a tiny woman, soberly dressed and sharp featured.

"Yes?" She scowled at him.

He touched the brim of his hat politely. "I was wondering if I could speak to Miss Mary Ann Trowbridge. I understand she lives here."

"Who are you?"

Murdoch hesitated, not sure whether revealing his identity at this point would get the door closed in his face. He felt squeamish at the idea of pretending to be a customer, however.

"My name is Murdoch. I'm an acting detective at number four station. I'm pursuing an investigation and I would like to talk to Miss Trowbridge."

She didn't look impressed or alarmed. "What sort of investigation?"

"I'd prefer to discuss that with her."

"She doesn't live here anymore." She didn't relent from the frown.

"Where is she?"

"I don't know. I'm not the post office keeper."

The woman's hair was pulled up tightly into a knot at the top of her head, accentuating her rather prominent ears. What he could see of her dress was a drab brown. She made him think of an elf, but without the endearing qualities one usually associated with the fairy world. She also was a kindred spirit to Beulah.

"Is there anyone else I can speak to then?"

"No."

Fortunately, he was saved from more aggravation by somebody speaking from the hallway.

"Emily, you are letting in the worst draft. Either invite the gentleman in or close the door."

The woman addressed was obviously about to follow the second injunction but Murdoch quickly got his knee in the way. He pushed his way forward across the threshold.

A young woman was standing at the bottom of the stairs. She was full fleshed and her white diaphanous gown was cut to reveal a considerable amount of bosom and bare arm. Her abundant brown hair was loosely pinned, her lips and cheeks rouged. She was Murdoch's idea of a whore.

She smiled. If the doorkeeper was a bad-tempered elf, this young woman was a flower fairy. At least in the dim light. He touched his hat again.

"Excuse me, ma'am, for disturbing you, but I am a detective and I would like to come in and ask a few questions."

The smile vanished and she looked alarmed.

"I, er…" She glanced over her shoulder for help and yet another woman appeared. The hall was becoming crowded. She was older, statuesque in build, magnificently corseted into a pearl-grey silk gown. The ivory satin draping her bosom would have done credit to any mantelpiece. Her full chin was pushed into further roundness by the high lace collar. Exactly what he imagined a bawdy house mistress would look like.

"Emily, what is the trouble here?" She spoke with complete

authority and the gatekeeper stepped back a pace. The young woman also moved halfway up the stairs but stayed to watch.

Again Murdoch introduced himself. "I would appreciate some of your time, ma'am."

He saw her consider all of her choices, then she smiled. Her teeth were startlingly white, and faultless. He was reminded of Dr. Stevens's denture display case. She held out a mittened hand, leaning across Emily as if she were a piece of furniture.

"How do you do? I'm Mrs. Clara Doherty."

He took her hand, a little uncertain as to what was expected of him. She was wearing a large emerald ring on her index finger and the gesture was almost papal. He refrained from kissing it, however, and half-squeezed, half-shook the palm.

"Please come in. We can talk in my chambers." Her accent was quite English.

He wasn't sure how he was going to get past the recalcitrant servant without embarrassment to both of them, but Mrs. Doherty saved him.

"Emily, I'm sure Mr. Murdoch needs something warm. Bring us some Turkish coffee. Is that agreeable to you, sir?"

Murdoch nodded appreciatively. His search for Mary Ann Trowbridge was introducing him to some exotic culinary tastes.

"Give me your things," said the housekeeper and he obeyed, struggling in the confined space to divest himself of his sealskin coat. Finally he was free and she took the coat and hat and trotted off down the hall, where she dumped them on a tall oaken stand. The young woman, who had giggled prettily during this transaction, was still watching, but with a quick nod of the head from her mistress, she too left, ascending the stairs with a certain degree of melodrama and her dress lifted well above ankle height. The effect was marred, however, by her need to sneeze violently. She didn't let go of her skirt but sniffed back whatever snot she could.

"Mr. Murdoch?" Mrs. Doherty said.

He blushed, annoyed at himself for being distracted.

"This way." She pulled aside a red velvet portiere to the left, opened the door, and ushered him in. He immediately banged his shin against the corner of a low table that seemed to be placed directly in the doorway. Mrs. Doherty sailed ahead, navigating an astounding amount of furniture – lamp tables, plant stands laden with large potted ferns, purple plush armchairs. She took a seat on one of the couches by the fireplace and indicated he should sit across from her. The carpet was thick, fawn coloured, patterned with large pink and yellow roses. Mrs. Doherty glanced at his feet and he was aware that his boots were wet and he shifted like a schoolboy. He'd conducted many interviews in his career but he didn't remember feeling so ill-at-ease and clumsy. He didn't know if it was his own consciousness of his lack of sexual initiation or if Mrs. Doherty had perfected the art of keeping the male half of the population off balance.

"I know that Mary Ann Trowbridge lives here. I would like to talk to her."

His harsh tone apparently startled Clara, who had obviously been intent on keeping up pretences as long as she could. She frowned.

"I'm afraid she's moved out."

"When?"

"Yesterday, as a matter of fact. But I must insist you explain yourself, sir. Why do you want to speak to her?"

Her voice changed; the false English intonation dropped away.

"As you no doubt are aware, Miss Trowbridge testified recently at an inquest into the death of a young constable. The investigation is not complete and I would very much like to ask her some questions."

She chose to look affronted at his lack of manners.

They were interrupted by Emily, who without a knock or any other warning opened the door and entered the room. She was carrying a silver tray on which sat a silver coffeepot and two cups and saucers. They were delicate but normal size, unlike the ones at the Avison house.

"I've just took out some plum cake, shall I bring it in?" she asked Clara.

"No, this is quite adequate."

Murdoch would have dearly liked some plum cake, as his stomach had been growling for the last hour, but he had offended Clara by his lack of tact and she was punishing him. There was a stiff silence while Emily put down the tray on the sideboard, shoving aside a porcelain lamp that tinkled musically as the crystal droplets shook. She poured out some dark, thick liquid into the china cups and handed one to Clara, the other to Murdoch. Then she herself took a seat on the couch beside Mrs. Doherty, who immediately sipped avidly at her drink. Murdoch tried his. The brew smelled all right, but tasted so harsh and bitter he almost spat it out. He was aware Clara was watching him.

"Hm...hm."

Surprisingly she smiled her perfect smile. "I prepare the essence myself. I have heard there is none quite like it."

Murdoch nodded in acknowledgment, not sure how he was going to swallow the rest of the poisonous brew. He felt as if he had lost a layer of skin off his tongue.

"Horrible stuff," said Emily. "Burn a hole in your stomach."

Mrs. Doherty ignored her and he wondered again what the status of the bad-tempered elf was in this household. Not servant surely. She took too many liberties.

His hostess opened a drawer in one of the plant stands that was on her right. She took out a small silver flask, unscrewed the top, and held it out to him. "A little brandy, Mr. Murdoch. It is a very dull morning."

He wouldn't have broken the fragile truce even if he'd taken the pledge.

"Thank you, ma'am. A spot would go down well."

Emily snatched the flask from Clara's hand and poured a generous shot into his cup. She then added a much smaller amount to Mrs. Doherty's cup. Murdoch tasted the coffee again. The brandy definitely improved the flavour and he managed to gulp back most of it.

He heard the faint sound of a bell ringing from the rear of the house. Emily immediately stood up. "I'll leave you to your business," she said, and she gathered up the two cups, put them on the tea tray, and left. As soon as the door had closed, Mrs. Doherty bent over, fished beneath the skirt of the couch, and pulled out a wooden pail. She took off the lid.

"Would you care for a sweet?"

"No, thank you, ma'am."

She paused, scrutinised the contents of the pail, and selected a bright pink egg-shaped candy.

"Now, sir. You were saying?" asked Clara. The English inflection was back in place, slightly muffled by the crackling of her chewing. He decided to come in on a more oblique tack.

"Are you acquainted with Mr. Sam Lee, a Chinaman?"

She didn't speak until she'd finished off the candy egg. "No, I am not."

"He says he has been a visitor here."

"Is that so? Unfortunately, Mr. Murdoch, as all of my friends will tell you, I have a most appalling memory. In my capacity of music teacher, I see many people but I could not tell you who they are. If we were ever to meet on the street, I do not acknowledge them. I regret to say, I will probably forget you, yourself, tomorrow."

So that was going to be her line, was it?

"But you do remember Oliver Wicken? He was engaged to Miss Trowbridge."

"How extraordinary. But these days young women are so independent. They don't share their lives at all, not the way we used to when I was a girl."

Murdoch was certain she had never been young, that she had sprung fully dressed and bejewelled out of her father's head.

"You are saying he never came here to see her?"

"No, he did not."

"What is your relation to Miss Trowbridge?"

"She is my niece by marriage."

He leaned forward, trying to force her to look him in the eyes.

"Mrs. Doherty, at the inquest which is under the jurisdiction of Her Majesty, Queen Victoria, Miss Trowbridge produced a letter supposedly from her aunt. She named her as a Mrs. Avison. That good lady has informed me that they are not related and that, in fact, Miss Trowbridge was her maid some years ago. Her name then was Trotter. It seems that the poor girl was got in the family way and was dismissed."

"How unkind of her employer."

"Madam, I must remind you we are dealing with the law. This is very serious. It seems that your niece produced a document which was a forgery. She will be open to charges."

"I understand that."

Frustrated, Murdoch stood up, although there wasn't very far to move.

"You are saying, unequivocally, that you have no knowledge

of a constable named Oliver Wicken or any engagement that existed between him and Miss Mary Ann Trowbridge?"

She shrugged and delicately probed underneath her dentures to remove a fragment of icing. "I am saying that, with such a bad memory as I have, I am utterly unreliable as any sort of witness."

He knew he would not shake her. Even in such ridiculous lies she was imposing.

"Why did Miss Trowbridge leave your house?"

Again the shrug. "She was a little bored with Toronto. She has relatives in Montreal and it seemed more exciting to her, I presume. She rarely confided in me."

He returned to the couch, sat down, and took out his notebook.

"Where is she staying in Montreal?"

"Alas, Mr. Murdoch, I don't know. She never said."

He closed the notebook with a snap. "Was Miss Trowbridge at home on Monday evening?"

"Yes, I believe she was."

"All evening?"

He'd made a move she hadn't expected. She bought time by sifting through the candy pail.

"I cannot say for certain. I was rather unwell; I retired early."

A yellow egg was popped into her mouth. More crunching.

"Did you say good night to your niece?"

"Yes, of course."

"What time was that?"

"I cannot be precise."

"Just within an hour would help. Eight o'clock? Nine?"

She hesitated, trying to sort out the least compromising answer. "Perhaps closer to nine. As I say, she is an independent young woman. She must have slipped out, not wanting me to worry."

"Would you have forbidden her if you had known?"

"Of course. Which is why she was probably so cautious. I doubt anyone else would have seen her."

"In other words, nobody will deny or corroborate her statement?"

"I suppose you could put it that way."

She offered him the candy pail.

"Can I tempt you?"

"No, thank you." He waited for her attention. "Miss Trowbridge said under oath that she met with Wicken the night he died."

"Indeed!"

"But I have a witness who says he saw the constable in the company of a different woman at that exact time. His fiancée."

"Really? Another? Is he setting up to be a bigamist?"

"I don't think so. I believe he had only one, the young woman who met him on his beat. You see, according to my witness, Miss Trowbridge is a prostitute."

He'd wanted to shock her but she was ready.

"There are always people ready to smear a young woman's reputation."

"And yours then, ma'am. My witness says that you run a bawdy house here and that Mary Ann Trowbridge is one of your doxies."

She smiled; she was on safe ground here. She'd dealt with this before. "As I already said, I am a music teacher. I run a music academy for adult students. People are only too ready to gossip."

As if to validate her statement, a piano started up from somewhere in the house. The sound was execrable, out of tune and spasmodic.

She was as implacable as the stuffed couch she sat on. Murdoch sat forward.

"Mrs. Doherty. At this time I am not too interested in how you earn your living. I am more concerned with trying to find the truth about what happened to Oliver Wicken. Let me put it this way. I will give you until tomorrow evening to locate the current whereabouts of Miss Mary Ann Trowbridge. If I receive that information in good time, I will not proceed any further with the complaint we are going to receive about you and the music academy. Is that clear?"

For answer, she reached over and pulled at a bell rope that hung beside the fireplace.

"I will ask Emily to see you out."

He didn't move and they faced each other like two opponents across a chess board. She lowered her gaze first. "I'll think about what you have said, Mr. Murdoch. If I do obtain the information you need, I will send a messenger to the station."

"Number four, the northwest corner of Parliament Street and Wilton."

The door opened and the housekeeper came in carrying his sealskin coat and hat. He took them from her and headed for the door, negotiating his way around the chairs. Mrs. Doherty and Emily both watched him.

There was a lamp beside Nathaniel's bed, the wick turned low. The old man's face was dark with shadows, but there was a glisten of saliva dribbling from the corner of his mouth. His eyes were open. Jarius leaned over the bed, placing his hands on either side of Nathaniel's head as if he would embrace him. He stared into the unmoving eyes.

"I don't know if you can hear me or understand what I am saying but I don't care. Listen to this, Nathaniel. It is time you died. You should have gone years ago. You won't recover from this, don't even hope that you will. So it is time to make right some wrongs. You are going to make a new will."

The old man made grunting sounds in his throat and his eyelids flickered.

"Does that little fart mean you understand me? I dearly hope so. I want you to make your last journey knowing the truth. You can take it to hell with you because that is surely where you are going." Jarius picked up the cloth that was on the pillow and wiped away the dribble. Then he bent down until he was so close, it was almost a kiss.

"I hate you! You think I loved you but you fooled yourself. I have never for one moment felt any feelings toward you other than disgust. You destroyed my mother, my dear mother, as surely as if you had put a revolver to her temple. She wanted to die because her life here was unbearable."

He caught Nathaniel by the chin and jerked his head higher.

"You do understand. I can see that you do. You look shocked. I don't know why you should be. We reap what we sow. You are fond of proverbs, aren't you? *Spare the rod and spoil the child. Waste not, want not.* Lots of them, all impressed on my bare backside."

Nathaniel made a feeble attempt to move his head away but it was impossible. Gibb squeezed his chin even tighter. "Frank hates you too, but you probably know that. The surprise must be me."

He let go and stepped back, pulling aside the quilt. "You stupid, revolting old man. At your age, to think you could still stop your beak in some poor woman." With a tug, he lifted the nightshirt. "Look at you. A chicken gizzard has more life in it than that." He leaned over him again. "Listen to me good, Nathaniel. Your little jade was as light-heeled as they come. She wanted to hump with me from the moment she came in the house. And she did. She slipped between my sheets many a night when you were snoring. Oh, she is as willing a tit as I've ever had. She was spent over and over. Quite wore me out. I only told you the half of it."

It was all lies, of course. Peg had done no such thing. Except for the single desperate visit to his room, she had kept her distance. Jarius had enjoyed contemplating which course of action he would take. Tell the truth and make the old man face his mistake, or send him to eternity with a lie to make him squirm. The latter had seemed more likely to inflict pain.

The gurglings from Nathaniel's throat were louder. Jarius smiled. "Don't like to hear that, do you? She'd almost convinced you she was innocent, hadn't she? Well, take it to your grave, dear Stepfather. May it torment you for all eternity."

He reached inside his waistcoat and took out a folded sheet of paper. "This is your new will. I have written it out according to your instructions. I'll read it to you."

He opened the paper, shook it in mock seriousness. "*This is the last will and testament of Nathaniel Joseph Eakin Esquire of 295 Gerrard Street in the city of Toronto and the county of York. Being of sound mind...*Debatable, but never mind, I'm going to predate it. *I hereby bequeath my goods and chattels in the following manner. To my beloved children* – I call that a poetical conceit – *To my beloved children, Francis John Eakin and Augusta Louisa Curran, I leave the sum of one thousand dollars each.* Not what they are hoping for, of course. *To my wife, Margaret Eakin, I leave likewise the sum of one thousand dollars, to be used for her care and maintenance as long as it is necessary.* Don't worry, she won't need that much longer. *I leave to my faithful servant, Janet Cullie, the sum of two hundred dollars.* See how kind you are in your dotage, Nathaniel. Now here's the nub. *To my dearest stepson, Jarius Gibb, whom I have ever loved and been loved by as a son of my own flesh and* *blood*. That's good, isn't it? Another poetical conceit. *To Jarius, I hereby leave my estate and all money that does accrue from the same, my insurance policies, and savings bonds*. A goodly sum, Stepfather, thank you. Nobody would have suspected you had such a fine dowry. I welcome it, and as we both know, it is only fair and just that it go to me. Augusta has her own husband to take care of her, Frank would piss it away on whores and horses within a month, and dear Stepmother won't have any need. So there we are."

He had brought in his scribe's lap desk and he opened the lid, took out a pen, and dipped it in the inkwell. Then he lifted Nathaniel's flaccid hand and wrapped the fingers around the pen.

"Sign here."

Slowly, he drew the old man's signature on the paper. "Good, that will do nicely."

He blew on the ink to dry it, then replaced the paper in his pocket. "I know what you're thinking, Stepfather, but I have taken care of that. The date on the will is two days ago. Before you became incapacitated. How fortunate for us that you had the foresight to take care of your affairs. And I know Frank won't balk at getting one thousand dollars. That is better than a rope necklace."

He bent over and kissed Nathaniel on the cheek. "Good night, Stepfather. Sleep well."

He left, closing the door as softly as if he were leaving a nursery. Good. He was fairly certain the document was watertight, but just in case, there was one more thing to take care of. It was time some member of the family went to visit the unfortunate Mrs. Eakin.

CHAPTER THIRTY-FOUR

THE BRANDY MURDOCH HAD DRUNK AT THE BAWDY house was racing through his body, and there was a jauntiness in his step as he headed toward Queen Street to catch the streetcar.

When he took his seat, however, the false energy left him abruptly. The car clattered along, and before he knew it, his head drooped forward on his chest and he began to doze off.

"Sir! Sir!" The conductor was shaking his arm. "Here's your stop. The provincial asylum."

He was speaking in a hushed voice as if it were impolite to say the name out loud.

Murdoch scrambled to his feet, and conscious of the curious

gaze of the other passengers, he made his way to the front. The car slowed down and halted in front of the gates. He was the only one to get off.

He hadn't been here before and didn't know what to expect. However, at first sight the asylum appeared imposing and dignified rather than frightening, although he could see the windows were barred and there were sharp-looking railings on top of the surrounding wall. The building was long with two wings, each four stories high, and a higher central block. There was a cupola over the centre pediment that gave the building an ecclesiastical appearance, but which he'd heard actually housed a water tank. Although there was currently a lot of gossip about the bad air and need for repairs, originally the asylum had been designed with pride and care and it still showed through.

The tall iron gates were open and he walked in and along a winding path to the front doors. In the garden were two fine marble fountains, now turned off for the winter. Probably in summer the aspect was as pleasant as a public park.

He had telephoned the asylum earlier to see if it was all right for him to come, and the matron herself said she would meet him in the receiving area. He was relieved at that. As he entered the building, a uniformed doorman with impressive grey side-whiskers greeted him.

"Good day to you, sir. What is your business?"

"I am Acting Detective Murdoch. Miss Bastedo is expecting me."

"Ah, yes. Come this way, if you please."

He led Murdoch across the marble-tiled hall and up a flight of stairs. The place seemed deserted and Murdoch remarked on it.

"On a day like this we don't get many visitors," answered the doorman. "Pity really. Makes a change for the inmates to have some family company. They like variety same as everybody else."

At the top of the stairs was a wide corridor with windowed rooms opening onto it. A sign said FEMALE PATIENTS ON LEFT. MALE PATIENTS ON RIGHT. He glanced into one of the rooms on the right. A man, head bent to his chest, was seated between a woman of middle age, quite well dressed, and a younger woman. They must have been mother and daughter by the similarity of their posture, and they were staring straight ahead, not speaking or touching the man, each lost in her own misery.

In the centre of the corridor was the matron's office. It rather reminded him of the bridge on a ship. Windows on all sides gave her a view of the comings and goings in the reception rooms. She was writing at her desk but she looked up at their approach and came out at once to greet them.

"Mr. Murdoch, I'm Miss Bastedo. We can talk in my office. Thank you, Landry."

The doorman bowed slightly and left them. Must have been a butler in his earlier employment, thought Murdoch. The matron, however, had none of the polite airs of a lady of leisure. She held out her hand as straightforwardly as a man might and her grip was firm indeed.

"I have arranged to have Mrs. Eakin brought down. She will be here shortly."

She indicated he should sit down and she went behind her work table, a severely plain piece of mahogany that took up most of the space in the small office. She opened a cloth-bound daybook.

"I thought we should talk about her condition beforehand. This note was completed by the attendant this morning. I'll read it to you. 'Mrs. Eakin continues to show signs of improvement. She is keeping herself clean and is generally pleasant to the staff and other inmates. She has agreed to do some light sewing and has already completed two tray covers. She is eating well and taking her tonic without complaint.' Good."

She paused. "One of the reasons Mrs. Eakin was committed to the asylum was because she was convinced somebody was trying to poison her and she had not eaten in days."

"Who is it that Mrs. Eakin thinks is trying to kill her?"

Miss Bastedo frowned. "That is the terrible thing about illusional insanity, Mr. Murdoch. The poor lunatic fears and suspects everybody. She said at first her entire family was involved, then she suspected the doctor and even perhaps the staff here, although that suspicion seems to have disappeared."

"I suppose it is not entirely impossible – that somebody is trying to poison her, I mean."

Miss Bastedo smiled at him. "That is a detective talking, Mr. Murdoch, not a physician. Many of our inmates sound quite convincing because they are sincere in their own beliefs.

However, Mrs. Eakin's family has shown great concern for her well-being. It is a rather unusual situation, as perhaps you know. She is a good deal younger than Mr. Eakin, and his own children are her age or even older. I would think there might be some tension brought about by this inequality. Her only son by her first marriage died suddenly and it was after this that she began to show the first signs of instability."

So far, what the matron was saying concurred with what he'd heard from Mrs. Curran. "I understand the boy died from peritonitis."

"That is the case. Dr. Ferrier was in attendance. The poor boy's appendix burst and nothing could be done."

"I was told by her husband that she could also be suffering from what he called erotomania."

She glanced at him sharply. "Did he now?"

"What is that exactly?"

"The patient will approach men in a lascivious and seductive manner, or express an inordinate sexual appetite often manifesting in self-abuse."

She spoke as if she were quoting from a medical textbook. It was quite different from Eakin's, "She will lift her tail to any man."

"We understand there was some inappropriate behaviour toward a family member, but she has not shown any evidence of that here. There is a possibility of surgery," she continued. "Her doctor is recommending a hysterectomy but Dr. Clark likes to proceed conservatively. We will keep her under observation for at least a week or so longer."

"Not speaking as a detective, Miss Bastedo, but simply as a man, is such an operation effective?"

She wasn't happy about the question but she was an honest woman. "Some doctors believe so, others do not."

"And you?"

"On a conservative estimate from witnessing several female patients who have been so treated, I would say it is too early to tell. Dr. Clark himself is a great believer in fresh air, regular exercise, and a calm setting."

Murdoch was about to ask her about the efficacy of that particular treatment, but she consulted the large gold watch that hung from her belt. "I have to do my rounds shortly. You can interview her in this office. There is always an attendant within call. Please try not to overly excite the patient, Mr. Murdoch. She is just settling here." She sighed. "I should tell you that we received a telegram this morning from the senior member of the family. Apparently, Mrs. Eakin's husband has suffered a severe stroke. The doctor does not think he will recover. We have not told her yet. The daughter is planning to come in later today and we will tell her then. So, please, Mr. Murdoch, don't upset her. I suggest you make no comment if she does bring up any of her delusions."

Murdoch wondered what he should do or say if she displayed signs of erotomania, but he didn't quite know how to ask the matron about this.

She stood up and looked through the window. "Ha, here

they are."

He turned and could see one of the attendants leading in a patient. Small and thin, her hair in a long braid, Mrs. Eakin could have been taken for a child.

"Excuse me a moment, Mr. Murdoch," said the matron and she went out to meet them. She had a short conversation with the attendant that he couldn't hear. He realised the glass windows of the office were a double glaze, giving some measure of privacy. Mrs. Eakin was looking toward him the entire time. There was something about her expression he couldn't quite identify. An eagerness perhaps, again reminding him of a child. The matron brought her into the office. He got to his feet.

"Mrs. Eakin, this is Detective Murdoch. He is conducting a police investigation and he would like to ask you some questions. You don't need to be alarmed in any way. It is simply a matter of routine. Miss Shelby is outside if you need her. Sit here." She pulled forward a second cane chair. "I will return in one half an hour."

She smiled at Peg, patted her arm, and bustled off. Both Murdoch and the young woman remained standing until, hesitantly, she sat down in the chair the matron had indicated. Murdoch resumed his seat facing her.

She was watching his face anxiously and he had the impression that she was straining every sense to read his countenance. "I beg your pardon, sir. Miss Bastedo did say your name, but I did not quite register it."

Her speech was quite rapid but the words were enunciated

precisely, as if she were holding them tight in case they slipped away. Her accent was English.

"Murdoch. Acting Detective William Murdoch. I am pursuing a police inquiry and I hoped you might be able to help." He hesitated, searching for the right words. How could he ask her bluntly if she were awake and crying out the night Wicken died? She was sitting very still, watching him. She did not seem insane to him or in the least irrational but she was expecting something. Keeping his voice low and even, he continued.

"The matter concerns one of our constables."

Unexpectedly, her eyes lit up and she interrupted him. "Thank the Lord. He has spoken to you, then?"

"About what, ma'am?"

Murdoch had no idea why what he said was so distressing to her but the brightness on her face disappeared, replaced by something else, a look of such despair he wanted to reach over to her and make it go away. Her voice dropped so low he could hardly hear her.

"Why have you come to see me, Mr. Murdoch?"

There was no way around it. "Last week one of our officers, a Constable Wicken, was found dead in the vacant house on the corner of Gerrard and Parliament, close to your house. The circumstances of his death are not completely clear. I thought you might help me with my inquiry."

He thought she had been sitting still before but now she seemed to freeze.

"What do you mean, he was found dead?"

"He was shot. Apparently by his own hand."

"When?"

"Monday night last."

"Was this constable fair-haired?"

"Yes, with a full moustache. Constable, second-class, Oliver Wicken. He was on duty."

She moaned and began to rock slightly back and forth in the chair. Suddenly, he had an image of a young cougar that a sailor had brought into the village when he was a boy. For five cents you could go into the hot, musty tent and view the animal. For a further penny, the sailor handed you a stick and you could poke her through the bars of the cage and "make her roar". The expression in the eyes of Mrs. Eakin and the tormented animal were the same.

He glanced out of the window, wondering if he should send for the attendant.

"Can you tell me what is the matter, ma'am? Did you know the constable? Did you see him?"

She didn't answer and he tried to find a way to reach through her fear. "What did you mean just now when you asked if he had spoken to me?"

"They must have killed him after he left. So he wouldn't talk." She was whispering as if she had no energy left to propel her voice.

"I'm afraid I don't understand. Talk about what?"

Suddenly, she jumped up and rushed at him. She was so fierce he involuntarily put up his arm to shield himself, expecting a blow, but she stopped short and caught at the lapels of his coat.

"They murdered him..." Her voice was high-pitched and tight in her throat but her grip was strong.

Murdoch forced himself not to back off. Her pupils were dilated; there was some froth at the corner of her mouth. "Who did? Who are you referring to?"

Before she could answer, the door to the office opened and the attendant swept in.

"Now, now, Mrs. Eakin, calm yourself, please. Leave the gentleman alone."

She grabbed Peg by her wrists and snatched her away from Murdoch. Peg pulled back, trying to twist herself free.

"No, you've got to believe me..."

Shelby spun her around so she could pin Peg's arms to her sides but, as she did so, Peg arched her back and her head jerked upward. She caught the attendant under the chin, causing her to bite through her lower lip.

Another attendant rushed in, sized up the situation at once, and ran over to a cupboard near the door. She took out a restraining jacket.

"No!" shrieked Peg. "I'll be good. I swear. I won't fight." Miss Shelby ignored her and forced her arm into the sleeve of the jacket. Murdoch could only watch helplessly while the other attendant assisted, and within moments, Peg was fastened into the restraining jacket and the strings tied behind her back. She was crying now, tears she could not wipe away. "Please, please let me out. I'll be good, I promise. I'm sorry."

"Bit late for that, isn't it?" said Miss Shelby grimly. Her white bib was spattered with blood from her bitten lip and Murdoch pulled out his handkerchief and gave it to her. He felt dreadfully responsible and wished he had never attempted the interview.

"Come now, Mrs. Eakin," said the attendant and they began to lead her away. Peg looked at him beseechingly over her shoulder, just as she had that morning. "Help me," she said.

Augusta Curran seated herself in the reception room of the asylum. There was another woman visitor in the next room who was talking to an elderly inmate. Augusta tried not to look at them, although she glimpsed some affectionate exchange. Another woman, who was wearing the institutional uniform, was down on her knees by the door, scrubbing the floor. There was a sharp smell of carbolic in the air. Augusta hoped she wouldn't meet up with anybody she knew. She had hired a cab to bring her to the asylum, but she'd got him to let her off two blocks away so he wouldn't know her true destination. As a result, her cloak was wet and the hem of her skirts was muddy from dragging through puddles on the way. She sat, chilled and miserable, clutching her basket on her lap, staring ahead. She thought it was most unfair that she was the one sent to deliver the bad news, but Frank flatly refused and Jarius claimed the sight of him or Peter might inflame Peg's already unstable mind. "Do your duty, Aggie. There's a good girl. And why don't you make her one of those lemon cream tarts she likes? It might make the visit go a little easier."

Jarius had sent Cullie off on some silly errand, which meant Augusta had to do the baking herself, and although he kept her company and tried to soothe her with sweet words and compliments, she resented it.

She had been waiting about ten minutes when the door to the reception room opened and a woman in the severe blue dress of a nurse came in. She was dark-complexioned, strong-featured, and had an indisputable air of authority.

"Mrs. Curran, I'm Miss Bastedo, the matron."

"How do you do?"

The matron sat down in the chair next to her. "I regret to say that Mrs. Eakin has had a bad spell. She is still quite unsettled and we think it better if she doesn't have visitors at the moment."

"What sort of bad spell?"

"A police detective came to interview her. Unfortunately, I had no idea it would upset her as much as it did. She became quite hysterical and she has had to be restrained."

"I knew he shouldn't have come. He insisted. He doesn't realise how unstable she really is."

"I am of the opinion that any mention of death completely unnerves her," said Miss Bastedo. "It brings back her memories of the sad demise of her son. We must be very careful what we say to her and only discuss the most cheerful topics until she is much stronger. It will be wise not to mention the illness of Mr. Eakin at this point."

"Yes, of course."

"Perhaps you could come back in two or three days? We have every confidence she will be quite improved by then."

"Yes, yes, I will." Augusta was eager to make a good impression on the matron, as she had an uneasy feeling Miss Bastedo did not approve of her. She took a cake tin out of the basket.

"I brought her a lemon tart."

"You can leave it with me. I will make sure she gets it."

Augusta thanked her and took her leave. She was only too glad not to come face to face with Peg. The woman terrified her.

CHAPTER THIRTY-FIVE

IN PART BECAUSE DETECTIVE MURDOCH HAD DECLARED the blow to the attendant was an accident, Peg was released from the restraining jacket and had been given only a mild chloral sedative. She had fallen into a restless sleep where images surfaced and sank and surfaced again. Shelby dabbing at her cut lip, glaring at her; Mr. Murdoch in his long coat, brown eyes troubled as he talked to her; Miss Bastedo, grave-faced, telling her that Augusta had come to visit, although Peg was certain she hadn't actually seen her.

She could hear somebody moaning, *oh, oh,* but she couldn't sort out what the sound was. The cry was sharp and Peg sat up in bed.

Emma Foster was also sitting up. She was clutching at her stomach and it was she who was moaning. Suddenly, she vomited on the coverlet.

"Oh, oh," she groaned and another spasm gripped her. The vomitus was mixed with blood. She cried out and rolled onto her side, the violent momentum sending her crashing to the floor. Peg jumped out of bed and rushed over to her.

"Mrs. Foster! What is it?"

The old woman couldn't answer but lay thrashing in spasms that shook her entire body. A rush of watery diarrhoea came from her bowels. The smell coming from her was vile. Peg looked around desperately for something to use, and as she did so, she saw the cake tin sitting on the bedside cupboard. It was black with red and white flowers painted on it. The last time she had seen it was in the kitchen of the Eakin house. The knowledge stabbed at her chest, so that for a moment she could hardly breathe. Hurriedly, she pried off the lid. Inside was a cream tart, one large piece missing. Panting now, she bent over the sick woman.

"Mrs. Foster, did you eat the tart?"

But she knew she had. One of the attendants must have put the tin in Peg's cupboard and Emma had stolen it in order to help herself to some of the delicacy.

Both Miss Anderson and Mrs. Mallory were sitting up.

"One of you, bang on the door for Reid."

Miss Anderson started to sing 'We Will Gather by the River' and Mrs. Mallory pulled the quilt over her head, whimpering.

Peg got up and ran to the door. "Mrs. Reid! Help!"

She heard footsteps outside the door, saw the attendant's alarmed face in the window, and the key was turned in the lock and the door flung open.

"What on earth...?"

She saw Mrs. Foster's plight and rushed over to her. The floor was slippery with vomit and blood and she gasped as she trod in it.

"She's been poisoned," cried Peg. "She ate some of the tart. Look!"

Reid waved her hand. "Never mind that now. Go and fetch Miss Corley as fast as you can. She's in the sitting room."

"It was meant for me."

"Nonsense. Please do as I ask, Mrs. Eakin."

Suddenly, Peg felt as if her mind were functioning on its own with no connection to her body. The fragile sense of security that had been growing while she was tucked away in the asylum shattered like glass. She was safe nowhere. She had to escape.

She ran from the bedroom. Outside in the corridor, the wooden warning flag in the ceiling dropped down. Reid must have pressed the electric button in the room to signify there was trouble. Peg knew an attendant would be coming soon. The only place to go was the dining room directly across from her. She tried the door and it was unlocked. Quickly she slipped inside and leaned against the door, listening. The blood was pounding in her ears, making it difficult to hear anything else.

She tried to will herself to be calm. She didn't have a lot of time before Reid realised she hadn't done as she was told.

Even through the closed door she could hear Mrs. Foster's cries.

The dim room was unlit but she could see sufficiently to make her way over to the dumb waiter, which was in the far corner. She slid open the doors and pulled hard on the rope that brought up the lift. It was light and came up easily. For a moment, as she gazed into the small cupboard-like space, her resolve almost failed. *Now! Do it!* She climbed in, hoping desperately it would hold her weight. There was barely enough room but she curled up tightly, and except for a slight shaking, it held. She pulled the doors closed. As soon as she did, she was in pitch darkness. A wave of fear grabbed her but she forced herself to concentrate on the task. She caught hold of one of the ropes and began to pull hard, hand over hand. With a creak, the lift began to descend. There was another access on the second floor but she pulled steadily past it, her arms aching in the cramped space. *Just one more floor to go.* At last, with a bump, she reached the kitchen level. There was no handle on this side of the doors and she scrabbled at the wood, trying to open them, breaking her fingernails. She was sweating, fighting back panic. She couldn't get out. Could she breathe? Was there enough air? There was a sharp pain in her back from being bent over but there was no room to move around. Finally, the doors yielded sufficiently for her to make a space wide enough to get her fingers through. Then she wriggled her hand in and she could push the doors back.

She had gambled on the fact that there would be nobody working in the kitchen at this hour, but she didn't know for certain. However, the place was in darkness. Stiffly, she climbed out of the lift and immediately fell to the ground as her knees gave way. She knelt on the floor, listening. There were no sounds of racing footsteps, no voices calling an alarm. She stayed where she was, crouching like a dog. She had no idea where she would go even if she did manage to get out of here. She'd seen all too clearly the expression on the detective's face. He had been kind but she knew he thought her mad. She should have been calm, talked reasonably, but the shock of what he said was too much. She had been waiting for Wicken to come and she was sure he was investigating her accusations as he had promised. She sank even lower to the floor. She couldn't struggle any more. It was all too big for her. They were too powerful.

Probably only a minute had elapsed but she felt as if she had been lying here on the flagstones for a long time, her cheek pressed against the cold surface. *If only she had some proof. Something more than the word of a deranged woman against that of a respectable family.* Bitterness was like bile in her mouth. They were hypocrites all of them. Nathaniel, Frank the cheater, and especially Jarius Gibb. She sat upright. Jarius's diary! Shortly after Charley died, desperate, she had started to prowl around the house whenever she had the opportunity, looking for evidence. She already knew of the existence of Jarius's journal, because one evening she went to call him to dinner and accidentally interrupted him. He was writing in a ledger and he closed the book at once. "I do value my privacy, Stepmother." Words said in a tone so biting, she had shrunk away. After that, she'd observed him and his habits. She knew how often he left late at night, how furtive he was. Not too long ago, she had decided to risk going back to his room. She'd found the key under his chair and unlocked the scribe's lap desk. The ledger was his private diary and what she read there made her face burn with shame. He had recorded the events of her entry into the household and had not tempered his utter contempt for her or his dislike of her son.

She had the sense he wrote down everything that happened. Surely there would be something there that would help her, something revealing she could show to the detective who had come today.

She got to her feet, shivering. None of the ranges were lit, waiting for the early morning workers to rake them out and start them up. It was easier to see now, and frantic, she looked around for something she could use. She was barefoot and clad only in her nightgown. *Thank God*. Over by the door was a row of hooks for the kitchen workers to hang their coats and hats. There were two things, a pair of felt slippers and a rubber waterproof cloak. She thrust her cold feet into the slippers, which for that moment seemed as luxurious as anything she had ever worn. The waterproof was too long for her and dragged on the floor but she had to use it.

Hurry, hurry. She ran over to the window and pushed up the sash. There were no bars. Encumbered by the heavy waterproof, she climbed over the sill, dropping quickly to the ground, soft and muddy from the unrelenting rain. She almost lost one of the slippers in the dirt and she took them both off and stuffed them in the pockets of the waterproof. Barefoot, she ran toward the path that was just visible in front. She knew it must lead to the stables and the far end of the garden. Not too distant, there was a dark tree, leafless now but broad and thick-branched. She halted here, panting and gulping for air. From the shelter of the trunk she peeked toward the building. Lights were lit on the east wing where she'd come from, but so far, the rest of the institution was in darkness. They wouldn't want to sound an alarm yet. They'd search the ward first. She might have at least an hour before they realised she had got out. She set off again. She had to be careful as she approached the stable, because she knew there would be one or two men sleeping there, but she got past without incident and then she was at the wall. There was a low iron railing along the top, making the entire height about eight feet. She stopped again, breathing hard. *A ladder. There must be a ladder*. She turned around and jogtrotted to the shed that was at the edge of the vegetable garden. Against the wall she could see a tarpaulin that was draped over some long object. Almost crying with the hope of it, she fumbled with the rope that was tying down the end. Her fingers were clumsy with cold but she finally undid the knots and was able to pull back the covering. There were three ladders underneath and she tugged at the one uppermost. It was heavy and difficult to move but her fear gave her strength and it finally slid free. She dragged it to the wall, hoisted it up, and climbed up. The top rung reached just below the iron railings that surmounted the wall. Here she hesitated, looking down the steep drop. But she had only one option. She held onto the railing, hoisted herself up, and swung one leg over so that she was balanced astride on the narrow toehold. For a moment, she swayed dangerously but she clung to the railing and began to lower herself until she was dangling. She let go and landed awkwardly on the muddy ground. She had to wait a moment to get her breath, then she got to her feet and put on the slippers. They were useless for protection against the wet but they would make her less conspicuous. Head bent into the pelting rain, she set off as fast as she could manage around the outside of the wall toward Queen Street.

The macadam pavement was black with rain and the streetcar tracks glistened in the flickering gas lamps. There was not a soul abroad. She pulled up the collar of the waterproof to hide the fact that her hair was unpinned and began to walk away from the asylum. She could not allow herself to think what would happen if her plan didn't work – if Jarius was at home. Her teeth were chattering uncontrollably and her entire body was trembling. But she was out.

CHAPTER THIRTY-SIX

EDDY TINGLE BLEW HARD INTO HIS GLOVE, TRYING TO get some warm air onto his fingers. His thoughts about his passenger were becoming decidedly unchristian. She must have been gone for a good ten minutes by now. Had he been conned, he wondered? She didn't look too respectable but she spoke good, sounded like a lady's maid, which is what she said she was. She'd flagged him down on Queen Street, practically weeping with the relief of seeing him.

"I was afraid I would have to walk all the way home," she said. "I've been watching my sister, who is poorly from childbed, but I've got to get back. My mistress doesn't even know I'm out. I'll be dismissed without a letter if she finds out. But what could I do? She's my only sister and all alone except for the one girl to tend her."

This had poured out of her, unasked. Tingle hadn't really hesitated. He was going that way home anyway and another fare was gravy on the pie. Not that he completely believed her story. She was a bedraggled scrap of a girl without hat or gloves. More like she was visiting a sweetheart, had a quarrel, and ran out all of a huff.

"Where do you want to go?"

She gave him an address on Gerrard Street east of Parliament.

"It's extra charge after midnight, you know."

"That's all right."

"Hop in, then." And she had jumped right fast into his cab. He got a bit of a trot out of Blackie and they were up at Gerrard in about a half an hour. Just as they were approaching the number she had given him, she opened up the small trap in the roof of the cab.

"Cabbie, I've just discovered I have left my purse at my sister's house. You will have to wait while I go in and get some money. How much is it?"

"It's fare and a half after midnight and you were also in the second zone. That makes it three dollars."

He pulled up in front of the house. It was set back a bit from the road and looked quite grand. His passenger got out of the cab and scurried off, her long cloak dragging on the wet pavement.

She went through the gate, walked quickly down the path,

and disappeared around the side of the house to the servants' entrance. Tingle waited. He gave her enough time to get in, go to her room, which would be on the third floor, get her money, and come right out again. He tucked his hands between his knees under the beaver throw that covered him. He was ready for a kip. He didn't like night fares, but earlier, he'd picked up a gentleman outside the National Club on Bay Street and brought him out to the west end of the city. Swell of a fellow, evening dress, cloak, but full as a soldier. He'd delivered him to a house on Jane Street and left him to the not-so-tender mercies of his wife. Tipped well but it made for a long night. So this girl's fare had seemed a bit of a blessing. Until now. Blackie shifted restlessly. He wanted the comfort of his stable. Stiffly, Tingle climbed down from his perch. Time to investigate Miss Lady's Maid.

He followed in her footsteps through the gate and around to the back of the house. There was not a light to be seen, the household was asleep. He tried the back door but it was firmly locked. He banged hard on the door. "Anybody at home?" Bang, bang. "Hey, in there!"

He saw a light flare in a second-floor window and he knocked again. In a few minutes, the door opened and an elderly man in a flannel dressing robe appeared on the threshold.

"What the devil do you want at this time of night?"

"My fare, that's what. I just delivered a young woman to this house. She's your mistress's maid and she owes me three dollars."

The man leaned forward and ostentatiously sniffed the air.

"Are you drunk? You've come to the wrong house. There is no mistress, only my master and he doesn't have a maid; never did nor never will."

"What are you gabbling about? She said she lived here. She came through the gate. Said she had to get her money. She was watching her sister over on Queen Street and left her purse there."

"She's told you a nailer, my lad," said the butler with some satisfaction. "The only person of the female persuasion in this house is my wife, Mrs. Bezley, and she's in bed, until a few minutes ago enjoying a well-deserved sleep."

Tingle looked around him. "But where'd the girl go then?"

"She's done a bunk. Must have been trying to avoid ponying up."

He went to close the door but Tingle stopped him. "What about the neighbours? Anybody close by have a lady's maid?"

"Not on the right nor the left. The Eakins, two houses down, have a general servant that's a girl. What did your one look like?"

"A titch. Spoke good."

"That's not Cullie. She's a big lass. Anyway, no sense in me catching my death standing out here. You've been bamboozled and that's all there is to it. Good night to you."

He closed the door.

"Arse crawler," said Tingle. He was tempted to knock again but knew it wouldn't get him anywhere. The girl must have gone through the rear gate to the laneway at the rear of the house. She'd be well on her way now.

He made his way back to his cab. Sod it. He was going to make a report to the police. He hated his good nature being taken advantage of and this girl had gulled him. He climbed back into his seat, clucked to Blackie, and they turned around and headed off down Parliament Street toward the police station.

Peg had done exactly what Tingle surmised. She had run along the laneway, which ended at the Eakin property, two houses down. Here, she crouched by the gate, afraid to move until she was sure the cabbie wasn't going to pursue her. She could hear him banging on the door and, shortly after, the sound of voices. Silence, only the soft patter of the rain, until finally she heard the clop of the horse's hooves as the cab moved off. As soon as the sound had faded completely, she opened the gate and ran across the cobblestone yard to the rear door of the house. She was inside at once. The door opened into a small passageway at the end of which was the back staircase. She knew this was the way Jarius went when he left at night. For these excursions, he always wore a shabby overcoat of dark English tweed, quite unlike the formal black business coat of the day. She could barely make out the coat stand that was beside the door, and feeling almost more than seeing, she checked whether the tweed coat was there. It was not and the flood of relief she felt made her dizzy. Jarius had gone out.

Immediately, she took off the cumbersome waterproof and hung it on the stand. There was an old green cape belonging to Augusta on the peg and she slipped it on, burying her face in the soft fur trim and hugging herself tightly to feel the warmth of the flannel lining. She knelt down, searching for the boots that were usually kept on a rack beside the stand. There were four pairs, one of them her own, a pair of red kid. She kicked off the soaking felt slippers and pulled on the boots, not stopping to button them. The warmth from the cloak and the boots gave her renewed strength, and she hurried as quickly as she could up the stairs to the second floor. Here, she waited briefly but there was no sound in the house, nobody had been disturbed. Carefully, she pushed open the door that led onto the landing. There was a candle burning in the hall sconce and she could see another faint light shining beneath the door of Nathaniel's bedroom. Her heart lurched. Was he still awake? She stood still, listening. Faintly, she could hear his windy snores. He must have fallen asleep with the candle lit. She crossed the landing, pressed her ear against Jarius's door, and hearing nothing, she went inside.

The curtains were closed and the room was dark. She would have to risk lighting a lamp. Forced to move more slowly, she felt her way to the mantelpiece. Here she fumbled for the box of matches, found them, and struck one. Jarius's bed was made and tidy. The room smelled like him. She lit the lamp, turning the wick low, and crossed over to his chair where the key was hidden. For a moment she couldn't find it and almost panicked but there it was in the leather pouch. Rationally, she knew she had only been in the house a very short time, but her fear was mounting. She had to hurry.

The lap desk wouldn't open at first and she fiddled desperately with the key. Finally, the lock yielded. The ledger was inside and she took it out, hugging it to her chest as if it were a beloved infant.

She had already started toward the door when she heard a footstep on the landing outside.

The door opened and Augusta stood on the threshold. Her hand flew to her mouth in shock. "You! What are you doing here? Where's Jarius?"

For a second, Peg stared at her, transfixed.

"Why are you wearing my cloak?" gasped Augusta.

Peg bolted. Augusta was taken off guard and the force of Peg's charge sent her reeling to the floor, so that she dropped her candlestick. Peg raced back the way she had come, out to the yard. She was heading for the front gate when she saw a man coming along the street. A tall man in policeman's uniform. She swerved away and ran toward the barn, the only place she could hide.

Murdoch was dreaming he was in his childhood bed. Somehow, his mother had got herself locked out and she was knocking on the door. *Wake up, Will! Wake up, I've got to get your father's tea going.* He was trying to open his eyes, straining to see, but the room was too dark. He had to get up and let her in before his father came home, but he couldn't move.

Suddenly, he was awake and in the present. Somebody was knocking at the front door.

"Mr. Murdoch! Mr. Murdoch!"

He jumped out of bed, grabbed his trousers from the chair, and pulled them on over his nightshirt.

Again the persistent knocking and the half-hissed call. "Mr. Murdoch!"

He opened his bedroom door and at the same time, Enid Jones appeared on the landing. She was holding a night candle and, in spite of the circumstances, his heart jumped at the sight of her. She was dressed in a red flannel robe and her hair was down, loosely braided. She looked still soft from sleep.

"What is it? Who's knocking?" she asked.

"I'm just going to see."

He hadn't waited to strike a light and she held out her candlestick.

"Take my candle."

He did so and hurried down to the hall. Mrs. Kitchen emerged from her room.

"Who on earth is here at this time of night?"

Murdoch opened the door.

A tall, gangly young constable was standing outside, his dark lantern pointed downward.

He touched his forefinger to the rim of his helmet in greeting.

"Constable Dewhurst here. Sorry to disturb you at this hour, sir, but Sergeant Hales thought I should fetch you. We've heard from the asylum that the lunatic lady, Mrs. Eakin, has managed to run away. It seems like she's come back to her home."

"Good heavens! Have you got her?"

"Not yet, sir. The matron had only just telephoned. She wanted us to go and notify the family. The sergeant was about to send me over there when up shows a cabbie, name of Tingle." The constable's words were rapid and excited. The drama was spicing up an otherwise dull evening. "He came in right at that moment to report on a fare who had gammoned him. We knew from his description it was one and the same woman. He'd picked her up on Queen Street not far from the loony bin and dropped her off right near the house."

"Did the matron give you any more information?"

"Only that the woman has lost all of her slates. One of the inmates was taken ill in the night, gastritis probably, and Mrs. Eakin took it as a sign she was being poisoned. The matron thinks she could be dangerous. To herself or to her family. Sergeant Hales decided to go over himself. He wanted me to get you, seeing as you know the woman in question."

Murdoch was already dragging on his boots.

"Here!" Mrs. Kitchen, who had heard all this, handed him his hat and coat. "Please be careful." He gave a quick glance up the stairs and saw Enid was still standing on the landing, watching. The concern on her face warmed him.

"The cabbie's waiting outside," said Dewhurst. "We requisitioned him."

He led the way.

"Did you telephone the asylum?" Murdoch asked.

"Yes, sir. They're sending somebody right over."

Like the constable, Eddy Tingle was finding this quite an

adventure, and he grinned at Murdoch as he climbed into the cab.

"Where to, sir?"

"Corner of Gerrard Street and Parliament. Can you get that nag of yours to at least trot?"

"Looks are deceiving. He can run like a thoroughbred when he needs to."

"This is one such occasion then."

Dewhurst got onto the step, holding on to the door handle.

"Scorch it, Tingle," said Murdoch. The cabbie cracked his whip over the horse's head and they lunged into a gallop up the sleeping street.

CHAPTER THIRTY-SEVEN

SERGEANT HALES PUSHED OPEN THE GATE AND WENT into the yard. As he did so, a man and a woman in night clothes appeared at the rear door. He recognised Peter Curran from the inquest. When the woman saw him, she cried out.

"Officer! There's a madwoman on the loose. Did you see her?"

"Yes, ma'am, I believe I did. She has just run into the barn."

Mrs. Curran gasped. "My brother is in there. You must do something. She'll kill him."

She made as if to run to the barn and Hales caught her arm. "Hold on, ma'am."

At that moment, another man came through the gate behind him. It was Jarius Gibb. He went over to the woman.

372

"Aggie, what on earth is the matter?"

"She was here, Jarius. In your room. She knocked me down."

Mrs. Curran was almost incoherent with fear. Her husband made no move to comfort her and stood like a simpleton, staring at the sergeant.

"You mean Stepmother?"

"Yes. Oh, she's quite mad, Jarius. She was standing there, in my cloak. She ran at me."

Gibb turned to Hales.

"Officer, what is going on?"

"We've had a telephone message from the asylum, sir. Apparently, Mrs. Eakin has run away."

Augusta interrupted him. "Oh, what a shock she gave me. I thought it was you in there, Jarius. She stole your ledger. Why would she want that? And my cloak?"

"Hush. Peter, is Frank in the barn?"

"S'far as I know. He went over there at midnight, same as usual."

"She'll kill him," repeated Augusta.

"Ma'am, try to calm yourself," Hales interceded. "She's a slip of a woman and he's a strong grown man. I doubt she'll hurt him."

"We can't count on that, Sergeant," said Gibb. "My brother often drinks himself into a stupor. There are many knives available to her if she wants to do him harm. And a shotgun. It is still there by the door, isn't it, Peter?"

Curran nodded. "S'far as I know."

Gibb turned to Hales. "I'm going to go into the barn,

Sergeant. We must do something."

"Begging your pardon, sir, but I don't think that's a good idea. A doctor is on his way from the asylum. He's better to handle it."

"She's terrified of doctors. He will only make her more disturbed. I'm the one who should talk to her. She knows me and trusts me. Isn't that so, Aggie?"

"I, er...oh, Jarius."

"I'll come in with you then, sir."

"No, Officer. Absolutely not. She fears police even more than she does doctors. You can wait outside. If I need help, don't worry, I'll call for you."

"Jarius, what about Frank?"

"Be quiet, Aggie. I'm doing what I can." His voice was sharper, impatient. "Officer, may I take your lantern?"

Rather reluctantly, Hales handed over the light. Leaving the Currans at the door, he and Jarius hurried across the wet cobblestones to the barn. When they reached the doors, Gibb stopped, cocking his head to listen. There was no sound from inside except the soft snicker of a horse, no indication that the sleeping Frank had awoken. With a nod at the sergeant, Gibb swung open the door and stepped inside.

Hales heard the sound of the bolt being closed behind him.

Jarius waited for a moment, swinging the lantern high above him.

"Peg? Stepmother? Don't be afraid. You can come out." Gibb

wanted to make his voice pleasant and reassuring, but even to his own ears, it didn't sound that way. He walked over to the corner of the barn where Frank slept in a partitioned-off room.

His brother was fast asleep, face-down on his bed and fully dressed. The room reeked of stale beer. Jarius shook him awake, hard and roughly.

"Get up, you sot. Come on, rouse yourself."

Frank blinked into the light. "What's the matter?"

"Our dear stepmother has escaped from the loony bin. She's hiding in the barn somewhere."

"In here?" Frank was still stupid with drink. "How'd she get in here?"

"Never mind that now. Get on your feet. There's a police sergeant outside. I said I'd bring her out nice and quiet."

He put the lantern on a wooden box beside the bed, took off his overcoat and threw it across the bed, and went over to a shelf where Frank kept his shotgun.

"Where are the shells?"

"Why? What are you doing?"

"You know damn well what I'm doing. I'm going to save your arse for the second time. Where are the shells?"

"In that box."

Jarius snapped a cartridge into the shotgun. "You look in the stalls. I'll do the tack room."

"Jarius –"

Gibb swung the gun around so that it was pointing at Frank. "It will be quite easy to have two accidents instead of one. She aimed this gun at you, you struggled, boom. You both die."

"My God, are you going to shoot her?"

"Do I have a choice?"

"She doesn't really know what happened."

"It's got nothing to do with that."

"What then?"

"For Christ's sake, Frank. Why are you always so stupid? You know the woman is in the way."

He tucked the gun under his arm and gave his brother a shove. "Come on. We don't have much time."

Peg saw Jarius come into the barn and heard him call to her. She had run into the carriage room and was crouched in the far corner. He must have gone to wake up Frank because she heard voices. She crept to the edge of the partition that separated the carriage room from the rest of the barn. She peered through a crack in the wall. Frank and Jarius emerged and Jarius was carrying a shotgun.

She ran for it.

In front of her was the ladder to the loft and she was up it in a flash.

"There she is," Jarius shouted.

Peg tripped and sprawled on the floor. She knew Jarius must be close behind her and she turned, cowering against one of the hay bales. She heard somebody climbing up the ladder and Jarius's head and shoulders appeared.

"Please don't shoot me. You can have the book. I won't tell

anybody." But she wasn't even sure she had spoken out loud. If she had, the words made no impact on Jarius. He turned sideways, leaning against the ladder so he could take aim. There was a terrifying deliberation in his movements, as if he were on a duck shoot and preparing himself.

Frank came up close behind him holding a lantern.

Peg tried to press herself into a bale. Jarius raised the gun and she heard the click as he cocked the trigger. She covered her head with her arms.

CHAPTER THIRTY-EIGHT

TINGLE HAD JUST PULLED UP HIS CAB IN FRONT OF THE Eakin house when Murdoch heard the boom of the shotgun. Sergeant Hales was standing in front of the barn doors with Augusta Curran and her husband. He saw Murdoch.

"This way," he shouted, and he started to run along the side of the stable. Murdoch raced after him, Constable Dewhurst at his heels. They were at the side door in a moment and into the barn. Horses were screaming and the air was thick with the smell of cordite. Frank Eakin was lying on his back close to the wood stove. Jarius Gibb was almost on top of him. Somebody was moaning dreadful sounds of pain. As Hales and Murdoch approached, Jarius tried to get to his feet but his leg splayed out at an angle, and with a cry he fell forward.

Murdoch felt rather than heard the whisper from above his head. Peg was looking down at him.

"Here. I'm up here," she said.

Peg was not injured but in such a state of terror, she was unable to move. Murdoch hoisted her over his shoulder, fireman style, and carried her out of the stable, while Hales tended to Gibb and Frank. He sent in Tingle to calm the horses and ordered the Currans into the house under the supervision of Constable Dewhurst. Augusta was weeping ceaselessly, her antagonism for her brother apparently forgotten. Her husband said nothing.

Peg was seated on the bench in the yard and it took several minutes before she could stop a kind of dry, choking sob. She kept repeating that she had dropped Jarius's diary in the barn, and it was only Murdoch's firm insistence that he would get it that calmed her down. He chafed her hands and kept talking to her and finally she was able to tell him what had happened. When she tried to relate how Jarius had stood and aimed the shotgun at her as if he were at a hunt, she broke down again, and Murdoch had to wait patiently for her to recover. She was not entirely sure what had happened next, but she had the impression Frank had grabbed Jarius to stop him and they had both fallen from the ladder.

At that point, Dr. Clark arrived with two burly attendants from the asylum. Fortunately, he was a sensible man and, when he saw how Peg was with Murdoch, he made no attempt to interfere. Murdoch accepted responsibility for his charge and the doctor hurried into the barn to tend to the injured men.

As soon as Tingle had dealt with the horses, Murdoch persuaded Peg to go with the cabbie to the Kitchens'. He made her promise she wouldn't try to run away, but he knew she wouldn't. She was still dreadfully shaken, but as far as he could see, she was quite sane. He knew that Mrs. Kitchen would take very good care of her, and if Peg needed anything, it was some motherly attention.

That done, he went into the barn.

Dr. Clark had just finished administering morphine to Jarius Gibb, who was propped up against the knee of one of the attendants. Sergeant Hales had brought out more lamps and the scene was bathed in light.

"Mr. Gibb has dislocated his hip," said Clark when he saw Murdoch. "We can take him to the hospital, momentarily."

"And Mr. Eakin?"

"He cannot be moved. I fear his back is broken."

Frank looked dreadful. His skin was ashen and his face was already swollen, his eyelids puffed to the point of closure.

Murdoch crouched down beside Jarius Gibb. "Can I ask you what happened, sir?"

Jarius scowled. "I've already talked to the sergeant. I'm not going to repeat it."

"As you wish." Murdoch stood up and pointedly beckoned

to Hales, drawing him off to one side, out of earshot.

"According to Mrs. Eakin, she was up there in the loft and Gibb climbed up and was about to shoot her. She thinks Frank saved her bacon by grabbing Gibb and they both fell. What did he tell you?"

"He said she was the one with the gun and that he climbed the ladder so that he could talk to her. Persuade her to come down. She aimed at him. He managed to wrest the gun from her, in the process of which it went off. Then he lost his balance and fell off the ladder, taking his brother with him."

"Is that likely, do you think?"

"Dog droppings, if you ask me. Look over there." Hales pointed to a low, splintered hole in the next partition. "I'd say the gun hit the floor and discharged and I'll wager it was him was holding it when he fell. He intended to kill the woman, I'm sure of it. When I got to the house, I saw Mrs. Eakin running into the barn. Just then Gibb came up. Said he could look after it." Hales frowned in chagrin. "I shouldn't have allowed him to go in but he was soft as shite. I've seen lunatics before and I know how riled up they get at the sight of a uniform. So I let him. But as soon as I heard him throw the bolt behind him, I knew something wasn't right. I'd have gone after him at once but Mrs. Curran got all hysterical and I had her to deal with."

"There's some kind of diary of Gibb's that Mrs. Eakin came to get. She thinks she dropped it in here somewhere. I'll have a look."

Gibb had been watching them while they talked, but he was

distracted by the pain of Dr. Clark trying to immobilize his hip with a makeshift splint. Murdoch crossed in front of him and went into the tack room. A black official-looking ledger was lying in the straw. He picked it up, opened it, and glanced at the contents. He saw enough to think that Peg was right. Holding the journal, Murdoch returned to the doctor. One of the attendants had laid out the stretcher and they were about to lift Gibb onto it. He scowled at Murdoch.

"That's mine, I believe. May I have it?"

"I'm afraid not, sir. Police property until this case is cleared up."

"What case is that, officer? You saw her. She's insane. Can't help herself. I won't press charges."

"That's not what I'm referring to," said Murdoch, and he tapped the ledger. "Let's see if this gives us some answers."

"Lie down, if you please, Mr. Gibb," said one of the attendants. "We're going to lift you."

Reluctantly, Jarius obeyed and the two men heaved him onto the stretcher. Although the movement must have caused him great pain, Jarius only grunted. He had expressed no concern for Frank, or Peg for that matter. He lay looking up at the ceiling but Murdoch knew there had been fear in his eyes and he was glad of it. The attendants carried him out to the ambulance.

Murdoch turned his attention back to Frank Eakin.

"How is he?" he asked the doctor.

Clark shook his head for an answer. He took a small bottle

out of his bag, unscrewed the top, and held the vial underneath the injured man's nose. Frank opened his eyes, flinching. He couldn't move his head away from the stinging smell.

"Can you get this weight off my chest?" he whispered. "I can't breathe."

Dr. Clark shook his head. "Mr. Eakin, there is no weight, you have been injured."

"I can't seem to move my arms. Have you tied them down?"

"No, we haven't, sir."

A look of panic came into Frank's eyes. "I must have hit my back on the stove. Jarius was on top of me."

He licked his lips. "Could I have a drink of water?"

"I'll get him some," said Hales.

"Am I dying?" Frank asked; his breath was raspy.

Dr. Clark was a decent man and his voice was gentle when he spoke. "If you wish I can send for a minister immediately."

"No. I thought I heard that detective. Is he here?"

"Yes, I am." Murdoch knelt down, leaning in close.

"I must talk. Tell you the truth."

Hales had returned with a dipper and a bowl of water. The doctor dribbled water on Frank's mouth. Murdoch bent over again.

"Mr. Eakin, Frank. Do you want to make an official statement?"

"Yes, I do."

"I am sorry to say this, but for such a statement to be valid in a court of law, I must ask you if you are fully aware of your present circumstances."

Frank blinked. "That I'm a goner, you mean?"

"Yes. That you realise you are dying and that what you are about to say is a true statement on your deathbed."

"I understand."

"Sergeant Hales, please write down what Mr. Eakin says."

Murdoch waited for the sergeant to take out his notebook and pencil. "According to Mr. Gibb, Mrs. Eakin had the shotgun and was about to fire at him. Is this true?"

Anger seemed to give Frank strength. "No! Other way around. He's a cold-hearted devil as ever walked on the earth and I ain't going to die without him getting his comeuppance, same as me...He was going to shoot her. I stopped him. I couldn't bear seeing her like that. Scared witless. I suppose you might say, the worm turned. He didn't expect that. I grabbed his legs and we fell." He managed to meet Murdoch's eyes. "Is he hurt?"

"Yes. He's smashed his hip."

"Too bad it wasn't worse. And her?"

"She's in good hands. She will be all right...Frank, Mrs. Eakin says Constable Wicken came to the house the night he died..."

"Yes, he did. We'd all had a terrible barney the night before. Cooked up by Jarius, of course, and she was barricaded in the upstairs room. She'd called to Wicken from the window and he'd come to see what was the matter."

He gagged and yellowish spittle ran from his mouth. Clark

took a sponge from his bag and wiped him.

"Joke was, the three of us, Peter, him, and me, had been having a talk about what to do with her. Jarius kept saying as how she was a loony and should be shut away. Didn't seem like that to me but he was pushing it. Then in comes the frog and she starts to tell him she was being poisoned…"

"Was she?"

"Not by me, nor Aggie, I'm sure. But I wouldn't put anything past Jarius. He hated her from the first moment she come here. Thinks she's going to whelp and cut him out."

His breath was so harsh Murdoch wondered if he could keep on. He glanced at the doctor, who put his fingers on Eakin's pulse. He used the vial of ammonia again and Frank continued, his words faster, as if he were trying to outrace death.

"I could tell the frog was swayed. Told her he'd look into it. Then she said other things. About me and the horses. Fiddling. He said he wanted to see the stables. He insisted and we all marched over. When he examined the horses, he got his dander up, 'cos he saw what I'd been doing. Him and me had words. It made me hot. I hit him. Hard. Side of the head…He fell down."

Tears started to spill from under the swollen eyelids. "He was just a young fella…I didn't mean to do for him…Will I go to hell for it?"

Murdoch winced. "Our Father is ever merciful."

He wasn't sure if Eakin even heard him but his urgency pushed him on. "Jarius took over as always. 'You've killed him, Frank,' he says, but did I? Did I? He looked bad, white as paint, but maybe he wasn't dead, I don't know. Jarius made us wrap him in a blanket and carry him over to the empty house. He had the key. 'I'm doing this for your sake,' he said, and he got Peter to prop him up. Then he shot him with his own revolver...he aimed it at the place where I'd hit him. He said it would be easy to make it look like suicide. He wrote the note and he got one of his whores to testify. The one you saw."

His voice died away and Dr. Clark wagged his finger at Murdoch, warning him.

Murdoch took the sponge, wetted it, and bathed Frank's face and mouth. That seemed to revive him sufficiently for him to continue.

"That bastard shouldn't get away with it. He kept saying he was protecting me but he wasn't. It meant he had me good then, forever. He made me put the revolver in between the officer's legs. He thought it was a good joke. I'm sorry I did that; it wasn't right."

Again the tears spilled out and down his cheeks.

"Funny, ain't it. Papa's up there not able to move and I'm down here in the same way. Like father, like son. What a laugh. Well, at least he can say I'm following in his footsteps now."

There was a sob that couldn't get past the paralysed walls of his chest and Murdoch could see the light was leaving his eyes.

"I think you've got all you need, Mr. Murdoch," said the doctor. "His sister should pay her last respects now."

Murdoch stood up. He wanted to say something to the dying man, something that might ease his soul into the next life, but even as he looked down at him, he saw it was too late.

Dr. Clark put the back of his hand under Frank's nose to check for breath. After a moment, he shook his head.

"He's gone."

He lifted Frank's wrist to confirm there was no pulse and then laid the dead man's hands across his chest. "Sergeant, will you be so good as to bring in Mrs. Curran and her husband."

Hales put away his notebook and with a nod at Murdoch he left. The patrol sergeant was a man vindicated.

"We'll need to send for a coroner and gather a jury," continued Clark.

"I'll see to that."

There was no more to be done here, and Murdoch thought Augusta was owed some privacy in her grief. He'd wait until she had finished before he spoke to Peter Curran.

He went outside to the yard. After the brightness of the barn, the night seemed dark. He took a deep breath, shivering in the cold air. A horse whinnied softly nearby. Tingle had brought two of the horses out of the barn and they were tethered to the hitching post. Murdoch went over to them. The mare turned her head to look at him and he patted her neck.

"What a piece of work we men are, my girl. But you don't care, do you? You just want some mash and a warm stall." She tossed her head.

As for him, he felt sick at heart with the awareness of how much pain human beings were capable of inflicting on each other. He, too, wanted to get home as soon as he could. He needed some evidence that love could have as much power as hatred.

ACKNOWLEDGEMENTS

THERE ARE ALWAYS SO MANY PEOPLE WHO HELP ALONG the way in the process of writing a novel. I would like to thank Cindy Boht, who helped me with the horse material; Dr. Jerome Chen, who was my generous resource person; my brilliant dentist, Dr. Stephen Forgacs, who checked my facts and also sent me over to the archives of the Toronto School of Dentistry, where Dr. Dale and I literally climbed over old dentist chairs so she could show me the wonderful collection of dentures; and Larry and Eileen Richard, who kindly instructed me in the finer points of Catholicism. I am grateful that Dr. Geoffery Rheaume made his doctoral thesis on the history of the Queen Street Mental Health Facility available. It gave me invaluable material. I am particularly indebted to Cheryl Freedman, who read the book in manuscript form and gave me extremely helpful feedback. As always, I am grateful to my agent, Teresa Chris, and my editor, Ruth Cavin, for their patience and perspicacity.

ABOUT THE AUTHOR

MAUREEN JENNINGS WAS BORN IN BIRMINGHAM, England and emigrated to Canada at the age of seventeen. Jennings's first novel in the Detective Murdoch series, *Except the Dying*, was published to rave reviews and shortlisted for both the Arthur Ellis and the Anthony first novel awards. The influential Drood Review picked *Poor Tom Is Cold* as one of its favourite mysteries of 2001. *Let Loose the Dogs* was shortlisted for the 2004 Anthony Award for best historical mystery. *Night's Child* was shortlisted for the Arthur Ellis Award, the Bruce Alexander Historical Mystery Award, the Barry Award, and the Macavity Historical Mystery Award. And *A Journeyman to Grief* was nominated for the Arthur Ellis Award. Three of the

Detective Murdoch novels have been adapted for television, and a Granada International television series, *The Murdoch Mysteries*, based on the characters from the novels, is entering its fifth season on CityTV and Alibi. She lives in Toronto, Canada, with her husband Iden Ford.

Let Loose the Dogs

Detective Murdoch's life and work become tragically entwined when his sister, who long ago fled to a convent to escape their abusive father, is on her deathbed. Meanwhile, the same father has been charged with murder and calls on his estranged son to prove his innocence. But, knowing his father as he does, what is Murdoch to believe?

AVAILABLE APRIL 2012

Night's Child

After thirteen-year-old Agnes Fisher faints at school, her teacher is shocked to discover in the girl's desk two stereoscopic photographs. One is of a dead baby in its cradle and the other is of Agnes in a lewd pose. When Agnes fails to attend school the next day, her teacher takes the photographs to the police. Murdoch, furious at the sexual exploitation of such a young girl, resolves to find the photographer – and to put him behind bars.

AVAILABLE MAY 2012

TITANBOOKS.COM

Vices of My Blood

The Reverend Charles Howard sat in judgment on the poor, assessing their applications for the workhouse. But now he is dead, stabbed and brutally beaten in his office. Has some poor beggar he turned down taken his vengeance? Murdoch's investigation takes him into the world of the destitute who had nowhere to turn when they knocked on the Reverend Howard's door.

AVAILABLE JUNE 2012

A Journeyman to Grief

In 1858, a young woman on her honeymoon is abducted, taken across the border to the US and sold into slavery. Thirty-eight years later, the owner of one of Toronto's livery stables has been found dead, horsewhipped and hung from his wrists in his tack room. The investigation endangers Murdoch's own life – and reveals how harms committed in the past can erupt fatally in the present.

AVAILABLE JULY 2012

TITANBOOKS.COM

WEARING NOTHING BUT HIS HELMET, HIS SWORD, HIS WAISTCOAT AND A TEENY-WEENY PAIR OF HAIRY SWIMMING TRUNKS, HICCUP HORRENDOUS HADDOCK THE THIRD HAS BEEN KIDNAPPED!

But his outfit is the least of his worries. Trapped on *The American Dream II* with his friends Fishlegs and Camicazi, Hiccup must **ESCAPE** the barbarian Norbert the Nutjob, and somehow dodge the cruel **POLAR-SERPENTS** in the icy waters below.

If **ONLY** Hiccup hadn't promised to help the Wanderer slaves on board escape too! **HOW** will Hiccup save himself, his friends and a hundred and twenty-two Wanderers off a ship **WITHOUT** their terrifying captors noticing?

You don't **HAVE** to read the Hiccup books in order.
But if you want to, this is the right order:

1. How to Train your Dragon
2. How to be a Pirate
3. How to speak Dragonese
4. How to Cheat a Dragon's Curse
5. How to Twist a Dragon's Tale
6. A Hero's Guide to Deadly Dragons
7. How to Ride a Dragon's Storm
8. How to Break a Dragon's Heart
9. How to Steal a Dragon's Sword
10. How to Seize a Dragon's Jewel
11. How to Betray a Dragon's Hero
12. How to Fight a Dragon's Fury

JOIN HICCUP ON HIS QUEST
(although he doesn't quite realise he is on one yet...)

THE PROPHECY OF
THE KING'S LOST THINGS

'The Dragontime is coming
And only a King can save you now.
The King shall be the
Champion of Champions.

You shall know the King
By the King's Lost Things.
A fang-free dragon, my second-best sword,
My Roman shield,
An arrow-from-the-land-that-does-not-exist,
The heart's stone, the key-that-opens-all-locks,
The ticking-thing, the Throne, the Crown.

And last and best of all the ten,
The Dragon Jewel shall save all men.'

Hiccup

Toothless

Stormfly

Snotlout

BIG
BOOBIED
BERTHA

MadGUTS
the
Murderous

Gumboil,
Madguts'
assisstant

NORBERT
the
Nutjob

Fishlegs
(Hiccup's
best
friend)

Camicazi

Stoick the
Last →

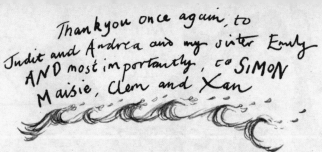

Thank you once again, to
Judit and Andrea and my sister Emily
AND most importantly, to SIMON
Maisie, Clem and Xan

HODDER CHILDREN'S BOOKS

First published in Great Britain in 2008 by Hodder & Stoughton
This edition published in 2017 by Hodder & Stoughton

5 7 9 10 8 6 4

SPECIAL EDITION

Text and illustrations copyright © 2008 Cressida Cowell

The moral rights of the author have been asserted.

A CIP catalogue record for this book is available from the British Library.

ISBN: 978-1-444-93982-8

Cover design by Jennifer Stephenson
Background cover illustration by Christopher Gibbs

Printed and bound by Clays Ltd, St Ives Plc

The paper and board used in this book are made from wood from
responsible sources.

MIX
From responsible
sources
FSC® C104740
FSC
www.fsc.org

Hodder Children's Books
An imprint of Hachette Children's Group, Part of Hodder & Stoughton
Carmelite House, 50 Victoria Embankment, London EC4Y 0DZ
An Hachette UK Company
www.hachette.co.uk

To Stephen, Joanna, Chloe,
Nell and Michael, my American
cousins, with love

Great
West
Ocean

How to Ride a
Dragon's Storm

written and illustrated by
CRESSIDA COWELL

Hodder
Children's
Books

A division of Hachette Children's Group

THE LAND OF THE POLARSERRENTS

the
Murderous

Mountains
↓

the
little
isle
of Berk

THE BARBARIC
ARCHIPELAGO

~ CONTENTS ~

THE CURSE OF BEARCUB'S GRANDMOTHER

A long time ago, a small boy was dreaming.

He was dreaming of running through the beautiful white wilderness that was his childhood home, running and running through snow so perfect you could hardly bear to touch it. But suddenly his legs grew tired and so heavy he could hardly move them… something was pulling him back… what was it?

And then he awoke and opened his eyes, and he was about as far from home as he could possibly be, lying in the darkness below the decks of a great ship.

The boy was called Bearcub. He belonged to a people called the Northern Wanderers, and he had not always been a slave. Only two weeks before, he had had miles and miles of glorious icy desert to play in, as free as the polar bears and seals that his people harpooned to eat and keep them warm.

But then the Vikings came.

They had surprised the Wanderers by attacking while they were asleep, dragging them aboard their Viking ships and taking them away from their

15

homeland. Since that time, Bearcub had not had a proper meal, and worse still for a boy full of fidgets and used to running, he hadn't taken more than a couple of steps.

Bearcub's father had been out on a hunting party when the Vikings struck so he had not been captured.

'Please father,' Bearcub whispered into the blackness. 'Save me, father...'

'HA!' rasped the doom-filled furious voice of Bearcub's scary Grandmother, who was lying chained beside him. 'Your father cannot rescue you, for he does not know where you are. And the gods must have forgotten us, to let this happen. Vikings are vermin, every single one of them,' she spat into the darkness. 'I never met a good one. Murderous, wicked, evil people... oh, if I had one here I would do such things. I could eat their livers I really could. I am Cursing this voyage and everyone aboard this ship...'

'WE are aboard this ship,' Bearcub pointed out. 'Do not Curse this voyage or you may be Dooming us, too.'

'YOU do not contradict your elders and betters,' cried his Grandmother sternly (it is not pleasant to be chained to a cursing Grandmother). 'We are DOOMED already... No, the only thing left for us

16

now is to Hate, and to Curse...'

And so Bearcub's Grandmother had ALL of the
Wanderers Hating, and Cursing, and wanting to eat
people's livers, baying out their fury in the rocking
darkness below the decks of the ship.

'YOU BETTER WATCH YOUR STEP UP THERE!'
screamed Bearcub's Grandmother, howling up at the
ceiling like a wolf. 'IF ONE OF YOU MISSES YOUR
FOOTING AND FALLS DOWN THAT HATCH, I'M
TELLING YOU, WE'LL TEAR YOU APART!'

Only Bearcub was quiet, and in the blackness no
one could see the tears slowly rolling down his cheeks,
which was lucky, because Wanderers have the hearts of
polar bears and they do not cry.

And inside his head he repeated over and over
again, 'Please, father,
please, help me... please,
gods, please, please, help
me... please... *anybody...*
if you're listening...
help me... help me...
help me...'

help
me...

tick
tock
tick
tock

1. A PROPER VIKING SWIMMING RACE

One chilly spring day in the Barbaric Archipelago, Hiccup Horrendous Haddock the Third, the Hope and Heir to the Tribe of the Hairy Hooligans, was standing miserably on the West Beach of the Murderous Mountains with absolutely nothing on but his helmet, his sword, his waistcoat, and a teeny weeny pair of hairy swimming trunks.

The Murderous Mountains were not the kind of place you wanted to visit at the best of times. They gave Hiccup the shivers. Tall, cruel-looking, dizzyingly high peaks that were home to some unspeakably dangerous dragons and mutant wolves, not to mention the Murderous Tribe, the fiercest and most ruthless Vikings in the uncivilised world.

The Murderous Tribe did not often receive visitors. Perhaps it was their uncomfortable habit of sacrificing unwelcome intruders to the Sky Dragons at the point of Mount Murderous that kept people at bay.

But on this occasion, Madguts the Murderous had taken it into his head to be hospitable, and to invite two of the other Tribes, the Hooligans and the Bog-Burglars, over to his island for a jolly little

19

Inter-Tribal Friendly Swimming Race.

It was a traditional *Viking* Swimming Race, and the Vikings were a little bit crazy, so they were going swimming with their weapons on: swords, axes, daggers, that sort of thing.

It did not seem to have occurred to them that this would make them less floaty.

So there they were, the entire Warrior populations of the Murderous, Hooligan and Bog-Burglar Tribes, hopping up and down on the uncomfortable shingle beach, trying to pretend they

weren't freezing their horns off, with the mutant
wolves howling cheeringly up in the mountains above.

There was a strong easterly wind that brought
goose-bumps to Hiccup's skinny, freckled arms, and
whisked off helmets, cloaks and swords, and sent
them bowling briskly down the beach. Hiccup's tiny
hunting-dragon, Toothless, was having difficulty
flying without being blown away.

Toothless
was a particularly
small Common-
or-Garden dragon
with large,
innocent greengage eyes.

'Toothless w-w-wouldn't go swimming today if Toothless was you,' he advised Hiccup. 'Is very ch-ch-chilly in there, Toothless has been in already and it nearly froze Toothless's wings off.'

'Yes, thank you, Toothless,' said Hiccup. (Hiccup was one of the very few Vikings, before or since, who could speak Dragonese, the language in which the dragons speak to each other.) 'Very helpful, I'll bear that in mind.'

Gobber the Belch, the teacher in charge of the Pirate Training Programme on Berk, had stripped down to his smalls, and was breathing in the gale as if it were the loveliest of summer breezes. 'Lovely swimming weather!' he roared delightedly, beating his chest with his fist like a great red-headed gorilla. 'Gather

T-t-t-othless want to go H-home... Is ch-chilly.

round and stand to attention,
boys, and I'll explain the Rules
of the Race...'

The twelve boys stood
before their teacher in a
shivering line.

Toothless was in a big grump

'Now boys!' boomed Gobber.
'A Proper Viking Swimming Race is not like
those pathetic little competitions they carry out on the
mainland. It is a test of your ENDURANCE, your
STRENGTH and your SUICIDAL BRAVERY...'

'Oh brother,' moaned Hiccup's best friend
Fishlegs, who was the only boy on the Programme who
was even worse than Hiccup at all the Viking activities.
He had legs as limp as two strings of spaghetti, and he
couldn't swim. 'I don't like the sound of this...'

'In a proper Viking Swimming Race,' continued
Gobber, 'the winner is the person who is LAST.'

There were gasps of surprise, and 'oh sir, please
sir, that can't be right, sir,' from the line of boys.

'In which case,' sneered Snotface Snotlout,
a great bullying brute of a boy whose muscly arms
were covered entirely in skeleton tattoos, 'Hiccup the
Useless will win, no problem. *He's* always the last
at everything...'

23

Hiccup stood on one leg, tried to smile, and fell over in the sand.

'*Aha*,' grinned Gobber, his beard bristling with keenness. He laid one finger to his nose. 'But think carefully about this, boys… we all set out from the beach and start swimming, and from then on it's a game of Chicken. Who can swim out the furthest, the longest, into the deepest ocean, and still return? Many are the Warriors over the centuries who in their pride have misjudged the swim BACK, and who have drowned as a consequence…'

'Oh yippee…' moaned Fishlegs.

'But on the plus side, anyone who drowns in the course of a Swimming Race will automatically go straight to Valhalla,' smiled Gobber, in the manner of someone giving everybody a great big birthday present.

'Ooooooooooooh,'
exclaimed the boys in a
pleased way.

'MAD,' groaned Fishlegs,
swaying in the wind like a
small skinny tree about to
snap. 'We are the only
sane people in a Tribe
of total LOONIES.'

Fishlegs

'Any questions?' roared Gobber.

Hiccup put up his hand. 'A small point, sir. Won't we freeze to death in about five minutes?'

'Don't be a softy!' roared Gobber. 'The Blubberwing fat you have rubbed all over you SHOULD keep you warm enough to prevent actual DEATH... but it's all part of the game, of course. Can you use your skill and judgement to stay out long enough to win the Race... but not SO LONG that you freeze to death?'

Gobber walked up and down the line of boys inspecting them before they went out to join the competition. 'Very smart, Snotlout... Chin up, Tufnutt Junior... Haven't you forgotten something, Clueless?'

'I've got my sword, sir,' said Clueless.

'You do have your sword,' admitted Gobber, 'but you DO NOT have your swimming costume. Put it on quick, boy... I don't think that Thor will be welcoming you into Valhalla in the altogether. It really doesn't bear thinking about...'

He moved along the line until he stopped dead in front of Fishlegs. 'WHAT,' roared Gobber in an awful voice, 'WHAT in Thor's name are THESE?'

'Armbands, sir,' replied Fishlegs, looking straight ahead.

26

'Fishlegs can't swim, sir,' offered Hiccup in defence of his best friend. 'So we made him these out of a couple of pig bladders. Otherwise he sinks like a stone.'

'Like a stone,' repeated Fishlegs helpfully.

'Oh for Woden's sake,' blustered Gobber, 'what are the Murderous Tribe going to think if they catch sight of THOSE? I'll lend you my cloak, Fishlegs, and you can drape it over them, and let's just hope nobody notices. Thor give me strength…

Luckily, the Hooligan boys were very sensitive about these things…

HA! HA! HA! HA! HA!

'Now, has everybody got their hunting-dragon?' bellowed Gobber.

The boys had brought their hunting-dragons. They were huddled on the beach, their wings over their heads, shielding themselves from the rain.

'Your hunting-dragon can fly over your head as you swim. It makes you easier to spot from the beach, and they can maybe fight off any predators... sharks, Darkbreathers, that sort of thing... OK, you can fall out now and get ready, and I'll see you at the start line in about five minutes.'

The boys began their last-minute preparations, chattering excitedly.

'Hi there, LOSERS,' sneered Snotlout, a tall, mean boy with nostrils so large you could stick a cucumber up them (Toothless had actually DONE this once) and the repellent beginnings of a moustache sprouting on his upper lip like a little hairy caterpillar. 'I hope ickle baby Hiccup has been practising his doggy-paddle then...'

He gave Hiccup a big shove that sent him sprawling in the sand.

'Her her her...' snorted Dogsbreath the Duhbrain, Snotlout's equally unpleasant sidekick. Dogsbreath looked rather like a gorilla in goggles who had been over-doing it with the doughnuts.

'Very funny, Snotlout,' replied Hiccup, spitting sand out of his mouth.

'You guys are normally so good at coming in last…' sneered Snotlout. 'In fact this may be your only opportunity ever to come in FIRST, for once… Just try and at least go out of your depth, won't you, before you crawl back to the beach like the pathetic cowardly little plankton you are? You don't want to embarrass us PROPER Hooligans more than you actually have to… Nice armbands, Fishlegs, by the way…'

And Dogsbreath took the pot of slimy green Blubberwing goo Fishlegs was holding in his hands and poured it over Fishlegs's head, before strolling off with Snotlout, who had a rather basic sense of humour, and was laughing so hard he could barely walk.

'I hope a Darkbreather gets him,' said Fishlegs gloomily, taking off his glasses and trying to rub off the Blubberwing fat

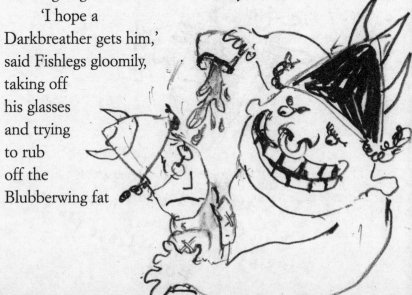

with the edge of his swimmers, but only succeeding in smearing it all over the glass so that they were impossible to see through.

'It would just spit him out again,' replied Hiccup even more gloomily, trying to rub the sand off himself, but completely failing because the Blubberwing fat was so sticky. 'I bet he tastes horrible.'

PAAAAA-AARAAAP!

A musician from the Murderous Tribe sounded the horn to summon the competitors to gather for the beginning of the Swimming Race...

The Blubberwing goo had so attached itself to the glass that it was like looking through a dense pea-green FOG

2. MAY THE FATTEST (AND LEAST STUPID) MAN (OR WOMAN) WIN

Hiccup's father and grandfather came over to the boys to wish them luck.

Hiccup's father, Stoick the Vast, O Hear His Name and Tremble, Ugh, Ugh, was the Chief of the Hairy Hooligan Tribe. He was built in the traditional Viking mould, six-and-a-half-feet high, belly like a battleship, eyebrows blowing in the breeze like a couple of large hamsters doing cartwheels. He was horribly hearty, and full of the joys of spring.

'Fabulous day for a Swimming Race!' he roared happily.

'I'm not sure I agree with you,' wheezed Old Wrinkly, Hiccup's grandfather, who was one of the Judges in the competition. He was a wrinkled old oyster of a man, whose ancient back had been blown into a hoop by ninety years of Archipelago gales. His long tangly white beard trailed behind him, picking up shells and seaweed as it dragged in the sand.

Old Wrinkly had been trying to persuade Stoick not to take part in the Race.

'I have been looking into the Future and the Omens are not good,' whispered the old man.

'NONSENSE!' pooh-poohed Stoick the Vast. 'Everyone knows you're hopeless at looking into the Future, Old Wrinkly. Now, *I'm* obviously going to win this Race,' said Stoick, who didn't do modesty, 'but, Hiccup, I would like YOU to beat Snotface Snotlout and that sort of thing...'

Snotface Snotlout was Hiccup's cousin. He was a good foot-and-a-half taller than Hiccup, incredibly muscly and tough, and better at Hiccup at practically everything. Hiccup had no chance of beating him in a Swimming Race.

But Stoick often didn't notice things like that.

Stoick gave Hiccup a kindly biff on the shoulder. 'I KNOW you can do it, son!' he said enthusiastically. 'You may be small, but you're wiry! And your legs might be just a trifle on the skinny side, but you've got the old Horrendous Haddock *fight* in those knobbly knees! All you have to remember, lad,' said Stoick, taking Hiccup by the shoulders and looking into his eyes, 'is *one thing*. Repeat after me: KEEP KICKING!'

'Keep kicking,' said Hiccup slowly.

'LOUDER!' bellowed Stoick, punching the air.

'KEEP KICKING!' shouted Hiccup, punching the air too.

'That's the spirit!' beamed Stoick. 'I know you'll make me proud, so don't let me down, now!' And he marched off, beaming happily.

Both Old Wrinkly and Hiccup sighed as they watched Stoick bustling off.

'He's a good lad Stoick, really,' wheezed Old Wrinkly, 'but he never EVER listens.'

'No,' agreed Hiccup sadly, 'he doesn't. I haven't got a HOPE of beating Snotlout.'

Old Wrinkly turned his bright, razor-shell-sharp eyes on his grandson. 'We'll see,' said Old Wrinkly. 'Now, this is very important, Hiccup. *Have you got your ticking-thing?*'

'Yes,' answered Hiccup, surprised.

The ticking-thing was a strange round object, with a front that was hard and transparent, like ice. Behind it were all these rune numbers set in different circles, and at least seven arrows, all different colours.

Hiccup had discovered many uses for the ticking-thing. One arrow seemed to tell the time. Another always pointed north, which was extremely useful if you were lost. And since it was quite a changeable day, with the prospect of this strong easterly wind blowing you off course, Hiccup thought it might be handy on this occasion. The ticking-thing was waterproof, too.

Hiccup's only worry was that he was going to LOSE it, so he had attached it to his wrist with a long piece of rope, and then tucked it into his waistcoat pocket.

'Excellent!' said Old Wrinkly. 'Hand it to me, for a moment...'

Hiccup took the ticking-thing out from his pocket. Old Wrinkly opened the back of it and began to fiddle with some of the little buttons inside.

'Now, Hiccup,' said Old Wrinkly, 'I haven't got time to explain, but you have to return to this beach within THREE MONTHS, FIVE DAYS AND SIX HOURS, do you understand me?'

'THREE MONTHS, FIVE DAYS, AND SIX HOURS?' gasped Hiccup. 'What ARE you talking about? I'm not going to last more than *fifteen* minutes out there!'

'I've set the alarm for you,' said Old

Hiccup's ticking thing.

tick tock tick tock tick tock tick tock tick tock tick

Wrinkly, putting the ticking-thing back into Hiccup's waistcoat pocket. 'When you have less than six hours left, it will start to tick louder. And if the alarm goes off, well, then you will know you are too late... DON'T BE LATE now, Hiccup, will you? I'm counting on you, boy...'

And Old Wrinkly hurried off to the Judges' Table, with Hiccup staring after him with his mouth open. 'Mad as a banana,' said Hiccup.

All the competitors were crowded at the start line drawn in the sand twenty metres from the sea, chatting with each other.

Big-Boobied Bertha, the Chief of the Bog-Burglar Tribe, was slapping Blubberwing fat on to her arms, her gigantic boobies flapping so buoyantly and joyously in the wind that it looked as if any second they might carry her up into the sky like a couple of hot air balloons.

Bertha had a foghorn voice with the kind of carrying quality that could be heard several islands away. She was telling everyone within a two-mile radius that SHE was Bertha the Unsinkable, the Archipelago Swimming Champion, and that everybody else might as well go home right now.

Bertha
the
Unsinkable

The Murderous Tribe were passing their swords and axes and spears and hammers from hand to hand in a thoughtful fashion. They reminded Hiccup uncomfortably of a load of hairy cannibals waiting for their dinner.

Madguts the Murderous, the head of the Murderous Tribe, stood with his arm muscles rippling menacingly. Even with a brisk wind blowing, he was reeking like a three-week-old seal corpse. He was a stinking seven-foot giant with unattractive blue-black skull tattoos covering his cheek-bones.

One of the most terrifying things about Madguts was that he never spoke. Nobody quite knew why. Some say he lost his tongue wrestling a Stormdragon with his bare hands. Others said that it was merely a nasty cold caught when a small baby. Who knew the reason, but he had never been known to do more than grunt. His repulsive assistant Gumboil, an unpleasant little pimple of a man, did all the speaking for him.

There were three Judges, one of whom was Hiccup's grandfather, Old Wrinkly, whose job was to mark the timing of the race.

The Chief Judge, a sad, unbelievably wrinkly little Bashem-Oik, cleared his throat and announced in a high quivery voice:

The Judge's Hut

'O Hear Ye, Vikings of the Tribes of the Archipelago! He who is the last to return back to this beach from the moment I blow this trumpet shall be declared the Last Man Back. He must be able to Swear, according to ancient tradition, that he "did not seek aid by Float or Boat". And as a prize for this contest he may make a single demand of the other two Chieftains. Do you Chieftains swear that you will agree to this demand?'

'We swear,' swore Bertha, Stoick and Madguts the Murderous.

Camicazi, Big-Boobied Bertha's tiny tangle-haired daughter, trotted over to wish Hiccup luck. One of the best Burglars in the Archipelago, Camicazi wasn't afraid of anything or anybody.

'Lovely day for a swim, isn't it?' she said cheerily. 'I can't wait to get in the water.'

Around Camicazi's legs curled a beautiful Mood-dragon called the Stormfly. A Mood-dragon, as its name suggests, is a chameleon that changes colour according to its mood, and this particular Mood-dragon was unusual because it not only spoke Dragonese, but also NORSE, the language of the humans.

"hello less" Toothless drawled Stormfly

'Hello, Toothless,' drawled the Stormfly, batting her beautiful long eyelashes at him.

Toothless turned bright red.

He had a bit of a crush on the Stormfly and immediately he began to show off, turning cartwheels in the air and blowing complicated smoke rings that went down the wrong way and gave him a coughing fit.

Toothless turned bright red. He had a bit of a crush on the Stormfly.

As they were standing there, Snotlout sneaked up behind them and whisked Gobber's cloak from off poor Fishlegs's shoulders, revealing the armbands for everybody to see.

'Whoops!' grinned Snotlout. 'Silly me!'

'HA HA HA HA HA!' roared the crowd, pointing at Fishlegs and jumping up and down in joy. 'THERE'S A HOOLIGAN OVER HERE WHO'S WEARING *ARMBANDS!*'

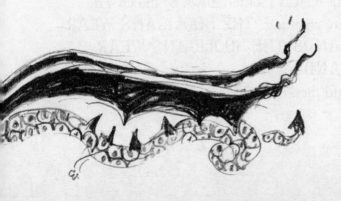

'These aren't armbands!' shouted Hiccup, desperately trying to save the situation. 'They're *weapons*! Inflatable shoulder armour! Very strange and deadly!'

Stoick the Vast blushed purple and swelled up with anger and irritation. That ridiculous fish-legged boy was bringing dishonour on to the Hooligan Tribe.

'Isn't that your SON, Stoick, standing next to the little loser?' grinned Gumboil.

Hiccup was quite a funny sight himself. Covered in shingly sand from head to toe, he resembled nothing so much as a skinny little breadcrumbed kipper ready for the pan.

Stoick tried to stop himself from thinking, *Why does Hiccup always have to make such a spectacle of himself? Why can't he be friends with somebody suitably violent and normal? And why is he covered head to foot in sand?* before yelling loudly and loyally: 'My son is right! The weird little Warrior is wearing the latest in inflatable defence-wear!'

But he was shouted down by the crowd, who were chanting: 'THE HOOLIGANS WEAR ARMBANDS! THE HOOLIGANS WEAR ARMBANDS!'

And then to Stoick's intense relief:

PPPPPPPAAAAAAAAAARRRRRP! went the
horn to announce the start of the race, and the Viking
Warriors forgot about teasing the Hooligans, and the
crowd went wild as the Viking Warriors stampeded
through the wind and into the water like a herd of
runaway buffalo, plaits flying, bellies wobbling.

'GO, BOG-BURGLARS GO!'

'UP THE MURDEROUS!'

'HOOLIGANS HURRAH!'

Snotlout sprinted through the shallows, flexing
his muscles and waving to the crowd, before making a
fancy swallow dive into the slightly deeper water and
setting off in a horribly efficient crawl.

Stoick tried hard to control his temper, and keep
the disappointment out of his voice as he walked over
to Hiccup and reproved his son sternly, 'You are a
Warrior-in-Training now, Hiccup, and this is NOT the
moment to be playing in the sand.'

'But I'm not!' protested
Hiccup. 'I'm just covered
in sand because...
because...'

... but Stoick
had already stalked
off.

HA! HA! HA! HA!

'Oh, jumping jellyfish!' exclaimed
Fishlegs, in a wriggle of anxiety. 'I can't see a THING
through these glasses now!'

The Blubberwing goo Snotlout had poured over
Fishlegs's head had so attached itself to
the glass that it was indeed like trying
to peer through a dense pea-green
fog. Poor Fishlegs staggered forward,
in completely the OPPOSITE
direction to the ocean.

'Hang on,' grinned Camicazi,
'isn't the sea the other way?'

'Fishlegs!' hissed Hiccup
anxiously. 'You're going
the wrong way!'

The
crowd was
divided
between cheering on the
Warriors and laughing at the
sight of the only three who hadn't set
off yet, which were Hiccup, Fishlegs and Camicazi.

Fishlegs was running increasingly fast in
completely the opposite direction to the ocean,

Ooooh...
where am
I going?

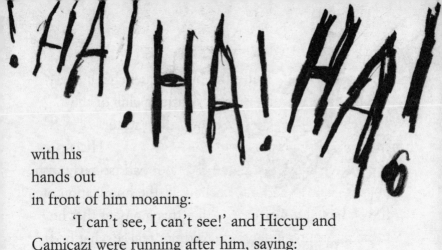

with his
hands out
in front of him moaning:

'I can't see, I can't see!' and Hiccup and
Camicazi were running after him, saying:
'It's this way, Fishlegs, this way!'

So: 'HA HA HA HA HA!' yelled the watching
crowd, parting to let poor blind Fishlegs blunder on
up the beach.

Eventually Hiccup caught up with Fishlegs,
who tripped over somebody's discarded trousers,
and with the help of Camicazi he managed to
steer his friend back
in the direction of
the ocean.

And such was
Hiccup's embarrassment
at the whole situation,
that he was almost
RELIEVED to

this is so
embarrassing

enter the breath-quenching, chest-
burning chill of the
water.

Hiccup
was so busy with
the humiliation of
this moment that he
did not realise what had
happened to his father and
Big-Boobied Bertha.

What had happened was this. Stoick the Vast,
Big-Boobied Bertha and Madguts the Murderous
swaggered out into the surf in a more leisurely way.
All three of them were certain they would win. Stoick
forgot about his disappointment with his son as he
remembered something amusing.

'Tell you what, Bertha,' whispered Stoick, giving
Bertha a friendly poke on the shoulder, 'let's agree,
whichever of us wins, we teach that Madguts a lesson.
We'll get him to row across the Sullen Sea in a
bathtub, with his underpants on his head!'

Big-Boobied Bertha roared with laughter until
the tears ran down her hairy cheeks. 'For once in your
life, Stoick, you old warthog,' she bellowed, 'you've
had a good idea! It's a plan, then…'

When they were just entering the water, Madguts grunted at Gumboil, his eye alight with sneakiness, and Gumboil said craftily, 'Madguts can't help but notice that you're wearing that old-fashioned **BLUBBERWING FAT**... it doesn't keep out the cold half as well as the Deepest Purple Fleshfang Oil that Madguts is wearing... you put this on and you're never cold again. Lasts until next winter.'

'Oh Toenail Clippings of Thor!' exclaimed Bertha, staring down at her luminous green body in disappointment. 'I thought I'd got the very latest thing!'

Madguts the Murderous

HATE

HATE

Gumboil

tee-hee

Stoick gazed at Madguts's glowing violet chest in admiration and envy. Madguts was so warm under his coating of Deepest Purple Fleshfang Oil that a light steam was rising off his tattooed chest and blowing away in the wind.

'Madguts wants this to be a fair fight,' smiled Gumboil silkily. 'Why don't you try some of his stuff, to make it all equal? We've left the pot just behind you at the edge of the water... we didn't need it any more, because just the one application is sufficient...'

'Well that's mighty kind of you, Madguts!' beamed Stoick. 'But hang on, can we go back there? Hasn't the Race already started?'

Gumboil waved the thought away with one airy hand. 'Oh no...' he reassured the Chieftains cheerily, 'no, the Race doesn't start until you actually start swimming... didn't you know that?'

Stoick and Big-Boobied Bertha said, 'Ah, yes, of course,' and nodded wisely as if they had really known that all along, and turned back and waded out of the sea to pick up the little black pot of Fleshfang Oil that was sitting just a couple of feet beyond the water's edge...

'That trickster Madguts!' said Stoick, tut-tutting in mild disgust. 'Fair fight indeed! *Look!* There's absolutely nothing left!'

Nor there was, just the merest little purple smear at the very bottom, hardly enough to cover Stoick's big toe.

It turned out that that wasn't the *only* thing Madguts had been tricky about.

Stoick looked up as he realised that all around him the crowd was gasping in astonishment and disappointment. The Hooligans, in particular, were wrenching their beards in dismay. And standing right in front of Stoick and Big-Boobied Bertha was the Chief Judge, looking more depressed than ever, his spectacles perched on the end of his nose.

'Commiserations,' said the Chief Judge, gloomily scratching their names down on the parchment in front of him. 'YOU are the First Man (and Woman) back. A dead heat. How do you spell Bertha?'

Stoick laughed and patted the Chief Judge on the head. 'Oh no! Oh *no*, my good little Oik, I think you do not understand the rules. The Race doesn't start until you actually start *swimming*...'

'Of course I understand the rules,' said the Chief Judge calmly. 'I am the *Judge*. If you get out of the water, you've ended the race.'

'But... but... but... of course we're going back

IN again!' spluttered Big-Boobied Bertha in horror.

'Oh, no, you're not,' said the Chief Judge. 'My decision is final.'

Stoick and Big-Boobied Bertha looked like they were going to explode.

'Old Wrinkly!' gasped Stoick. 'Tell him! We can't possibly have LOST the Race!'

Old Wrinkly surveyed the twenty sand-timers in front of him. 'I'm afraid you have,' he said sadly. 'And in three minutes twenty-two seconds exactly. A new Competition Record.'

'But *I'm* the Archipelago Swimming Champion!' shouted Big-Boobied Bertha, raising her great fist in the air. 'Bertha the Unsinkable!'

'AND MADGUTS THE MURDEROUS SAID IT WOULD BE FINE!' yelled Stoick. Even as he said the words, it finally dawned on Stoick and Big-Boobied Bertha (who were not the brightest Chieftains on the block) that they had been taken for a ride.

Two minutes before, Bertha and Stoick had been strutting on the sand, all proud and puffed up like a couple of fat cockerels, so certain had they been of victory.

Now they deflated like the air leaking out of a couple of large and handsome balloons. Bertha's boobies drooped, Stoick's magnificent biceps sagged.

'That rotten, low-down, cheating, Murderous stink-pot!' said Stoick from between gritted teeth. 'He's only gone and tricked us into losing the race!'

3. ISN'T THAT SNOTLOUT A LOVELY GUY?

Hiccup and Fishlegs and Camicazi didn't see what was happening behind them.

They had some problems of their own.

Hiccup had set off as fast as he possibly could, still hot with embarrassment at the scene on the beach.

'Wait up,' begged Fishlegs, sploshing after Hiccup and Camicazi in a clumsy dog-paddle,

'it's really tricky trying to swim in these beastly armbands. We don't have to go *too* far you know, we're not Warriors, we're only in this competition for the fun of it… always supposing your idea of fun is freezing your horns off in Sharkworm-infested waters, of course…'

As soon as Hiccup got out of his depth, the weight of his helmet and his sword made him drop abruptly, and it was only by kicking madly that he was able to keep his chin out of the water.

Even Camicazi was finding that swimming fully armed took a lot of concentration. Her sword and daggers weighed her down so far to the right that she had a tendency to swim round in circles.

'Oh **BOTHER!**' complained Hiccup. 'How am I possibly going to beat Snotlout at this rate?'

They were so busy trying to keep afloat that they
hadn't noticed Snotlout and Dogsbreath the Duhbrain
swimming up behind them. (Which shows how
distracted they were – Dogsbreath's splashy crawl was
as noisy as a hippo in a bathtub.)

The two bullies overheard the last bit of the
conversation, and Snotlout was
laughing so hard he was in danger
of drowning. 'You said it, Hiccup,
you loser!' crowed Snotlout.

One of You three? Beat ME???

'One of *you* three? Beat *me*?
I've never heard anything so
funny in my life!'

'Her Her Her,' grunted
Dogsbreath, snorting seawater
out of his nose.

'The thing is, Hiccup,' sneered Snotlout, 'you
heard everybody laughing on the beach... you guys are
just an embarrassment to the Tribe.'

Snotlout's eyes were alight with real murderous
malice. He looked over his shoulder to check that
nobody could see what he was doing. 'I am now going
to give *you*, Hiccup, a lesson in being a Viking Hero,
and *you*, Fishlegs, a lesson in how to swim without your
armbands on...'

'No!'
shrieked Fishlegs,
trying to swim away.
But he hadn't a hope of escaping.
Both Snotlout and Dogsbreath were
big, burly adolescents and they caught him easily,
ducking Hiccup and Camicazi along the way. Snotlout
popped the right armband with his dagger and
Dogsbreath removed the left.

'Now, Hiccup,' purred Snotlout. 'You can just
about make it back to shore on your own, but if
you try to do it holding Fishlegs, I don't fancy your
chances. So… what do you do? I suggest you do us all
a favour, and ditch the LOSER, but it's up to you,
of course.'

And the two bullies swam away, laughing.

Hiccup resurfaced,
gasping, and thrashed
through the water towards
poor Fishlegs, who was going
under for the second time. With the help of Toothless,
Stormfly and Fishlegs's hunting-dragon Horrorcow, he
got the boy upright with his head out of the water, but
Fishlegs was so terrified he was struggling and in danger
of dragging Hiccup under with him.

'STOP PANICKING AND RELAX!' shouted
Hiccup sharply.

'RELAX!' shrieked Fishlegs. 'HOW CAN I
RELAX? *I'M DROWNING! DROWNING ISN'T
VERY RELAXING!*

But he stopped struggling, and forced himself to
go limp, and floated on to the surface with Hiccup and
Camicazi holding him by the shoulders.

'OK,' said Hiccup, in his I'm-trying-to-stay-calm-
but-really-I-want-to-run-around-in-circles-screaming voice,

'*now* I think we might have a bit of a problem…'

As Hiccup bobbed upwards on the waves, he could see the shoreline, and suddenly it seemed very distant. Hiccup wasn't sure that he could make that swim back carrying Fishlegs all the way, even with Camicazi helping.

This is the trouble with a Proper Viking Swimming Race. It's a game of judgment as well as endurance. You have to be very careful that you don't go out so far that you run out of energy to make it back.

'We'd better get Fishlegs back to the shore, then,' Hiccup said with a confidence he was far from feeling.

'Carrot, anyone?' smiled Horrorcow, sensing a crisis and swooping down from above in a motherly way. 'It will help keep your strength up for the swim...'

'Not now, Horrorcow,' said Hiccup, and then (trying to sound extra casual), 'Horrorcow, maybe you should just flap back to the shore and tell them to send out some Rescue Dragons for us...'

'Righti-ho,' replied Horrorcow cheerily, and she flapped off. 'Keep kicking...'

'Keep kicking... keep kicking... keep kicking...'

Hiccup lost count of the amount of times he said this in the next half hour.

For a strange thing was happening. The more they kicked, the FURTHER they seemed to be getting from the beach. During the confrontation with Snotlout and Dogsbreath, they had drifted into a tide that was carrying them out to sea.

They could no longer hear the friendly shouts of other Vikings. Apart from the sound of their own splashing, they were alone. Alone in a stone-cold sea that stretched out for miles around them.

'I'm getting tired,' said Camicazi, who was never tired.

It is a little difficult to see how their situation could get any worse.

But that, as anybody who has read Hiccup's memoirs before will know, is often a sign that things are going to get REALLY, REALLY bad.

Suddenly Toothless, who had been fishing for mackerel, shot shrieking out of the sea only centimetres from Hiccup's ear.

'What is it, Toothless?' gasped Hiccup, as the little dragon hovered above him.

'S-s-s-something n-n-nasty...' stammered Toothless, spiralling upwards on shaking wings, 'something nasty down there!'

'What sort of nasty?' swallowed Hiccup.

'Toothless not know...' replied Toothless. 'NASTY sort of n-n nasty... didn't wait and see... something b-b-black...'

'What's wrong?' shivered Fishlegs. 'What's he saying?'

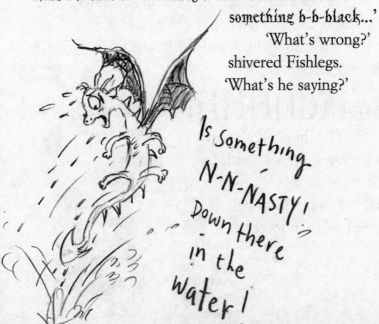

Is something N-N-NASTY! Down there in the water!

'Oh, nothing,' lied Hiccup carelessly. 'You know Toothless, he's easily spooked... *Keep kicking, keep kicking,*' whispered Hiccup, looking all around him, 'but kick *softly...*'

'Why softly?' squeaked Fishlegs, beginning to panic and sinking as a result. 'There is something, isn't there? What is it? DARKBREATHERS? SHARKWORMS? TERRORFANGS????'

'It's nothing,' whispered Hiccup soothingly, 'you just concentrate on floating, Fishlegs...'

Then, suddenly Camicazi let out a piercing scream.

'AAAAGHHHH!'

She thrashed around in the water for a second, and then she was dragged underneath by some unknown force.

'*Camicazi!*' shrieked Hiccup, trying to hold up
Fishlegs and look underneath the water at the same
time. '*Camicazi! Camicazi!!!!*'

But she was gone.

4. A REALLY, *REALLY* BAD SITUATION

'Oh for Thor's sake, oh for Thor's sake…' cried Hiccup, looking desperately around him. But there was no sign of Camicazi.

Just the silent mists, and below them… why, below them, there could be **ANYTHING** down there in the water. It could be Darkbreathers, that liked to drag their victims underneath the water and suck out their blood. It could be Sharkworms, that killed with their foot-long fangs, or grabbed a take-away of a dangling limb, and swam on.

'*Where is she? Where is she? Where is she?*' Fishlegs kept repeating, as if Hiccup knew the answer.

One terrified minute passed.

And then Fishlegs, too, screamed, and was dragged under, out of Hiccup's arms.

'*Fishlegs!*' yelled Hiccup.

Hiccup was alone in the cold grey ocean.

Never had his poor flapping feet felt so vulnerable.

There was nothing he could do. He could not run, or fly away (although Toothless was valiantly trying to haul him out of the water by the back of his waistcoat).

And then he felt the first searching nibble on his ankle…

Hiccup screamed, and tried, clumsily, to splash forward.

But whatever-it-was took a firm grip on his leg and pulled him underwater.

Hiccup just had time to take a big lungful of air. The water around him turned swiftly from green to grey to black as he was dragged down into the sea.

So this is it… thought Hiccup… as he went deeper still… *This is what it is like to die…*

Just as his lungs were about to burst, he was pulled back the other way up, the water turned from black to grey to green to white again, and he was hauled out of the sea and into the sky.

Hiccup was being carried upside-down through the air by a gigantic dragon, with a wingspan of about seven metres.

All around him, with great
rasping shrieks, a whole pack of the
creatures was leaping out
of the sea, shooting
upwards as if they
were arrows being shot
out of Neptune's bow.

The dragon holding
Hiccup was flying so low
that Hiccup's fingers were
scraping the surface of the
water. It swung him
upwards as
if he were
a piece of
mackerel and let
him go, sending Hiccup
cartwheeling through the
air, and as he was JUST
about to hit the sea, another
dragon dived and caught him,
this time by the arms.

Out of the corner of his eye, Hiccup
could see Fishlegs and Camicazi being carried
by other dragons in the pack in a similar fashion.

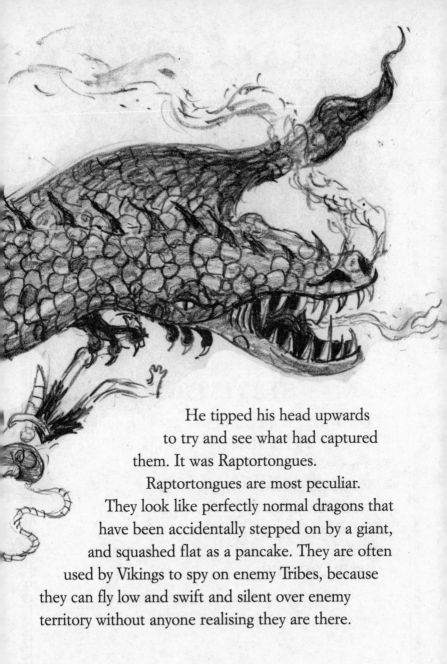

He tipped his head upwards
to try and see what had captured
them. It was Raptortongues.

Raptortongues are most peculiar.
They look like perfectly normal dragons that
have been accidentally stepped on by a giant,
and squashed flat as a pancake. They are often
used by Vikings to spy on enemy Tribes, because
they can fly low and swift and silent over enemy
territory without anyone realising they are there.

Raptortongues

A Raptortongue swooping over enemy territory

~ STATISTICS ~

COLOURS: Raptortongues are chameleons
ARMED WITH: The usual fangs and talons.
FEAR FACTOR:...............................7
ATTACK:.......................................7
SPEED:...7
SIZE:..7
DISOBEDIENCE:.........................5

Raptortongues live hidden in the deep crevasses of the Murderous Mountains or the Gorge of the Thunderbolt of Thor. They have an extraordinary ability to flatten themselves, which means they can squeeze through surprisingly small spaces. They make excellent spy dragons.

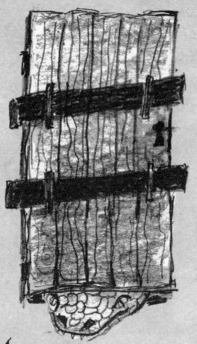

A young Raptortongue squeezing under a locked door.

The pack was about fifty strong, and they were carrying the three young Vikings out into the Open Ocean.

This was surprising, for Hiccup knew that Raptortongues were Archipelago dragons, not Ocean creatures at all. WHERE, for Thor's sake, were they taking them? The Raptortongues flew on and on. Every now and then, when Hiccup's arms were aching so hard he thought they would pull out of their sockets, the Raptortongues would fling him upside-down again.

Hiccup attempted to talk to the Raptortongue who was carrying him, but it merely adjusted

its grip, and snapped, 'You say one more word, and I will remove your head.'

Hiccup was an intelligent boy, and he judged that it might be wiser to shut up.

Eventually a smudge appeared on the horizon, gradually growing bigger and bigger as they drew nearer. At first Hiccup thought it was an island with a volcano on it, for it was belching out a thick grey-green smoke. But as they grew nearer and nearer Hiccup realised it wasn't an island at all, but a boat.

And what a boat it was.

Steam Balloon The keep-the Boat-From Sinking-and Scare Away the Big Sea Dragons Machine

cages

chimney

slave hatch

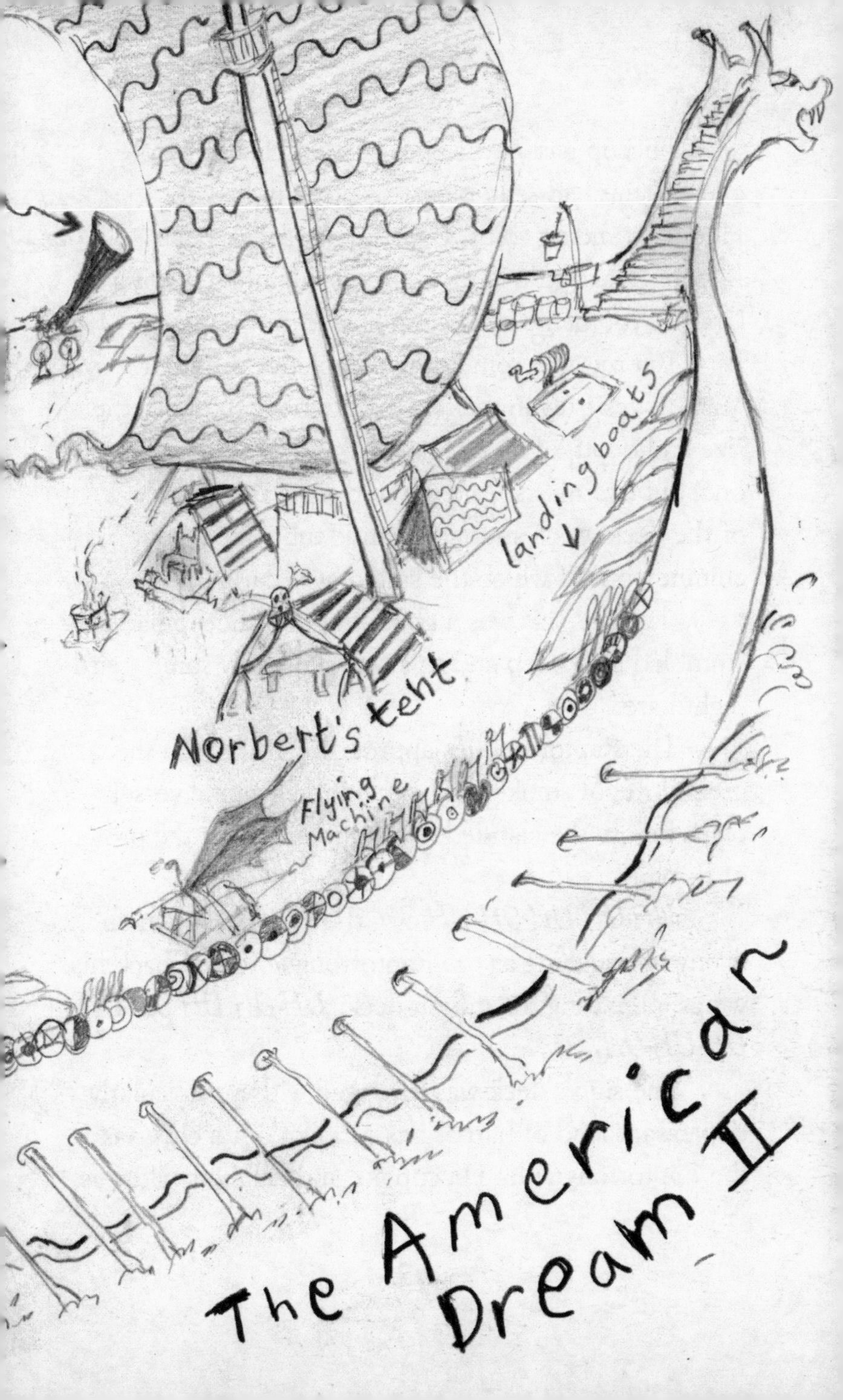

landing boats

Norbert's tent

Flying Machine

The American Dream II

Hiccup had never seen anything like it before, and Hiccup had seen plenty of boats in his life. Hooligan raiding ships, Bog-Burglar sneak-boats, Roman Dragon-Rustling Galleons, Uglithug Slaving Craft... you name it, Hiccup had seen it.

But *this* was something completely different.

It was truly immense. It was about six times the size and depth of an ordinary Viking ship. It had not one, but *two* masts. And planted right at the back of the deck was a strange gigantic tube like a bent chimney, out of which the smoke was curling.

Perhaps this was a ghost ship, or Hiccup had stumbled into sleep and this was all merely some weird nightmare.

The Raptortongues approached it through the great drifts of smoke, and circled the gigantic vessel twice before they landed, swooping low over the prow of the ship.

UH-OH-UH-OH-UH-OH, thought Hiccup in an agony of coughing as the Raptortongue folded back his wings, preparing to land on deck. *UH-OH-UH-OH-UH-OH-UH-OH...*

The ship's deck was thronged with a particularly unpleasant load of barbarians, who let out a cheer as the Raptortongue let Hiccup go, and laughed wildly as he sprawled on the deck, with Camicazi and Fishlegs being dropped beside him.

'COME BACK AND FIGHT LIKE *VIKINGS*, YOU COWARDLY BATS!' shrieked Camicazi, in a twist of fury at being kidnapped by the Raptortongues, and their new captors only laughed the more.

The young Vikings were wound around with ropes as securely as chickens trussed up for slaughter and tied upside-down to the central mast of the ship.

Even Toothless and the Stormfly had been captured, and tied up next to their Masters.

So the mood of the three young Heroes was gloomy, anxious, even terrified. They didn't know what their captors were going to do to them.

What was a VERY bad sign, however, was that the entire crew was chanting, 'KILL, KILL, KILL, KILL, KILL! *KILL* THE CHILDREN, KILL, KILL, *KILL*!'

Even Camicazi, who liked to look on the bright side, could tell that this didn't look promising.

'Do you think they're talking about US?' whimpered Fishlegs.

'Well, we're the only children *here*, aren't we?' Hiccup pointed out, teeth chattering together like crabs' claws.

73

'We should probably be planning our escape,' chirped Camicazi, cheerily listening to the cruel laughter and jeering of the brutes, who were now merrily lobbing fish at the poor captives.

'You're right, Camicazi,' admitted Hiccup, 'but it looks like there are at least two hundred of them… They're heavily armed… and I don't know about you, but at the moment *I* am dripping wet, unarmed, and tied securely upside-down to a mast. I'm not sure *how* we're going to escape from this position. I guess we could try reasoning with them, but they don't look all that reasonable to me.'

"LET US GO, YOU PLANKTON HEARTED, JELLYFISH MUSCLED SLIMY SONS OF SHRIMPS! OR I'LL GRIND YOUR BONES To SAND AND THROW YOU BACK IN To THE SEA WITH THE EELS WHERE YOU BELONG! YOU CAN'T KEEP A BOG-BURGLAR UNDER ROPE AND CHAINS!"

… shouted Camacazi.

The growling and chanting increased to double the volume, and the air rained down with fish thrown in their direction.

Shouts of, 'You and whose army, blondie?'

'Nice reasoning, Camicazi,' said Hiccup.

One of the barbarians strolled over to a tent built in the centre of the ship and shouted, 'Bo-o-o-o-ossss! They're he-e-ere!'

'It appears,' said Hiccup grimly, 'that we're expected. That's not a good sign.'

'NONE of this is a good sign!' shivered Fishlegs. 'Who do you think has kidnapped us?'

Hiccup wracked his brains. Who hadn't been at the Friendly Inter-Tribe Swimming Race? Bashem-Oiks? Uglithugs?

'I *do* hope it's not Uglithugs,' whimpered Fishlegs.

But it was much worse than Uglithugs. For the barbarian shipmates drew back the curtains on the tent in the middle of the ship, and there, sitting having a little light supper together, were three men who were three strokes of Very Bad Luck Indeed.

Reading from left to right, they were Madguts the Murderous, Norbert the Nutjob, Chief of the Hysteric Tribe, and Gumboil, Madguts's lovely assistant.

5. AN UNPLEASANT OLD ACQUAINTANCE

They were sharing a deer between them, and Norbert and Madguts made a disgusting sight, sitting there with their hands dipped scarlet in blood as they tore the poor thing limb from limb.

Gumboil was a little more delicate in his manners, and he was nibbling daintily at a piece of deer liver on the end of a long pointed black fork.

Norbert the Nutjob swallowed the last bits of wine that he was drinking out of a skull, chucked some fleshy bits of deer over his shoulder, and rubbed his bloody hands on his shirtfront.

'Oh well done, Madguts old chap,' said Norbert enthusiastically, 'your Raptortongues have brought us the victims.'

Hiccup didn't like the sound of the word 'victim'. 'What's going on?' he stammered.

'Why have you brought us here? We need to get back to our Swimming Race... And why is Madguts here? He's supposed to be in the Swimming Race too...'

Norbert got up and

thrust his face into Hiccup's face. One mad
eyeball stared straight at Hiccup, red veins
bulging all over it like lines on a lunatic
map, a violent tic sending the pupil
quivering and trembling in a wild dance
of rage.

'*Your* race is over,' said Norbert
with satisfaction. 'Madguts and
I have made a little agreement.
Madguts has brought me YOU,
and I, in return, have put him up
on my ship here for a couple
of hours. He will then swim
back to shore well after the
others, making sure that
HE is the Last Man
Back…'

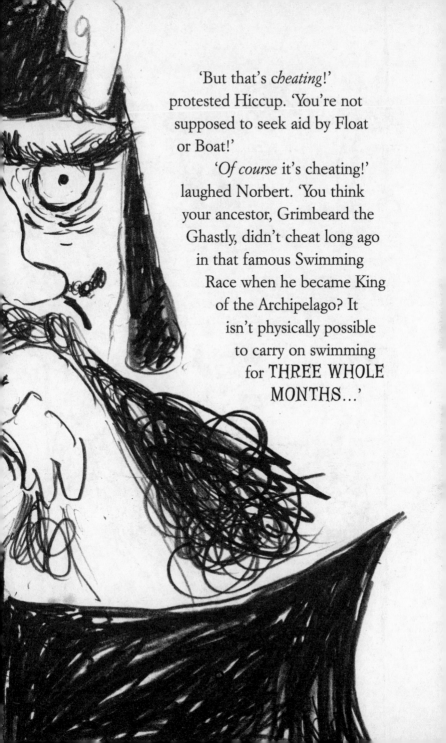

'But that's *cheating*!' protested Hiccup. 'You're not supposed to seek aid by Float or Boat!'

'*Of course* it's cheating!' laughed Norbert. 'You think your ancestor, Grimbeard the Ghastly, didn't cheat long ago in that famous Swimming Race when he became King of the Archipelago? It isn't physically possible to carry on swimming for THREE WHOLE MONTHS...'

'That *is* a long time,' grinned Gumboil. 'I'm sorry to interrupt, but we'll be off now, since you've got what you wanted, Norbert. Madguts has rested enough, and he has a race to come last in.'

Madguts the Murderous grunted and wiped his bloody palms on the front of his waistcoat. He shook Norbert the Nutjob by the hand, and did a few leg stretches, before swallow-diving off the edge of the boat, followed by the repulsive Gumboil, holding his nose and doing a bomb. The Raptortongues unfolded their bat-like wings and followed them.

'Well, well, well, if it isn't the weird little red-haired boy,' smiled Norbert the Nutjob. 'When last we met, I seem to remember that you stole my ticking-thing, burned down my Great Hall, chewed off my moustaches, and fed Papa to the Squealers.'*

'That was an accident!' protested Hiccup. 'An unfortunate SERIES of accidents which we deeply regret, don't we guys?'

'Mmff,' snorted Norbert. 'Didn't I warn you that the next time we bumped into each other I would KILL you?'

'Well, *lovely* as it is to see you again,' said Hiccup tactfully (you should always be polite to madmen carrying axes), 'I didn't exactly PLAN this meeting…'

---

*See *How to Cheat a Dragon's Curse.*

'My Chopper has been *aching* to bite your head off ever since...' Norbert lovingly stroked the double-headed axe that he carried with him everywhere. One side of the axe was bright and shining gold, the other a blackened twisted mass of rotting metal. 'And you guys too, of course.' He generously included Camicazi and Fishlegs, in case they were feeling left out. 'But I can't quite decide whether to kill you right now, or take you on our little expedition and THEN kill you... dear oh dear... life is full of tough decisions...'

'KILL THEM NOW! KILL THEM NOW!' shouted the watching Hysterical crew gleefully.

'Expedition?' said Hiccup, his heart sinking lower still. 'What do you mean *expedition*? Where are you going?'

'Oh… not far…' Norbert the Nutjob gave a peculiarly nasty grin. 'Just a little light sailing, to try out my new boat… I thought we might drop in on AMERICA, you know…'

'But there's no such place as America!' objected Fishlegs. 'The world is as flat as a pancake and if you sail too far to the west you fall off the end of it!'

'SHUDDUPPPPP!!!' roared Norbert, a fanatical gleam in his mad eye. 'The world is round as an orange, and I know there's such a place as America because I've BEEN THERE! I shall return in GLORY, with WARRIORS and MIGHT, and I shall found a great EMPIRE! Just picture me, Norbert the Great, Emperor of the New World!'

Hiccup *was* picturing it. It was a horrible thought.

'I shall call this new country *Nutjob-Land*,' said Norbert with satisfaction, making a grand gesture with his axe. 'But in order to get to America in the first place,' Norbert continued, 'I need that ticking-thing that you stole from me the last time we met. Only *that* can show us the way. So… which of you has it?'

He jabbed his axe at them, one at a time.

'Is it the funny-looking kid with the red hair and the freckles… the little blonde lunatic… or the boy with a face like a fish?'

'It's *me*, Hiccup Horrendous Haddock the Third,' said Hiccup, 'and you're standing on it right now.'

Hiccup was hanging upside-down, so the ticking-thing had fallen out of his pocket, and it was now lying on the deck with Norbert's great big maniac foot on it.

'My ticking-thing!' cried Norbert delightedly, untying it from Hiccup's wrist and clasping it to his chest.

'And now, Hiccup,' smiled Norbert, reminding Hiccup that he had more important things to be thinking of by pressing the blackened edge of his two-headed axe against Hiccup's throat, 'as I said, I can't quite decide whether to kill you now, or once we get to America... understand?'

'Perfectly...' gulped Hiccup.

'The Axe of DOO-OO-OOM will decide!' roared Norbert, throwing wide his arms. (Wild cheers and stampings of feet from the bloodthirsty crowd.) 'I shall throw it up in the air, and if it lands gold side down, you come with us to America. But if it lands black side down... why, if it lands *black* side down you *die on the spot*!' yelled Norbert the Nutjob. 'How lucky are you feeling today, Hiccup Horrendous Haddock the Third?'

'Well I've been thinking about that,' muttered Hiccup, 'and so far I reckon this has been just about the unluckiest day I've had in *years*.'

'Oh goodee,' grinned Norbert the Nutjob, 'I HATE waiting for my treats.'

'THROW THE AXE! THROW THE AXE! THROW THE AXE!' yelled the Hysterics joyously.

'DEATH OR AMERICA!' shouted Norbert the Nutjob.

'DEATH OR AMERICA!' screamed the Hysterics back at him.

'Death or America,' groaned Hiccup, Fishlegs and Camicazi.

Hiccup closed his eyes as with a manic scream Norbert the Nutjob threw the great axe high, high in the air.

The Hysterics scattered in all directions.

The axe swooped upwards, turning over and over, first the gold side up, then the black... up and up it soared...

And then it seemed to hover for a moment before it began the plunge downward towards the deck. Was it the gold side down or was it the black?

Hiccup squinted anxiously through his salty strands of hair, trying to see.

'It's the black! It's the black!' shouted Norbert the Nutjob with mad glee. 'Prepare to die!'

And with horror Hiccup realised it **WAS** the black side plunging towards the deck. And there was absolutely **NOTHING** he could do about it.

It's the BLACK! it's the BLACK!

6. THE AXE OF DOOM DECIDES

Hiccup's mind raced desperately.

He couldn't move, but inspiration suddenly struck...

'CAN YOU *READ* THE TICKING-THING, NORBERT?' screamed Hiccup.

Norbert looked at the ticking-thing... *Curses!*... *He couldn't*...

Curses.
He couldn't.

... but the axe was steaming towards the deck of the ship, and the Axe of Doom was never allowed to be wrong... So Norbert the Nutjob gave Verociously Violent a big shove so that Verociously got in between the axe and the deck, getting a nasty scratch on his arm in the process.

'NOW LOOK WHAT YOU MADE ME DO!' roared Norbert the Nutjob. 'OK, untie the wretched little burglars!'

Muttering with disappointed bloodlust, the Hysterics unwound the ropes tying Hiccup, Fishlegs and Camicazi, who fell on to the deck, deeply relieved to be the right way up again, but very dizzy.

'Follow me,' barked Norbert the Nutjob.

Hiccup followed Norbert to the central tent in the middle of the deck.

This tent was Norbert's cabin. Now, Vikings normally travelled very light on board ship. And they didn't generally have cabins at all, just maybe a couple of upturned landing-boats to shield them from the wildness of the wind.

But Norbert was intending to sail to America FOR EVER, so he had packed this ship with every possible thing that a Future Emperor might need over there in a New World. Tables, chairs, chessboards, smashsticks-on-ice sticks, bashyballs, skis.

The walls of this tent-cabin of his were covered with crazy drawings of Norbert's latest inventions, and also with maps. Norbert jabbed a fat finger at one particular map with some little squiggly numbers drawn on it.

'THIS was the Map my father Bigjob used to go to America,' said Norbert.

Here is what

The funny round TICKING THING can DO:

This arrow here always points to the NORTH

These arrows tell the time.

Hiccup doesn't yet know what the question mark and the lightning arrows do.

This arrow tells you how far to go EAST

This arrow tells you how far to go WEST

This arrow is a LIE DETECTOR
Tell a lie when you are holding the ticking-thing and it whirls round and round crazily.

'He read those funny little numbers, and he checked the ticking-thing, and that would tell him which way to go.'

Norbert handed Hiccup the map and the ticking-thing. There were nine arrows on the dial.

The two little ordinary arrows told the time much

more accurately than Old Wrinkly's complicated candlesticks. The little fat arrow always pointed to the north, like the North Star. The one with the round circle on the end was a lie detector. Hiccup didn't yet know what the one shaped like a question mark did, or the funny little jagged one like a piece of lightning.

But the remaining two told him how far to go upwards, and how far to go westwards.*

He sat there staring back and forth from the ticking-thing to the Map for such a long time that Norbert grew impatient, and roared:

'HURRY UP BOY, HURRY UP! We haven't got all DAY!'

'The quickest way to America, if such a place really exists, is in *that* direction.' Hiccup pointed over towards some distant storm-clouds to the north. 'But we'd have to go through the Ice Islands and there are some really unpleasant Ice-Dragons we could meet that way—'

---

*This suggests that the ticking-thing contains a device for calculating LONGTITUDE (what Hiccup describes as 'going westwards'). It was previously thought that the first device for predicting longtitude was the chronometer created in 1773, but Hiccup's memoirs show otherwise.

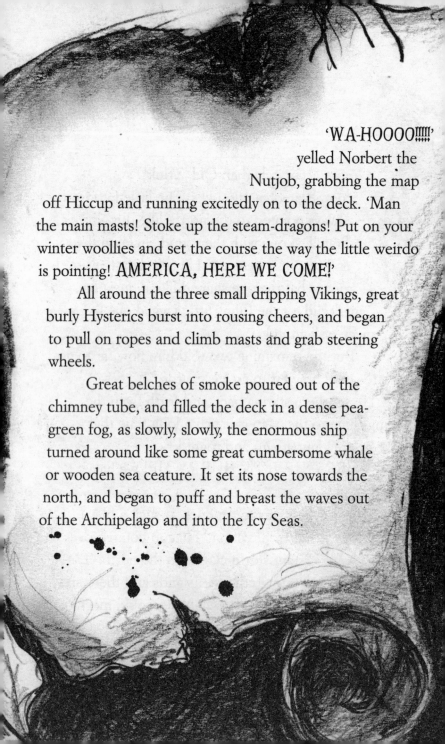

'WA-HOOOO!!!!!'
yelled Norbert the
Nutjob, grabbing the map
off Hiccup and running excitedly on to the deck. 'Man
the main masts! Stoke up the steam-dragons! Put on your
winter woollies and set the course the way the little weirdo
is pointing! AMERICA, HERE WE COME!'

All around the three small dripping Vikings, great
burly Hysterics burst into rousing cheers, and began
to pull on ropes and climb masts and grab steering
wheels.

Great belches of smoke poured out of the
chimney tube, and filled the deck in a dense pea-
green fog, as slowly, slowly, the enormous ship
turned around like some great cumbersome whale
or wooden sea creature. It set its nose towards the
north, and began to puff and breast the waves out
of the Archipelago and into the Icy Seas.

the DARK SIDE of THE AXE

(a moving little lullaby)

Come and dance the Deathwalk
Beneath the grinning moon..
We'll do the dance together
In the dying afternoon...

The Deathwalk looks so tricky,
But I think you'll learn it quick,
Just step into my Axe's arms,
She'll teach you in a tick..

See the jolly skeletons
A dancing on the seal
They haven't got no cares now
Not like you and me...
They went and did the
DEATHWALK
That crazy night-time
beat...

And now they partner ghosts and whales
On bony pearly feet...

7. THE QUEST TO DISCOVER AMERICA

So this was how Hiccup, Camicazi and Fishlegs got themselves kidnapped by Norbert the Nutjob, and found themselves in a boat that was sailing out of the Archipelago, never to return.

Of course, Hiccup, Camicazi and Fishlegs did not want to go to America. Besides which, there was the tiny problem of crossing the Great West Ocean which, Hiccup knew, was full of Sea-Dragons so large and fearsome that they could swallow the ship they were standing on in one gulp.

'So... what do we do *now* then, Hiccup?' asked Fishlegs slowly.

'Well,' said Hiccup, through chattering teeth. 'Let's dry our wet things, first of all.'

The chimney at the back of the deck out of which the smoke was pouring was hot to the touch, so they leant against it for a couple of hours, letting the lovely warmth penetrate their frozen bodies. The green streaky remains of the Fleshfang oil on their cheeks and arms made them look like three cold-blooded little lizards baking in the sunshine. Their salty clothes were stiff as cardboard, but at least they were dry.

When they had finally stopped shivering, they began to explore their floating prison.

Hysterics are a Tribe of dreamers, lunatics and inventors, so the *American Dream II* was not your ordinary Viking ship.

The steam pouring out of the chimney was a distinctive grey-green, so Hiccup suspected it was dragon-smoke, probably coming from dragons hidden within the belly of the ship. Hiccup would have loved to see by what mechanism this steam powered the boat.*

The dragons weren't the *only* mad thing about this vessel. There was a weird thing with wings sprouting out of the side that a Hysteric called Red Ronald told them was Norbert's attempt at a Flying Machine. Unfortunately it didn't really work yet.

Several times during the day, Norbert ordered three unfortunate members of his crew to try it out, hauling the Machine all the way up to the top of the Mast on ropes, and then launching it from the crow's nest.

It only stayed up in the sky for a couple of minutes, before crashing spectacularly into the Ocean,

---

*Hiccup's memoirs seem to suggest that Norbert had built a steam-ship, many, many centuries before steam was used to power marine craft. Similarly, the artist Leonardo da Vinci drew designs for a helicopter, a trench-digging machine, a deep-sea diving suit, a revolving bridge, a calculator, a hang-glider and a tank, four hundred years before any of these things were 'invented'.

Wind Powered Flying Machine
Fig. E

This one could work.
Get Violent, Goggle Eyes
and Ronald to try out
and see if they can
make it back over
the hill this time. No No

Steam-Powered Machine.
Perhaps not this one.

Fig. P

and the crew members had to be rescued, and the Machine mended again.

And then there was an extraordinary Machine with a wheel that the crew took in turns to pedal with their feet, which was attached to a large trumpet-like funnel. It was very difficult to work out what the purpose of this Machine was. At the moment it was Verociously Violent's turn on the Machine, because his arm was still recovering from the gash he had received from the Axe of Doom incident, so he wasn't much good at pulling on ropes and other tasks around the boat at the moment.

Hiccup was so curious about what the Machine did that he approached Verociously to ask what he was doing.

'Oh, this is the Keep-the-Boat-From-Sinking-and-Scare-Away-the-Big-Sea-Creatures Machine,' explained Verociously Violent, stopping pedalling for a second to answer Hiccup's question. 'It stops the boat from sinking and it also scares away the Sea-Monsters, Great Terrorwings, Seadragonus Giganticus Maximus, that sort of thing.'*

'KEEP PEDALLING! KEEP PEDALLING!' screamed Norbert the Nutjob, marching up, and the Hysteric hurriedly resumed, so fast his feet were a blur.

---

*Some of Norbert's inventions were more practical than others, because the line between genius and total loopiness is quite a fine one.

'And *YOU*,' Norbert turned to Hiccup, 'STOP DISTRACTING THE CREW! If this man here stops turning this wheel for even *one second*, the boat will sink, and we could be attacked by one of the Ocean Dragon-Mammoths.'

'Fascinating,' said Hiccup, very politely, thinking, *nutty as an absolute fruitcake*.

'Is there any chance,' gulped Fishlegs hopefully as they walked away, 'that that thing could work?'

'Yeah, right,' replied Hiccup. 'Like a revolving tube with a funnel attached is *really* going to stop a boat from sinking…'

At the end of the first day of The Quest to Discover America, the sun sank in a glorious technicolour display of pink and gold streaked with red. The three young Vikings sat and worried…

and worried… and worried. (Actually, *two* of them worried; Camicazi just played with Toothless.)

They worried until it was late at night, and the Hysterics had built a fire on deck, and were singing songs to the rising moon. The songs were about the life of a Viking. You have to imagine Norbert the Nutjob adding the *HO!*s, while banging his axe on the bottom of an iron bucket.

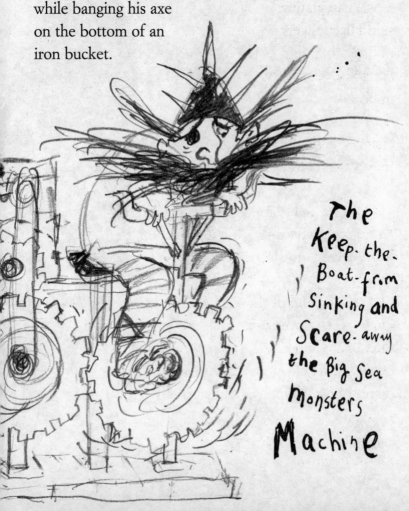

The Keep. the. Boat-from Sinking and Scare-away the Big Sea monsters Machine

'We could be safe at
hearth and home
Around a fire with loved ones near
Instead we brave the cold dark wave
The salty kiss of a Hero's grave
Looking for a land we saw…
Once before… long ago…
HO!

Norbert the Nutjob was sitting, a twisted shadow watching the singers, his cabin shrouded close around him. Only his eyes gleamed in the firelight, as he watched and smoked from a long thin pipe that sent a crooked plume of smoke up into the sail billowing above him and on into the night sky.

'We could take the easy way
Stay at home with loved ones dear
But here we are on rocking waves
Sails spread out like dragons' wings...
Lost out in a hurricane...
Looking for a land we saw...
Once before... long ago...
HO!'

As the Hysterics sang on in the warm night, Hiccup's eyes began to close.

But they opened again with a start when the deck beneath Hiccup's feet began to vibrate with a new noise. Strange voices were beginning their own song. Weird voices, singing in a language that Hiccup did not understand, the sound of something so Other and unfamiliar that they were as alien as the music of whales or dolphins calling to each other.

104

Voices coming from deep within the belly of the ship.

'What is *that*?' whispered Fishlegs to Hiccup, with round, scared eyes.

Hiccup's heart plummeted.

He suddenly realised what it might be.

'I wonder,' replied Hiccup slowly, 'if this ship is carrying *slaves* on it?'

The Hysterics stopped to listen too. And as they listened the song changed, to something much more sinister. A shiver went slipping down Hiccup's spine like a cold drop of water. You did not have to understand the language the slaves were speaking to understand what they were saying.

Toothless let out a whine of fear, as if he were a spaniel, and covered his ears with his paws.

They were laying a Curse on the ship. A Curse on the voyage. A Curse on every single Viking man, woman or child who was keeping them there, under those decks…

The hairs stood up on the back of Hiccup's neck.

They went right on singing, that fierce terrible Curse, until Norbert strode to the centre of the deck, and struck it with his axe three times, and shouted:

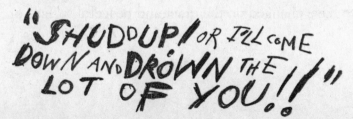

"SHUDDUP! OR I'LL COME DOWN AND DROWN THE LOT OF YOU!!"

And then it was quiet again.

Hiccup lay in the darkness, his heart beating quick. Oh how he longed to be Home...

It was very late when he fell asleep again, the Hysterics still singing:

> 'Glory comes not to the weak
> A treasure land shines out so strong
> We see it clear from far away
> O Great and Brave and Mighty Thor
> I *hope* that that was land I saw
> Once before... long ago...
> *HO!*

The ship sailed on through the moonlit night.

Apart from four crewmen (one steering the boat, one looking after the Steam-Dragons, one keeping lookout, and one laboriously turning Norbert's mad Monster-Scaring Machine), all the human beings aboard the *American Dream II* had fallen asleep now: Hysterics, Hooligans, friends and foes, all.

What none of these little sleeping human beings knew was how tiny they were compared to the vastness of the world they were about to enter. Nothing seemed to have changed on the quiet and peaceful surface of the water... but in fact they had moved out of the safe, shallow seas of the Archipelago, they had crossed an invisible line in the ocean, and they were now sailing over very deep waters indeed.

Waters fathoms and fathoms deep, a sunless, black and watery desert.

But could it be that *something* was about to stir down in the darkness? The unimaginable enormity of the Open Ocean holds such strange and terrible things, things which we cannot even dream of.

If you were a fanciful person, you could imagine that something dreadful was about to happen. Some dragon-giant of the abyss, sleeping all coiled up like an unwoken tornado, was about to gain consciousness and would move inexorably on the little ship puffing its way across the water.

But we are not fanciful people, so we know that cannot be true.

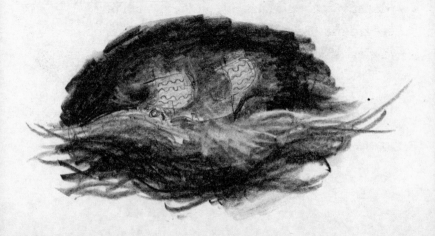

LEARNING TO SPEAK DRAGONESE
TOOTHLESS WANTS A PET

please
please
please
Please

Nee-ah, Toothless, ta NA aca
un sweetie ickie tootsienipper
par un fluff-squees.
No, Toothless, you CANNOT
have a dear little rat for a pet.

Parsk me pappa na likeit.
Because my dad won't be pleased.

Na un moonhowler, oo un deathscuttler plus DOUBLY
DOUBLY na un fangboggle-limb-scruncher.

Nor a wolf, or a scorpion,
and DEFINITELY
DEFINITELY not a
shark.

When Toothless is in
a mood he puffs out so
much black smoke you
can hardly see
him.

Yow is a snakenipper
Yellfatter, plus
yow squeezeblood
ist conja da
sniffersludge.
You are a very mean
Master, and your
heart is made out
of bogeys.

8. THE SLAVEMARK

Hiccup was right, the ship *was* carrying slaves.

Hiccup asked Red Ronald about it the next morning, and Ronald said there were one hundred and nineteen slaves being kept in the hold, all of them Northern Wanderers. Wanderers were very fierce and wild, and they detested Vikings.

It made Hiccup shiver to hear the noise of their Cursing, floating up out of a heavily barred Hatch in the centre of the back deck, all day and all night.

Two days passed.

Each morning Hiccup would read the ticking-thing for Norbert in his cabin, and then the three young Heroes spent the rest of the time dreaming of escape as the ship chugged steadily north and the weather grew colder and colder.

There is no more exciting place for a lively young dragon than a ship in full sail.

The two little dragons were now having a *lovely* time, flying through the rigging, getting tangled up in ropes, sliding down the sails, trying to nick things from the Cooking Cabin without getting caught by the Cook, dashing after mice in the hold, chewing the arms off Norbert's shirts and the bottoms out of his shoes, and in the Stormfly's case, flirting with the hunting-dragons who were lined up, very dignified on the mast-head.

But both dragons avoided the Slave Hatch. Every time Toothless passed it, his hackles rose, and he hissed with fear and alarm.

The three young Heroes had had time to think, and so they were now quite optimistic about their chances of escaping.

It was just a question of agreeing on a plan.

'OK,' said Camicazi breezily. 'I've thought of several ways to escape. I might dress up as a Hysteric and trick one of those idiot guards into launching one of those little landing-boats by saying we'd hit an iceberg.'

'That Hysteric guard isn't going to think you're another Hysteric!' scoffed Fishlegs. 'However stupid they are they're not actually *blind*! You're only four foot tall, Camicazi, you're blonde, you're female, you have no facial hair…'

'A*ha*,' said Camicazi, laying a finger against her nose and looking very cunning, 'but if I wear a very long coat, and stand on your shoulders, and I'll stick one of Norbert's bearskin knee-pads on to my chin as a beard—'

'There's no way *in a million years* that that is going to work,' argued Fishlegs.

'OK, so what's YOUR idea, then, Mr Clever Clogs?' said Camicazi crossly. 'I'm telling you, I've escaped from more Uglithug Dungeons and Murderous Cage-Mazes than you've had hot dinners...'

Meanwhile, in the background, Norbert was watching the crew feeding the Wanderer Slaves by opening up the Slave Hatch and throwing food down below.

'Not TOO much of that bread,' Norbert roared greedily. 'They're refusing to row, and slaves that are on strike should not be fed.'

Unbeknownst to Norbert, Toothless was showing off his excellent hunting skills to Stormfly.

He had been chasing a fly through the rigging for the past five minutes. He was now hovering about a metre above Norbert's head, only his wings and his narrowed eyes moving as he watched the fly.

'Bzzz... bzzzzz... bzzzzzz...' buzzed the fly, zig-zagging drunkenly around Norbert's head.

Toothless crept ever so softly down in the air as his muscles poised, ready to pounce.

The fly made a few more aimless buzzes...

… and settled on the end of one of Norbert's sticking-up hairs.

'W-W-Wrrrewwwowwwwwrrrrrrrrr!!!!!!!'

With the smothered yowl of a kung-fu kitten, Toothless launched himself, claws out, on to Norbert's head.

Norbert was not a relaxed personality. In fact, you *could* describe him as 'tightly wound'. So his reaction when a dragon suddenly landed unexpectedly on his head was to shriek like a fire-engine and spring into the air, as if stung by a bee. One of his flailing arms pushed over one of the Hysteric crew-members… who then cannoned into Hiccup… and Hiccup slid over, plunging down into the Hatch, *just* managing to grab hold of the edge of the Hatch as he fell, so he was still hanging on by one hand…

… until with a cry of 'Hiccup!' and Toothless still attached to his head, Norbert blundered forward

to try and help, and in the process trod heavily on
Hiccup's clinging fingers.

So that Hiccup let go and fell down the Hatch...

... the Hatch that Bearcub's Grandmother only
the day before had been warning that no Viking should
fall down OR ELSE...

... down that very same Hatch Hiccup fell, the
door clanging shut behind him.

There was a short silence.
Then pandemonium broke out.

'Aaaarrgh!' screeched Norbert the Nutjob, seeing his guide to America lost, and his journey going up in smoke. 'Get him out! Get him out! They'll kill him!'

But the crew could not open the Hatch. Somebody had lost the key and had to run off and find it.

Frantically, Camicazi and Fishlegs and Norbert pulled and pulled at the bars, and tried to squint down to see what was happening.

There was a horrible noise of shouting and screaming going on down there in the darkness.

What was happening to Hiccup?

Hiccup fell down, down, down, into the blackness of the hold, landing on the wood with the carrots, and the bread, and the cabbages the Wanderers were starting to eat.

There was a shocked silence for a moment.

Then came a roar of rage.

'It's a Viking!' yelled one big Wanderer, shaking his chains in fury.

'Kill him!' shrieked Bearcub's Grandmother, showing her sharp pointy teeth and seizing Hiccup by the leg. 'Crush him to death!' She made a growling noise like a wolf.

'It's quite a *small* Viking,' said the big Wanderer more uncertainly as he grabbed hold of Hiccup, and he paused his raised hand.

Hiccup knew that all Wandering Peoples
could speak Dragonese as well as they
spoke their mother tongue.*

So he spoke to them directly
in the Dragonese language.

'Please don't kill me...'
whispered Hiccup.

There was
a moment's
astonished
silence.

Vikings are
VERMIN!

---

*Unlike Vikings, who had mostly lost the art of speaking
with serpents.

'It's a Viking that speaks Dragonese,' said Bearcub's Grandmother in amazement.

'Please don't kill me,' repeated Hiccup.

'Why should we not kill you?' asked Bearcub's Grandmother in a dreadful angry voice, her eyes as wide and staring and hypnotic as those of a king cobra.

'Your people have killed *my* people for as long as my people can remember. They have robbed us, and cheated us, and sold us into slavery. All of history is against you, Viking. Why should we not kill you?'

Hiccup had never met a Wanderer before, and she was an awful sight, her hair all askew like a bundle of hay, and those terrible grim and gloomy eyes, always staring into the far distance as if she'd just spotted something terrifying.

She took Hiccup by the neck in one of her skinny hands. 'You are a Viking, and all Vikings are vermin, wicked and brutish enslavers of dragons and humans. You may be young, but you should be killed *now* before you grow into a rat, or a fox,' she said, her voice shaking with fury. Her long fingernails dug scratches into Hiccup and he was petrified she was going to strangle him.

'We're not ALL like that,' protested Hiccup.

When Hiccup fell down the Hatch his helmet

had fallen off, and it was lying on the wooden floor beside him. Little Bearcub had been staring fixedly at Hiccup's bared head, and now he piped up, pointing at Hiccup's hair.

'Look, Grandmother, he hasn't got any horns.'

'What do you mean?' snapped Bearcub's grandmother.

'You said that Vikings were devils that had horns growing on their heads, which was why their helmets were such a funny shape,' said Bearcub. 'But look, this one doesn't.'

'Humph,' snorted Bearcub's grandmother, feeling through Hiccup's shaggy red hair. 'Perhaps they are too small to see yet. But, trust me, they are there. There's a few lumps and bumps here that could easily grow into horns.'

'If you don't kill me,' pleaded Hiccup desperately, 'I will help you.'

Bearcub's Grandmother gave a bitter laugh and shook her chains. 'Nobody can help us,' she said in Dragonese, opening up her gloomy eyes. 'We are DOOMED... we are ALL Doomed, for I have put a Curse upon this ship.'

'Yes, I heard,' said Hiccup nervously, thinking, *not another fruitcake*. 'But we are travelling north, where your

117

people come from, and when we get closer to your country, I will help you to escape.'

There was a moment's silence, and then the listening Wanderers broke out in a chatter of excitement.

Bearcub's Grandmother was more sceptical. 'How can you do that?' she spat in disbelief. 'You are far too small...'

'I will find a way,' said Hiccup. 'I'm pretty sure I will, anyway. I've done this sort of thing before.'

There was a long, long silence. Everyone looked at Bearcub's Grandmother. She was staring at Hiccup, boring into him with her eyes, as if a tiny hope was struggling with a lifetime's bitter experience.

'You are a Viking,' she said at last. 'I think that you are saying this so that we will let you go, and you will climb back to freedom, and then forget about us.' She jerked her head up at the Hatch above, which the Vikings were still banging and clanging in their desperate attempts to open it.

'I give you my promise,' said Hiccup.

'A Viking's promise is worth nothing,' spat Bearcub's Grandmother. She looked at him thoughtfully. 'What is your name, Viking?' she asked.

'Hiccup Horrendous Haddock the Third,' replied

Hiccup. 'I am the son of Chief Stoick the Vast, of the Hooligan Tribe.'

'Viking *royalty*,' said Bearcub's Grandmother, sarcastically, but Hiccup had made her pause, and she was thinking hard. 'How interesting. We are honoured indeed. *King* Rat. *King* Fox.'

Her eye caught a long, sinister-looking metal tool leaning against one of the beams that propped up the ceiling of the hold. It ended in the shape of an 'S', and it was dipped in a dark blue ink.

'OK then, Viking,' said Bearcub's Grandmother, 'you have got yourself a deal. But it will come at a price. In return I will give you the Slavemark. Hold him fast, Wildthing and Lonefox...'

the Slavemark

'No!' screamed Hiccup, struggling frantically.

'The Slavemark is easy to give,' said Bearcub's Grandmother slowly, approaching him with the pointed stick, 'but impossible to remove.' She pointed bitterly at the blue Mark on her hand.

119

'Take off his helmet,' Bearcub's Grandmother ordered Wildthing and Lonefox. 'And then he can hide it from those devil-Vikings up there. We do not want them to suspect that he has an understanding with us.'

So Bearcub's Grandmother put the Mark on the side of Hiccup's head, some way above his left ear. One second later and the Slavemark was there, a livid blue mark that would stay for ever, a bit like a tattoo.

'You will not be able to forget us now,' said Bearcub's Grandmother with gloomy satisfaction.

The Hatch above Hiccup's head finally burst open and a great shaft of light poured into the dark room.

Norbert the Nutjob's furious red screaming face appeared in the space. 'IF YOU'VE TOUCHED A HAIR ON HIS HEAD I'LL FEED THE LOT OF YOU TO THE LOBSTERS!' he roared. 'CLIMB UP *QUICK* THERE, BOY!'

A rope flopped down into the hold.

'Swear by this Mark that you will help us escape, or we will not let you go,' hissed Bearcub's Grandmother.

'I swear,' gasped Hiccup, nearly crying. And then he put both hands upon the rope, and was hauled up through the Hatch.

'You see, Grandmother!' said Bearcub excitedly, 'We are not Doomed after all! I asked for someone to rescue us and he *has*!'

'You are not rescued *yet*,' said his Grandmother sternly.

The Hatch clanged shut and they were left in darkness again.

'And wipe your nose,' came the voice of Bearcub's Grandmother in the blackness. 'It's running most dreadfully.'

We're saved!

9. THE LAND OF THE POLAR-SERPENTS

The *American Dream II* puffed its way steadily north, and the weather got colder and colder, and darker and darker, until they were travelling through total blackness, day and night, and this was the home of the Wanderers.

It was an eerie place. Icebergs drifted by, taller than the masts of the ship itself, cracking and splitting and creaking around them in the mist.

The crew fell silent as they went about their work, and even Norbert managed to lower his voice to a menacing whisper as he scolded and shook his axe threateningly at his men.

For they had entered the world of the Polar-serpents.

The Polar-serpents were great white dragons slumbering on the ice like over-sized walruses. They reminded Hiccup of the Sabre-tooth Driver Dragons the Vikings used to pull their sleds back in the Archipelago. Except that instead of sabre-teeth, out of the nose of each Polar-serpent grew a long white tusk like a unicorn or a narwhal.

Polar-serpents swam under the icebergs, and when they found shoals of unwary seals and penguins resting on the surface above, they sawed great holes in the ice, so that the unsuspecting prey fell into their open jaws below.

A Polar-serpent feeding frenzy was a terrifying sight. They could strip a mammal down to the bone far quicker than a shoal of piranhas, and as far as they were concerned, a human was just as tasty as a seal.

Perhaps even tastier.

Of course, the Polar-serpents weren't a threat when you were aboard a boat… but nonetheless,

polar-serpents

~STATISTICS~

COLOURS: White with faint grey markings
ARMED WITH: Talons and spear-like horn
FEAR FACTOR:..............6
ATTACK:........................7
SPEED:................................7
SIZE:..5
DISOBEDIENCE:................6

Polar-serpents live in the north, basking like
seals on flat icebergs. Their beauty hides a
cruel streak. A pack will even attack a polar
bear. They nest in snowdrifts, crevasses
and on the tops of icebergs. They windsurf
across the ice on their tummies and reach
extraordinary speeds doing this.

Hiccup swallowed hard as they steamed quietly past the creatures. And he noticed that all of Norbert's hunting-dragons were careful to stay close to the ship as well.

They roosted on the masts like a row of malevolent starlings, watching the Polar-serpents, with the Polar-serpents watching them back.

After a while Norbert slightly lost it with the Polar-serpents.

'STOP LOOKING AT ME, YOU BIG WHITE MAGGOTS!' he yelled, waving his axe at the dragons. 'OR I'LL CLIMB OVERBOARD AND CHOP OFF YOUR HORNS!'

He grabbed the cauldron with the remains of lunch and shook it over the side of the boat.

The statues on the ice sprang instantly to life. They slid into the water like big white crocodiles: thirty, forty, fifty, sixty, three hundred of them.

Within about five seconds the water behind the boat was a thrashing, churning, manic froth of red as the Polar-serpents went into their feeding frenzy.

They were so crazy in their bloodlust that they even attacked each other, tearing each other from limb to limb.

Norbert went back to whispering.

The Slavemark
is easy to give
but impossible
to remove.

All day long, Hiccup
could feel the Slavemark
pressing against his helmet.
He hadn't told Fishlegs and
Camicazi about it, because he
knew he had to keep it a secret.
The Law of the Archipelago
was quite firm upon the matter.
Anybody with the Slavemark
was automatically an Outcast,
whether it was their fault
or not.

And they certainly couldn't
become a *Chief*. No, if Hiccup ever
got back home (and it was a
big 'if' at this point), this was
a secret that Hiccup would
have to keep to himself
for the rest of his life. He
couldn't tell anybody, because
if someone like Snotlout were to
find out...

Hiccup pushed the thought to the back of his
mind, because he had to concentrate on the more
pressing problem of escaping.

And now, escaping had been made that much more difficult. As Camicazi had so helpfully pointed out, it was all very well trying to escape when there are three of you, but trying to get a hundred and twenty-two people off a ship without their captors noticing required a little more forward planning.

'We could escape so easily on our *own*,' complained Camicazi. 'Why are you suddenly bothering about those people? They're not even Vikings, they're WANDERERS, for Thor's sake, we might set them free and then they might kill us, you know what people say about Wanderers.'

'I told you,' said Hiccup grumpily. 'I had to make them a promise.'

Hiccup sat up in the crow's nest of the *American Dream II*, and thought and thought and thought, his legs swinging as Stormfly and Toothless chased each other round and round in circles.

In the middle of the night...

Me has b-b-buckets di belly-scream.
I am very hungry.

I am very hungry

Me isna burped si ISSA middling o di zuzztime.
I don't care if it IS the middle of the night.

Me needy di grubbings SNIP-SNAP!
I want food RIGHT NOW!

Oo mes'll do di yowlyshreekers too fortissimo theys'll earwig me indi BigManGaff.
Or I'll scream so loudly they'll hear me in Valhalla.

Me needy di S-S-S-S-SALTSICKS.
I want OYSTERS.

Yow g-g-grabba di saltsicks low indi Landscoop. Sna staraway.
You can get oysters from the Harbour. It's not far.

M-M-Me gogo ta yowlshreek...
I'm starting to scream...
(three quarters of an hour later)

Yow me p-p-peepers undo!
You woke me up!

Wah is DA?
What is THAT?

Da na goggle com s-s-
saltsicks...
That doesn't look like oysters...

THAT looks like bogeys

DA goggle com sniffersludge...
THAT looks like bogeys...

Sniffersludge p-p-plus di squidink tiddles...
Bogeys with black bits in them...

Me no likeit di squidink tiddles.
Issa y-y-yuck-yuck.
I don't like black bits. They're disgusting.

They're disgusting

Watever, me is tow zuzzready
por di scrumming.
Anyway, I'm too
tired to eat.

Why are you in a bad mood?

10. TOOTHLESS'S ADVENTURE IN THE COOKING TENT

It was Toothless who provided the answer to the Escape Problem.

One afternoon Hiccup looked down from the crow's nest and spotted Stormfly and Toothless creeping out of the Cooking Tent. They had sneaked in there while the Cook was having a thoughtful chat with Norbert, as Norbert checked his Great Map of America.

Both dragons were flying extremely erratically. Stormfly had turned every colour of the rainbow, and was letting out little hiccups in fiery explosions of golden smoke as she somersaulted and cartwheeled through the air.

Toothless appeared to be flying upside-down.

He too was hiccupping, and with every hiccup, a little stream of golden bubbles blew out of his nose.

'What ARE they doing?' asked Camicazi, in danger of falling off the mast as she peered down at the little dragons' eccentric progress.

'They look like they're DRUNK,' said Fishlegs in amazement.

Toothless got entangled in the rigging, and the

Stormfly was so helpless with giggles she could barely free him.

'Isshh v-v-very TANGLY, thish air,' Hiccup could hear Toothless saying.

Eventually they got going again, and they flew past Hiccup's perch.

'Who ISH this tall gentleman?' asked Toothless, as he bashed into the mast for the second time. 'He keepsh getting in my way.'

'Toothless! Stormfly!' Hiccup called out. 'Come over here!'

'That b-b-boy over there s-s-seemsh to be calling you,' Toothless advised the Stormfly. 'Hic... whoops... shorry...'

They flapped over to where Hiccup and Camicazi and Fishlegs were sitting, and they were burping and swaying and exploding with bubbles.

'What *have* you been doing?' scolded Hiccup. 'I TOLD you not to go near that Cooking Tent...'

'I haven't been anywhere near the Cooking Tent, have you, Toothless?' drawled Stormfly.

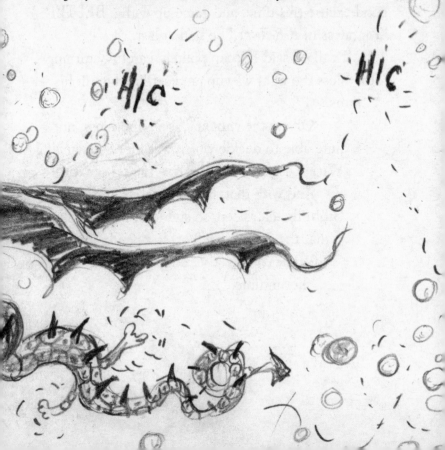

The upside-down Toothless nodded so hard great streams of golden bubbles poured out of his ears.

'Absholutely NOT,' he said solemnly, his eyes crossing. 'T-t-toothless NOT go into the Cooking Tent... Toothless N-N-NOT open the lovely shcrum-diddly-delicious j-j-jar of lemonade with the l-l-lovely tickly bubbles... oooh... hic... tee hee... there goes another one... Toothless not there... Toothless... Toothless...'

He searched his rather addled brain for a really good excuse this time, and came up with a BELTER. 'Toothless in R-R-Rome,' he said at last.

'Really?' said Hiccup politely, carefully turning Toothless the right way up, and settling him in his arms.

'OR up the chimney,' said Toothless, not quite able to decide which was more convincing. 'With Toothless's *good friend*, the s-s-senator.'

And with that, both Toothless and the Stormfly fell asleep, so suddenly and deeply that the Stormfly fell off her perch, and Camicazi only just caught her in time.

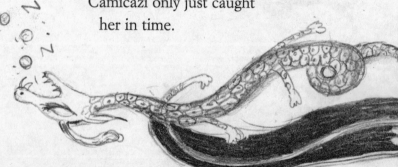

They were both snoring like two little hibernating grizzly bears.

All around their mouths was a slightly sticky browny-yellow substance.

'*Dragon-nip*,' said Hiccup thoughtfully. 'There must be a jar of dragon-nip down there in the Cooking Tent.'

Dragon-nip was a perfectly harmless but sleep-inducing substance gathered from the sweat glands of the Loafer dragon.

'A spot of dragon-nip in the dinner, and anybody who eats it will be out for the count for the next twelve hours...' said Hiccup. 'OK, guys. I think this could be a good night for us to escape.'

11. THE ESCAPE FROM THE AMERICAN DREAM II

The full moon shone down on the great boat steaming through the icebergs. The crew of the *American Dream II* feasted well that night, on a stew which, unbeknownst to them, was heavily laced with dragon-nip.

Hiccup had crept in to the Cooking Tent, and poured it into the bubbling cauldron of dinner.

For a while the Hysterical crew ignored their spooky surroundings, and sang out loud songs to the moon above, banging their dinner plates on the deck, and Norbert the Nutjob fiddled madly on his Viking violin, and the Hysterics did wild jigs, and the Polar-serpents sat on their icebergs, quiet statues, only their eyes following the mayhem.

And then, one by one, the dragon-nip's heavy fumes overcame the Hysterics. Sleep overtook them so quickly that they dropped as they stood, in the middle of whatever they happened to be doing at the time, and fell to the deck in grotesque attitudes of slumber.

Norbert lay snoring, the violin still tucked under his chin. Goggle-eyes the Gory was clasped fondly to the breast of Verociously Violent, who was under the sleepy delusion that he was three years old again, and this was his mother.

Red Ronald was pedalling the wheels of the Keep-the-Boat-from-Sinking-and-Scare-Away-the-Big-Sea-Creatures Machine slower and slower until he stopped entirely and drooped snoring over the handlebars.

And the Ship's Cook collapsed face down in his snail and jellyfish pie. (He would still be picking bits of snail shell and egg out of his nostrils three days later.)

Hiccup, Camicazi and Fishlegs waited till everybody on the deck was completely still – and then they waited five minutes more, just to make sure. Then slowly, quietly, they slipped down the rigging of the mast. Hiccup was carrying the sleeping Toothless in his breast pocket, and Camicazi had the slumbering Stormfly draped around her shoulders like a scarf.

They tip-toed across the deck of the *American Dream II*, carefully, *carefully* picking their way through the sleeping, snoring Warriors lying strewn on the boards, the sweet yellow-brown smoke from the cauldron billowing across the ship and making their eyes water. Cautiously, gently, Hiccup took the ticking-thing from around Norbert's wrist, and tied it back again to his own.

Quietly, softly, Camicazi removed the large bunch of keys from Norbert's waistband with her quick, light little fingers, and she opened the lock of the Hatch that led down to the hold where they were holding the Wanderers. It took all three of them to lift up the Hatch, which they did with a whining C-C-C-CREAK! And then they threw down a rope and the keys to the Wanderers below, Hiccup whispering as loud as he dared to tell them to unlock their chains and climb up, one by one.

The first two out were Bearcub and his Grandmother.

Bearcub was in a state of high excitement, and danced round his Grandmother squeaking, 'I TOLD you! I TOLD you he would rescue us! You see! You see! Not ALL Vikings are wicked, and we're not DOOMED after all!'

Bearcub's Grandmother was torn between her delight at being rescued, and her annoyance that her prophecy of DOOM wasn't being fulfilled. 'Mff,' she sniffed. 'We're not rescued YET. If just one of those Vikings wakes up, we're all as dead as dinosaurs... DOOMED, the lot of us... a one-way ticket to the happy hunting grounds...'

'Can you work out how to get back to your home

140

from here?' asked Hiccup, consulting the ticking-thing anxiously. 'And take us back to Berk when you've got there?'

The scary white wilderness all around them seemed an unlikely sort of home to Hiccup, but there was a happy glint in Bearcub's Grandmother's wild eyes, although she tried to hide it. She breathed in the air, as cold as needles, and peered through the mists as if looking at something very familiar. She nodded. 'A Wanderer is never lost,' she said. 'We don't need that silly little bauble of yours to take us home. I could have showed that ridiculous Viking with the axe the way to America, if he'd had the intelligence to ask me...'

Hiccup tried to organise launching the landing-boats in a QUIET sort of way, which was impossible, and Hiccup hopped from foot to foot in anxiety as the Hysterical Warriors mumbled in their sleep with every crash of the oars. They were heavily armed, with swords, and wicked axes, and every sort of dagger, and Bearcub's Grandmother did have a point: Hiccup had no doubt that if awoken, they would deal out death with a vengeance.

But it seemed that luck was with the escapers.

The seven landing-boats plopped into the water without any of the Hysterics opening their eyes.

The Wanderers filled the boats, and the first boat began to row through the mists, Bearcub's Grandmother standing up straight and tall at the front, pointing the way with one outstretched arm.

The last landing-boat had filled up, apart from Hiccup, Fishlegs and Camicazi.

Fishlegs was watching Hiccup, as Hiccup got ready to climb down over the rim of the *American Dream II* and into the last landing-boat.

There were flat icebergs very close to the left and right of them. Camicazi had taken over from the snoring Red Ronald, and was steering the *American Dream II*, making sure the ship was moving forward in a straight line so that it didn't bump into the icebergs. She had tied the slumbering Stormfly to her chest, and the little dragon suddenly stirred violently in her sleep, jogging Camicazi's arm on the steering wheel... the *American Dream II* swerved suddenly and violently to the left...

... *just* as Hiccup was dangling over the edge on a rope, preparing to let himself drop into the little boat filled with Wanderers below.

'Wooooahhhhh!' gasped Hiccup, as the rope swung him forward, leaving the landing-boat behind. 'Watch where you're going, Camicazi!'

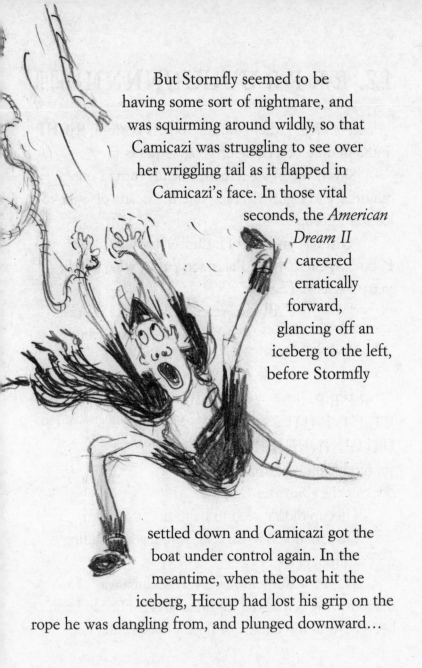

But Stormfly seemed to be
having some sort of nightmare, and
was squirming around wildly, so that
Camicazi was struggling to see over
her wriggling tail as it flapped in
Camicazi's face. In those vital
seconds, the *American
Dream* II
careered
erratically
forward,
glancing off an
iceberg to the left,
before Stormfly

settled down and Camicazi got the
boat under control again. In the
meantime, when the boat hit the
iceberg, Hiccup had lost his grip on the
rope he was dangling from, and plunged downward…

143

12. R-R-R-R-UUUUNNNNNN!!!!!!

… and landed, rather painfully, on his bottom, RIGHT in the middle of a circle of Polar-serpents.

Slowly the Polar-serpents' heads turned one hundred and eighty degrees, like the heads of owls, to look at Hiccup.

'OK…' stammered Hiccup. 'Easy now… nice Polar-serpents… *sweet* Polar-serpents… what lovely sharp horns you have…'

'All the better,' whined the nearest Polar-serpent, 'for spearing you with.'

'R-R-R-R-R-U-U-U-U-U-U-U-UNNNNNN!!!!!!' shouted Camicazi from the deck of the *American Dream II*.

Hiccup didn't need to be told.

He scrambled to his feet, slipping and sliding on the slippery ice.

The Polar-serpent has a very strange way of manouvering across the ice floes, and if Hiccup hadn't been right in the middle of fleeing for his life, he might have admired it. Half the pack of Polar-serpents spread out their wings like the sails of ships, braced their talons, and then shot forward on their smooth bellies, rocketing after Hiccup, their noses pointed straight toward him like darts for a dartboard. The remaining Polar-serpents slid into the water, swift and silent as alligators, and joined the chase from under the ice.

'Don't fall over, don't fall over, don't fall over!' begged Hiccup, clasping Toothless to his chest to stop him falling out of his waistcoat as he ran. He could hear the Polar-serpents whirring closer and closer, their nails screeching on the ice.

Now the shadows of those that were swimming under the ice swooped like swallows under his feet.

The *American Dream II* was still steaming alongside the iceberg.

'Hang on, Hiccup!' shouted Camicazi at the steering wheel. 'We're coming to rescue you!'

But Hiccup had no intention of hanging on. He was running faster than he ever had done in his life.

'**Mfff**,' sniffed Bearcub's Grandmother. '**It doesn't look good.**' She tut-tutted. '**He's not long for this world, you mark my words.**'
She held up a skinny finger. '**He's DOOMED, I tell you, DOOMED.**'

It seemed a fairly safe prediction, under the circumstances.

CCCC-CCC—RRUNNNNNK!

A great horn speared up through the ice right in front of Hiccup.

He swerved around it in the nick of time.

CCCC-CCCCRUNNNNK! CRRRUNNK! CRUNNNNKK!!!!

Three more appeared, and Hiccup slalomed round *them* too.

'*Kill them!*' shrieked Camicazi.

Fishlegs had got hold of one of Norbert's great bow-and-arrow harpoons.

tick-tock

It is unclear how he thought he was going to kill FIFTY Polar-serpents with the one harpoon, but he was pointing it in the general direction of the Polar-serpents with the bow upside-down, and his eyes shut.

As the harpoon went off Fishlegs fell backwards, letting go of the bow, which ricocheted across the deck, and jammed itself under the rim of the boat.

The harpoon sailed through the air, missing the Polar-serpents by at least ten metres.

But it was right bang on target for Hiccup, and would have hit him splang in the chest if the rope hadn't run out and pulled it to a sharp halt, sending it crashing to the ice with a clang.

'Why are you shooting at *me*?' howled a sprinting Hiccup. 'Haven't I got enough problems?'

The harpoon clattered in front of him, setting off little sprays of snow as it bounced across the ice.

'Oh *I* see...' panted Hiccup, and he launched himself at the harpoon as it dragged off...

But he *just* missed catching hold of the rope with both hands.

'Great God Thor... *ow!*... I could do... with some HELP here...' begged Hiccup, his chin in the snow.

But it seemed the Great God Thor was

temporarily deaf. The Polar-serpents were closing in for the kill, sending out thunderbolts of flame that only just missed incinerating poor Hiccup.

Hiccup scrambled to his feet. The harpoon was way out of reach now, his last hope of getting back on board the boat. The iceberg stretched out flat in front of him. He knew he couldn't outrun the Polar-serpents, who were already gaining on him. To his left there was a gigantic cliff of ice, with an enormous dark Cave at the bottom of it, like the open mouth of a monster.

Hiccup ran full tilt into the Cave.

The Polar-serpents followed.

He could hear their talons clicking and scraping on the ice, and their quick, fast breathing, so close that they were trying to grab hold of the ticking-thing bouncing along behind him, like great cats pouncing on a tasty morsel tied to the end of a string.

What's that up ahead? thought Hiccup. *Oh Woden the Great and Magnificent, I am begging you, please don't let that be a wall, the finish of the Cave, a dead-end, in which case I really* am *dead…*

It *was* a wall.

But as Hiccup ran closer still, he could see it was a rough and craggy wall with nooks and crannies and ledges and knobbly bits, and if he could climb up it before the Polar-serpents caught him, surely there would be a tunnel up there somewhere...

O Bending Biceps and Quivering Quadrapeds and Twitching Toenails and Little Hairy Curly Bits of Thunderous Thor!!!!!

It wasn't a wall at all. It was a DRAGON.

He was running straight, full-tilt, as hard as he could towards a truly immense sleeping Sea-dragon, so huge that its head filled the entire cave in front of him.

Hiccup put the brakes on.

He skidded abruptly, screeching on the ice, slid forward, arms waggling desperately, trying to stop

before he bumped into the thing, because he really did NOT want to wake it up...

... and he came to a halt just in the *nick* of time, feet away from the dragon's sleeping chin.

Hiccup stopped.

But the ticking-thing attached to Hiccup's wrist did not stop.

Momentum carried the ticking-thing UP from the ice where it had been bouncing along behind

Hiccup, sailing o-o-o-over Hiccup's head, and on
and on and up… and landing, sharp and precise, on
the closed eyelid of the sleeping dragon, as if it were
politely, but firmly, knocking on a door.

'Oh brother… oh brother… oh brother…'
whispered Hiccup, reeling the ticking-thing in and
around his wrist.

The eyelid fluttered.

It stayed down, as Hiccup backed slowly away.

'Please stay closed… please stay closed… please
stay closed…'

And then the eye opened.

In the darkness of the Cave it was like turning on
a great yellow searchlight, and Hiccup was blinded by
the glare.

How quickly the hunters become the hunted.

Hiccup was now running TOWARDS the Polar-serpents, confusing them considerably... until they too realised that that bright light was in fact the eye of an enormous, no-longer-sleeping, dragon.

Yowling and screeching like a pack of wolves, the Polar-serpents came tumbling and somersaulting to a stop and turned to run back the other way, with Hiccup belting after them, arms and legs going like pistons.

And behind them the terrible beginnings of a great rumbling R-R-R-ROAR...

The *American Dream II* had passed on from the iceberg now,

and was some distance away, and Camicazi was trying to get it to turn around.

Fishlegs looked over his shoulder to see the entire pack of Polar-serpents shooting out of the great Ice Cave like arrows shot from a bow.

Followed by Hiccup, running flat out.

'What's... going... on?' asked Fishlegs, knowing that whatever it was, it was Very Bad News.

The flat iceberg stretched out in front of Hiccup, far too big for safety. There was nowhere to go, no trees to hide under. No rocks, no tunnels for shelter.

So there wasn't really any point in running.

But the young Viking and the Polar-serpents still ran, nonetheless, hoping to put off their deaths for one moment, one *second* even.

For to Fishlegs's horror, two great yellow eyes slowly appeared in the darkness of the mouth of the Ice Cave.

Whatever it was, it was *huge*.

Something
like a moving
mountain with
wings exploded
out of the Cave.
The cliff erupted
into a volcano of
snow, as this *Something* burst out
of there. A great mass of raw
energy, a roar of wild triumph
screaming from its throat,
sending snow and ice
exploding in all
directions.

It was so big it momentarily blotted out the moon as it sailed through the air, and landed, screaming, on the iceberg Hiccup was running across.

So big was this Thing, that when the Thing landed, it crashed through the entire iceberg, sending great slabs of ice, and fountains of water, shooting up into the air. And Hiccup and the Polar-serpents were catapulted upwards.

The Polar-serpents ricocheted off in all directions like fireworks.

And up and up Hiccup sailed... o-o-o-o-o-over the surprised, sinking Monster's head... across the sea... up and towards the deck of the *American Dream II*... where he *just* missed catching on to the rim of the boat with his flailing fingers, and fell down, down, the side of the boat, and into the sea.

Where he would have remained if the harpoon that Fishlegs had shot earlier hadn't snagged into the back of his waistcoat, and dragged him along as if the boat had caught itself a fish.

Hand over hand, Hiccup heaved himself up the rope, and Camicazi and Fishlegs hauled him up and on to the deck of the *American Dream II*, steaming westward with its still-sleeping crew. And as he clambered, dripping, over the edge of the boat, heart racing like a rabbit, scarcely able to believe that he was still alive…

'The Machine!' he gasped, and immediately ran to the Stop-the-Boat-From-Sinking-and-Scare-Away-the-Monster-Sea-Creatures Machine. 'Help me get this guy off it, Fishlegs.'

The two young Vikings dragged the dead-to-the-world Red Ronald off the Machine, and Hiccup looked fearfully over his shoulder. The Monster had disappeared underneath the broken remains of the iceberg it had shattered. But was it his imagination, or could he see a racing, shooting, white line of water, beginning to TURN AROUND, and move back in their direction…?

Hiccup thrust his trembling feet into the pedals of the Machine and circled them furiously, making the ridiculous trumpet-like thingy revolve like a whirligig.

'I thought you said that Machine was useless,' panted Fishlegs.

'Well, hopefully I was wrong,' gasped Hiccup. 'Because otherwise we are DEAD.'

'Full steam ahead!' shouted Camicazi, rushing back to the steering wheel of the boat, and the *American Dream II* surged away from the iceberg.

'I… think… it's… working…' panted Hiccup.

Thor only knew *how* the Machine worked,* but that white wake of water seemed to slow down… and slow down… and slow down… and finally turn away. So whether or not Norbert's Machine would prevent a boat from sinking, it did seem that it was not quite as loopy as it looked, and it really *could* scare away a Monster Sea-dragon.

With a massive sigh of relief, Hiccup turned and he looked back over his other shoulder… to see the seven boats of Wanderers oaring away from them as quickly as possible in the other direction.

'Hey!' cried Hiccup in alarm. He showered Fishlegs with drops of seawater as he waved his arms at them. 'Fishlegs, take over, and for Thor's sake DON'T STOP PEDALLING…'

Hiccup swapped places with Fishlegs, and ran up and down the deck shouting: 'Don't leave us! What are you doing? Come and get us! What are they doing?

---

* In his later memoirs, Hiccup suggests that the 'trumpet' attachment emitted an unbearable noise at a pitch too high for the human ear to hear. Other sources say that the hearing of the larger Sea-dragons was so acute they could pick up the noise of a shrimp breathing several miles away, and this would certainly explain why the Machine worked on the 'Dragon-Mammoths', but not on smaller dragons such as Polar-serpents.

Camicazi, turn round and go after them.'

'Are you CRAZY?' interrupted Fishlegs. 'What about that THING? We have to get out of here as quickly as possible.'

'*WHERE ARE YOU GOING?*' Hiccup cupped his hands and shouted through the swiftly descending sea mist at the Wanderers, fast disappearing in the other direction. Hiccup's heart sank. He couldn't believe the injustice of it. After ALL that he had done, ALL that they had risked to save them from slavery, the Wanderers were running away, abandoning them!

'COWARDS!' yelled Camicazi over her shoulder. 'YELLOWBELLIES! *TRAITORS!*'

For a few minutes, Hiccup could still see
Bearcub's Grandmother, standing straight and tall on
the edge of her boat.

And then she disappeared into the mist.

13. THEY WERE IN *ITS* TERRITORY NOW...

So that was the end of the last hope of Escape from the Quest to America.

All hundred and nineteen of the Wanderer Slaves escaped.

But Hiccup, Camicazi and Fishlegs did not.

Hiccup saved Bearcub.

But who would save Hiccup?

They had their work cut out over the next five hours or so, trying to prevent the great boat from crashing into an iceberg in the mist. And by the time the mists lifted it was nearly morning, they had steamed out of the land of the Icebergs and into the Great West Ocean, and the Hysterics were beginning to stir in their sleep.

It was astonishing that they had all slept through the whole thing, but they had, even Toothless, who had snored happily through being chased by Polar-serpents and bumping over icebergs and submerged in ice-cold water, without so much as opening an eyelid.

Red Ronald was the first to wake up, to find Camicazi pedalling the Keep-the-Boat-from-Sinking-and-Scare-Away-the-Monster-Sea-Creatures Machine.

'*I* won't tell Norbert, if you don't,' said Camicazi, climbing off the Machine and letting Red Ronald climb back on again. Red Ronald was so pathetically grateful he practically cried, for he knew if his Boss found out he had fallen asleep on the job he would quickly find himself on the wrong side of the Axe of Doom.

Hiccup re-tied the ticking-thing to Norbert's wrist, so that Norbert would never know he had tried to steal it, and then he judged it best that the three of them should be out of the way when Norbert made the discovery that all of his slaves had escaped into the night.

So, once Hiccup's clothes had thoroughly dried on the chimney, they crept back up to the crow's nest, where they fell asleep, curled around the comforting warmth of the two dragons, who gave out lovely waves of heat like two little hot water bottles. They were only awoken by Norbert's great roar of rage.

At first Norbert was sure that it was all Hiccup's fault.

'THAT WRETCHED WEIRD LITTLE RED-HAIRED BOY! I SHOULD HAVE KILLED HIM WHILE I HAD THE CHANCE!' screamed Norbert the Nutjob. 'HE'S MADE OFF WITH ALL OF MY SLAVES!'

Hiccup put his head over the top of the crow's nest.

'No, I haven't,' he called down. 'I'm up here…'

Norbert was so furious, he swiped at the mast with his Axe as if he were chopping down a tree, taking a big slice *out* of it. 'WHAT HAVE YOU DONE WITH MY SLAVES???!!!' he roared.

'I haven't done ANYTHING with your slaves,' Hiccup called down. 'If I *had* done, I would have run away myself.'

This was quite a good argument, but Norbert wasn't in a listening kind of mood and he took another swing at the mast.

'Now, now,' Hiccup shouted, 'we need that mast, you know, and I'm the only one who can read the ticking-thing and get us to America, aren't I? So without *me*, you can't create your Land of the Nutjobs… your Empire…'

With a massive effort, Norbert managed to stop himself from cutting down the mast. But nonetheless, Hiccup thought he might stay up in the crow's nest until he felt Norbert had calmed down.

Toothless and Stormfly both woke up much, much later, when the sun was high in the sky, and the two little dragons had absolutely no recollection of what had happened.

The ship was way out in the Great West Ocean now. The world around them had turned to water.

Nothing but water, water everywhere.

It was as if a Great Flood had taken place and washed over every precious piece of land. And now there was nothing but sea below and clouds above, and their tiny little speck of a boat crawling across it, like a bug across a window pane.

It was as if they had left this world entirely and were sailing through space, looking for another star. There was no way of contacting other humans. They were on their own, in a universe of water that went on for ever.

And what was worse, was that the ship now seemed to be being *followed* by something.

From high up in the crow's nest, Hiccup, Fishlegs and Camicazi saw it first.

It was the white wake of a GIGANTIC *Sea-Monster*.

'SEA-DRAGON ON THE EASTERN HORIZON!' screamed Norbert from down below on the deck. *'GET PEDALLING!!!!! OR I'LL FEED YOU TO THE MONSTER WITH MY OWN FAIR HANDS!!!'*

The crew took it in turns to pedal the Scare-Away-the-Big-Sea-Creatures Machine so fast that the Machine's spokes and wheels whined a screeching, creaking, out-of-control complaint, and the trumpet-attachment thingy whirled so crazily, it looked in danger of falling off.

But the Sea-dragon was not scared away. The sound the Machine made was so physically unbearable to the Monster that it kept a safe distance from the boat. But it did not stop it from following them.

All of the rest of that day the Sea-dragon followed the *American Dream II*, and all of the night.

The crew went to sleep at their battle-stations, upright in their armour, harpoons at the ready.

As they closed their eyes in sleep, it was the last thing they saw on the horizon, the long thin line of a white wake, and the great spiny back of one of the Great, Deadly Terrors of the Deep, rising and falling as it swam inexorably after them like some ghastly Fate.

They were in ITS territory now…

… and IT knew it.

All it had to do, was to be patient.

The only thing preventing the Sea-dragon from moving in for the kill, and tearing apart the *American Dream II* with its mighty jaws as if it were a child's toy, was a dilapidated, cranky, over-worked little Machine.

A Machine that was looking increasingly creaky and wonky as each crew member pedalled it furiously to death.

If a screw came loose on one of those wobbling wheels, that whirligig trumpet thingy would come whizzing off and...

It didn't bear thinking about.

EVERYBODY had nightmares that night.

And it made Hiccup's heart skip a beat or two when he woke to see the wake of the Sea-dragon on the horizon. It was still following them.

Hiccup crept down from the crow's nest, and over to the Steering Deck where Norbert was staring at it too, through his looking-glass thingy.

'Norbert,' said Hiccup nervously. 'I just have a feeling that that Sea-dragon doesn't like us for some reason. Don't you think we should go home?'

For a moment, Hiccup didn't think Norbert had heard him, for Norbert carried on looking at the horizon, muttering to himself slowly: '*That*... is the largest Sea-Monster I have EVER seen...'

And then Norbert took his looking-glass thingy from his eye and looked straight down at Hiccup.

'No dragon, however big, is going to take away

my dream,' ground out Norbert the Nutjob from between clenched teeth, shaking his fist in Hiccup's face. 'I'll jump down that Thing's throat and personally remove its wishbone with my axe if I have to. You understand me, boy?'

Hiccup nodded.

'**DEATH** or **AMERICA!**' roared Norbert the Nutjob. 'Now read me the ticking-thing, and stop talking treachery.'

Hiccup climbed despondently back to the crow's nest, and relayed the bad news to his friends.

'This just gets worse and worse, it's like some sort of nightmare...' moaned Fishlegs. 'We could have escaped on our own, but, oh no, you have to choose to try and escape with a hundred and nineteen Wanderers, very subtle, and they aren't even Vikings...'

'I made them a promise,' replied Hiccup automatically.

'And look how they repaid you!!' Fishlegs pointed out. 'So you've saved a hundred and nineteen not-very-nice complete strangers, but you've doomed your two best friends in the process. Nice choice, Hiccup. Any escape plans, Camicazi?'

Even Camicazi, who had escaped from practically every Tribe in the Archipelago, seemed to have run out of hope that she could escape from this situation. 'I think the safest place to be right now is on this ship,' she said. 'Because out there, is that Sea-dragon. Do you think it's the same one that chased you in the land of the Polar-serpents?'

'Definitely,' said Hiccup. 'I recognised the spines on its back. Those kind of spikes are mostly seen on dragons that are now extinct.'

'What kind of dragon is it, anyway?' asked Fishlegs.

'I don't know,' said Hiccup slowly. 'It was difficult to tell because it was so dark, but it wasn't a species I recognised. It reminds me of some of the ones that I've heard about in the ancient Sagas. A Leviathorgan, or a Gorgenghast.'

'Aren't those just mythical creatures?' asked Camicazi. 'You know, made-up, like unicorns and mermaids and things?'

'Maybe they're *not* made-up,' said Hiccup. 'Maybe they just haven't been seen for a long time. Just because we don't know *how* that Machine works, doesn't mean that it *doesn't* work. Just because we've never *seen* America, doesn't mean it isn't *there*. We're in waters that we're not used to now, the waters of the Great West Ocean. There could be all *sorts* of terrible things down there in the fathoms below us, who knows?'

It was not a cheerful thought.

To keep their spirits up, they thought about what everybody would be doing back at home.

The Hooligan Tribe would be back on Berk now, playing Bashyball in the mud, preparing for the spring shearing, painting the boats for the summer sailings.

'I wonder who won the Inter-Tribe Friendly Swimming Race?' mused Fishlegs.

'My mother is the Archipelago Long Distance Swimming Champion, Bertha the Unsinkable!' said Camicazi. 'She'd have stayed out there for *days*!'

'And why wouldn't my father have won?' argued Hiccup loyally. 'He's just as good at swimming as Bertha...'

'NO WAY!' insisted Camicazi.

And so they argued, back and forth, not that it mattered, of course, but it passed the time, and it helped to be thinking of what might be happening at home.

They did not realise, of course, that in fact neither of their parents had actually *left the beach*, let alone *won the Competition*, on that fateful morning several weeks ago...

14. WHAT HAPPENED BACK IN THE MURDEROUS MOUNTAINS

Several weeks earlier, back in the Murderous Mountains, it looked like Madguts would have the glory of being Last Man Back. He lasted for forty-one hours out there in the water, which, even when covered with a thin layer of Deepest Purple Fleshfang Oil, is an almost superhuman feat.

He was greeted by a cheering crowd of Viking Tribesmen on the Long Beach as he strode out of the waves, arms held above his head in victory, Gumboil trotting a few steps in front of him.

The Chief Judge, the sad little Bashem-Oik, rushed up the beach to meet Madguts. He gave him a golden medal, and a pipe that Madguts jammed between his lips as he made a Victory Lap of the Beach, acknowledging the cheering.

Gumboil bowed towards the Inter-Tribal Friendly Swimming Race Committee. 'My Master greets the Judges, and claims the Victory of being the Last Man Back in this Swimming Contest. And as Last Man Back, according to the Rules, he may make a single demand of the losing Chieftains, Stoick and Bertha.'

Poor Stoick was sitting with his head in his hands. Stoick was not a natural worrier, but he was now terribly concerned about the fate of his son, Hiccup. Now he got to his feet and roared, 'But Hiccup is not back! My son may yet return and claim the prize himself!'

It was a desperate hope, but Stoick was clinging to it. Madguts grinned an unpleasant grin with not enough teeth in it. He whispered in his assistant's ear.

'My Master points out, respectfully,' Gumboil bowed in the direction of Stoick and Bertha, 'that Stoick's son, Hiccup, Bertha's daughter, Camicazi, and the odd looking boy they call Fishlegs, are most likely to have DROWNED in the very first hours of the Competition...'

'*NO!*' bellowed Stoick, with an anger born of fear.

The Inter-Tribal Friendly Swimming Race Committee nodded wisely and sadly to each other. It did seem likely at this point.

'This is true,' admitted the Chief Judge solemnly. 'For Snotface Snotlout here reports that he and Dogsbreath the Duhbrain saw Hiccup and the other two in difficulties. He tried to help them...'

'We did our best,' said Snotlout, sorrowfully and nobly, 'but we were swept away by the force of the current, weren't we, Dogsbreath?'

Dogsbreath grunted, and removed his helmet out of respect for the dead.

'It's a tragedy,' sighed Snotlout. 'Hiccup was like a brother to me...'

Stoick gave a groan of sadness, terrible to hear, and turned away.

'Don't worry, Stoick, my dear chap,' Bertha comforted him awkwardly. 'Camicazi is with him, and, trust me, *she* always turns up all right... *She* could escape from Valhalla itself...'

'And so Madguts demands his prize,' smiled Gumboil silkily. 'And he demands... *the kingdoms of Stoick and Bertha, who should be taken immediately from this beach, and up to the Sky Burial Place on the clifftops to be sacrificed to the Sky Dragons*!'

'Whaaaaaaaaat?' roared the Hooligans and the Bog-Burglars in fury. Uproar on the beach.

'But… but… but this is outrageous!' stuttered Bertha. 'He can't ask for *that*!'

'I hope you're not going to go back on your word, Bertha,' Gumboil wagged a warning finger at the apoplectic Bog-Burglar Chief. 'Don't be such a bad sport. I am presuming that if YOU had won, you would have expected Madguts to do YOUR bidding…'

'This is just a Friendly Swimming Race! *We* were only going to ask for Madguts to cross the Sullen Sea in a bathtub with his underpants on his head!' yelled Bertha indignantly.

'More fool you,' smiled Gumboil. Madguts is only asking what *Stoick's* ancestor, Grimbeard the Ghastly, asked of *Madguts'* ancestor, way back in the bad old days…'

Old Wrinkly had been trying to interrupt for some time. He got to his feet and cleared his throat.

'A small technical point, Your Wheeziness,' said Old Wrinkly to the Chief Judge. 'Let me tell again that story from the bad old days, the Saga of Grimbeard the Ghastly and the Swimming Race. Just in case there are some people here who do not know it.'

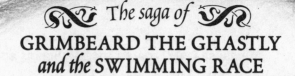

The saga of
GRIMBEARD THE GHASTLY
and the SWIMMING RACE

Grimbeard the Ghastly was Stoick's great-great-grandfather, a wicked, successful pirate who became the last King of the Archipelago. One day, Murderous the Magnificent challenged Grimbeard the Ghastly to a swimming race, and the two chiefs agreed the winner should be granted a single demand.

So one cold morning they set out from the Western Beach of the Murderous Mountains. Murderous the Magnificent finally swam back to the same beach in seventy-one hours and forty-two minutes, nearly three days in total. His face had swollen to twice the size and his body was so covered in wrinkles he looked like he had been pickled in the brine.

The Hooligan Tribe waited on the beach hoping and hoping for their chief to return. After a week, they accepted that he must have drowned, and conceded the victory to the Murderous Tribe. Murderous the Magnificent claimed the Kingdom of the Archipelago, and that, everybody thought, was the end of the matter. However, three months later, Murderous the Magnificent was conducting a night-time banquet on that very same beach. The highlight of the banquet was the human sacrifice under the stars.

Just before the sacrifice took place, Grimbeard the

Ghastly came staggering out
of the surf. He was barely recognisable.
Half-human, half-monster, with skin like a
dragon, all entwined with seaweed, and he had shark's
teeth around his calves like bracelets.

Grimbeard the Ghastly staggered up the
beach and collapsed. Murderous the Magnificent
raised up his sword to kill what he thought was some
kind of demon... then he saw that the monster was
wearing around its waist Grimbeard the Ghastly's
famous sword, the Stormblade!

The next words that Grimbeard spoke, as he lay
gasping for breath on the sand, can be repeated proudly
by every Hooligan schoolboy, so well-known are they:

"Stay your hand, Murderous the Magnificent.
I am no ghost. It is I, Grimbeard the Ghastly, who
have the Greatest Stomach after all. I have survived the
Open Ocean, by the will of Thor, without seeking aid
from float or boat, I am the last man back, and I am come
to claim my Kingdom for the Hooligan Tribe!'

I am afraid that Grimbeard the Ghastly, who
was not a nice man, then insisted as his demand that
Murderous the Magnificent should be sacrificed
to the Sky Dragons. The Annual Inter-Tribe
Swimming Race has been held every year in memory
of this historical event, but over the years it has
become more of a friendly competition.

'There you are, you see!' said Gumboil triumphantly. 'For one hundred years the Murderous Tribe have been waiting for our revenge, and now finally, the time has come, and our pride shall be restored.'

'Stop interrupting!' snapped Old Wrinkly 'Now, Grimbeard was, among other things, a terrible trickster, a practical joker and an all-round cheat. But however he achieved this extraordinary stunt, he returned to this beach, Last Man Back (the Committee might like to check the Sagas for this), exactly THREE MONTHS, FIVE DAYS AND SIX HOURS later! There ARE still three members of the race unaccounted for, namely Hiccup, Fishlegs and the very small Bog-Burglar they call Camicazi. I would propose that if *Grimbeard the Ghastly* could stay out that long, then, technically speaking, *they could too…* so we need to wait three months, three days and eleven hours before Madguts can claim his prize.'

Gasps from the crowd.

The Judges went into a 'Thinking Scrum' to consult upon this matter.

'OK, then,' said the Chief Judge, emerging from the Scrum and banging on the drum. 'HERE IS THE VERDICT of the Inter Tribal Swimming Race Committee. As long as Madguts has stuck to the Rules of the Competition, trickery played within those Rules is a perfectly repectable Viking characteristic.'

Cheers of greedy joy from the Murderous Tribe.

Howls of sadness and fury from the Hooligans and the Bog-Burglars.

'I haven't finished!' cried the Chief Judge. 'Madguts the Murderous is granted temporary custody of Big-Boobied Bertha and Stoick the Vast. And we Judges will stay on the beach to keep watch for the three missing competitors. But the rest of you can go home. And you will return back to this beach exactly three months, five days and six hours from the start of the race. If in that time no one has returned alive from these waters, Madguts the Murderous will be declared Last Man Back, the Berk and Bog-Burglar islands will fall into Murderous hands, and Stoick and Bertha, I am afraid, will be sacrificed to the Sky Dragons...'

The Chief Judge banged his staff upon the ground. And so it was.

The three old Judges sat patiently on the beach, through wind and rain and storm, looking out to sea.

The rest of the Bog-Burglars and the Hooligans sailed sorrowfully back to their islands.

And poor old Stoick and Big-Boobied Bertha were not playing Bashyball in the mud, or supervising the spring shearing, or painting the boats for the summer sailings, as Hiccup had imagined.

They were incarcerated in the deepest and darkest Murderous Cave Dungeons, so cramped and dark that they could barely move a muscle.

There was a tiny barred window in Stoick's dungeon, which had a good view over the Great West Ocean and Stoick would fall asleep sometimes, looking out over this view, and dream that his son was alive, and swimming back to him across the sea. But then he would wake up, and it was nothing but a dream, and all there was was water, water, stretching out for ever, and the cold lonely cry of the seagulls.

15. IT'S A LONG WAY TO AMERICA

Now follows the part of the story in which Hiccup travelled across the Great West Ocean.*

It would take far too long to tell you what happened every minute, every hour, every day.

Thousands and thousands of miles the Great Ship travelled, the puffing fiery furnace sending them skimming across the water far quicker than sails alone. Thousands and thousands of miles across the Ocean, sometimes in sunshine and glass-flat sea and windless skies, sometimes in gales and hurricanes and driving rain, surging up and down on the back of the white-topped waves as if they were aboard a great galloping horse.

Travelling across the Great West Ocean is a VERY long way indeed.

It is indeed *such* a long way, it seemed to Hiccup to be like stepping off the edge of the World and into Forever. And through wind and sun and frost and rain, this Sea-dragon followed the doomed ship, constant as a meteor orbiting the earth, just as if the ship were a planet that had its own particular moon, slowly and predictably circling it.

---

*The Atlantic Ocean, as we now call it.

The Hysterics were still hale and hearty, wolfing down their smoked reindeer with gusto, and washing it down with a nice dose of bull's blood and strong cabbage BEER.

They were in fine, violent spirits, joking with one another, and sometimes going too far, and so the whole deck erupted into fisticuffs, and Norbert had to break up the fights by storming into the centre of the trouble, whirring his axe above his head like the propeller of one of his mad inventions.

The Hysterics sang all day and night long, of their sweethearts at home, of Jellybelly's bright eyes, and Grimhilda's magnificent chin, and fortunes to be made, and blood to be spilt, in the New World called America.

And at night, as they slept, their dreaming minds drew maps of America and each map of this paradise-on-earth was drawn according to their own desires.

To Nutjob it was a place of GOLD, where all his inventions worked like clockwork, and he could rule on a golden throne with a golden crown on his head and a golden axe in one hand.

To lazy little Toothless, it would be a land of FOOD, with small furry animals in such abundance that you barely had to raise a claw to catch them.

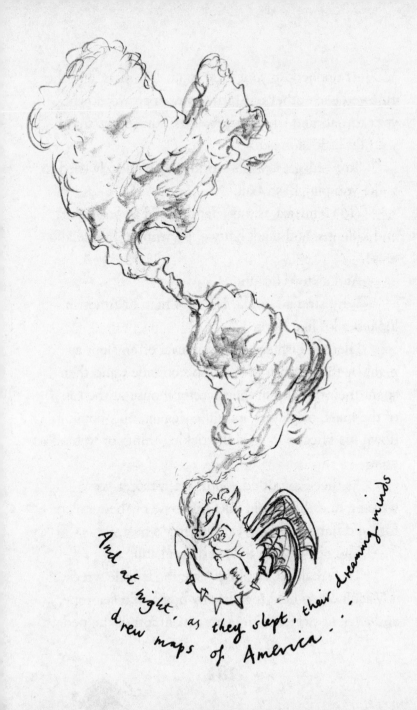

And at night, as they slept, their dreaming minds drew maps of America . . .

You just opened up your little tooth-free jaws, and they elbowed each other out of the way to crowd down your throat, and troop downwards, squeaking, into your fat little stomach.

To Fishlegs, it was a world where nobody tried to make you play Bashyball.

To Camicazi, it was a land full of sword-fights, and kidnaps, and mad, hairy opponents to burgle and tease.

And as for Hiccup...

Why, strange to tell, *Hiccup's* map of America looked a lot like Berk.

Hiccup, Fishlegs and Camicazi often slept at night by the warmth of the ship's chimney, and then spent their days up in their treetop house at the top of the mast, or played upon the rigging, only coming down for Hiccup to read the ticking-thing, or to have a meal.

As the ship puffed south, the weather grew warmer, and they could take off some of their stolen furs and hang them out on the crow's nest.

The Sea-dragon followed them still.

The creaking, clanking, shambolic little wreck of a Machine was held together by bits of old sea rope, and ancient twine. With every revolution of the pedals,

the trumpet-thingy seemed in trembling danger of
falling off...

... but by some miracle, the wheels still turned,
and it hadn't fallen off...

... *yet*.

Every evening just at sundown, Norbert would
summon Hiccup to his tent to read the ticking-thing.
There he would be, pacing up and down on the
rocking deck in front of his maps, all spread out on the
bearskin tablecloth, and as the days went on he grew
more and more impatient, clapping his great hands
together, and muttering to himself, 'Nearly there now!
Nearly there!' before Hiccup told him the reading for
the day. Norbert wasn't a very patient man, and this
waiting was killing him.

He had a tiny replica of the *American Dream
II*, exquisitely made in every detail, but only about
eight centimetres high. It had a real working sail, and
the writing on the side was so tiny it looked like it
had been drawn by a flea. Norbert used his axe to
push this boat across the surface of his great map,
according to Hiccup's reading of the ticking thing, so
that he could see where they might be on the Great
West Ocean. Every day it drew nearer and nearer to
the great landfall Norbert had drawn on it and called

'AMERICA', until it was now, according to the map, only a day or two's sail away, and Norbert could barely contain his excitement.

Hiccup was very uneasy. He remembered what Norbert had said about how they were only safe for as long as Norbert needed him to read the ticking-thing for him. Now they were so close to America, a nasty look came into Norbert's eye when it rested on Hiccup. Norbert had taken to polishing the dark side of his axe until it gleamed like ebony, whispering to it as if it were a precious pet: 'Not long now my darling… soon you shall be fed…'

Hiccup did not like the sound of this *at all*, and he took the precaution of getting Camicazi to steal them back their weapons. He had a nasty feeling they were going to need them.

So there was a great knot of anxiety in Hiccup's stomach. Especially as he watched the crew while they were having breakfast outside the Cooking Tent the next day. The Hysterics were in an excitable mood, singing their songs with great gusto:

'There's LAND ahead lads, LAND ahead, a LAND of milk and HONEY,

'We'll soon be off these rocking waves and rolling in the MONEY…'

16. LAND AHOY!!!!!!

A storm was brewing.

Ominous clouds were building up in the skies above, like a god with a headache, and the boat was already beginning to rock beneath their feet as the swell grew larger, and the wind picked up.

Suddenly, there was a great flash of lightning that lit up the sky.

Hiccup could see distinctly in that sudden flash the black back of the great Sea-dragon on the horizon.

And *just* as the lightning struck, there was a great gleeful cry of JOY from the lookout on the first mast: 'NUTJOB-LAND AHO-O-O-O-O-O-O-O-Y!!!!!!!!!'

And the Hysterics rushed to the edge of the boat, jostling and trampling and elbowing each other out of the way.

They wanted to be the first to catch a glimpse of that glorious, mythical, land, that mysterious place they called 'America'.

That first sighting was just as wonderful as they could possibly have imagined.

Above them, the storm was breaking, and rain poured down on their heads, as the ship bucked up and down on the back of the plunging waves.

But on the horizon, the long grey smudge of land
that seemed to stretch infinitely from west to east was
bathed in sunshine under the bluest of blue skies.

America.

The land of dreams, it really *did* exist, and in that
wonderful moment, it was just as it should be.

No sooner had Norbert clapped eyes on this
country that he had waited so long, and journeyed so
far, to find, that he drew his axe in order to exact an
old revenge.

'*Now*, Hiccup Horrendous Haddock the Third,'
grinned Norbert the Nutjob, with the light of triumph
glowing in his manic eye, 'I have no need of YOU any
more… and *now* you will feel the sharp end of the Axe
of Doom… PREPARE TO DIE!'

Hiccup leapt up on to a barrel so that everyone
could see him. 'DON'T KILL ME JUST BECAUSE
I'M A RED-HEAD, NORBERT!' shouted Hiccup as
loud as he could.

The Hysterics crowded at the ship's rail turned
around.

'What's going on?' asked Verociously Violent,
whose hair was a great shock of scarlet, flaming like a
fiery furnace.

'What *are* you talking about?' blustered Norbert.
'*NORBERT, HERE, DOESN'T WANT ANY
RED-HEADS TO BE LIVING IN THE PROMISED
LAND!*' yelled Hiccup. '*HE'S GOING TO KILL US
ALL WITH HIS AXE OF DOOM!*'

It just so happened that, by coincidence, quite a
lot of the red-headed members of the Hysteric Tribe had
suffered at the hands of Norbert's wild temper and his
experiments. (For instance, Norbert had sent Verociously
Violent and Goggle-eyes the Gory up in the air to try
out his Flying Machine experiment TWENTY-SEVEN
TIMES, and *every single time*, the Flying Machine had
crashed into the sea two minutes after it took off.) So
the red-heads drew their swords with an angry rumble of
revolt.

For their part, the Hysterics with blond hair had
always had a secret feeling of superiority. Now that
Norbert had brought it up, what could be better than
a whole Tribe of blonds, storming into the Future, hair
brighter than the cornfields?

So they too drew their swords, and within
a couple of seconds, to Norbert's open-mouthed
amazement, the entire Tribe of Hysteric Warriors were
fighting *each other* as if they were desperate enemies.

It was a terrible battle indeed. Thor's thunder
rolled out across the black and angry stormclouds,
and great jagged splinters of lightning cracked open
the skies and punched down on to the swelling seas
all around them. Huge frothing waves spilled over the
sides of the boat and across the deck, upsetting the
combatants as they fought in the drenching rain.

Camicazi joined Hiccup in fighting Norbert.

'YOU, Norbert,' teased Camicazi, 'have the
mental capacity of a jellyfish with a lobotomy. You
have the leadership skills of a lemming with a head
cold. You couldn't run an Empire larger than my toilet
without making a complete dog's breakfast of it...
which is a bit of a problem for a dictator...'

Hiccup lunged forward with a Left-handed
Heartseeker, and Norbert was so distracted by
Camicazi's insults that he only just parried it in time.

And while he was occupied with the parry,
Camicazi leapt in and tickled him under the armpits.

'Oooh, nice muscles, Norbert, have you been
working out?'

With a howl of fury, Norbert shook her off, and
Camicazi sprang backwards, and ducked his furious
swing of the axe.

'Temper, temper...' she scolded, and so mad
with rage was Norbert that he didn't even
see Hiccup's Twirling Double-Point until it
removed the bottom half of his beard, and
meanwhile, Camicazi sneaked in under his
left arm, and stole the ticking-thing from
out of his pocket, cutting the rope that tied it to
Norbert's wrist.

'Is this yours?' asked Camicazi,
dangling the ticking-thing in front of him.

'Tut, tut, you need to be careful with it, or someone might steal it…'

'Give it here!' roared Norbert, slashing away at her randomly.

'Come and get it…' sang Camicazi, twirling the ticking-thing around her head, and bonking Norbert on the nose with it, before she threw it to Hiccup, who caught it neatly.

The only problem with Camicazi's fighting method was that it tended to make the opponent REALLY REALLY MAD.

Norbert turned as red as a tomato, and LAUNCHED himself at the two young Vikings, howling like a dog.

The swords flashed together, in and out, lunge and parry.

Norbert was a terrifying opponent, with his sword in one hand and his axe swiping in the other.

But even though they were young, as you can see, Hiccup and Camicazi were a formidable fighting duo.

Who knows *what* would have happened, if Toothless hadn't taken it in his head to be helpful.

Toothless grabbed Norbert's big map of America from the table in his Tent, and flapped unsteadily, like

a large ungainly moth, over to the scene of the fight.
He hovered for a second over Hiccup, Camicazi and
Norbert, and then shook his head as he dropped
the map, so it spread out nicely as it fell, and
floated gently…

… on to the head of Norbert the Nutjob,
covering him from the top of his helmet to the bottom
of his midriff, like a mysterious lady of the Eastern
deserts.

'Oh well done, Toothless!' Toothless
congratulated himself, clapping his wings together in
an ecstasy of excitement. 'Nice swooping!'

The deck heaved violently on the swell of a wave.

Norbert staggered, trying to regain his balance,
but with a map upon his head, he couldn't see where
he was going…

He lurched violently to the left… and then wildly
to the right, bashing into Red Ronald, still pedalling
faithfully away on the Stop-the-Boat-from-Sinking-
and-Scare-Away-the-Big-Sea-Creatures Machine, with
such force that… Red Ronald… and, most importantly,
the MACHINE… the creaky, cranky little Machine
that had by some extraordinary chance held together
all this way…

… fell over the rim of the boat and into the sea.

There was a mighty pause.

'Oh, Toothless...' moaned Hiccup, with his hands over his eyes.

They were *so close* to America that it had ceased to be a pale grey outline, and was a long swoop of white beach, with great grey waves crashing upon the shoreline, and trees above, and you could even see tiny little mysterious figures moving upon the sand.

But now the Machine was no longer giving out that unbearable high-pitched noise, the Sea-dragon on the horizon – the Sea-dragon that everybody had forgotten about in the heat of the fighting – was *finally* released.

And with a mighty, terrible shriek, it shot towards the boat.

Having regained his balance, Norbert took the Map off his head and blinked twice, first at the spot where the Machine had disappeared over the rim of the boat, then at the Truly Gigantic Dragon moving purposefully towards them.

Nobody was fighting now. Red-heads, blonds, lunatics, *all* had recognised a greater danger, and were crouching down on the deck in fear.

'*HERE IT COMES!*' shouted somebody.

17. THE LEVIATHORGAN STRIKES

The Hysteric nearest to Hiccup fell to his knees, gasping: 'Thor save us!'

All they could see of the Creature were the spines on its back drawing closer and closer in the water.

It was aiming straight for the boat.

But at the very last moment, it changed direction, and swam alongside it. And it was only then that they realised how truly enormous it was.

It was IMMENSE.

As the Dragon passed the boat, it rolled slightly on its side, and one terrible yellow reptilian eye stared at Hiccup, pinpointing him, picking him out. There was a curious expression in that eye, of intelligent humour mixed with the purest fury. It was as if it hadn't forgotten the incident in the Ice Cave, and something in that eye seemed to say, 'You're going to pay for that, boy, and I'm going to enjoy it... You can't get away from me now.'

And then it moved on, muscles rippling, as it swam sinuously as a panther through the water. It swam so close to the boat, that it was almost as if it were showing off how big it was. That long, glorious back with the cruel, primeval spikes, went on, it seemed like, for ever...

Oh for Thor's sake, thought Hiccup, his heart in his mouth, *it must be twice, no nearly* three *times as long as this boat...*

It was a Leviathorgan, all right.

Like all the ancient Sea-dragons, it had probably been alive since the age of the dinosaurs, and it had the look of something dug up from the past. Blackened crustacea festooned its spiny armour like rust. Parts of its body were so encrusted with coral, and trailing with long drifts of seaweed, that it was like a living, moving reef.

The heart-stoppingly huge length of the Leviathorgan swam beside the boat. And then it turned away, and swam on past them, and disappeared below the water, the casual, contemptuous flip of its tail creating such a great white washing powerful wake that it swamped the deck with a wave that covered their knees.

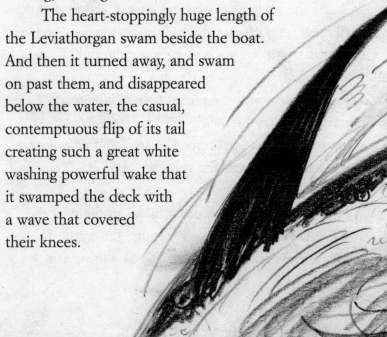

'Where's it gone?'

Many voices called out the same question from the ship.

There had been a look in that Dragon's giant eye which Hiccup had seen in the expression of Toothless when he had cornered something smaller than himself, like a mouse or a rabbit.

We're going To need a bigger boat...

Like cats, dragons have a cruel streak, and they like to play with their food, before they kill it.

'*It's going to play with* US...' thought Hiccup with foreboding. 'Grab on to something on the boat!' he yelled out, winding a rope attached to the mast firmly round his wrist.

'Oh brother,' moaned Fishlegs, as he did the same, 'how did this happen? We just went out for a simple little SWIMMING RACE, is there NO safe activity in this uncivilised world?'

The dragon had dived under the water, and there was no sign of it, just the roaring of the wind, the crashing of the thunder, the drenching rain.

'WHERE IS IT? WHERE'S IT GONE?' someone shouted frantically.

There was an explosion of white water to Hiccup's left, as the Leviathorgan LEAPT out of the sea. It flew right over the boat, and hovered there.

Again, it was almost as if it were showing off how big it was.

It was so enormous that hovering above the great ship's mast, the tips of its great wings *just* grazed the surface of the water as they beat downward on either side.

Its eyes bored down at the Viking ship. Gently

it reached out its gigantic talons, and took hold of the mast of the *American Dream II*, like an eagle grasping a stick.

And then it lifted the entire ship completely clear of the water...

It looked down into the boat to see the reaction of the inhabitants.

Most of them were screaming.

The great Sea-dragon gave the ship a little shake, sending the Vikings inside it catapulting around the deck like marbles... and then it dropped the *American Dream II* back into the water again.

The Monster hung above them still, blotting out the sky, and now it stretched wide its great ancient mouth, far wider than would have seemed physically possible, so that it became a great black cavern, opening up in front of their eyes.

Like an enormous spitting cobra, the Sea-dragon began to hiss.

First a gentle sssssss... getting louder and louder, SSSSSSS, until it built up into such a sinister, angry intensity that it was as if the entire ship were crawling with nests of serpents about to strike. The sound sent goosebumps all over Hiccup's body, and every individual hair on his head stood up as if charged with static electricity.

The Creature's eyes bulged, its throat worked.

It was looking straight at Hiccup, and instinctively, Hiccup ducked behind the mast.

Something flew through the air, and sunk itself quivering into the wood.

With round, terrified – no, *petrified* – eyes, Hiccup peered round the mast to look at it.

It was the sting of the Leviathorgan.

Hiccup had heard of this in legends. Like a gigantic bee, the Leviathorgan carries stings within its body, but in its throat, inside the fire-hole rather than its abdomen. It can propel these stings from its mouth at astonishing speed, like a rocket launcher.

The sting of a bee is no more than a couple of millimetres long. The sting of a Leviathorgan is roughly the length of a spear.

It had sunk quite eight centimetres into the wood, and remained there, shivering and on fire. It seemed to be made out of some kind of bone as hard as metal, but it was difficult to tell because the flames flickered along its length. A great scarlet-black stain was spreading out on the mast as the poison from the tip leaked out, and Hiccup was just taking off his jacket to smother the flames before they set fire to the mast, when the Leviathorgan entered the water on the other side of the boat.

This time it slapped down its tail with such deliberate force that a wave tipped the boat violently to the left, so much so that the tip of the mast itself nearly reached the water.

Barrels, the Cooking Tent, cauldrons, brooms, Norbert's precious Map Table, his table and chairs, his rugs and his birdcages, Hysterics, forks, pails, and vegetables, all were washed away in a flood of thigh-deep water as the boat dipped so crazily that it almost seemed in peril of tipping over entirely.

Both Fishlegs and Camicazi had lost their grip on what they were holding on to and were washed off by the force of the wave. But the ticking-thing had caught around the mast, and Hiccup remained on the boat.

For a second it seemed as if the boat would up-end completely… and then it righted itself again, and swung back, equally wildly, in the other direction, flinging Norbert back over the edge and spinning him to the centre of the deck.

Again it seemed uncertain that the ship would find its centre of balance, but it rocked back eventually, and rolled drunkenly forward, direction-less now that there was no one at the wheel.

Most of the crew was washed off into the stormy seas.

The deck was ankle-deep in water, stained a bloody red (I'm SORRY for those of you who are squeamish, but it was).

Those crew that remained were either concentrating in putting out the fire on one of the sails before it spread (the Leviathorgan had shot out another flaming sting before it dived back into the sea, and it had passed straight through the end sail, setting it alight), or they were on their knees praying to the great god Thor.

Some, indeed, thought that the Leviathorgan was the incarnation of Thor himself, come down in judgment upon them for their temerity in daring to cross the Uncrossable Waters, and its stings were Thor's lightning bolts raining down upon them.

Many had now abandoned the *American Dream II* as a hopeless cause, a lost ship, and were even now striking out for land as their only hope of survival.

Camicazi and Fishlegs were in the sea.

Fishlegs had got hold of one leg of Norbert's Map Table, which was floating upside-down in the water, and he looked down, and found himself staring at the great black form of the gigantic Leviathorgan swimming just ten metres below him.

'It's all right!' screamed Camicazi. 'It's going for the boat!'

And then they both turned white.

Hiccup was still on the boat.

Hiccup had unfortunately tied the ticking-thing to his wrist a little *too* carefully, with one of Stoick's Foolproof Never-Go-Wrong Slip-Knots, and he was having difficulty *un*tying himself.

'Come on... come on... come on...' he muttered, desperately trying to untangle himself.

'Help me bite it apart, Toothless,' he said, and the little dragon worked at the rope with his sharp little gums, to no avail.

'Hurry up, hurry up!' screamed Hiccup.

'OK, that's it,' said Toothless, folding his wings, and stopping biting. 'Toothless not help the big Mean Master if he be cross with p-p-poor Toothless.'

There was a great crash from below of splintering wood, and the boat rocked crazily, and another crash, and the boat listed to the left and then sank a couple of metres into the water.

OK. that's IT

'*Aaaaghhh!!!! It's holed the boat, it's holed the boat! ABANDON SHIP!!!*' yelled one of the crew, belly-flopping over the side.

'Toothless! Help me!' shrieked Hiccup, scrabbling frantically at the rope, trying to untie it, and only succeeding in making a complete bird's nest of the thing. 'I didn't mean to sound cross, I was just frightened!'

'Is no r-r-reason to be RUDE,' complained Toothless, in a huff. 'And Mean Master still sounding cross.'

'I'm not cross!' squealed Hiccup. 'Get biting! Get biting!'

Toothless wagged a wing at Hiccup. 'First, Mean Master say he *v-v-very* sorry...'

'I'm very sorry!' screamed Hiccup. 'Very, very, very sorry! I couldn't be sorrier!'

'Say, I am a big, wingless idiot and T-T-Toothless the handsomest, cleverest *k-k-kindest* dragon in the WHOLE WORLD...' said Toothless, giggling naughtily.

'I-am-a-big-wingless-idiot-and-Toothless-is-the-handsomest-cleverest-kindest dragon-in-the-whole-world!' gabbled Hiccup.

Norbert was lying in the centre of the deck in a crumpled heap, and for a moment Hiccup hoped, as he frantically worked at the knot, that he was actually, finally, completely dead.

But Norbert seemed to be indestructible. He quivered a little, and then rose like a nightmare from the deck, as he did in so many of Hiccup's dreams, a limping sack of bones and muscles with murder in his eyes.

His clothes were in dripping tatters around him, his face was contorted in fury.

Hiccup could tell from the crazy light in Norbert's eye that he had lost the plot. He no longer cared about escaping the frightful peril of the Creature determined to destroy the boat, or about reaching the American shore, so temptingly close, and yet still so far away.

All he wanted now was the head of Hiccup.

'YOU...' spat Norbert, as he staggered forward, panting hard. 'You, Hiccup Horrendous Haddock the Third are my nemesis... my Curse... If YOU were not in this world I would be a RICH man, counting my American gold... an Emperor perhaps, of the New World... but you and your wretched little flying lizard have foiled my dreams once more. I mean, can't a man

DREAM for Thor's sake? All of my dreams YOU have turned to ashes, time and time again.' Tears of self-pity rolled down Norbert's furious face, as he waded through the knee-deep water.

He staggered forward, his sword raised above his head.

'... and when we get home, I am going to let Toothless have his very own p-p-pet, a dear little rat...' finished Toothless.

'And-when-we-get-home-I-am-going-to-let-Toothless-have-his-very-own-pet-a-dear-little-rat-help-me-Toothless-or-I-am-going-to-DIE!' screeched Hiccup.

At the very last minute, Toothless *finally* unwound the ticking-thing from the mast. Hiccup looked desperately around him as the lightning shook the sky... there was no escape now, nowhere to go but... UP.

In an instant, a Plan popped into Hiccup's mind. The Archipelago was a dangerous place to live, and Hiccup had spent many years coming up with one desperate plan after another, but this was a plan too crazy even to be given the name 'desperate', so let us call it the Suicidal Plan.

Sheathing his sword, the Endeavour, Hiccup began to climb the mast of the *American Dream II*.

18. UP THE MAST OF THE AMERICAN DREAM II

He shinned up the mast like a little monkey, as it reared up and down like a great plunging tree on the back of the waves. He was in terrible danger of being blown off by the shrieking wind that tore at his clothes, and froze his fingers till they nearly lost their grip, but up, and up he climbed.

Norbert halted at the bottom of the mast for a second. He was laughing as he did this, shouting up the mast, 'Where are you going, you small boy? Don't you know you're going to run out of mast, and I shall get you in the end?'

And then he began to climb after Hiccup.

Up and up Norbert climbed in pursuit. He was surprisingly quick, for he had an interesting technique. Every few metres or so he let out a scream of effort as he sank his axe deep into the mast above. And then he hauled himself up, almost entirely with the strength of his upper arms, worked the axe out, and dug it into position a few metres further up.

Hiccup had run out of mast.

He curled the rope of the rigging around his arm

(he was careful not to tie it this time), drew his sword again, and waited for Norbert.

Down in the sea, Fishlegs and Camicazi were watching him, open-mouthed.

'What is he DOING?'

'I think,' said Fishlegs slowly, 'he's going to fight Norbert on the mast.'

Hiccup's fight with Norbert on the mast top has passed into Viking Legend.

Never had a fight been undertaken in such difficult circumstances as these, on top of the rigging and mast of a ship that was rapidly sinking, in the middle of a thunderstorm, and under attack from below by one of the major Monsters of the Deep. Norbert drew his blade with his left hand as soon as he was level with Hiccup, and aimed a great swinging swipe at the boy, which Hiccup parried at the last moment, and the two great swords rang together.

'It's not too late, Norbert,' panted Hiccup, as he parried a Flashburn Fancy-Thrust, and nearly fell off the rigging while doing so. 'Can't we put this off till later? This boat is SINKING.'

As if in response to this statement, the boat gave another lurch downward, and Hiccup was hanging only by one arm for a second before he got his feet back on the ropes, slippery in the drenching rain.

'I've BEEN patient!' howled Norbert, slicing through the air with a Double-wristed Heartbreaker. 'Fifteen years stuck on Hysteria! And then two *American Dreams* built and destroyed by YOU! Everything was all going to plan, if YOU hadn't come along.'

'Well, be fair,' argued Hiccup, steadying himself on the mast as he performed two quick Wristflickers and followed them up with a Grimbeard's Grapple, 'we had to defend ourselves, because you were going to kill us, weren't you?'

'Oh you're always full of excuses,' howled Norbert furiously.

'*Maybe* I wouldn't have done. I will *now*, of course,' and as if to emphasise this point he narrowed his mad eye, and followed up a Perfectpiercer with a wild lash with the axe.

Hiccup desperately avoided the axe, helped by a gust of wind that threw him backwards a little. He lost his footing, was hanging on by one hand again, and Norbert bashed away at the fingers with his foot.

Camicazi and Fishlegs could hardly bear to watch as they bobbed in the sea below.

But Hiccup threw the ticking-thing upwards, and it whipped through the air, and the rope wound itself around the horizontal beam of the mast a little further down. Just at the moment that his hand gave way, he swu-u-ung on the rope, yelling out the Hooligan War Cry, and landed safely a little distance away.

'Oh Bravo, Hiccup!' cheered Camicazi excitedly, 'That was a really cool move.'

Toothless flapping into Norbert's face gave Hiccup the time to regain his footing on the rigging. Hiccup followed up with some graceful Left-Hand Lunges, one of which was so close to disabling Norbert's sword arm that it ripped off the right sleeve.

'I think he's winning, you know, Fishlegs,' chirped Camicazi.

It was an extraordinary sight.

Great crashes of thunder from Thor at his most furious, the distant grey outline of the American shore, the majestic half-sinking ship still pouring steam from its chimney, and then high, high on its mast, the two tiny figures, who had now climbed even higher, and were fighting in the crow's nest...

'Oh for Thor's sake,' gasped Fishlegs, as he clung like a half-drowned little spider to the Map Table. 'What's THAT?'

The Leviathorgan had been repeatedly battering the ship from below, and it must have been very well-made, the *American Dream II*, for it was only now that the hull gave way into splinters, and the head of the great dragon appeared through the deck, screaming in fury, and chomping away at the wood with its fangs. It threw back its head and let out a great roar, shooting three of its stings upwards simultaneously. One of the flaming spears of bone shot straight through the swordfight, the other narrowly missed Norbert's bottom. (*That* would have been uncomfortable.)

As if woken from a dream, Norbert looked down to see the deck destroyed, with the head of the Monster thrusting right through it, and looking up at him and Hiccup.

An appalling stench of long-dead seal and rotting porpoise reeked off its fangs (these large Sea Monsters always smell bad, I'm afraid, owing to their carnivore diet), and the feet of an unfortunate Hysteric crew-member could clearly be seen disappearing down the black cavernous gullet.

Norbert's concentration wavered for a second as he realised he had been carried away by his own anger, and Death was now staring him straight in the face.

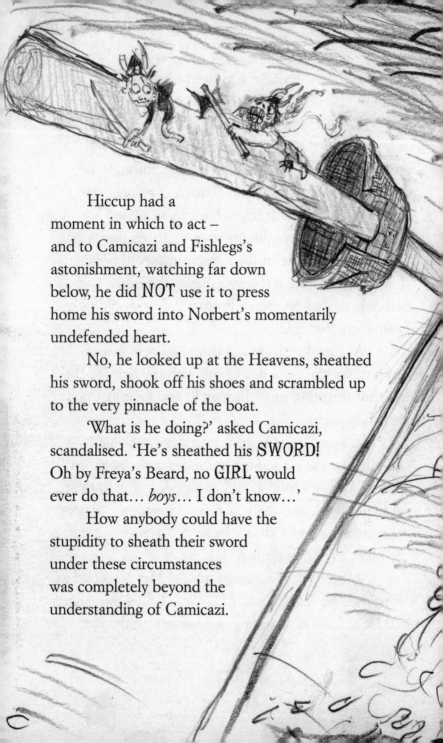

Hiccup had a
moment in which to act –
and to Camicazi and Fishlegs's
astonishment, watching far down
below, he did NOT use it to press
home his sword into Norbert's momentarily
undefended heart.

No, he looked up at the Heavens, sheathed
his sword, shook off his shoes and scrambled up
to the very pinnacle of the boat.

'What is he doing?' asked Camicazi,
scandalised. 'He's sheathed his SWORD!
Oh by Freya's Beard, no GIRL would
ever do that... *boys*... I don't know...'

How anybody could have the
stupidity to sheath their sword
under these circumstances
was completely beyond the
understanding of Camicazi.

Hiccup edged out on to the mast like a tight-rope walker, the wood cold beneath his bare feet, his arms flapping outwards for balance, the wind tearing at his clothes.

He put up his face to the furious storming black Heavens. 'OK, THOR!' shouted Hiccup. 'THIS IS YOUR CHANCE TO SHOW ME. ARE YOU ON MY SIDE, OR ARE YOU NOT?'

The small boy wobbled, teetered, on the mast of the sinking ship, with his arms stretched up and out, it wasn't quite clear whether for balance or in prayer to the storming skies above.

For one second, the boat seemed to stop sinking. The Leviathorgan, with its paw hauling its great body up the mast, greedy jaws a-gape, froze like a statue, even the storm seemed to ease for a second.

'Norbert!' shouted Hiccup above the howling of the wind. 'If it is, as you say, all my fault, then Strike me Down Now, for then at least one of us shall die happy!'

Another pause.

And then everything happened very quickly.

Norbert hauled himself up high on the pinnacle.

Hiccup was right, at least he would go to Valhalla in a moment of triumph.

He raised the Axe of Doom above his head with a scream of victory, ready to bring it down on the unarmed boy with the outstretched arms and upturned head. The air above fizzed with electric energy, crackling, bursting, searching, *seeking* for a path down to the sea.

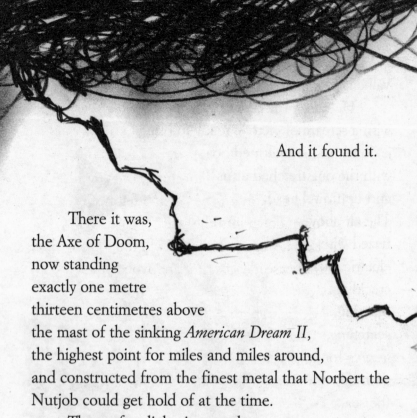

And it found it.

There it was,
the Axe of Doom,
now standing
exactly one metre
thirteen centimetres above
the mast of the sinking *American Dream II*,
the highest point for miles and miles around,
and constructed from the finest metal that Norbert the
Nutjob could get hold of at the time.

The perfect lightning conductor.

A crooked bolt of tremendous lightning jagged
down from the clouds, and struck the blackened point
of the axe.

The second before it struck, Hiccup's toes left
the mast as he sprang off and out in a (not quite
perfect) swallow dive.

The lightning struck the Axe of Doom, and
three-hundred-thousand volts of electricity ran
sparkling down the arm of Norbert the Nutjob,

bristling down the mast, and straight through the body of the Leviathorgan.

Sparks flew from Norbert's nose and jumped crazily off the wood of the mast, setting it alight, and frazzled around every spiny tip of the Leviathorgan's jerking body, in a beautiful impromptu firework display.

The body of Norbert the Nutjob fell from the peak and down, down into the sea.

The Leviathorgan crashed down too, through the hull in another cascade of water and wood splinters. And then DOWN went the *American Dream II*, and down in style, with her sinking mast in flames.

Down went the largest, most technically sophisticated boat that a Viking has ever built, already turning into a wooden skeleton, a ghost, as she

sank slowly
through the cold,
grave fathoms to
the sea-bed below. And
nestled within her in
the darkness, as if she
were his coffin, was
the dead body of the Leviathorgan.

It had tried to eat the boat, but ended up
with the boat eating it, its white picked-
clean bones sleeping for ever more in
the belly of the ghost ship on the
sea-bed. And a boat like that
has never been made again
by the Vikings, as far
as I know.

Norbert the Nutjob may have been a maniac, but lunacy and genius are very close together, and it had to be admitted, he was a great Dreamer.

Perhaps the inventor-madmen of the Future will dream its like again.

But for now it was no more, and down it went, the death of Norbert's Dream, the sinking of all his hopes.

And, incidentally, the only way they had of getting back to the Archipelago.

19. KEEP KICKING, IT'S A LONG SWIM HOME

What happened to Hiccup?

As I said, he jumped off the mast in a not-very-perfect swallow dive. Toothless dived after him, folding back his wings. It was a long way down, and by the time Hiccup reached the breath-stoppingly cold sea, he was moving at quite a speed.

Momentum took Hiccup quite a way downward, and as he resurfaced, he hit his head on a cauldron, which was slowly sinking down to the bottom. Hiccup spat out water, gasping and confused, not sure where he was, or *who* he was or what was going on. Blood was pouring into his eyes, and he fainted.

Toothless let out a scream of alarm to Camicazi and Fishlegs, and dived down to pull his Master up so that his face was out of the water. Camicazi immediately set out in her sprawling crawl to try and help, but she was some distance from where Hiccup had landed, so she was never going to be able to reach him in time. Fishlegs, on the other hand, was very close.

As Hiccup disappeared under the water for the second time, Fishlegs let go of the table, and splashed haphazardly across to his friend.

He hauled Hiccup up, still unconscious, and heaved him a couple of metres or so to the relative safety of the floating table.

'Oh for Thor's sake, oh for Thor's sake... is he all right?' asked Camicazi as she reached them. Hiccup was sprawled floppily on his back, still breathing but with his eyes closed, and one arm trailing into the water.

'I don't know...' replied Fishlegs anxiously. 'He's still alive, but he's been knocked out. I think he hit his head on something under the water.'

'We need to get him out, *fast*,' cried Camicazi. 'and get him warm.'

The storm had passed as suddenly as it arrived, and was already moving on to the land called America, leaving chaos in its wake. It was as if an angry god had turned the ship upside-down, shaken out its contents, and tossed the boat to the depths. All around them, the surviving Hysterics were striking out for the American shore, swimming around the myriad of objects floating in the waters.

Saucepans, chairs, tables, hammocks, chessboards, stools, fishing equipment, pairs of trousers: Norbert had been very ambitious about the amount of STUFF that he was taking to America.

226

And they were all now strewn about the waves, and would be washed up for many years on those white beaches, and I wonder what the native American peoples made of them when they found them.

Camicazi tried to pull the table towards the land, but Fishlegs was wondering what the little figures walking about on the beaches would make of THEM when they swam up the shore.

It is one thing to turn up in a new country in all the pomp and circumstance of a great big boat, heavily armed, and laden down with good things to eat and trade. It is quite a different thing, as poor refugees throughout history will tell you, to turn up practically naked, unarmed, defenceless and with nothing in your hands.

As strangers from an alien nation, would they be greeted with interest and mercy? Or would they be greeted with fear, and a hail of arrows?

'No!' cried Fishlegs, pulling in the other direction. 'No! I think we should swim over there!' And he pointed out to sea.

'Are you out of your tiny little mind?' asked Camicazi. 'The Archipelago is thousands and thousands of miles away across the Great West Ocean. You think we're going to SWIM to it?'

'No, of course not,' gasped Fishlegs, accidentally swallowing a big gulp of sea-water. 'But I think I can see the outline of a boat on the horizon... I just have this really strong feeling it wouldn't be a good idea for us to land on that beach...'

The faint noise of shouting coming from the beach in question seemed to underline that feeling.

'Oh I don't know,'
shivered Camicazi, faint with
weariness and cold.

'OK, let's swim out
a little further, we can
always change our minds,'
she agreed.

So they began to
swim away from the
beach.

tick
tock
tick tock

'But *you* can't live in the ocean! Humans haven't got gills!' Stormfly pointed out.

Toothless fanned Hiccup's face with his wings, to try and get him to wake up. 'We n-n-need you M-m-master! These h-h-humans don't know what they're doing!'

The thing is, after a while, as they swam out further and further, it became clear that they couldn't necessarily change their minds.

They were so weak with cold and exhaustion that they weren't swimming fast at all, particularly because between the two of them they had to push the table along the water and over the waves. And there must have been a strong, unseen current beneath them, for they were moving out to sea at a very rapid rate. And the sails that Fishlegs thought he had seen seemed to vanish in the sea-mist as they swam towards them,

230

until Fishlegs began to doubt he had
ever really seen them at all.

They didn't speak of it, though they both knew
what was happening.

They were too frozen and too tired to speak, and
they needed all their energy to keep kicking.

'Keep kicking... keep kicking... keep kicking...'
Fishlegs muttered.

Strange how a story sometimes seems to end just
how it started, in a circle.

They had set out, swimming away from the beach
at the bottom of the Murderous Mountains, many
weeks before.

And now here they were, swimming out into the
very same Ocean, from the opposite direction, and
from a very different shore.

After a while, the land behind them had been
covered by mist. And they had become just another
strange floating object in an alien environment, two
Viking children pushing a table with another child's
body on it across a vast and lonely Ocean.

Above them hovered two dragons, wings spread
wide and tossed up by the wind.

231

There was still quite a swell, so they were riding up the waves, and then having to hold their heads up high as the wave washed over them, until they dropped down and were picked up by another one. Their feet were so cold they could barely kick now, and they had lost all feeling in their arms.

Toothless tried to help by catching fish and offering it to them, but poor humans, they are so helpless, they didn't even seem to want to eat it.

After about half an hour Camicazi said through numb and frozen lips, 'You DID learn to swim there, though, didn't you? You pulled Hiccup out without holding on to anything. I *told* you you could do it!'

'I did didn't I?' gasped Fishlegs. 'I didn't even think about it.' He gave a shaky laugh. 'Well, *this* has all been worth it then, hasn't it? What a way to learn to swim!'

Camicazi started laughing, hysterically and faintly, and then she said, 'Maybe we should go back now.'

'In a little while, perhaps,' said Fishlegs. 'Keep kicking... keep kicking...'

After another twenty minutes, Camicazi said, 'I think I might have a little nap, I'm feeling very tired...'

'All right then,' said Fishlegs, 'We'll just

sleep a little while, and then we'll carry on.'

The two dragons fluttered down, and landed on two of the table legs, sitting up straight and stiff like two guardian angels on a bedstead. The two Vikings laid their tired frozen heads on the table, and Fishlegs was just dropping off when he saw through half closed eyes…

… a ship, surprisingly close, looming out of the mist.

'Over here,' he whispered, his voice-box so cold that noise could barely come out of it, and then a bit louder, and dragging himself up on to his elbows, 'OVER HERE!'

He shrugged off his waistcoat, and half-stood up on the table, waving the waistcoat over his head. 'OVER HERE! OVER HERE! OVER HERE! Camicazi, wake up, there's a ship, there's a ship!'

'Oh go away and leave me to sleep…' muttered Camicazi, not opening her eyes. 'It isn't morning time yet.'

The people on the ship seemed to hear the shouting, for there were cries in a strange language from aboard, and it moved towards them, nearer and nearer.

'Wake up, Camicazi, wake up! There really *is* a ship!' cried Fishlegs. 'In fact, more than one ship!'

And when Camicazi opened her eyes, there they were, seven ships, and standing on the front of the deck of the first one, straight and tall as a figurehead, and holding aloft a flare in her right hand so they could see through the mist…

… was Bearcub's Grandmother.

234

'I hope we're not too late,' she said. And then she saw Hiccup's prone body on the table. 'But I see we may be,' she said, with sorrow, but also perhaps a certain amount of gloomy satisfaction.

There were seven Wanderer ships that had followed the *American Dream II* across the Great West Ocean. Wanderers are the best trackers in the world, so they are good people to have following you.

They had known they were getting close to the *American Dream II* for the past hour, because they had begun to pick up a trail of the wreckage strewn in the sea. Candlesticks, barrels of vegetables and jars of beer, chairs, oars, maps, cups, swords and saucepans – all the mad remains of a doomed voyage.

They picked up all that they could find, in case it would be useful or valuable, because Wanderers are not a wealthy people, and this was riches to them.

One of the ships had even retrieved Norbert's defective Flying Machine, and balanced it on the back of its deck, so that it looked as if it were about to take off into the sky.

Bearcub's Grandmother had begun to think that Hiccup had drowned, or landed on the shore of America, when they spotted the floating table in the distance.

235

It turned out that Bearcub's Grandmother was a surprisingly good nurse, for one so good at Cursing. She was much better at it than Old Wrinkly, the doctor of the Hooligan Tribe, whose cures and potions of seagulls' droppings mixed with spider webs often made you feel somewhat worse than you did before you went to see him.

A couple of hours and some of Bearcub's Grandmother's medicine later, and Hiccup's eyes opened, to see the faces of Fishlegs, Camicazi, the Stormfly, Toothless, Bearcub and Bearcub's Grandmother looking down at him.

'I thought you had left us,' said Hiccup to Bearcub's Grandmother, in surprise.

'Why did you think that?' snapped Bearcub's Grandmother. 'We could not follow you in those titchy little landing-boats, we had to fetch some proper ships. We Wanderers are a people of our word, unlike some other people I can mention.'

20. THE TICKING THING STARTS TO TICK LOUDER

Again, I will not weary you with the details of the long journey home, the dragons they saw, the storms they survived, the perils of the crossing, or we would be here for ever.

Every day, Hiccup checked the ticking-thing. As they grew closer and closer and closer to home, their hearts were lifting with excitement.

But something had begun to worry Hiccup. It was something that Old Wrinkly had said on the beach, on the day of the Inter-Tribal Friendly Swimming Race. He had told Hiccup that he had to be back within three months, five days and six hours.

Now, why would Old Wrinkly say that?

It may seem obvious to you, dear Reader, for you know all the facts, but it never occurred to any of *them* that the Race they had been participating in was either particularly important in itself (it was only a Friendly, as far as they were concerned, after all, and there were always Competitions going on in the Archipelago), or that the Race could still be *going on* all that time later.

So Hiccup didn't know why Old Wrinkly would say such a precise time. And it was concerning him, because according to his reading of the ticking-thing, they had now been gone for three months, four days and thirteen hours, and they were still at least two days' sailing away from the Archipelago.

'I don't know why you're worrying about this,' said Fishlegs, who was in a hugely happy mood now they were nearly home. 'It probably didn't mean anything at all. You know Old Wrinkly, he's not that great a soothsayer, and he's sometimes a bit batty.'

'But what if it *did* mean something?' insisted Hiccup. 'What if Old Wrinkly had seen what was going to happen to us... he knew we weren't going to come back that day, didn't he? And look, we're nearly coming in at exactly the time he said, it's just that we're going to be a bit late, and he *particularly* told me not to be late...'

The next day, Hiccup was even more worried, and the ticking-thing began to tick louder, as Old Wrinkly had said it would.

TICK-TOCK-TICK-TOCK-TICK-TOCK.

'Look!' said Hiccup anxiously. 'That means there's only six hours left, and even though it's a very windy day, we're at least...' he checked the ticking-thing, 'TWENTY-FOUR-hours' sailing distance away... we're going to be late!'

239

'Late for *what*?' asked Fishlegs in exasperation. 'There's nothing we can do about it, anyway, and Old Wrinkly probably didn't mean anything when he said it.'

Hiccup fiddled and fiddled with the ticking-thing as he worried, and the back of it fell open, and for the first time he noticed, along with the little delicate moving wheels on the inside, there was a tiny little inscription. Two letters. G.G.

Hiccup's heart beat a little quicker, for he had seen those letters before, and he knew what they stood for.

Grimbeard the Ghastly.

Hiccup had assumed that this ticking-thing had been made by Norbert's father, Bigjob, and he had always felt a little guilty about stealing it from Norbert.

But it seemed that Bigjob had perhaps stolen it himself.

For this ticking-thing, surely, belonged to the Heir of Grimbeard the Ghastly, and the Heir to Grimbeard the Ghastly was...

... Hiccup.

And now he was *absolutely* sure that there was a precise reason for the time that Old Wrinkly had given him. He did not yet know what the reason was, but he was certain that somehow there was some kind of pattern to it that he did not yet understand.

Some way in which everything interconnected, like the little tiny wheels revolving in the instrument in front of him.

Six hours.

TICK-TOCK-TICK-TOCK-TICK-TOCK went the ticking-thing, a little louder still.

They were never going to get there in six hours... *by boat.*

Hiccup looked up and his eye caught Norbert's defective Flying Machine, salvaged from the sea by the prudent Wanderers, and now lashed to the figurehead of one of the other Wanderer boats.

There was a very strong wind today.

Hiccup knew from the time that he had spent in a Roman Observation Balloon (it's a long story, don't ask)* that flying was much quicker than sailing.

If only that Flying Machine actually **WORKED**.

Fishlegs saw what Hiccup was looking at, and guessed what he was thinking. 'Oh no, Hiccup, oh, seriously, you have got to be **JOKING!** Remember how many times they tried that thing out on the journey? And how many times it fell out of the sky like a stone? That Flying Machine *doesn't work*.'

---

*Please read *How to Speak Dragonese*.

'We thought the Stop-the-Boat-from-Sinking-and-Scare-Away-the-Big-Sea-Creatures Machine didn't work, didn't we?' Hiccup pointed out. 'And we were wrong.'

'But we're so close now… so close… and so ALIVE which is the important thing,' gasped Fishlegs. 'what is the POINT of risking it all right now, after all that we've been through, when we're so very nearly there? No, I'm putting my foot down this time, Hiccup, I can't let you do it…'

TICK-TOCK-TICK-TOCK-TICK-TOCK-TICK-TOCK went the ticking-thing.

21. THE END OF THE SWIMMING RACE

On the windy clifftops of the Murderous Mountains stood the proud figures of Stoick the Vast and Big-Boobied Bertha, their arms in chains, surrounded by Murderous Warriors. They were too dignified to show fear. They would show Madguts the Murderous how bravely a Chieftain could die. Before them was the Sky Burial Place, where they would be strapped down and left, helpless, for the Sky Dragons to attack them. Nothing would be left of their remains.

Above their heads, the Sky Dragons were already massing in their hundreds, with shrieking, hungry vulture cries.

Down on the beach, the Tribes of Hooligan and Bog-Burglar stood, depressed and silent, holding burning flares in their hands, looking up at the silhouettes of their Chiefs on the clifftops.

The deaths of their Chieftains were not the only things at stake here for the two Tribes. Madguts was about to take over their lands. The Hooligans and Bog-Burglars had packed up all their belongings, and loaded them into their own ships standing in the Harbour. These ships were piled high with every

possession they owned:
favourite swords and armour,
stools and clothing,
clucking hens and pigs
and goats.

The Hooligans
had never intended
to settle on Berk in the
first place. Berk was not the
most comfortable, the most
luxurious, the most civilised place
to live in the world. It was a funny,
boggy, shaggy little heap of heather and
rock, where the wind buffeted so strongly
that you might as well be on the sea in a
ship, and when it wasn't raining it was often
snowing.

But Berk was where they had grown up,
where they met their sweethearts and brought up
their children, and when it came down to it, they
found that they didn't want to leave.

So they stood there, sunk in the profoundest melancholy.

The sun was going down on this day, and Old Wrinkly's big sand-timer was running out of sand, and his complicated candlesticks were running down to little stubs, marking the Final End to the Competition. The three Judges sat solemnly at the table.

Three months, five days, three hours and twenty-*four* minutes… Three months, five days, three hours and twenty-*five* minutes…

*   *   *   *   *   *   *

Norbert's defective Flying Machine worked rather better than Fishlegs had expected.

But he hadn't expected *much*, it had to be said.

Fishlegs and Camicazi insisted on going in the Machine with Hiccup, Camicazi because it was the kind of crazy thing she particularly enjoyed, Fishlegs because despite all the complaining he wasn't going to desert Hiccup, who was the closest thing to family that Fishlegs had.

The Wanderers had to haul the Machine up to the top of the mast so they could take off in it, and Bearcub's Grandmother predicted Doom and

Destruction would be the outcome. 'Vikings – they're all mad... even the small ones...'

But Doom and Destruction did not follow – not immediately, at least.

It was a very windy day, and when the Wanderers let go of the Machine, lift-off was instantly successful. The wind caught underneath the wings and launched the Machine almost vertically up into the air, like a kite.

'Wahooooooooo!' cried Camicazi, as they soared, legs dangling, hair blown back in the wind, up and up into the big blue sky.

'If Thor meant humans to fly, he'd have given them wings,' recommended the Stormfly, swooping alongside them in an amused way.

The wind was strong, the young Vikings were light, and they quickly left the seven boats with the cheering, waving Wanderers on them far, far behind. They were heart-stoppingly high.

Hiccup had flown on the backs of dragons before, but never at this height.

They were so far up in the sky that it was difficult to see how fast they were flying, apart from the marker of the little boats, now only specks way behind them in the distance.

It was cold up there, so cold that Hiccup
was glad that they had tied themselves to
the Machine, because their fingers were so
numb they might have fallen out, and the sea
was a very long way down.

And they were up there for such a long time,
that after a while, even Fishlegs began to feel that they
weren't going to plummet out of the sky like a stone,
and opened up his eyes to look about him, at the blue
above and below, stretching out for ever.

**TICK-TOCK-TICK-TOCK-
TICK-TOCK-TICK-TOCK** went the
ticking-thing, getting louder and louder and more
insistent with every passing moment. *I hope we're going
to make it…* thought Hiccup.

And after a long, long time, a grey smudge appeared on the horizon before them, and Hiccup shouted over the wind, and pointed towards it, and as it slowly became larger and greener, it was clear that it was the Murderous Mountains.

'HOW ARE WE GOING TO GET *DOWN?* shouted Fishlegs, because they were still so high that he had a sudden vision of them sailing right over the Archipelago and beyond. But a sudden SNAP! from one of the wings of the Machine above them provided the answer to Fishlegs's question.

The Machine lurched violently to the right.

They lost height with such rapidity that Hiccup's stomach lurched and his ears popped. And Norbert's defective Flying Machine folded up its wings, and plunged in a nose-dive towards the sea.

'AAAAAAAAAAAaaaaaaaaaagggggghhhhhh!' screamed Hiccup, Fishlegs, and Camicazi.

*　　*　　*　　*　　*　　*　　*

Madguts the Murderous strode up and down the beach, his cape whirling, Gumboil trotting after him, rubbing his black-gloved hands together.

In fifteen minutes, the Murderous Tribe would

have the revenge for which they had waited a hundred years…

Fourteen minutes… whispered the Judges together, staring at the sand-timers.

Thirteen minutes…

On the stroke of thirteen minutes, Old Wrinkly thought he caught a sound coming from out to sea. He shielded his eyes from the rays of the setting sun with one gnarled and wrinkled hand, and cupped the other behind his ears. Was it just his imagination playing tricks on him? Was it just the beat of his old heart making the sound that he so longed to hear?

For the first time in three months the old man got to his feet, his ancient legs shaking as he leant heavily on his staff. He stumbled forward in the sand, straining, longing, *willing* it to be the sound he wanted it to be… and there it was.

Coming from out of the sea, soft but getting louder every second.

TICK-TOCK-TICK-TOCK-TICK-TOCK

To the astonishment of the watching crowds, the old man let out a cracked old laugh, and began to dance in the sand on his bent old legs, his clothes flapping around him like a scarecrow doing a jig.

251

He's really lost it… they thought, as Old Wrinkly bustled back to the Judges' Table, his eyes now brimful of merriment and excitement.

And then came a shout from the clifftops.

Stoick shouted out something, and pointed, and the crowd could not hear what he was saying, but they looked where he was pointing, towards the long rolling waves coming in from the West. There was nothing there but the path of the setting sun lighting up the tops of the long waves rolling in from the west.

But then there came a cry, from Nobber Nobrains maybe, 'Look! Over there!'

And there, distinctly, far into the bay, were three little heads bobbing in the waves.

'What is this?' snarled Gumboil, screwing up his eyes to try and see what they were looking at out there in the water. 'Those are just SEALS.'

'Seals with horns?' asked Gobber the Belch, with hope rising in his chest.

'Deer, then,' argued Gumboil.

But as the little heads swam nearer and nearer it became clear that they were not deer. Those were VIKING helmets on their heads, and hovering protectively above them, were the distinct shapes of two small hunting-dragons. And as they came nearer and nearer still, Old Wrinkly cried out: 'Remember! They must land here unaided!'

His warning was unnecessary for it was as if the crowd had been turned to stone, so dumbfounded were they.

The three figures swam closer and closer until they got into their depth, and then they put their feet down on the sand of the Archipelago, and they waded waist high through the crashing waves.

Hiccup, Camicazi and Fishlegs staggered out of the water of the Great West Ocean, exactly three months, five days, five hours, and fifty-eight minutes after they had entered it.

They were totally bewildered to find everybody on the beach, flares in their hands, apparently waiting for them, and absolutely silent and stunned.

They had entered the Ocean all that long, long time ago, a laughing-stock. The smallest contestants in the Race, jeered at, pointed at, humiliated and embarrassed. Now the same crowd that had laughed them so uproariously into the water, greeted them with awed, wide-eyed wonder and amazement.

Slowly, the huge adults on the beach removed their helmets as they passed, the ultimate sign of respect. They fell back in wonder at the soft footprints in the sand. They murmured their astonishment as great hairy forearms were raised in admiring salute.

It was the proudest moment in Fishlegs's life. He had left this very beach an object of ridicule, unable to swim and wearing those ridiculous armbands. Now all those who had laughed had watched him as he swam, entirely unaided, up the whole depth of the bay. Even though he was so tired he could barely put one foot in front of another, his back was straight, his head held high.

As he passed he heard one Hooligan whisper to a Bog-Burglar… 'That's Fishlegs, there, the one on the right…' in a tone of recognition and admiration.

A proud moment for Fishleg

Imagine that, for a boy used only to being ignored or laughed at!

Fishlegs, Hiccup and Camicazi had equalled Grimbeard the Ghastly's record, but they did not look like they had spent the time pickled in the sea. Their hair was so stiff with salt water it stuck out like broombrushes. Their faces tanned dark brown. They were a little taller maybe. (Well, it *had* been three months, and pre-teens can grow a great deal in three months.)

They were, without question, this skinny, unlikely threesome, the last three competitors to return alive to the Archipelago.

The Last Men (and Woman) Back.

Hiccup staggered forward to the Judge's Table, too tired to ask questions, almost too tired to think, the ticking-thing dragging behind him in the sand,

TICK-TOCK-TICK TOCK-TICK-TOCK TICK-TOCK...

He stopped at the Judges' Table, and wound the rope of the ticking-thing around his wrist, placing the ticking-thing carefully before the dumbfounded Committee.

Softly, the two small hunting dragons folded their

wings, and landed on the Table their eyes fixed on the ticking-thing in the centre.

TICK-TOCK
TICK-TOCK...

… and the alarm on the ticking-thing finally went off, in a peal of tiny clockwork bells, ringing to the sound of the Hooligan National Anthem.

A typical Grimbeard the Ghastly touch.

You had to admit it, the guy did have STYLE.

Old Wrinkly reached out and turned it off.

'I wasn't late,' said Hiccup.

'No,' said Old Wrinkly. 'You were just in time.'

The Bog-Burglars and Hooligans were so amazed they just stood there, eyes open wide as saucers, staring at them.

Madguts was looking like a thundercloud.

'I do not believe this!' spluttered Gumboil. 'Madguts does not believe it… These are just CHILDREN… and quite odd looking children at that. They can't possibly be the LAST MEN BACK.'

Nobody could believe it. Snotlout was lost for words. How did Hiccup DO it? Yet again, it had seemed certain that he had kicked the bucket, and yet here he was, turning up very much alive and in a horribly glorious manner. Even that weed Fishlegs seemed to have somehow taught himself to swim.

'Yes, well they're *not* the Last Men Back are they, unless they are able to take the Oath that they did not seek aid by Float or Boat,' Snotlout pointed out meanly, so eaten up with jealousy that he spoke without thinking.

Snotlout's own father, Baggybum the Beerbelly, shouted: 'Shut up Snotlout!' and there were cries of 'Shame!' and 'Whose side are you on, Big Nose?' And even the Murderous Tribe booed and hissed him, for nobody likes a traitor to their Tribe. Snotlout turned a bright and unattractive red, and muttered sullenly, 'I was only *saying...*'

'Yes, as Snotlout so *kindly* reminds us,' said Old Wrinkly, shooting Snotlout a venomous look, 'for any of you to be declared Last Man Back, you have to take the Oath. Can you take the Oath?'

Hiccup, Fishlegs and Camicazi at last realised the significance of what was happening. They looked up at the clifftops, at the long line of little figures standing silent below the wheeling, shrieking Sky Dragons. They looked around at the serious, intent faces of the Tribesmen. They looked at each other.

Well… the Oath said that you were not allowed to 'seek aid' from Float or Boat.

None of them had *asked* to be kidnapped by Norbert the Nutjob. And only Fishlegs and Camicazi had 'sought aid' from the Wanderers, to take them back to the Archipelago. Hiccup had been knocked out, unconscious at the time, not in a condition to seek aid from anyone. And a Flying Machine was neither a Float nor a Boat.

So, *technically speaking*, Hiccup COULD take the Oath.

Fishlegs and Camicazi pushed Hiccup forward.

Hiccup put up his left hand.

Total silence from the crowd.

'I solemnly swear by this my sword-arm,' said Hiccup, 'that I did not seek aid by Float or Boat… I did not plan to win this Race by trickery or deception… and that any assistance I received was by the favour of Fortune, and the gracious will of the great god Thor.'

The crowd erupted with joy.

The Chief Judge signalled to the Murderous Warriors on the clifftops, and reluctantly they let Bertha and Stoick the Vast free of their chains, and the two Chieftains walked proudly down the cliff-paths to the beach, heads held high.

Cheers rang out along the bay, and 'SILENCE!' yelled Old Wrinkly, bursting with pride, for it is not every day that a grandson returns to you from out of the water, a Competition is won, and a prophecy is fulfilled.

(And he was rather proud of his soothsaying skills on this occasion – Old Wrinkly's soothsaying did not always turn out this well.)

He turned his grandson around to face the crowd.

'He did not seek aid by Float or Boat,' cried Old Wrinkly solemnly in his ancient old quavering voice. 'And therefore I declare that the winner of this Competition, and the Last Man Back, to be... *HICCUP HORRENDOUS HADDOCK THE THIRD!*'

Old Wrinkly held Hiccup's arm up in the air victoriously.

'This is preposterous!' spluttered Gumboil. 'This is impossible! He can't have done it! He must have cheated!'

Gumboil found himself grabbed around the throat and lifted up in the air, his little legs dangling like a frantic beetle.

'Are you suggesting, that *MY* ancestor, Grimbeard the Ghastly, and, more importantly, *MY SON AND HEIR*, Hiccup Horrendous Haddock the Third, are *LIARS?* spat Stoick the Vast, pressing his face menacingly into Gumboil's.

'Erm… no… not exactly…' gargled the strangled Gumboil, his voice squeaking like a five-year-old.

Oh, how the Hooligans and Bog-Burglars cheered then, throwing their helmets up into the air, and clapping Hiccup and Camicazi and Fishlegs on the back, and Bertha and Stoick hugged them hard, and they all made ready to leave for their boats moored in Wrecker's Bay, because, frankly, they had had enough of the Murderous Mountains to last them a very long time indeed.

'Wait!' called the Chief Judge, the sad little Bashem-Oik. 'Before you go, there is just one more thing,' he said. 'And that is the question of the demand of the Last Man Back. According to the Oath declared by all, the Last Man Back may demand a request that cannot be denied from the Chieftain of the opposite Tribe.'

The cheers died down and the mood darkened. And Madguts had gone very silent and still, as he realised his trick had turned on himself, and he had played into his Enemy's hands. Stoick's grin turned to a thunderous frown, Bertha's hands were on her hips.

'What is your request, Hiccup? You can ask anything, anything at all.'

Madguts the Murderous had turned rather white, and he fiddled nervously with his sword. He did not have a leg to stand on, and he knew it. He only had himself to blame for the situation in which he now found himself.

The faces of the Bog-Burglars and the Hooligans were hard and set and seeking Revenge. They drew their weapons and tapped them on their thighs, and the air was filled with menace. Up on the clifftops the Sky Dragons circled. *They* didn't care WHO they ate.

'What will it be, Hiccup? What is your demand?' asked Old Wrinkly.

Hiccup thought for a long, long time, looking out over the waters.

The thing about history is that it has this nasty habit of repeating itself. If he did to Madguts what Madguts was intending to do to *them*, well, Madguts would only be getting his just desserts. But then the cycle of revenge would just start anew. In a hundred years' time, did he want Madguts' Heir and his own Heir to be playing out the same tragedy all over again?

At some point it might be a good idea to say goodbye
to the Bad Old Days...

'I demand,' said Hiccup slowly, 'that Chief
Madguts the Murderous should sing a love song
at the next Thing* while dressed as an ickle pretty
shepherdess.'

A pause. Everybody looked at Stoick to see what
his reaction would be.

For a moment Stoick remained purple with fury,
the angry flush of the Blood-Rage still engorging his
face, his hand shaking with righteous wrath.

And then Stoick's thunderous brow lightened,
he sheathed his sword, and threw back his head in a
tremendous guffaw. He patted his son on the back
affectionately. 'That WOULD be
funny,' he admitted.

---

*'The Thing' was a meeting of all the local
Viking Tribes.

'Very funny,' grinned Big-Boobied Bertha, her great biceps rippling in her amusement. 'Even better than the bathtub-and-underpants idea!'

And the Tribes of Hooligan and Bog-Burglar put away their weapons, their love of a good joke turning away their anger. Tragedy turned to comedy in an instant.

History, you see, is like the interlocking wheels turning in a ticking-thing. Something unexpected happens, some sort of *hiccup*… the wheels are jogged… and then they set off again, beating out the time in a new pattern.

'So there you are then, Madguts!' yelled Stoick the Vast. 'My son has made his demand, and you'll just have to carry it out… No hard feelings, eh?'

Madguts the Murderous shook Stoick's hand, unable to believe his good fortune. He'd thought that he was a dead man for certain.

You couldn't say that he was *happy* at the prospect of standing up in front of 'The Thing' dressed as an ickle pretty shepherdess.

The pride of the Murderous Tribe winced at the thought of it.

But on the whole, it was better than being picked to death by Sky Dragons.

And the Hooligan Tribe made their way down to their ships and returned to Berk.

Going back to Berk now, when they thought they had lost it for ever, in their boats laden with all their belongings, it was as if they were discovering it for the very first time.

A beautiful little island, all lit up under a canopy of stars.

Maybe it was a little rainier on Berk than you might wish for. Perhaps it was a trifle on the windy, boggy, rocky and heathery side. No doubt there were lands with bluer skies and richer soils, somewhere over the horizon. But Berk was the Hooligans' *home*, and perhaps that is what really matters, after all.

EPILOGUE by Hiccup

So that is the story of how I went to the New World.

I crossed thousands and thousands of miles of ocean, starving and baking on the deck of the ship, slew monsters and fought battles with my life hanging on the thinnest of threads... I cheated death so many times on that journey... and then finally, FINALLY, I saw with my very own eyes, the dream land, the imaginary place, that was no dream after all... it WAS true!

Despite what it may look like, the world is not really as flat as a pancake. There is no waterfall at the corners. There are no edges to the globe on which we live and struggle and laugh and die.

The world is a circle that has no end.

I know that, I have been out to the West and seen with my very own eyes the white beaches and lush green trees of America... and yet I never *quite* landed. I was so CLOSE to landing, that if I swam just a *few* hundred metres more, I could have put my foot on American sand.

But I did not.

What Glory it would have been to have discovered America! To have founded an empire there!

To have your name live for ever in the history books…
to have little schoolchildren chant your name, saying
*'America was discovered by Hiccup Horrendous Haddock
the Third…'*

But within touching distance of the Ultimate
Quest, I turned back.

I went home. I took the quiet way, back into the
shadows, to be forgotten by future generations.

It may seem to you, perhaps, dear reader, that my
Quest was not a success.

To have travelled so far… such a very long, long,
long way… and at the last minute, within sniffing
distance of the prize… to have *not* discovered America
after all.

What a failure!

But this is not how it seems to me. Again and
again I have been on Quests that I thought were
for one thing, and turned out to be something quite
different.

For it was on that Quest that I first truly
discovered MYSELF, and my destiny.

We were not ready to build a New World.

How can you make a fresh start in a New World
when you are carrying with you on your boat all the
same problems, the same frustrations and inequalities

of the *Old* World?

Let's face it, any country ruled by Norbert called 'The Land of the Nutjobs' would have turned out to have the same problems as the Barbaric Archipelago quicker than you can say the words 'half crazed lunatic carrying a double-headed axe'.

What that trip taught me was just how very many things were wrong with that Old World of ours. And I returned the long, long, way back to the Inner Isles with a new determination. The boy that went into the Atlantic Ocean that day was a very different boy than the one who came out three months, five days and six hours later. I had been immersed in the waters of the Western Seas, and came out a different person.

I had always known that I had, one day, to take over my father's job. I had always felt reluctant, even cross, about this. Always felt that it was something I didn't really want to do. Now, for the first time in my life I really wanted to be a Chief. And not just a Chief, but a KING.

I knew for the first time that *I* was Grimbeard the Ghastly's True Heir... and I would be such an Heir that he had never dreamed of.

I wanted to be a King who would found a New World, not in some misty country far across the seas, but right *here*, right *now*, at home. I would make the Barbaric Archipelago a place in which Might was no longer Right. Where the weaker Tribes could have their say and their vote at 'The Thing'. Where small children would not live in daily fear of death by wolves, by dragons roaming wild, by starvation and by war. Where the rule of Law would apply to bully boys like Snotlout and Nutjob himself. And, the first thing I would do as a King, would be to abolish slavery for ever from the Viking Lands...

The Slavemark has been a great burden to bear, and made my task so much the harder. But Thor was right to give me the Slavemark. I could never rub it away, never forget the promise that I made, because there it was, in indelible purple on the side of my head. Maybe all Kings should bear the Slavemark, to remind them that they should be slaves to their people, rather than the other way around. And to help them never to forget what it feels to be a child... to be small and weak and helpless.

Perhaps my vision does not seem so revolutionary to readers of the Future. But you have to remember the savage wildness of the world in which I grew up. It is quite extraordinary for one small boy with red hair and nothing very remarkable about him to think that he can change the world to that extent.

I did not realise at that time what a gigantic task I was setting myself, what a huge enterprise, so much larger than merely crossing the Western Ocean and back again... How much easier it would have been to have rubbed along as my father had, shrugging at the injustices, closing an eye to the Bad Things... But that way is not my way. My story is all about being a Hero the Hard Way.

We are all not so very different from Norbert the Nutjob. We need a vision of a New World to help us carry on. And in all that I have done, I have been dreaming of those white beaches. All my life I have struggled to found a New World, a better world, for us to live in. I have struggled to make us ready, to make us good enough, to return once again to that country that I saw, long ago, across the sea.

We are still not ready. Maybe we will never be ready. But we are a bit closer now than when I was young.

Now I am an old, old man, the world that I created has no need for dragons. They have retreated from the civilisation that I brought, along with the wolves, and the Berserks, and the monsters of my childhood.

But when I sleep, I am no longer a Great King but a child again. I slip into a longship that sets out across the oceans far far away, sails spread out like dragons' wings.

On and on we sail, unimaginably far. And if the dream is a good one I see again those white beaches, those green trees, with the bluest of blue skies above. Always sailing, sailing, sailing… *never quite reaching…*

Glory comes not to the weak
A treasure land shines out so strong
O Great and Brave and Searching Thor
I *hope* that that was land we saw…
Once before… Long ago…
HO!

This is all stirring stuff, but how is Hiccup going to keep the Slavemark a secret for ever and ever? If Snotlout finds out about it, Hiccup will never get to be a **CHIEF**, *let alone a* **KING**.

And why does Fishlegs appear to have no family?

And is that the last we shall see of that inventive maniac, Norbert the Nutjob? And what about Hiccup's arch-enemy **Alvin the Treacherous,** *who we last saw being swallowed by a Fire-Dragon that dived down into the burning waters of the Earth's core?*

I have a nasty feeling that Alvin might have survived that frightful experience, Thor only knows how...

Watch out for the next volume of Hiccup's memoirs,
How to Break a Dragon's Heart

So many

questions,
and not enough

answers. . . .

This is Cressida, age 9, writing on the island.

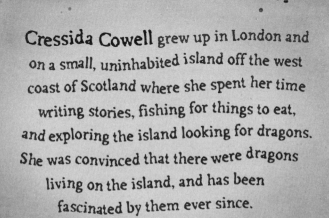

Cressida Cowell grew up in London and on a small, uninhabited island off the west coast of Scotland where she spent her time writing stories, fishing for things to eat, and exploring the island looking for dragons. She was convinced that there were dragons living on the island, and has been fascinated by them ever since.

www.cressidacowell.co.uk

HOWDEEDOODEETHERE!

For your latest news on all things dragon and Cressida Cowell please follow:

 @cressidacowellauthor

 @cressidacowell

 facebook.com/
cressidacowellauthor

 Toodleooon for now...

'Exciting adventures, great characters and plenty of jokes and funny drawings make Hiccup's adventures some of our favourite books.' **TBK Magazine**

'Cowell's Dragon books are proper modern classics.' **Sunday Express**

'This series is one of the greatest ever written for those between eight and twelve. Buy them all and your holidays will be blessed with perfect peace.' **The New Statesman**

'Cowell has crafted a modern classic ... every bit as consuming and deep as Harry's in Hogwarts ... And so the fight – part Doctor Who, part biblical epic – begins.' **The BIG Issue**

'One of the greatest pleasures of children's literature. Staggeringly clever and funny mash of Beowulf and Potter, with a truly unusual and "heroic" hero.' **Peter Florence**

'Hilarious and wise, it's never predictable, brilliantly illustrated and always delightful.' **The Times**

'Rollicking fun' **Guardian**

CRESSIDA COWELL
HOW TO TRAIN YOUR
DRAGON

ALSO AVAILABLE IN AUDIO
READ BY THE AWARD-WINNING ACTOR
DAVID TENNANT

'If you have six to twelve-year-olds, and you don't know
about David Tennant's readings of Cressida Cowell's
How to Train Your Dragon series, you don't deserve to be
a parent ... Simply the best of kids' audio-listening,
and just as much fun for parents.'
The Times

'This kept us all laughing on the edge of our seats.'
Independent on Sunday

AUDIO
Read by
DAVID
TENNANT

Want to listen to an extract?
https://soundcloud.com/hachettekids

Hodder Children's Books

READ HICCUP'S GUIDE
TO DRAGON SPECIES ...

Full of dragon profiles and tips on how to ride and
train them ... a **MUST READ** for anyone who wants
to know more about dragons.

THE WIZARDS OF ONCE

Once there was Magic...

This is the story of a young boy Wizard, and a young girl Warrior, who have been taught to hate each other like poison.